A C I D

Jeff Lovell

TotalRecall Publications, Inc.

TotalRecall Publications, Inc.
1103 Middlecreek
Friendswood, Texas 77546
281-992-3131   281-482-5390 Fax
www.totalrecallpress.com

Printed in the United States of America with simultaneous printings in Australia, Canada, and United Kingdom.

FIRST EDITION
1   2   3   4   5   6   7   8   9   10

To my friend and partner, Rebecca Pratt, owner of the Pratt Literary Group. I appreciate her help, her logic, her quest for excellence in everything more than I can express.

She gave me a chance.

Author Jeff Lovell

is a native Chicagoan, with 3 degrees from the University of Illinois and an earned doctorate from Vanderbilt University. Jeff taught high school writing and literature for thirty three years and sponsored the school paper, Student Council and several other activities. He ran the drama program at two high schools, teaching and directing and designing sets, lighting and costumes. His specialties in his career included Shakespeare, British Literature, and Writing as well as Computer Science. Since he retired from education, Jeff has served as a theatre and film critic for a television station and appears frequently to review theatre and literature.

Acknowledgment

Thanks to the girl I dated in the summer of 1968, just before I graduated from college. She used LSD and fell into a world of demons and terror, from which she struggled to recover the whole time I knew her.

Preface

In the late 1960s, American young people began a flirtation with mind-altering drugs, desperately evil drugs like LSD, then Angel Dust, and even heroin. We released a lot of demons in the Pandora-like 60s and some of them have never been placed back in the box. Here's the story of one such drug and what it does to four people who take it, unaware that they will be altered forever.

Introduction

The extent of the abilities of the human mind have never been fully realized. What would happen if an illegal drug, discovered by accident, could open pathways that have never before been opened? The characters at the heart of this novel seek to find their lives which have been reset by usage of drugs.

PART I

The University of Illinois
Urbana-Champaign, Illinois
March, 1968

Chapter One
Rachel

Keith smiled as he packed the little squares of blotting paper into a small plastic bag. Each square had a small discoloration in the center, where he'd deposited a drop of his masterpiece.

His professors, he smirked, thought he was brilliant and they'd let him go off on his own in his chemistry and biochemistry experiments. It worked out well for Keith. He could work in the lab all he wanted and use the stored chemicals as well as others that he'd purchased, to manufacture such saleable products as LSD, Benzedrine, Methedrine, and others. Not only that, he'd smuggled a lot of the university's lab equipment to his apartment and he had a thriving, if illegal, business going.

The money came in handy, to say the least.

One night, though, he made a mistake—just a little, almost imperceptible mistake—when he was mixing up one of his hell brews. He was about to destroy the mixture when he decided to see what would happen with it.

He had access to a few lab rats—white, innocent rats—and he used only the slightest amount of the new drug to spike a little bit of peanut butter, which these rats liked a lot.

After they consumed it, they looked okay for a few moments, but then collapsed into a coma. They were still alive, with steady heartbeats, but unresponsive and inactive.

Keith kept an eye on them for three days, then four, and saw them make a total recovery. He sat one night, observing them closely, each rat in a separate cage.

The rats, named Stony and Burke—after his favorite TV show, a drama about a rodeo performer—were quiet that night. Just before 9:00 P. M. however, Stony stopped, looked up at him—

And vanished.

Keith almost screamed, but caught himself just in time. A scream would have attracted attention from others at nearby work stations, and he knew he didn't want this to become public yet. He calmed himself down with an effort.

He went to Burke's cage and lifted him out. The rat seemed a little lethargic that night, but Keith lifted its head and looked into the rat's eyes. To his intense surprise, he found that he was looking at himself.

He knew, in a second, that he was seeing the world through the eyes of this rat. The thoughts of the creature were primitive, riddled with terror and a desire to get away.

With an intense effort, he pushed the little creature back into his cage and once again found himself staring at a white rat named Burke.

Keith stared back at the rat and sat down, stunned. He couldn't rid himself of the idea that the rat could read his mind. Its mind was too primitive to process what was happening, of course, but it saw what Keith was thinking.

As he sat, thinking through the situation, he became aware of a rustling sound from the next cage. He turned.

Stony was back. He prowled around his cage as if nothing had happened. Then, he disappeared again. The next night, Stony showed up again, then disappeared, then returned the next night, and vanished again.

Both rats died a week or so later. He dissected the brains of the two creatures but couldn't find anything unusual. They shouldn't be dead, he thought. Yet they were.

Okay, Keith thought. *I have to try this on a human.* Of course, no one would volunteer for such an experiment, and he sure as hell wasn't going to try it on himself. The only choice, Keith concluded, was the man who most closely approximated a friend.

Rolf Montjoy, a small, ferret faced chemistry major, lived next door to him and never locked his door. No wonder. He had nothing anyone would want to steal anyhow.

Rolf had a passion for coffee, Keith knew. He stopped at a small donut shop a few doors down from his apartment building and bought two coffees. He spiked one of them with a drop of the mixture and walked to Rolf's room. Rolf answered on the first knock and accepted the coffee with pleasure. Keith sat with him for a few moments.

Rolf passed out. Keith checked his pulse, his vitals, and knew that Rolf would wake up in a little while, like the rats did. Keith checked on him over the next couple of hours. He was fine, Keith was sure.

Two days later, Rolf spoke to him. "Hey Keith," he said. "You there?"

Keith turned, expecting to see that Rolf had slipped into his apartment. He wasn't there. "Where are you?" he asked.

"In my room," came Rolf's reply.

Keith ran next door. Rolf was grinning.

Rolf read Keith's mind without difficulty and discovered that Keith had slipped him what the old movies called a Mickey. It was something other than a narcotic and it had changed his mind forever.

Rolf wasn't upset, though. He saw it as an opportunity.

***

Keith's smile turned to a malicious grin as he packed up the little squares. He was going to try his hell brew on a couple of girls tonight at a fraternity party. He'd already picked them out. One girl, named Donna, was tall and beautiful and dated one of his best customers, an unprincipled lout named Dominick.

But he really was interested in another girl, one who had become another regular customer. Petite, with soulful brown eyes, and smart, Keith regarded her as an equal in intellect. She didn't know him, but she used a lot of drugs. Also, she didn't seem to have a steady boyfriend.

Keith licked his lips thinking about intimacy with her. Shouldn't be too hard, he figured. She'd try the stuff, for sure.

Her name was Rachel Farrell.

Keith smiled to himself as he packed his little inventions up to take them to the party at the fraternity house. Some people were going to be changed forever tonight.

"I wonder what they'll learn how to do?" he asked Rolf.

"I don't know," said Rolf, though he didn't speak out loud.

He thought the answer to Keith. Both of them grinned.

Keith thought about sex with Rachel Farrell. It would be great.

***

Five days later

Rachel found herself lying in a field of grass. Strange, she thought. She'd never seen grass this green, almost an emerald color.

The sky also: she'd never seen a sky that blue. She had the feeling that she could reach up and touch the sky and embrace it.

A song lyric occurred to her. One of the girls on her dorm floor had bought Jimi Hendrix's album *Are You Experienced* last week and played "Purple Haze" over and over: "Scuse me, while I kiss the sky." She grinned as she thought about how the rest of the girls on the floor had begun discussing the merits of lynching.

Rachel climbed to her feet, and found that she wore a garment she didn't remember owning. She felt sure she'd never even seen this article of clothing. It didn't quite cover her feet, and the brilliant fabric surpassed white.

No, it transcended brilliance. The whiteness surpassed white, the color of purity. She felt warm, also—not hot, but comfortable.

Off in the distance, she saw some trees, or what seemed to be trees. Nothing, though, was what it was supposed to be, wherever this was.

The cool, healing breeze caressed her face, like the breath of a mother over a beloved child. This air's purity felt nourishing. She faced into the gentle wind, took a deep breath and exhaled. She felt clean and whole, at peace for the first time in—months?

Rachel walked for a few moments, and it dawned on her that she wore sandals. She looked down and pulled the garment aside. A pair of leather sandals encased her feet, but they weren't sandals she'd ever owned. Still they felt more comfortable than any shoes she'd ever owned. A master craftsman seemed to have fashioned them around her feet.

It occurred to her that she ought to be afraid. She stood in this land all alone, as far as she could tell, and heard nothing at all: no sound of the wind blowing over the field, no birds, and no insects.

Yet the stillness didn't terrify her. This world, she thought, sat waiting for her to speak it into life.

Rachel extended her arms and leaned her head back, letting this strange, lovely new world enfold her. She realized that she didn't feel scared, nor angry, nor any other negative emotion.

She let the sun warm her face and neck, and breathed the lovely, pure air. She asked herself, *Am I dead?*

"No, not dead, beloved," said a voice behind her.

Rachel jumped, startled, not expecting to hear the voice of anyone else in this world. She turned to see someone standing behind her.

He towered over her, slim with long white hair. His eyes stared back at her, and the expression appeared neither sad nor happy, nor judgmental. He didn't appear to be much older than she, but the eyes were old, ancient with wisdom, and she saw, to her surprise, that they were golden—not brown, not chestnut, but gold. The eyes filled with tears as she looked back at them.

As she watched, he seemed to flicker. Then, where a man had stood, a pillar of flame burned orange and black. She started to scream—

But then the man stood there again. The eyes again filled.

The first tear trickled down his cheek. Stunned, she realized that he shed the tears for her. She turned her eyes away and down.

"You have been very foolish, Beloved," the man said.

She didn't speak. Couldn't even look up. She knew what he meant.

"I know I have," she managed at last. "I'm sorry. Can you forgive me?"

"No, I cannot do that," he said. "You need to take that to the One who has the power to forgive. But you must face what you have done first."

He pointed to her left. Rachel turned and saw herself sitting in the lavish living room of her parents' mansion, built near the lake in Winnetka, a wealthy North Shore Suburb of Chicago. She recognized the scene as her parents told her that they intended to divorce. She saw herself weeping as Mom and Dad drank and snarled at one another. There had been affairs, excessive drinking, irreconcilable hurts on both sides. Her father intended to move out but swore that he would fight her mother in court with all the violent energy he could muster. Her mother, her face stone, echoed his determination to see her husband defeated and humiliated in the divorce action. Rachel just sat, weeping and devastated to learn that her family would soon cease to exist. She begged them not to take any action until she graduated from college in June, only a few months away. She heard again their bitter acquiescence—

Now she found herself in the field, and the man pointed to her right side. The scene shifted. Now, with dismay, she watched her boyfriend of more than two years standing with her on the front porch of her parents' home. It was a day before Christmas and he told her that he had met someone new. Not only was he sleeping with his new girlfriend, but they intended to marry. He asked Rachel to return his college class ring which she had worn as an engagement ring. The ring symbolized her devotion which had led her to give him her virginity, and to trust him with her most intimate feelings, thoughts, and fears. As she watched the scene, she felt once again the pain, the anger, and the sense of betrayal that accompanied the brief and unexpected confrontation.

And the scene shifted again. Now the visitor showed her the friendship with Hollis that began following her return to the University of Illinois after Christmas vacation. The vision gave her brief glimpses of herself using the drugs to which Hollis and her boyfriend had introduced her: the marijuana first, then Speed, then hallucinogens, and then even a few shots of heroin.

Then she saw the party—

Now she shut her eyes and stopped watching, feeling real fear rising. "What happened at the party, beloved?" the tall man asked. He opened his arms to her and she came into an embrace that comforted her and helped her overcome the fear. Still, it took a few moments before she could answer.

At last, she told him. "I met someone named Dominick," she said. "He came to the party with a girlfriend, someone named—"she faltered a little.

"Donna," he prompted. She nodded.

"Then we met Barry, Dominick's friend," she went on. "Dominick introduced us to someone named Keith. Keith offered us a drug he'd invented. He said we'd find it similar to LSD, but much better."

"You all took the drug?" asked the Man. He flashed into a pillar of flame for an instant. Then again he looked like a man.

"No," she said. "Just three of us, I mean, Donna, Barry and me."

"And did you find it to be like LSD?"

"No," she whispered. "It wasn't like LSD at all."

"Was it better, Beloved?

She shook her head. "No," she whispered. "It terrified me."

She enjoyed the drug at first. As it warped her senses, she saw

bright lights, exotic new colors, heard the music at the party swell and recede, and then—

"Yes?" said the man. "Why did you stop?"

"Excuse me," Rachel said. "You know me, it seems—"

"Yes," he smiled. "All your life."

"Will you tell me your name?"

He frowned. "Curiel will do, I think, for now," he said. "But continue your story."

Rachel saw nothing but black for a few seconds. Then, a fiery glow appeared in the distance and something pulled her toward it. As it neared, she found herself standing at the base of a mountain— no, a volcano, she realized. The mountaintop smoked and belched out fire, she could see. To her horror, a river of lava began to flow down the mountainside toward her. It would reach her in moments.

In the side of the mountain, she spotted a cave. She could run to this cave and hide, safe from the lava—

Now a new terror arose. She couldn't move. She couldn't even lift her foot. She was going to burn alive, enfolded in the conflagratory arms of the goddess Pele.

She smelled the hideous stench of sulfur and smoke, and felt the searing heat of the lava as it approached. The roar of the volcano almost deafened her.

The lava flowed down to her and split as it neared her into two streams, trapping her between the flows. She saw several dark figures rise up out of the lava.

As she looked, she heard a voice: "Rachel," it snarled. Then a chorus of other voices joined the first. "Come to us," the voices said.

Several black shapes emerged from the lava and rushed toward her. They seized her in moments, and lifted her into the air. They crossed the lava field, with Rachel suspended mere inches above the flame that threatened to sear her flesh off. She still could not move. The shapes—which seemed to be the shape of men, but made of smoke and fire—seized and dragged her toward the cave. They pulled at her clothing and dragged her into the cave.

Down, down into the blackness of the cave the creatures dragged her, laughing and mocking her screams, her terror and her pleas for mercy. At last they stood before two enormous doors, black and menacing. The doors swung open and a blast of icy air assaulted her flesh. More demons poured forth, tearing at her clothes until she been stripped naked and humiliated—

"Then what happened, beloved?" Curiel asked, when she couldn't continue.

"You know," she said. "It's so terrible."

"Yes, it is," he said. "But have courage. Continue with the narrative." She took a deep breath and the air seemed to calm her and infuse her with a sense of peace.

She felt again the terror of that evening. The creatures laid Rachel out on the icy stone floor of the cavern, with demons kneeling on her arms. Others stood around, screaming, dancing with lust and fury while two pulled her legs apart.

Rachel heard someone yell. "Let her go, you bastards!" The demons snarled and screamed in fury, but a man appeared above her, swatting at the tormentors and driving them off of her. Now the man helped her up, draped a robe over her shoulders, then stripped off his own coat and bundled her into it.

She had a memory of this man picking her up, carrying her up the passage. They came into a foyer where someone opened a door. He carried her out into the cold air and to an old car. She had brief memories of streets passing, lights coming toward her, horns honking. Yet she felt no fear now, as the man kept his arm around her as he drove. In those moments, everything had changed for her.

"You no longer felt afraid," said Curiel.

"No," she said. "The man treated me with gentleness, and strength, and he brought me here. He laid me out in this field." She paused and looked around.

"Yes?" he asked.

"Where did this field come from? I've never been here before."

He paused. "Beloved, you've come to a safe, secret place," he said at last. "You have always imagined this place."

Rachel nodded. As he talked, she realized that she had always imagined that heaven would be like this place: utter peace, no fear, calm and safety.

"Yes," he said. "But your body lies in a house of healing—"

"A hospital," she said.

"Yes," he agreed. "You must return to life. Several people wait for you to return."

"Who?" she asked.

"Your parents, a nurse, and the man who rescued you." He pointed behind her. She turned and she found herself in the basement of Kam's, a popular beer hall on the campus of the University of Illinois. A band performed rock music and her attention riveted on the guitarist—

"Rick," she said.

Curiel nodded. "Yes, beloved. He's the man who saved you, the one on whom you have doted, whom you have come to love, all without his knowledge."

"But he has a girlfriend," she mumbled.

The scene in the bar blurred, and then disappeared, and she found herself again in the green field.

"He has become unhappy with her," Curiel said. "He comes to your hospital room because he has told himself that he's concerned for you, but in reality, he has begun to return your affection. You must find him when the hospital releases you."

"All right," she said.

"One thing more," he said. "An issue of vital importance."

"Yes?"

"Your memory of this place will fade, but what you have done will have consequences," he said, and again she saw a tear on his cheek. "The drug you took at the party turned on a switch in your brain that gave you an ability you were never supposed to have. The chemicals will empower you to do something you were never intended to do."

"Tell me," she pleaded.

"You will see soon enough," he said. "If you do use it, you will surrender yourself to the fury of the demons that tormented you before the gates. No, they cannot have you," he asserted. "But they can and will cause you anguish."

"They can't have me?" she asked.

"No, beloved," Curiel said. He pointed. Again she saw herself stretched out in humiliation before the black gates, screaming for help. "As you lay on the ground before the gates, you called on the Name." The scene before the doors played before her eyes. Rachel watched as the demons stripped away her clothing and heard herself scream: "Jesus!"

"Yes, beloved," he said. "You committed your life to him in high school at your church's youth group. At the gates you begged Jesus to save you. He did."

"I see," Rachel said, and for the first time in several minutes she felt calm and peace steal over her, wiping away fear, doubt, and guilt. "I have ignored Him for some time, haven't I," she said.

"You know the answer to that, Beloved."

"All right," she whispered. He embraced her and she felt fear, doubt, and depression ease away.

"Are you ready, Beloved?"

"Wait," she said. "Will I see you again?"

"Yes, Beloved," he said. "One day you will walk with me here. At that time you will never again feel fear or doubt. But that is many years from now."

"I understand," she said.

"Goodbye for now, Beloved," he said. "Be strong and believe."

"Wake up, Miss Farrell," said another voice.

Chapter Two

Rachel opened her eyes. "How do you feel?" asked a voice. Rachel turned, her eyes still blurry from the unconsciousness, and saw a man sitting on a chair next to the bed.

Rachel considered. "Thirsty," she replied, her voice sounding like a croak. "A little groggy."

The man put a straw next to her mouth and she sipped a little water. "Thank you," she said, her voice better.

The man smiled at her. "You're welcome. You okay?" he asked. Now, her eyes focused and his voice registered. As her eyes cleared, she saw his long hair, and the exotic paisley of his shirt, which identified him as a member of a campus rock band. She knew who this person was.

She nodded. "I will be, I think." She smelled the antiseptic odor of a hospital and felt the stiff discomfort of institutional sheets against her skin. "Would you crank my bed up for me?" she asked.

He took the control from the table and pressed a button. The bed rose up until she was upright. She stretched, her muscles coming alive. "Thank you," she said. "That feels better."

"I'm glad to see your eyes open," he grinned. "I'm—"

"Rick," she said. "Rick Howell."

Rick's eyes opened a bit wider in surprise. "You know me?" he said. "I didn't think we'd ever met."

"We haven't," she said. "But, yes, I know you. I follow your band around. I'm one of your fans."

Again a little surprise. "That's nice to hear," he said. "We play all over campus, and Champaign in general, and we know a lot of the people who come to see us—"

"I just kind of stand in the background," she said, her voice sounding a little lame.

"Well, anyhow, I came by to make sure you're okay," he said. "The doctors say you're going to be fine. By the way, they seem to think I'm your boyfriend."

She nodded, not sure that she could speak without crying in abject humiliation. She'd wanted to meet this man for months, but now she reached up and stroked at her hair, aware that she had on no makeup, that she wore an ugly hospital gown and beyond doubt looked like a perfect wreck.

She reached out and took his hand. She pressed it against her cheek and murmured, "Thank you. Oh thank you so much. You saved me from those fraternity creeps. You were so brave."

He stroked at her hair a little, not speaking. She looked up and realized that she'd embarrassed him.

"Thanks for saying that," he said. "I'm glad I could help. But really, I'm no hero. The rest of the guys in my band, and my girlfriend, well, we all kicked in…"

"Please," she said. "Please come here." She embraced him and whispered, "Thank you, Rick."

He murmured something, his tone gentle and kind. *What would my life be like if I married a man like this?* She wondered. She had a vision of a Christmas tree, a living room, candlelight—

—And felt something happen.

Rachel felt like she was being torn in two, from the inside out. Her head ached and the pain spread like ignited gasoline through her body—

Then stopped.

She opened her eyes and found that she no longer lay in a starchy, uncomfortable hospital bed. No, she lay in a queen sized bed, as familiar as a lover's kiss. Rachel found herself in a bedroom—hers, she realized—surrounded by pictures of her family—

Her family? She breathed deep, enjoying the pleasant aroma of the candles she'd lit before she climbed into bed. She relaxed a moment in the man's arms. She noticed that the strange discomfort she'd experienced a few moments before now had disappeared and she felt much better.

Her memory, too, began coming back. The hospital bed had been fifteen or so years ago, forgotten for a long while, a miserable recollection that seemed far away now.

She drew back from the hug and looked at the man—her husband, she realized—who sat on the bed embracing her. "Ricky," she smiled.

"Did I wake you?" Rick Howell asked in an intimate whisper.

"It's okay," she said, sitting up and leaning against the headboard. "Welcome, in fact. I was dreaming that I'd gone back to the hospital in college. " He groaned at the memory. Her eyes focused on a framed object on the opposite wall, which she realized as a medal.

No, not just a medal, Rachel knew. A Congressional Medal of Honor, awarded to her husband for conspicuous bravery and valor by the President himself. Rick had given the medal to her, she remembered.

He stroked her hair away from her face and kissed her lips. "I'm sorry if I disturbed you. See, I just got that bike for Danny assembled, and then checked on the kids."

Things were catching up in a hurry. "*Please* tell me they fell asleep," she groaned. "They went to bed so excited I thought we might have to shoot them to get them to settle down."

"I know," Rick grinned. "Yeah, they're dead to the world. Your parents, too. I listened at the door. Not a sound, unless you count your dad's snoring."

Rachel smiled too. "And *they're* so thrilled to be here," she said. "I'm so tickled that they drove all the way up from Tampa to share Christmas with us."

"Meanwhile, I want to give you something," he said.

"Oh yeah?" she said. "What a shocker."

He understood the sexual jibe and grinned. "No, I mean I want to give you your main present tonight," he said. "And the—er—other, as well, of course."

"Of course," she smiled with mock sternness. "Well, if you think you can bribe me into showing you your gift tonight, you can just forget it, Buster. You can just wait for morning like the rest of us. No way—"

"No, no, I'm not angling for my gift," he said. "This is too intimate to be shared with everyone else. Here." He handed her a long, narrow package which a professional had wrapped, she could see. At once she realized that the box contained jewelry.

"Oh Rick, what did you do—" she began, fumbling to unwrap the gift.

"Just a little something," he said. "I saw it in State Street Jewelers and I thought it would look pretty good on you."

Now she had the box open. Rachel found a pendant necklace and gasped as she drew it out of the box and held it to the light. Even in the dim candlelight, she could see the exquisite sapphire stone, surrounded by small diamond chips. "I got a white gold chain," he said. He took the jewel from her, reached up and secured the delicate clasp behind her neck.

Rachel stood and pulled off her nightgown as she walked across to the mirror above her dresser. "Oh, Rick, how could you afford—" she fumbled. "It must have cost—" she couldn't go on. Tears flowed.

"Not that much," he said, embracing her from behind and looking at the jewel over her shoulder. "Besides, no gift could ever equal what you're worth to me." She turned and returned his embrace. In moments they were on the bed, embracing, and then making love.

"Nothing you could ever give me would be better than this," he whispered after several marvelous moments.

"I love you too," she managed. Then her climax hit Rachel hard,

delicious and powerful. She shut her eyes as it flowed over her—

"You're way too kind," Rick Howell said. "I was glad to do it."

Now Rachel opened her eyes.

She wasn't in her bed nor was she hugging her husband. She embraced a man she'd just met, though she'd had a crush on him for some time.

"What just happened?" Rick said, shaking his head.

Rachel breathed deep as the hospital room appeared around her. What on earth? She thought.

"I just had the strangest—" he began, and then stopped. In that moment, Rachel had a revelation.

Whatever happened, he came with me, she thought.

Rick released her hand and stood up. "Sorry," he said. "I just…"

"Can you stay for a while?" she asked.

"Well, I…" he began. Then he looked in her eyes.

Oh, please stay, she thought. *I'm not afraid with you here.*

He looked at his watch. "I have to play a gig at Kam's," he said.

"A what?" she asked.

He smiled. "Musician talk," he said. "Gig means an engagement, a job, like that. This is Wednesday—"

"Wednesday!" she gasped.

"Yeah," he said. "You've been out of it since late Saturday night."

"Oh my," she groaned.

"Anyhow, we start at nine, but I have to get there about twenty minutes early to set up. I've got a little time."

"I don't want to impose," she said, aware that she sounded hollow. She really wanted him there.

"No imposition," he smiled.

"Rick," she said. "Can I please take you to dinner?"

His eyebrows shot up. "What?" he chuckled.

"Yes," she said. "You saved me from being raped and hurt. You stepped in when I needed you the most. The least I can do is to take you to dinner."

"Well, I—"

"I'm thinking we could go to the gas station on Green Street. They have hot dogs on the roller, you can select whatever chips and soda you want, and they don't charge for condiments, you know—"

He looked up, saw the mischief in her grin and chuckled with her. "Okay, I can't pass up an offer like that. Come see me when you get out and we can have a beer or something."

The young man and woman talked for quite a while, getting to know one another and enjoying one another's company. At eight o'clock, he said, "Look, I like chatting with you, but I really do have to go. I've got to grab something to eat."

"I know," she said. "Thank you so much." She reached up to hug him. He leaned over—

And then they began kissing.

Rachel had never experienced such a kiss. They kissed with a profound passion but she couldn't call it a make-out type kiss.

Rather, it felt like the kiss of a husband and wife, familiar, lovely, and a major part of a long-term relationship.

The kiss ended with a slow reluctance several minutes later. He drew back, released her, said an awkward good night and left.

The nurse came in a few moments later. "Your parents are here," said the woman. Mom and Dad followed just behind her.

"You're awake, at last," said Dad.

"Oh, honey," said Mom, coming up and embracing her. "What have you done to yourself?"

Rachel began to cry at the expression on her mother's face. Still she managed to sneer: "What do you care? You two have become so self-absorbed that you don't give a damn what happens to me."

"That's never been true," asserted her father. "We still love you—"

The argument accelerated for a few minutes and would have become antagonistic to the point of nastiness if the nurse hadn't intervened. "We need to keep her calm for a few days," she said, addressing Rachel's parents. "Could you two wait for a few moments in the hall?" Rachel sobbed in pain, fear and regret as her parents went back into the hall.

Her parents retired to the hallway, and Rachel forced herself to calm down. She dozed off again for a couple of hours.

When she woke, the room had become pitch dark—

And she saw her parents sitting in the hall. She heard her mother speaking: "How long has she been unconscious?"

"About twelve hours," said a man who seemed to be a doctor. "They brought her in unconscious and raving. We put her in restraints. . ."

"That bad?" asked Dad, tears on his cheek.

"Yes," said the doctor. "She kept going on about being carried into Hell or something."

"When can we see her?" asked Mom.

"Now," said the doctor, and opened the door.

Rachel turned to look—

But the door didn't open. No one came in.

Rachel swung her legs over the edge of the bed and walked to the door. She opened the door and looked into the corridor.

Rachel saw no one there. No Mom, no Dad, no doctor.

She went back into her room. She pressed a button to summon a nurse.

A few minutes later, the duty nurse came in carrying a tray.

"Could you send in my mom and dad?" she asked.

"They left a few hours ago, when you dozed off, I believe," replied the nurse. "They went back to their hotel…"

"No," said Rachel. "I just saw them. They started to come in the room."

"Impossible, my dear," said the nurse. "They left the hospital. You must have been dreaming."

Rachel stared as the nurse eased her back into bed and covered her. "Here," said the nurse, pulling the little table over. "Eat something. You'll feel better."

Rachel managed a little jello and half a sandwich, but she felt not the slightest bit hungry. The nurse chided her that she needed to regain her strength.

When the nurse left, Rachel reviewed the vision. The doctor said she'd been in the hospital about twelve hours, so it must have been noon when her parents were outside the room.

But that couldn't have just happened. She glanced at the clock on the bedside table and saw that it was 8:43 p. m. No light shone in through the shades from the outside and days had elapsed since that conversation had occurred.

Then she'd had that precious few moments of being married to Rick that seemed to have happened in the future.

Rachel thought for a moment. She cast about for a memory and hit upon a vacation the family had taken to Anaheim, California to see Disneyland in 1955, when she was about nine.

She focused hard on the memory and . . .

She stood in Disneyland in front of her favorite attraction in Fantasy Land, *Mr. Toad's Wild Ride*. Next to her stood Mom, much younger and thinner, no trace of bitterness in her eyes.

"My goodness," said Mom. "You want to go on *Mr. Toad* again?"

Rachel, astounded, managed to find her voice. "Mom? What's going on? How did I get here?"

Mom looked at her, then at Dad, utter bewilderment on both of their faces.

Rachel shut her eyes and thought about the hospital—

And opened her eyes to find herself in the hospital room in Champaign, Illinois.

She gasped for air, out of breath and frightened.

What had just happened?

She'd focused on a memory and found herself in the recollection. But how—

Then she remembered the Man in the meadow. What had he said? "You opened a gateway that should never have been opened."

Oh, God. Did he mean that somehow she had acquired the ability to control time and space?

***

Someone knocked. She yelled, "Come in!" The door opened and a tall young woman came in, wearing a tie-dye t-shirt, jeans, a floppy hat, and suede boots. "Rachel," she said, struggling to maintain composure. Rachel could see tears in her eyes.

"Hi, Hollis," she said to the girl who'd become her best friend over the last couple of months.

"You okay?" Hollis asked.

"Yes," said Rachel. "I regained consciousness earlier this afternoon. I've been dozing on and off. What about you?"

"Oh, I'm okay," said Hollis with a wave of her hand. "I never took that stuff once we saw what happened to you and your friends—"

"I wouldn't call them my friends," said Rachel. "I'd just met them."

"Oh," said Hollis. "Well, anyway…"

Her voice trailed off. "Yes, Hol?" asked Rachel, a few moments later.

"I'm so sorry about what happened to you," said the young woman, and Rachel again saw the tears. "I never thought…"

"I know," said Rachel. "I don't blame you. I'm the one who took the stuff. I don't know how I could have been so stupid."

Hollis wiped her eyes with her sleeve. Rachel continued. "I'm through with the drug bit," she said. "I can't do it anymore."

"Me, too," said Hollis. "I've been acting crazy. I even tried heroin last week."

"So did I," said Rachel. "That doofus Clyde came to my dorm room."

"He what?" gasped Hollis. Rachel nodded. "How did he get in?" Hollis asked.

"He's a criminal," shrugged Rachel. "He found a way. Anyhow, we did a couple of shots of the stuff." She lowered her eyes. "I went to bed with him after that."

Hollis looked shocked. "With Clyde?" she sputtered. "You couldn't…"

"I'm not going to do it again," Rachel said. "No, not quite sex. I knew he'd want that if I saw him again and I tossed him out." The things she was saying to her friend amazed Rachel. She realized that since her overdose, she felt she had to put everything behind her, to erase the chalkboard and start again. "Rick came to see me," she added. "He was here when I woke up."

Now Hollis smiled. "And?"

"Well, we visited," said Rachel.

Hollis' smile widened. "And?"

"Okay," Rachel smiled. "He kissed me just before he left. It was great."

Hollis now lowered her eyes. "Something you should know," she said. "I broke off with Greg. I have to get away from him and the whole drug thing."

Rachel nodded her understanding. The two young women relaxed and the tension eased. They became friends again. They made arrangements to have dinner together as soon as Rachel got out of the hospital. Hollis hugged her just before she left.

As she left, Rachel dozed off again. She felt exhausted from the conversations, but when she thought about kissing Rick, everything felt better.

She came awake at midnight when someone knocked at the door. "Come in," she yelled.

The door opened and the man named Barry came in, dressed in the clothes he'd worn that evening they'd overdosed at the party. They greeted each other and talked for a few moments.

"What time is it?" she asked.

"About midnight," he said. She took a deep breath and nodded.

"You doing okay?" he asked.

"Yes, I think so," she said. "I've done drugs for the last time."

Barry agreed. "I've been in to see Donna," he said. "She'd like to speak to you. Could you go in to see her?"

"Sure," Rachel said. "Is she okay?"

"Yeah," he said. "So am I, at least in a physical sense. My heart, lungs, kidneys, all that are fine, the doctors say. But..."

When he didn't go on, Rachel prompted him. "Yes?"

"Something's changed with my mind," he said. "Something really big."

"What do you mean?" Rachel asked.

He paused. "I keep seeing the past, and the future," he mumbled. "I'm seeing visions so vivid, so real—"

"Same for me," said Rachel.

"Yes?" he asked, eyes wide. She nodded.

She saw him hesitating to go on and said, "Something else?"

He nodded. "I'm going to sound crazy," said Barry. "I can go to these places I keep seeing, past and future."

Rachel hesitated. Then, "I know," she said. "Same for me."

Barry stared at her. "Did you see someone while you were unconscious?"

"Yes," she said.

"Someone with golden eyes?" he asked.

She nodded.

Barry stood and paced for a few moments. "Same with me," he said. "That Keith character designed the drug to affect people that way."

"But how could he do such a thing?"

Barry shrugged. "Drug dealers don't have much patience with things like compassion," he said. "They only care about profit. This guy Keith not only loved profit, he wanted to experiment with peoples' minds."

He turned to the window. "I'm scared to say this," he said. A couple of minutes elapsed before he murmured, "You and I have to go back to that party." He looked right into her eyes. "We have to stop Keith. We can't let him continue in this insane experiment with human guinea pigs. "

Rachel stared at him for a moment. "What are you saying?"

"We—er—have to kill Keith," he said. "We can't let him keep going with this."

"What!" she gasped.

"Yeah," he said, his eye contact wavering. "They just brought in two more victims. They're raving and scared and the hospital put them in restraints. I guess we came in like that too."

Rachel understood. She realized that Keith had infected other people since the party. "But..." she fumbled to get the words out. "Barry, I don't think I can kill someone."

"I know what you mean," he said. "It's okay, I think I can. I just need your help."

"Why do we have to kill him?" she pleaded. "Why can't we just turn him in to the police?"

"Because he knows how to make that stuff," said Barry. "Think for a minute. If he goes to jail, it won't be for long. He'll always know the formula, and who knows what it can be used for?"

She thought for a second or two and saw the point of his argument. "He'll come out and ruin other people's lives, won't he?"

"You understand," he said. "It's no use, Rachel. I've thought this through from every angle I can. It's up to us."

Rachel hesitated a moment before she said, "Give me a minute to get dressed."

***

Rachel and Barry stood in front of the fraternity house and watched people leaving, scared about what they had seen: three people carried from the house, suffering severe intoxication or a drug overdose. Barry suggested a plan, and Rachel nodded. It sounded perfect.

Keith emerged, looking scared and somewhat shaken, having just poisoned three people. He looked both ways, up and down the street, and his glance fell on Rachel and Barry for a second. He looked startled at seeing them.

Then, he shook his head. They saw what he was thinking—that couldn't be them. No, not possible.

He turned away and started to run. They followed, but Barry was in no hurry. "I know where he's going," he said. "Don't worry."

They followed Keith down Wright Street, past the huge Library and Lincoln Hall. He ducked between two buildings and headed across the quadrangle toward Noyes Lab, the chemistry building. They saw him run into the building.

"Over here," said Barry. "It won't be long."

They hid next to the building and waited. The quad was quiet, only a very few people wandering across it. They only had to wait a few moments. Keith came out, again looked side to side and all over. This time he didn't see them. He started off across the quad, not concerned. Barry nodded to Rachel and they hurried up behind him.

Rachel walked up next to Keith. "Hi, Keith!" she said, with apparent enthusiasm.

He turned and his jaw dropped. "No," he said. "No, it can't be you—"

But he shut up as Barry grabbed him and pinned his arms behind him. "What—" he began, but shut up when Barry hit him on the side of the head with an open palm.

"Hello, Keith," Barry spoke into his ear. "Yes, it's us. Two of the three people you just poisoned." Keith tried to struggle.

"Where are they?" Rachel asked, trying to be calm.

"What?" stammered Keith.

Rachel snapped her fingers several times. "Oh," said Keith. "You mean…"

Rachel nodded. "My jacket pocket," Keith managed, only just able to speak. Rachel reached into one pocket, then the other one, and found a small bag. Inside were about a dozen of the small red squares of blotting paper. She extracted one.

"Let's see what happens, Keith," said Barry. Keith clammed his mouth shut and struggled, but he had no chance against Barry, who outweighed him by fifty pounds and was at least six inches taller.

"Open wide," said Barry. Keith shook his head. Barry grabbed his nose and held on until Keith had to open wide. Rachel popped a square into his mouth.

"Another one," said Barry. Rachel put another square in his mouth. Keith struggled, his eyes bulging with terror, unable to scream with the strangle hold Barry had clamped on him. "Maybe one more for good measure," he said, and Rachel complied. Keith struggled, trying to spit the squares out, but Barry clamped Keith's mouth shut with a wrestling hold.

At last, Keith went limp. His eyes widened and Barry let him fall to his knees. Rachel bent over and lifted his head so that he looked into her eyes.

"They're coming for you, Keith," she smiled. "They'll take you through the black doors. It's for eternity. Take this with you." As hard as she could, she slapped him across the face.

Barry released him and Keith fell forward onto his face. Barry and Rachel nodded at each other and prepared their minds to Step away.

The first scream resounded through the quad as they Stepped back to the hospital.

Chapter Three

The next morning, a police detective came to Rachel's room. "That guy named Keith who gave you the stuff," said the policeman. "Do you know anything about him?"

"Why?" asked Rachel.

"A campus cop found him about 3:00 A. M.," said the cop. "He was lying in the bushes near the library on the quad. He was nearly dead when they found him. They brought him here, but he was too far gone and he expired just before dawn. It seems to have been a massive drug overdose. His roommate reported him missing the day after the party."

"Huh," said Rachel, trying to look unconcerned. "Forgive me if I seem somewhat obtuse, but I don't see what that has to do with me. I'd never seen him before that night."

"We have a witness," the policeman said. "He came to us and claims he saw you and a guy named Barry follow this Keith right after the party. He claims you assaulted Keith on the quad. The witness got scared and ran off. He didn't tell us until today, in fact."

"What the witness says is impossible," said Rachel. "I just met that er—Keith—that night and he gave me the drug that put me here. I was insensible and delirious when they brought me in. I've been here for the last several days. I just regained consciousness last night."

"There's something else," the policeman said. "His friend claims Keith never touched drugs, at least to take them."

"Let me say this," she said. "The world is better off without him in it. He hurt me and my friends. He'd keep doing it, too."

He nodded. He asked a few more questions, then thanked her and left a few moments later.

Barry came to her room in about fifteen minutes. "Did you sleep last night?"

"Not much," she said. "Terrible dreams, all night."

"Same with me," he admitted. "'*Sleep no more! Macbeth doth murder sleep,*'" he quoted and paused. "How'd it go with the police?"

"No problem," she shrugged. "They know we were incapacitated at the time the witness says we killed Keith."

"Yeah," said Barry. "We're okay. Look, I just went to visit Donna. She told me she'd dumped her boyfriend Dominick."

"That guy who brought that Keith over to meet us?"

"Yeah, right," nodded Barry. Rachel shuddered. "She wants to see you."

Rachel nodded. "I'll go in. Did you find out what happened with the other two people they brought in after us?"

He smiled. "They never came in, Rachel. It worked."

She smiled too. It had worked indeed.

The hospital released her the next day. She fought with her parents for some time when they wanted to bring her home. They agreed to let her stay at the University when she assured them that she'd left the drug scene for good.

For the next several weeks, Rachel focused on her course work and got caught up with her studies. When not studying, she tried to sleep and relax. But sleeping almost never refreshed her. She struggled night after night with terrifying dreams of murder, Hell, and demons.

She found that her determination to leave the drug scene was far easier to articulate than to carry through. Again and again, she found that she longed to put aside her terror, her anguish, and her loneliness in the dark shadow of chemicals.

At one point, she found herself drinking too much and had to scale far back on her alcohol consumption. She came to understand that she couldn't substitute one mind-bender for another, and that she had to face the troubles she had.

The University referred her to a counselor who gave her significant help, and she found her desire to use chemicals to change how she felt begin to recede. She leaned on her friend Hollis, who was going through the same struggle.

But she found herself leaning more and more on her friend Donna, and the two became best friends as time went on, going places together, calling one another, studying together, and going to church together. Donna had not been as involved with drugs as Rachel, but the two of them supported one another.

And there was someone else.

When she'd wake up after a hideous nightmare of eternal perdition, she'd focus her thoughts on the guitarist named Rick. She thought about him and how he'd carried her away from the scene at the fraternity. She thought of how good his hand felt in hers, the embrace, the wonderful kiss they'd shared, the only pleasant memory she had of that wretched time in the hospital.

One night Hollis came to her room with a Bible. Rachel realized that she hadn't opened one in years. Together, they read many of the psalms, and Rachel found herself drawn to the 91st. She recited the psalm to herself over and over until she knew it by heart.

Then she started to pray. She recalled the Green Field, the healing wind, the calm hands and eyes of the person called Curiel. She would calm and drift into sleep.

Rachel had missed a considerable amount of class, but as her mind settled down, her grades went back up and she found herself almost back at the high level of scholarship she'd been achieving before she'd gone to student teach.

Rachel went to see the campus band called The Rockets as often as she could but stayed in the shadows, not speaking to Rick. The opportunity to chat with him just never seemed to present itself.

Meanwhile, she made some subtle inquiries about Rick. She found out as much as she could about the guitarist, learning where he lived and where his girlfriend lived. People who knew him considered him a good student, his professors liked him, and he worked several nights per week with his band.

Nonetheless, her sleep continued to be horrid experiences of terror. The dreams seemed to get worse and worse. Still she refused to take any chemicals to help her sleep.

Then, one Saturday night, she made up her mind. She dressed in her favorite skirt and sweater, and planned to go to see Rick Howell perform with his band at Kam's one more time. The band as a rule played at Kam's on Wednesday night and Friday night, but this week they were also performing on Saturday.

So she'd go to Kam's and watch the band, dance, and have as good a time as she could. Then she'd come home and take the sleeping pills. She'd saved them one by one and now had about twenty.

They'd do the trick, she had no doubt.

It almost seemed fitting. She screwed up her life with drugs. She could use drugs to end that life.

She reached into her closet, and at the back of the closet, she found the prescription bottle. She opened it and shook a few pills into her hand, then sat on her bed, just staring at them.

These things could take her back to the field, back to Curiel, her mind and body wouldn't hurt, she would never be lonely again. Mom and Dad would be upset, yes, but they had their own lives and they'd recover. The school would find someone to take her place this fall. The terror of the Black Gates would vanish forever. The dark creatures wouldn't come for her—

The phone rang. She picked it up on the third ring and said, "Hello?"

"Rachel, it's Barry."

Rachel swallowed hard and forced herself to cheer up. She said in as bright a voice as she could, "Well, hi, Stranger, how – "

"Wait," he interrupted. "Listen. You have to get out of your room right away. They're coming for you."

She felt a thrill of terror. "Who's coming for me?"

"At the party that night, do you remember meeting a little guy named Rolf?"

She shuddered, seeing the scene again. Keith had come over with the drug, accompanied by a little man with a shock of red hair and a nasty sneer on his face. She made eye contact—

In the next instant she found herself on a bed, tied to the head board and the foot board. Standing over her was this man named Rolf, leering and excited. She felt a scream building—

Then she stood in the fraternity house again, scared and wondering what had happened.

What on earth? She thought. *What was that?*

Rachel shook her head to clear away the dreadful memory and spoke again into the phone. "Yes," she said. "I do remember him." She put the pills back into the bottle and closed it up.

"He's behind this," said Barry. "He wants the—well, you know."

Rachel felt a chill of terror. "What could he do?"

"He's sending several people to your dorm," Barry said. "They'll be there any minute. You have to get out."

"Okay," she whispered.

"Run over to Campus Town," he urged. "Meet me behind Kam's. Quick."

He hung up and Rachel grabbed her parka. She started to go out the main door of her dorm, but changed her mind and ran down the steps to the back entrance.

Out into the cold night. She stayed in the shadows as she crossed campus, hiding whenever she saw a group of people. She arrived at Kam's and hurried around the building.

"Here," Barry whispered. She found him hiding behind a large dumpster and joined him. "Stay here, will you? I'm going to see what's happening. I think you'll be okay."

He stepped into the darkness and was gone.

Rachel shivered, not just with the cold. She was afraid. She didn't think she had a chance to defend herself against Rolf's henchmen. "O Lord," she whispered. "Please help me—"

She stopped when she heard voices across the alley. They were coming, looking for her. She knew that she was trapped, unable to help herself.

She forced herself to remain calm and decided that she had to use her new ability to Step away. Where? Where could she go to be safe?

She thought of returning to the Christmas Eve with Rick. No, no, she couldn't do that. That must have been a fantasy.

The high school. She had done her student teaching at Westbrook High School. She could Step there.

Right. Mrs. Benson, her co-operating teacher, told her that the faculty always gathered in the school theater for meetings and introductions on the first day of school.

She could go there. She could use that strange ability to slide into a new situation.

But it hurt so much. She'd have horrid, desperate dreams. On the other hand, she might be killed if they found her here tonight.

Full of fear, she stood up and heard someone yell. She focused her thoughts—

And took a Step. The fiery pain blasted through her body, her mind and body screamed with strain and fear, and her eyes saw terrifying visions of demons and evil—

Then it stopped. She opened her eyes and found herself in a hallway outside the Westwood School Theatre, where the faculty met for school opening meetings. She heard a voice next to her saying, "So we put this huge kid named Elvin at defensive end. I tell him, 'Look, Elvin, you shed the block like this, then when the ball carrier comes toward you, you go out to him, right?'"

Rachel, relieved, turned to the voice. Barry.

"The kid looks at me, a total blank," Barry went on. "He stammers for a few seconds, then says, 'Yeah, Coach, I get that, but when I get to him, what do I do?'

"I can't believe it. I say, 'Well, Elvin, when you get to him, you tackle him, right?' 'Oh yeah, right,' he says."

Barry laughed and Rachel joined in, shaking her head. Yeah, she knew the huge kid named Elvin, dumb as a rock but lovable with a heart of gold.

She looked around to make sure no one could hear. "Barry," she whispered. "I just Stepped here."

"What!" he gasped.

"Yes," she said. "I came from a night the last semester at school—" She stopped talking as someone walked up and stretched out her arms to Rachel.

"I'm so sorry," said the woman. "But I'm so glad you're back."

"Thank you," Rachel said. She hugged the woman and remembered that her name was Grace. "It's so good to see you, Grace. I missed everyone."

She took Barry's arm and whispered to him. "Barry, what has happened? What did she mean, she's sorry?"

Barry started to answer, but now Mrs. Benson, who had been her co-operating teacher during her student teaching, came over. Rachel felt tears come to her eyes as the older woman hugged her and also offered sympathy. As she walked away, Barry said, "Rachel. Please try to be brave. I…"

He paused, unable to go on himself. She took his hand and the tears in his eyes touched her heart. "Please tell me," she murmured.

"Rick died," Barry said. "The Viet Cong killed him in December, just before Christmas."

"Rick?" she said. Now it began to come back. "Of course," she managed. "He died in a sniper attack in Viet Nam."

"That's right," he said.

"Oh," she said. "I came from a night before we got together. I don't remember—"

"You took a leave of absence last semester," Barry said. She nodded. He took her arm and led her into the meeting. They sat together as the Principal began his yearly litany of changes in school rules and procedures. They whispered about what they'd do about the night in Champaign.

"I'm glad to see you all," said the Principal. "The school gets pretty lonely over the summer without all of you here." The teachers and staff gave an appreciative chuckle, but the Principal used the line every year, Rachel remembered. As her memories caught up now, she recalled one time when he'd discussed an experience the administrative staff had undertaken the previous week.

"The administrative team went on a retreat last week," he'd said. "We feel we really moved forward."

Rachel couldn't restrain a giggle. Barry turned to her, amused, but she waved him away. The Principal now said, "In particular, I know that you will want to join me in welcoming back one of our teachers who took a leave of absence last semester. You'll recall that her fiancé died just before Christmas and I know that you all agree that we're glad she's back. Will you join me in greeting her? Rachel Farrell, will you please stand up?"

Rachel sat stunned for a few seconds as the teachers began to applaud. Barry helped her up, and she heard cheers and whistles as she turned and waved, saying "Thank you" several times. Barry handed her his handkerchief and she applied it to her eyes.

She thought. Her name was still Farrell. So she hadn't married Rick yet. But what about that vision in the future, when she'd gone to a Christmas Eve, when she had been married to Rick, when they'd had children and she was reconciled to her parents, and …

Then she felt the sensation begin. In a moment she stood again in the alley behind Kam's. She shut her eyes and forced herself to go back to the school auditorium. When she opened her eyes, she found herself again in the high school theatre, with people clapping. Touched by the outpouring of kindness, she couldn't stop crying.

At last the Principal began to speak again and she sat down. "Oh brother," she whispered to Barry.

"Are you okay?" asked Barry.

"Yes," she said. "But I have to go back to the alley, Barry. I'm starting to feel pulled away."

"Okay," he said. "I'll Step back too. I'll get Donna and we'll join you."

She nodded. The two friends waited until a moment presented itself. They stood, took one Step—

And fell into the vortex of time and space, pain, colors, lights—

Then Rachel found herself in the alley again. One man shouted,

"Over there! I've got her!" Two thugs started toward her.

Just before they reached her, a voice behind them said, "Hey, Punk." The men turned and Barry punched one of them hard in the face. Rachel winced at the sound of the blow and the involuntary release of breath that sounded like "Whumpf". The man fell hard, stunned and unable to break his fall. He landed hard on his back, his head cracking against the pavement.

The other man turned to look at Barry, then Donna, and started to run. He stopped and stared hard into Donna's eyes for a moment.

His cry of terror reverberated down the alleyway as he fell to his knees, holding his arms over his head in self defense, unable to do anything except whimper with fear. Donna and Barry grabbed Rachel's arms and propelled her out into the street, then into the beer hall called Kam's.

"Are you okay?" asked Donna, hugging Rachel, trying to make herself heard over the incessant pinging of the pinball machines. Rachel smelled the noxious odor of a hundred cigarettes mingled with the stench of pizza and stale beer.

"Yes, fine," Rachel nodded. "Do you think you hurt those two men? The one hit his head on the pavement when he fell."

"I don't know how he is," said Barry. "I'm not really worried about them, though."

Donna and Rachel nodded. Now Rachel began to notice the sound of the band playing in the basement, The Rockets, with Rick Howell on lead guitar. "Will you be okay?" said Barry. "I want to walk Donna home."

"Yes," said Rachel. "Go ahead. I'm going to go and hang around and listen to the band downstairs."

Donna grinned. "You mean you're going to watch the guitarist, don't you?"

Rachel felt her cheeks begin to burn. She smiled and nodded, "Yeah, that's what I mean."

Her friends hugged her and left. Rachel gathered her thoughts in the ladies' room. She fixed her makeup and made her way down stairs.

The band had just started their last set, and Rachel made her way to the back of the crowded room. Several people in the Friday night crowd hovered near intoxication. Rachel sat and listened to the Rockets, watching the lead guitarist Rick. She danced with a few boys and chatted, and when one of them asked if he could walk her home, she almost accepted. He was a big guy who could protect her.

Then she shook her head and said, "No thank you," with a broad smile, hoping she wasn't hurting his feelings. "I need to hang around for a bit. I'm sorry. I would have liked that," she added, to dull the rejection. "Another time, okay?"

He looked disappointed but smiled and nodded.

The gig ended and the band played its break song, a rendition of *Dancin' in the Streets* by Martha and the Vandellas. She listened to the organist introduce the group and she smiled when he said, "And on lead guitar, Rick Howell." Rick waved and played a nice riff on his guitar.

The crowd departed, but Rachel stayed around as the band broke down the equipment. She began to consider suicide once more. It had come up in her mind many times.

She couldn't take the fear and the crippling paranoia any more. She took comfort in a vague memory of a beautiful field, a man with golden eyes, peace and safety. She remembered a promise Curiel had made to walk with her again in the field.

Curiel told her to seek out Rick, but she now thought his instruction seemed impractical, if not ridiculous. Many times she'd gone to see the Rockets play, but she'd never seen Rick apart from his tall blond girlfriend, the one who looked like a professional model.

Donna had come with her one night to see the Rockets and watched Rick interact with his girlfriend. "They've got problems," she told Rachel. "Just be patient."

Rachel knew that Donna spent her life afraid, too, but at least she had Barry. Donna and Barry had begun seeing each other after they came out of the hospital and Rachel felt pleased to learn tonight that they were becoming serious about one another.

Now the basement had almost emptied, and she saw the band packing up their instruments. Rachel had seen them do this many times, but this time seemed a little different. It looked like they were taking all their instruments and amplifiers with them rather than storing them in the back room.

But Rick hadn't packed up yet. On the contrary, he'd become embroiled in a major argument with his girlfriend. As she watched, Rachel saw the girlfriend draw back her hand. The crack of the slap echoed through the dingy basement.

The girlfriend stomped out of the basement and up the stairs. Rick, rubbing his jaw, sat down and pulled out his guitar case, looking a little stunned.

Rachel Farrell stared, shocked at the violence. The slap had been vicious.

Then she breathed deep, straightened her skirt, smoothed her hair and walked across the room to meet the man named Rick, who'd saved her life.

PART II

Musician

Chapter Four
Rick Howell

Rick Howell stood watching Janet storm out of the bar, tears on her cheeks. She'd stalked away and up the steps, furious after the quarrel.

Another fight with Janet, he thought. Damn it all, *another* fight. His cheek still stung from the slap. Not the first time she'd whacked him in the last few months.

She'd come back in a few moments and he'd take her into town for a pizza. Not that he wanted to. He was sick and tired of contention, disagreement, fights—all that the relationship with Janet had become.

He unhooked the guitar strap and set the instrument on its stand. He sat on the bench watching Bob break down his drum set.

Rick knew he'd have another big fight with Janet on the way to the pizza parlor. He couldn't see any reason that tonight should be an exception. As he thought about it, he realized things had been going south with their love affair ever since that gig at the fraternity house, when he'd taken the girl to the hospital—

"You play well," someone said.

He looked up and smiled as he recognized the young woman. He'd last seen Rachel Farrell in the hospital where she looked haggard, thin and beaten up. The girl who stood before him now, however, wore an attractive outfit, flattering hairstyle, and a warm smile. His mind fled back to a romantic kiss in a hospital room—

He shook his head. "Thank you," he said. "I'm flattered."

"Modest, too," Rachel teased. "Very becoming."

That smile healed Rick's anger. He looked into her eyes and felt himself calm down, the fight with Janet and his frustration forgotten for the moment.

But the brown eyes held a hint of. . .

What could it be?

Now he realized. Though she smiled at him, he could see fear in those eyes. No, not just simple fear. Terror. He shrugged away the creepy sensation.

Rick stood up. "It's been a while," he said.

"A little more than six weeks," she told him. She extended her hand and he took it. The hand felt marvelous in his and he again thought back to a passionate kiss in a hospital room. He had a difficult time letting go and started to feel that the situation was becoming awkward. She broke eye contact then and looked around at the amplifiers and drums as the band took apart their equipment.

"It's nice to see you again," she said, not looking up at him.

"Thanks," he said. "You too. Don't take this the wrong way, but you look a great deal better than the last time I saw you."

"Yeah," she smiled. "I imagine I do. I've been feeling a lot better. I wanted to let you see that I don't always look like an expatriate from a starving nation."

Rick laughed at the simile and assured her that no one would mistake her for a refugee. "So you're doing okay?" he asked.

"Yeah, much better," she nodded. "Thanks to you."

"Ah, you're being way too kind," he said, but the compliment made him feel much better. The fight with Janet seemed far away when he looked at this girl.

"You're a very compassionate person, to help me like you did," she said. "I wanted to remind you that you made me a promise."

"I did?" he blinked.

"Yep," she said. "You promised to have dinner with me so I could repay you for all you did."

"Remember, I told you I didn't expect anything like that—"

"Shut up," she said. "We've already had this discussion and you lost then. I'm taking you to dinner."

"Okay," he chuckled. "The Texaco station, I think you said?"

"Or we could splurge and go to the Shell station, you call it," she smiled.

"I can't wait," he said.

"Right," she nodded. "So what happened with your girlfriend?"

The blunt question took him aback. "What do you mean?"

"The spectacular blond I always see you with, the one who just ran off crying. I figured her for your girlfriend."

"Well, yeah," said Rick, surprised and flattered that Rachel had been watching him. "We had a big fight a few minutes ago."

"So I saw," she said. "You make it sound like you two fight on a pretty regular basis."

Rick grew uncomfortable with the direction of this conversation. "Rachel," he said. "We've never met aside from a few minutes in the hospital—"

"Ah," she interrupted. "You mean I don't need to concern myself in the least with your relationship with the tall blond with the sensational figure. None of my business. Right, I know. I didn't mean to press you."

"Okay, forget it."

"I apologize," she said.

"Look, don't—" began.

"I never should have asked."

"Really, please don't think—"

"No," she said. "I feel awful."

Rick decided to try one more time. "Rachel," he began. "I'm not upset—"

"Oh, good," she interrupted. "Then tell me about the fight."

He snickered. He liked this girl and grinned as he said, "I have to pack up my guitar. Please excuse me."

"Where are you going in such a hurry?" she asked.

"Out with the spectacular blond," he said. He opened the clasps on the beat-up guitar case and lifted the top.

"Why do I get the impression that doesn't make you happy?"

He leaned over and placed his Gibson, his prize possession, into the blue plush velvet of its old case. He laid the strap along the fretboard of the guitar. He debated with himself for a moment. Then he decided that he wanted to tell Rachel what was up.

"We—I mean, the band—we got an offer to play at a late night party. The money sounded pretty good, and the gig would only last a couple of hours."

"A job? In the middle of the night?" she asked, amused.

"I know, but it happens," he said. "Not only that, I could use the money."

"So I don't seem to get the problem," she said.

"Janet got mad. She said she'd planned for us to go out."

"And you didn't know the plan?"

"I guess I didn't think about it," he admitted.

"Some boyfriend," she said with a look of disdain which didn't quite work because of her smile.

"Yeah, I'm not much, I agree," he agreed. "Anyway, I'm taking her into town for a pizza. The band can play without me. More money for them."

"They can get along without their lead guitarist?" she asked.

"They just won't do any guitar solo songs, or Steve, the organist, can play the solo."

At that moment, Janet returned, but stopped short when she saw Rick chatting with another girl. Her facial expression soured and she gave Rachel a nasty look which Rachel answered with a charming smile. Janet took Rick's arm.

Rachel held out her hand to Janet. "I'm so glad to meet you," she said. "I can't begin to tell you how much I appreciate—"

"Don't mention it," Janet interrupted, ignoring Rachel's hand. "Let's go," she demanded to Rick.

"Goodnight, Rick," said Rachel. "I enjoyed seeing you in a normal situation." She extended her hand and Rick, smiling at her comment, took it. He again enjoyed holding the hand of the Time Changer. He felt Janet's withering stare of disapproval.

"Nice to see you again," he smiled.

"What did she want?" demanded Janet as they drove away from the bar.

"Nothing special," he said. "She just thanked me again for taking her to the hospital and complimented me on my playing."

"She wants you," said Janet. "She's nothing but a crummy junkie. Why would you even speak to her?"

"Oh come on," sighed Rick, weary at the prospect of the next fight. "We talked about the band." He wasn't surprised that Janet didn't go for it. Another fight ensued, as he'd expected. By the time they reached the pizza parlor, they'd settled into a sort of uneasy truce.

In mid-argument, he realized that Janet seemed to be right about Rachel. Rachel found him as attractive as he'd found her.

Chapter Five

At 2:30 A. M., Rick dropped Janet off at her dormitory. After the late night dinner, he suggested they go back to his apartment. Janet, still miffed with him, didn't want to make love, nor did she want to spend the night, so he drove her home.

He watched the dormitory door close behind Janet and heaved yet another sigh as he walked to his car.

He started to lower himself into the seat behind the steering wheel, but jumped when he saw someone sitting in the passenger's seat.

"Hi again," said Rachel, and even in the dim glow of a streetlight he could see that radiant smile.

"Omigod, you surprised me," he said.

"Sorry," she said, her voice cheerful. "How'd the date go?"

"What are you doing here?" He found himself feeling rather leery of this girl showing up in his car. She didn't seem to be dangerous, but—

Rachel shrugged. "I did some asking around and found out where—er—what's her name—"

"Janet?" he asked.

"Right, Janet—where she lives. So after you left Kam's I walked over here and waited. I saw you pull up and came over to wait for you."

"How'd you get in the car?" he asked.

"You left the door unlocked," she said. "And I got cold waiting. Now answer my question."

Rick almost told her to get out of the car but he paused and took a deep breath. He liked this girl and her smile healed Rick's terrible mood. "Okay, I will," he shrugged. "The date stank. We had another big fight and a terrible pizza to go with it—"

"Yeah, they don't know how to make pizza here in Champaign," she shrugged. "Except for Kam's. It's pretty good."

"—And then I asked her to come back to my apartment. She told me no, so I drove her home."

"Oh," she said. To his surprise he saw that despite the smile Rachel still radiated an aura of fear. She looked as if she might be ready to cry. "She thinks I'm nothing but a White Trash junkie, doesn't she." It was a statement.

Rick tried to equivocate. "Oh, I don't know—"

"I do," Rachel said. "I could see it in her eyes. She considers me a druggie and a loser."

"Well, I don't," he said. Rachel looked up with surprise. Then a little smile crossed her lips.

"Do you love her?" she asked in a voice so low he had to struggle to hear it.

He started to say yes, of course he did, but the words wouldn't quite form. He remained silent and gave a little shrug.

"Do you?" she persisted.

"We're engaged to be married," he said. "We've even set a date. July next year."

"You didn't answer my question," she said.

"Rachel—" he began.

"The question shouldn't be that difficult, Rick," she said. "Do you love her or not?"

He paused. "How do you know for sure if you're in love?" he said. "Janet and I spend a lot of time together, do lots of stuff. . ."

To his surprise he saw a little smile start across her face. "So what upset you about the evening?"

"I dunno," he said, surprised that he didn't want to face the answer.

"Okay, let me tell you. You're still angry about not performing at the party."

He considered this for a second. "Yeah," he admitted. "I guess I am."

"Of course," she nodded. "Anyone can see how much the band and the music means to you."

"Well, yeah, that's true," he agreed.

"If you could do the last few hours over, what would you do?"

"No question. I'd go with the guys to play the gig."

"You're that desperate for money?" Rachel asked, peering into his eyes.

"Money wouldn't be the most important thing," he said. "The music—well, I—" he stumbled, trying to form a coherent answer.

"I get it," she said.

"Er—" he began, then stopped. "You do?"

"Sure," she said. "I play piano. I took private lessons for eleven years, beginning when I was six. Playing music means a lot to you. You're an artist."

"Thank you," he said, pleased at the compliment.

She sat for a few moments, staring out the windshield as if considering her options. "Okay," she said. "Come on."

She opened the car door and got out. "Come on," she insisted.

Mystified, Rick climbed out. He walked around to her and took her outstretched hand. She looked up into his eyes. "I'm going to give you a second chance," she said. "You won't remember any of this conversation. You won't even remember that you met me again tonight. Let's see how you do."

"Huh?" he mumbled, not sure what this was all about.

"I don't know if I can explain," she said. "It's going to sound strange. Well, no: beyond strange."

"Okay," he said. "Take a crack at it."

"You remember when you found me at the party," she said. "That's the night I and two others took some sort of drug. The pusher—" she paused and swallowed hard—"told us it was some sort of hallucinogenic."

"Right, I remember."

"Well, it wasn't a hallucinogenic," she nodded, not looking up at him. "That drug changed something in my brain, like it turned on a switch. Somehow I acquired the ability to alter time."

Rick stood dumbfounded for a few moments. "What in the blazes can you possibly be talking about?" he managed.

"I know that sounds weird," she nodded. "But I'm serious. And I can show you."

"My God, Rachel, what kind of crazy—"

"Please, Rick," she interrupted, almost begging. "Sure, this sounds beyond insane. But I swear it's true. I don't know what the drug did to me, or if it's permanent, but somehow I can control time."

He decided to humor her. "Okay, so how often do you do this?"

"I try never to do it. But there were a couple of very brief times."

"And what happened?"

"A couple of times I just Stepped back for a few moments," she said. "Twice I stepped forward. And then..." her voice trailed away and she looked uncomfortable.

"What happened?"

"I can't tell you about that," she said. "I made a promise."

"Uh, huh," he grunted, his skepticism obvious in his voice.

"Can I show you?"

"What did you have in mind?"

"We're going back to the end of the evening at Kam's."

"How in the..."

"Just tell me if you could go along with that."

He felt stupid, like she planned to play some sort of joke, and that she'd announce it, and a whole bunch of people would jump out of bushes laughing and taking pictures. But he managed, "All right."

She reached up and embraced him. "Expect some discomfort," she said. "Please, Rick?"

"Huh?"

She drew a deep breath. "Please try to remember to do what you want."

"I don't—" he stumbled, but she kissed him. Rick, surprised, almost pushed her away—

Except. . .

Except he liked the kiss. A great deal, he realized. He'd wanted to kiss her again for weeks. He returned the embrace and let the kiss deepen into passion for several moments. He felt as if a deep hazy fog swirled around him. He grew aware of sounds, lights, and . . .

Chapter Six

Rick Howell found himself standing in front of his amplifier, watching the Saturday night crowd leave. He felt a little dizzy, like he'd just climbed down from a roller coaster. Strange. What could have caused that? He lifted his guitar strap over his head and sat down.

Jeez, I haven't been drinking, he thought. *I don't smell any marijuana. .*

Janet came over. "Let's go," she ordered. "Pack up your guitar."

He started to say okay, but then he remembered something. He didn't want to go out with Janet. He wanted to play the late-night gig the band had just been offered. "I can't go out tonight," he said. "not for at least couple of hours."

Janet stared at him, fury starting to build in her face and posture. "What?"

"I hate to disappoint you," he said. "We just picked up a gig."

"What do you mean, a gig?" she said.

He explained and a full scale argument ensued. After several embarrassing moments Janet slapped his face hard. She grabbed her coat, shot him a nasty look and stormed out in tears.

Rick, on the other hand, just stood by his huge Standel amplifier with smoke coming out of his ears.

Another fight with Janet. *Another* fight. *Who needs this?* he thought.

Rick pulled his guitar case out and opened the snaps, hoping that the anger would ease a little. He breathed deep and packed the old Gibson away.

He closed the case. Then, he sat on the bench and leaned back against the wall, watching Bob break down his drum set. He noticed now that the dizziness he'd felt before the fight seemed to have dissipated. Maybe it went away when Janet hauled off and whacked him.

"You play well," said a girl's voice.

He looked up into the smiling eyes of a petite, charming girl. He smiled when he realized that Rachel, the girl he'd been thinking of for the last several weeks, stood in front of him. "Thank you," he said. "But I'm not very good."

"Yes," Rachel teased, "The modest bit works well. Very becoming."

Rick grinned and stood up. Rachel looked around. As she did, he noted that she had a trim lovely figure flattered by a skirt and a sweater.

He found her attractive at once, but something about her eyes bothered him. What was it?

Then he knew what he saw. This young woman's eyes, her posture, her clenched fists and a little quaver in her voice suggested that she had to struggle to hold down a mortal fear.

She seemed to summon up some courage. At last she said, "I had fun seeing you again this week."

Rick shook his head a little to clear his mind. For the last several moments, he'd found himself thinking that he'd done all this before.

Don't be silly, he told himself. "You've seen us before?" he asked her.

"Lots of times," she said. "Remember, I told you in the hospital? I'm one of your fans."

"Right," he said. "I remember you saying that. Well, thank you."

"And I'm still planning to take you to dinner."

Rick remembered the discussion. "Okay, then," he said. "The Texaco station, I think you said?"

"Or the Shell station," she giggled. "It's a little more upscale. You can take your pick." They grinned together. "Where'd your girlfriend go?"

He hadn't been expecting that question. "What do you mean?"

"The spectacular blond I always see you with. I thought she was your girlfriend."

"Well, yeah," said Rick, surprised that Rachel had watched him for some length of time. "We had a big fight a few minutes ago."

"You make it sound like that's an 'as usual,'" she said.

Rick shrugged. He chatted with her about his girlfriend Janet and their relationship, not sure why he felt so free to confide in the girl named Rachel. He also kept feeling so *strange*, like he'd done all this before.

He grinned a little and said, "I have to finish packing up my guitar and my amp. You'll excuse me if I—"

"Why the big hurry?" she interrupted.

"Karl—he plays bass for us—he has a friend who's having a party at his apartment and we're going to play it. Karl's buddy is bringing some guys to move our amps and stuff when he gets back—"

"So you're going to play at this party?" She asked.

"Yeah, I am," Rick assented. To his surprise, he saw her face blossom into a large, joyful smile. "Rick," she said, in a scolding tone, wagging a finger at him. "It's after midnight." He observed, though, that her eyes now looked much less scared. She looked happy.

Not only that, he noticed that he felt a rising compulsion to kiss this young woman. No. Not just kiss her. He found that he wanted to enfold her, stroke her brown hair, and stare into those deep brown eyes. Then kiss her for quite a while. He again remembered kissing her in the hospital—a dramatic kiss of devotion, familiar somehow.

He tried to shrug away the intense attraction. "I know it's late," he said. "Janet got mad at me for accepting the gig."

"Are you playing at this apartment for free?" asked Rachel, still puzzled.

"Hell no. We don't play any gigs for free. No, he's giving us a hundred bucks for a couple of hours at the most."

"I see."

"Yeah. We're only in it for the money."

"Frank Zappa and the Mothers of Invention," she said. He lifted an eyebrow in surprise. "*We're Only in It for the Money* is the title of their latest album."

"Right."

"Yeah," she grinned. "And you don't play for the money. I know better than that."

"What makes you say that?"

"You play with passion. You don't just play notes on the guitar. You try to speak through it."

"Thanks," he smiled.

"I mean it," she affirmed. "You love to play music."

"Do you play?" he asked.

"Isn't that kind of a personal question?"

He thought for a second. "Oh. I didn't mean—"

She laughed at his consternation. "I know," she said. "I play piano. Not great, but I took lessons for years."

"Me too," Rick grinned at her. "On the guitar, I mean."

"I sort of figured that," she teased.

"Er. . ." he fumbled.

"Yes?"

"Would you—ah—like to come along tonight to this gig?" There. He'd asked her, as he'd been wanting to. "I mean, I know it's late—"

"Sure, I'd love to," she beamed. "I enjoy listening to your band." The first date with the love of his life.

"We'll only play for a little while," he said. "Then maybe we could go to Mel Root's?"

"Where?" she said.

"A joint in Urbana. We go there for breakfast after gigs."

"An all night diner?"

Rick nodded, enjoying this girl. Petite with short dark hair, she now had an impish expression on her face. "I mean, I know we don't really know each other very well. . ." he stumbled, then trailed off and grinned, noting the way she held her hand in front of her mouth.

The mouth he kept on wanting to kiss again. *Get yourself under control*, He thought.

"Would you by any chance be laughing at me?" he asked her.

"Maybe a little. But yes, I'd love to come," she said. "I don't care that it's late. I never sleep much anyway."

The tone of the remark puzzled him. "What does that mean, Rachel?"

"It's complicated to explain," she said in a tone that asked him not to continue in this line of questioning. He shrugged it off.

At that moment, Karl's buddy and about five other guys showed up and whisked away amplifiers, drums, public address system, microphones and the other band paraphernalia.

Rick finished packing his guitar into the beat-up old case. He hoisted the instrument, touched Rachel's elbow and led her upstairs to the main entrance.

They looked around the beer joint called Kam's, located in the heart of campus town at the University of Illinois. "What a dump," he chuckled.

"Oh, I wouldn't call it a dump," Rachel said. "Kam's has a kind of *je ne sais quois.*"

"It does?" he asked.

"Yeah," she giggled, seeing his bewildered expression. "You just have to trust me."

"I suppose I'll have to. I don't know what it means."

She laughed out loud. He chuckled also, enjoying the delight he could hear in her laugh.

He opened the door—

And found his way blocked by a huge man.

"Excuse me," said Rick.

"Beat it," the man snarled at Rick, jerking a thumb over his shoulder.

"Well, just move a little and we—"

"You," the man interrupted, pointing a huge finger at Rick. "Hit the road." He pointed at Rachel. "You're coming with me."

Now Rick began to get mad. "That's up to her, Pardner," he said. "Now would you please—"

"I already told you to beat it," said the thug.

"Rachel, do you want to go with this man?" Rick asked, not taking his eyes off the huge man.

"No," she whispered. "Please—"

Rick turned to look at her. To his surprise, she looked terrified. "You heard her," said Rick, addressing the large thug. "Now please get out of our way—"

"Look, you're about to get your ass kicked," said the man.

"We don't want trouble," said Rick. "But I'll ask one more time."

To his surprise the huge guy took a clumsy, inexpert swing at him. Rick leaned back and the thug missed, the force of the inept punch heaving him off balance. Rick swung his guitar case into the thug's gut, driving out the man's breath with a loud "Oof." The man fell to one knee, gasping for breath.

Now two of Kam's bouncers hurried through the door, "What's going on, Rick?" asked one of them.

"I don't know," Rick replied. "This guy just threatened us and took a swing at me."

The bouncers grabbed the oaf and dragged him to the door. To Rick's surprise, the thug choked out, "Wait a minute. Where am I? What's happening—" Then the door shut behind him.

Rick turned to Rachel. "Are you okay?"

She nodded, but Rick saw the incident had scared her. "Yes, I'm fine," she managed.

"Gino and Vince will call the cops," Rick assured her. "It's all over." She nodded. "What did that character want?"

"I don't know," she said. "Let's go." She took his arm with both hands. The hands were trembling as he walked around the corner to his car.

Her answer stunned him. He tried to press her for a few moments, but Rachel made it clear that she had no desire to talk about the incident. He shrugged and decided to change the subject.

"Anyhow, Kam's finances college for me," said Rick. "Leo pays us $120 a night on Wednesday and Friday. We play on Friday afternoon as well. He kicks in an extra $60 for that."

Rachel took a deep breath. Rick saw that she was making an effort to be calm. "Split four ways?" she asked.

"Yeah," said Rick, unlocking his jalopy and holding the door for her. He shut the door and put his guitar into the back seat. "It pays for the car, too, such as it is."

"And you play other places too, I know. . ."

"Oh yeah. sometimes we play Sunday afternoon, Saturday night at fraternities or other beer joints, sometimes out of town—usually four, maybe five nights a week."

They pulled into the parking lot of the apartment building and went upstairs. Rachel took a chair off to the side as the band set up and tuned. Rick turned and grinned at her. She blew him a kiss. Again the desire to run over and kiss her almost overcame him.

Sometime later, he understood that at that moment he fell in love with the woman named Rachel. She gave him a tender smile that melted his heart.

"Rick?" said Steve, with a little grin.

He shook his head and got his mind focused. The band started with *I Feel Good* by James Brown. Rachel danced with several boys and had a good time, from what he could tell.

Somewhat to his surprise, he found that he was a little jealous of the guys who danced with her. *What is this?* He asked himself. *Why would I be jealous?*

The band played for a little more than an hour. The engagement ended when two members of the Champaign police department arrived at about 1:30. To Rick's relief, the police didn't arrest anyone, just told them to quit playing and beat it.

"Go ahead, Rick," said Karl, the bass player. "The guys can haul this stuff back to my place." He waved his hand at the amplifiers. Rick accepted the offer, relieved that he didn't have to spend the dreary time of packing amps and mikes and lights away.

Rick packed his guitar and drove with Rachel toward the all night diner.

"It seems like you ought to be tired," she said.

"Yeah, I'm worn out in a physical sense. But I won't be able to go to sleep for some time."

"Why not?"

He thought for a second. "Performing affects me like caffeine," he said. "When I play, the adrenaline flows. Performance high, I guess you could call it. It takes a while for me to unwind and come down."

"No kidding?" she asked.

"No kidding," he said. "You know how you always hear about musicians and actors getting involved with dope? They begin by taking things to come down from the high."

"Speaking of dope," she said.

"Huh?"

"Did you smell the reefer the guests were smoking in the bedroom at the apartment?"

Rick stared at her for a few moments. "What?" he asked, dumbfounded.

"Sure," she said. "Didn't you see how solicitous that Ron guy got when the police showed up?"

"Oh jeez," said Rick.

"Right," said Rachel. "If they'd gone into the bedroom they would have arrested the whole party."

Rick muttered a profanity.

"Well said," she agreed.

"That's all I need," he said. "Spending the night in the Champaign lockup."

Rachel didn't speak for a few moments. "Do you do drugs?" she asked, in an undertone.

"No," said Rick. "Never have. Not even reefer. I'm terrible at drinking, so I keep that to a minimum. I get sick and depressed if I have more than one beer."

She didn't speak, staring through the windshield. He hesitated, dying to ask.

"Want to tell me?" he said at last.

"You know I did," she said. "I went through a period where I took everything I could get my hands on."

"Ah," he said.

She turned and put a hand on his. "Does that freak you out?" she asked. She sounded anxious, like she worried about his approval. Strange, he thought.

"No," he said, entwining his fingers with hers. "With the band, I'm around the damn stuff all the time. I don't care if other people use drugs or drink. I just don't like the feeling of being out of control. "

"I understand," she said. "I promise you I'll never touch drugs again."

"Sounds serious," he said. She nodded and held his hand in silence. He felt her hand tremble a little and she bit her lip. A few moments later they arrived at the restaurant in downtown Urbana and he guided the car into a parking space. He put the transmission into Park and shut off the ignition.

She nodded. Rick turned and looked at her. A pall seemed to have fallen over her. She turned to look up into his eyes and a tear fell from her left eye. Then she stretched up her arms. He leaned toward her and embraced her.

Rachel slid across the bench seat to him and returned the hug, pressing her cheek against his. Rick, surprised, held her for a few moments, feeling tension in her body. "Okay," he mumbled, trying to be kind. "Rachel. It's okay."

She leaned back, looked in his eyes. "Thank you," she said, tears on her cheek. "I'm just so scared all the time…"

The kissing started with a subtle passion that grew for several moments. Sometime later, she drew back and stroked his face with soft, gentle fingers, staring into his eyes. "Oh Rick," she sighed. "I'm sorry."

"Sorry?" he said, surprised.

"Yes," she said, and kissed him again for just a moment. He looked into her eyes—

And again saw that subtle but jarring look of terror in her eyes.

Again he felt that eerie sense that she lived in desperate fear of something.

"I didn't mean to do that," she said.

"I'm glad you did," he said. "I wanted to kiss you since I saw you at Janet's dorm—"

He stopped, realizing that he hadn't seen her at Janet's dorm. No. He retraced the evening. He'd met her at Kam's, taken her to the party, they'd driven to Urbana, parked the car.

And started to kiss.

Chapter Seven

She stared at him in some surprise. "Janet's dorm?" she asked.

"No," he said. "I had this strange memory of seeing you at her dorm. I guess that's impossible," he said.

"Sure," she said, and leaned back with a weak little smile. She wiped her tears away and said, "I'm okay, really I am."

Rick nodded, then climbed out, walked around the car and opened the door for her.

Rachel took his hand in hers again and they walked in and found a table at the back of the restaurant.

He had a moment to consider how strange his behavior had been this evening: He'd kissed and held hands with this girl, he'd taken her on a date, and all while he remained engaged to Janet. Yet he felt no guilt, no remorse, nothing but an exhilaration at Rachel's presence.

She sat in silence as they scanned the menu. Rick found himself puzzled at the change in her attitude. The talk about drugs seemed to have upset her somehow.

The waitress, looking tired and bored, appeared carrying a couple of glasses of water. Rachel ordered tomato juice with extra lime.

"No coffee? No eggs?" he grinned. "They make a killer Coconut Cream Pie, if you're interested—"

"I'm not real hungry," she said. "You go ahead. I'll watch you eat. A vicarious thrill."

Rick ordered corned beef hash and fried eggs, with rye toast and crisp hash browns. She laughed and teased him about the amount of food he ordered. Her good mood returned.

They chatted about classes. She majored in English and planned to teach high school language arts. She'd done her student teaching during the first semester of the current school year and had a job offer from a school district when she graduated in a couple of months.

Rick smiled congratulations. He told her that he had an English minor but majored in history. They knew several professors in common and compared notes until his breakfast arrived.

He ate as they continued to chat a little.

"Want to tell me?" she said as he spread some grape jelly on his toast.

Rick looked up. "Huh?"

"No secrets, okay?" she said. "No lies?"

He understood. "You mean with Janet?"

"Yes, I do."

He thought for a few seconds, not sure how to explain. "We've been together for about two years," he said. "We—er—" he hesitated. He didn't finish the sentence. She nodded.

"I see," Rachel said, her voice subdued, not looking at him.

"She gets mad about how much time I spend with the band," he said. "She's been after me to quit and do something else. I know it isn't much fun for her. I mean, I work five, sometimes six nights a week until late."

"At least midnight," she nodded.

"Yeah," said Rick. "The band also has to rehearse and add a couple of songs each week. I have to practice every day, too.

"Practice?" she asked.

"Yeah," he said. "I run scales and chords on the guitar, and do vocal exercises too. I also have to figure out songs from sheet music, or playing by ear from the records."

"I see," she said.

"Then tonight, she wanted to go out for a while, just the two of us. Well, I hadn't made any firm plans with her when we got the offer to play and make some money."

"Money seems very important to you," she noted.

"I guess it sounds that way," he agreed. "I don't get the grades I ought to. I'm not in trouble with them and I'm not stupid, but I don't get any scholarship money, either. If I want to stay in college, I need to work. Playing in the band beats waiting tables or tending bar or working in the food service."

"You don't seem impoverished, though."

"No, but my parents wouldn't be called wealthy, either," said Rick. "I'm the oldest of four kids. I work in the steel mill in the summers and play guitar during the school year."

"So. . ."

"So, the grades suffer a little. I get by, but not what I ought to do."

"And your girlfriend resents the time you spend with the band."

"Sure," said Rick. "I don't blame her, but her parents have enough money that she doesn't have to work, either. I mean, she isn't real sympathetic."

The conversation continued until about four in the morning. Rick learned that her parents had a contentious, now nasty marriage. The prospect of her parents divorcing and no longer together devastated her.

At last he felt the fatigue creeping up. "I have to go home," he said. "I'm beat."

"I can see that," she said. "I appreciate you trying to hide the yawning."

He grinned. "Can I drive you home?"

"As opposed to leaving me here?" she smiled.

"I guess so," he chuckled and tossed some money on the table. He took her hand again as they walked to the car, thinking of how comfortable her hand felt in his.

He drove her to her dorm. She took his arm as he walked her to the door.

"Good night," she said, turning to smile up into his eyes. He put his arms around her waist.

"Can I see you again?" he asked.

"Do you want to?" she asked. He grinned. They agreed to meet at the Student Union for dinner the following evening. She gripped the front of his jacket and leaned up. She kissed him, a gentle warm press of her lips to his. The kiss, one of thousands they would exchange in their lives, struck him as chaste, not even flirtatious.

But precious. Then they put their arms around each other. He returned the kiss just as he'd been wanting to for hours.

As it had in the car, and in the hospital weeks before, the kiss became passionate and electrifying. He didn't want to stop.

They made an effort to stop kissing. She smiled, pecked his cheek and took a scrap of paper and a pen out of her purse. "Here's my phone number," she said. "In case something happens." She wrote on the paper and handed it to him.

"What could happen?" he asked, puzzled. But she turned and hurried through the door.

Rick felt strange as he drove home. He'd become so used to contention with Janet. A pleasant evening of conversation with a witty, personable girl invigorated him.

He'd never dated a girl like Rachel. He'd sensed a connection to her from the moment he laid eyes on her that night at the party: a pleasant connection, but a little eerie. The kisses had been something very special—

He sat behind the wheel of his car and pondered this idea for a second. He couldn't help feeling that he remembered sharing a kiss with her before that goodnight kiss at the door and in the car. Sure. Right by Janet's dorm.

He shrugged away the strange feeling. He couldn't have kissed Rachel at Janet's door. He couldn't imagine why he remembered it. Of course not.

Chapter Eight

Despite feeling dead tired, Rick had to struggle to fall asleep. His dreams, which began turning vivid and bizarre when he first met Rachel, tonight became downright eccentric.

Rick kept dreaming that he hadn't played the gig at the apartment. In the dream he quarreled with Janet after the gig at Kam's. He gave in, feeling resentment, and went out with Janet for a late night dinner. She started another fight in the car about a girl named Rachel. They had a cruddy pizza and Janet wouldn't come back to his apartment. Then he drove her home.

He woke up several times and tried to shrug off the strange dreams. No, he asserted to himself. The date with Janet hadn't happened. He hadn't given in during the tiresome fight with Janet nor had she stormed out of Kam's basement crying. Rachel came over and re-introduced herself. They spent the evening together.

Again and again he struggled back to sleep. Dinner with Janet. Arguments and contention. Drive her home. Rachel. Wake up. Again. Again.

At one point, he found himself dreaming that he stood in front of his car, face to face with Rachel. She told him that she could control time, that she had the ability to go back and forward in time, and that she could take him back to the end of the Kam's gig and change things—

He jerked awake and sat up. *What is this all about*? He asked himself as he looked at the clock. 8:00 A. M. He fought his way back to sleep. Again the bizarre dream. And again—

Now another dream interposed, one which he'd dreamed several times. He saw himself in a living room, kneeling beneath a huge Christmas tree, making a few final adjustments on a child's bicycle. Then he stood, walked to a closet and extracted a gift from the pocket of a little used overcoat. He walked to his bedroom and found Janet sleeping, her face turned away from him. Then he touched her shoulder and she turned to him—

But he found Rachel, not Janet, staring back at him, blinking away sleep, smiling...

And another dream started. He stood in an icy draft in front of two huge doors. Behind him he heard hideous shrieks of pain, misery and terror and understood, somehow, that he stood just outside the very Gates of Hell itself. He didn't know how he'd come to this awful place, which seemed to be dark as pitch although he could see without difficulty.

He saw a group coming toward him. Small, evil creatures were carrying and dragging a terrified girl down a passage. They tore at her clothes and left her naked and helpless. He saw that the creatures had captured her and held her tight, chattering with demonic glee, as she screamed with fear. They planned to rape her, all of them.

Rage rose up and he stepped forward to help her—

But felt someone shaking him. Dave, Rick's neighbor who slept in an adjoining bedroom, spoke. "Wake up, Scooter," he said.

"What time is it?" he groaned.

"It's 10:00," said Dave. "Janet's here, wants to speak to you."

"She came here? Now?" mumbled Rick, the horror of the dream not yet gone.

"Yes, now," said Dave.

Dave stood aside as Janet stormed in. "Here," she snarled. She dumped a few records Rick had loaned her on his head. "You miserable jerk," she screamed.

Rick sat up. "Thank you," he said, "for returning the records."

"Well?" Janet demanded.

"Well what?" he said.

"You could apologize," she scowled.

"Okay. Sorry."

"You don't mean it, do you?"

He paused and thought about kissing Rachel. He saw Rachel's face in his mind. "Sorry, no, I guess I don't."

Janet turned and stalked out. She would have slammed the door if Dave hadn't been standing there.

"Judas Priest," said Dave. "What just happened?"

"She's steamed," said Rick.

Dave stared at him. "Yeah, I got that," he said.

"Okay," Rick shrugged. "I played a gig after Kam's last night. Janet got mad at me for agreeing to do it. Hurt. Like that."

"You gonna do anything about it?"

Rick considered. "In a way, yeah I am," he said. "I'm having dinner with another girl tonight."

"Uh. . ." said Dave, rolling his hands to indicate that he wanted Rick to continue.

"That girl I took to the hospital, remember I told you?" Rick said. Dave acquiesced. "Her name is Rachel," Rick went on. "She came over and re-introduced herself last night after the gig at Kam's. We spent the night together. No, just talking," he assured his friend. "Well, we also did a fair amount of kissing. I liked that part best."

Dave snickered. "Okay," he said. "Look, I'm going home in a few minutes. I'll be back Tuesday night."

"Say what?"

"Yeah, my mom's brother died yesterday. We're holding the funeral Tuesday morning."

"I'm sorry, Bud. Want me to come with you? I can break this date and I don't have a gig until Wednesday. . ."

Dave shook his head. "No, don't bother. I appreciate it, but you've got to get after your grades, Scooter."

Rick sighed. "I know. I plan to spend the day studying."

"You know. . ." Dave began.

"What?" said Rick after a moment or two.

"I got to say," said his friend, "you don't seem too broken up about Janet."

Rick thought for a second. "You know, you're right. I'm not. I guess that makes me a complete jerk, huh?"

"Hell, I've always known that," teased his roommate.

Dave packed up some clothing and left while Rick dressed. He walked over to a local deli for a bite of breakfast and returned with a cream cheese sandwich and a bottle of orange juice. Then he broke out the books.

He felt sluggish from lack of sleep and turned on his stereo. He selected an LP Janet had just returned, *Fresh Cream*, and moved the needle to the last cut on the B side. He listened to Ginger Baker beat the bejeezus out of his drums on the song called *Toad*. Refreshed, he tucked into his work.

He jerked awake from a nap. He'd had a strange dream about a lousy date with Janet, followed by an even more bizarre dream about saving a girl at the gates of Hell.

Then he realized. He'd spent the previous night dreaming the same thing.

Puzzled, he glanced at his watch and groaned. 4:30. He still had to re-type a paper for a history class and had to turn in the paper at 3:00 the next afternoon. Damn.

He considered calling Rachel and calling things off for the evening but when he thought about kissing her in the car and at the dormitory door, he decided he didn't want to cancel.

He rationalized the date. After all, he had to eat dinner anyway, right?

Okay, he grinned to himself. He really wanted to see Rachel again.

He showered, changed and started to open the door—

And stopped when he saw the huge thug who had confronted Rachel and himself outside Kam's the night before.

Chapter Nine

"What do you want?" Rick asked. In the lingering winter daylight, he could see how big this guy really was. If this character wanted to make trouble for Rick, Rick saw that he was in for a bad few minutes.

"Are you Rick?"

"Yeah, that's my name."

The big man hesitated. "Look, I'm here to apologize," he mumbled. "I made an ass of myself last night, and I feel awful about it."

Rick was so surprised he couldn't talk for a moment. "I was over in the Union studying," the man said. "Then the next thing I remember two big guys were hauling me into Kam's and then the cops came, and I had to go to the station—"

"What did you want with Rachel?" asked Rick.

The big guy's face went blank for a moment. Then he nodded. "The girl, right?"

Rick nodded.

"I've no idea," said the man. "I don't know her, I've never seen her before. I've never been in a fight before either."

"You said you wanted her to come with you," said Rick.

"I did?" the man mumbled.

"Yeah," said Rick, surprised that the man seemed to have no memory of the episode. "You wanted her to come with you somewhere."

The big man shrugged. "I have no idea." He extended his hand. "Please accept my apology," he said. Rick hesitated, and then took the man's hand. He noticed that the man had a weak, flabby grip, and couldn't really meet Rick's eyes.

"Sure," said Rick. "No harm done."

The man nodded and walked away. *He's a big wimp*, thought Rick, baffled by the encounter.

He hurried over to the union, arriving about five minutes late. He found Rachel sitting at a table, a huge textbook open in front of her.

"Hi," he said. He leaned over and kissed her. The kiss took just a moment to become serious and he had to force himself to break away. He sat down on the other side of the table. "Sorry I'm late," he managed.

"Don't worry," she said, removing a pair of huge eyeglasses. "I've been here since two."

Rick noticed that he was having a hard time speaking. Seeing Rachel in the bright fluorescent lighting in the union cafeteria took him aback.

Rachel looked terrific. She had bright brown eyes that sparkled with laughter and accentuated her tender smile. A bulky sweater and jeans flattered her attractive figure. "Since two?" He asked, fumbling a little bit.

"Yeah," she said, looking amused at his consternation. "I have a paper due Wednesday. I'm trying to get ahead on it."

He pulled himself together. "Swell," he said. "I've got one due tomorrow, about five pages. I almost didn't come." *Except I really wanted to kiss you again*, he thought.

"I'm glad you did," she smiled, looking deep into his eyes. "So. . ."

"So let's eat, and then I've got to go home and pound away at it."

She took a deep breath. "Want me to come with you?"

He blinked. "You'd come home with me?"

"Sure," she said. "If you really intend to work on a paper," she added, giving him a mischievous smirk.

"I don't have much choice," he muttered, a bit rueful.

"Have you done anything on it?"

"Yeah, I've got a draft. It's about five pages."

"Okay," she said. "You type and I'll proofread."

"Proofread?"

"Yeah," she said. "I did my student teaching in English last semester. My cooperating teacher taught me how to proof student papers."

"Cool," he said, pleased at the prospect of working on the paper with her.

"Let's eat."

Rick lifted a hand. "Wait a second," he said. "I've got something to tell you." Rachel grinned, but her expression turned to amazement as Rick related the episode with the big thug at his apartment.

"So he just came over to apologize?" she asked.

"I guess so," he said.

Rachel shook her head and muttered, "Looney tunes."

"And you don't know what he wanted?"

"No, not a clue," she said.

Rick walked over to pull her chair out for her. As she stood, she looked into his eyes and gave him an affectionate smile.

She leaned up and kissed him just for a few moments. She drew back, grinned, and took his elbow as they walked over to the cafeteria line.

By midnight they'd finished with the paper. She'd been merciless in correcting the paper. She assailed his logic, corrected grammar, insisted on style changes.

"Good grief," he said. "I've never written anything better."

"Yeah, it's pretty good now, I think," she nodded. "Sometimes another set of eyes helps, I mean, proofreading."

"You're good at it," he acknowledged.

"The paper reads much better now," she agreed. "But I'm worn out and I've got an early class. I have to go home and get into my little bed."

"Okay," he said. "Uh—"

"Yes."

"Would you like to stay?"

She hesitated for several moments, thinking through the proposition. She looked at him, then the bed. Then the floor.

"Rick," she said. "I'd like to. But I can't let myself fall into this overnight."

Now he hesitated. "You're falling in love with me?"

"I'm well beyond that," she admitted. "I fell in love with you months ago."

"You what?"

"Yeah, I've seen you with your girlfriend lots of times. I've had a crush on you that whole time."

"You have?" He had a hard time talking.

"Let me handle this my way," she said. "Give me time. I don't feel confident that you've gotten past the blond yet. I don't want to make a mistake. I don't want you to make a mistake either."

"What mistake?"

"Sex would be a huge step for us," she said. "I couldn't bear to make that big a commitment to you if you can't commit to me."

"We wouldn't have to make love," he said.

"No, but we would, and you know it," she asserted.

He sat in silence for some time. "Okay," he said at last. "We'll handle this the way you want to."

She put on her coat. "Take me home," she said. "Let's walk, okay?"

He nodded. She smiled at him and said, "Look, I'll know when the time is right, okay?"

"Okay," he said.

"And I promise you'll be the first to know," she asserted. "Just be patient."

He nodded.

When they reached the sidewalk, she took his arm and they chatted in the cool air. When they arrived at the door of the dormitory, he asked, "Can I . . . kiss you?"

"Please do," she grinned.

The kissing, at first gentle and respectful, again became

passionate. Without thinking, he slid a hand to caress her breast and she pressed against him. The kissing went on for some time.

At last she put her hands on his shoulder and gave him a little push to make him stop. Both were breathing hard.

"Sure you don't want to reconsider?" he asked. "About spending the night, I mean?"

"You still don't understand," she said. "I wanted to stay. But I can't right now, Rick. Let this be enough for tonight. Please let me take it easy."

He smiled and said good night. He walked back to his apartment, his mind reeling.

Outside his door he fumbled with his keys. Finding the right one presented a little difficulty since he kept thinking about kissing Rachel.

He thought about caressing her breast. She hadn't drawn back, or stopped him, however. On the contrary, she had pressed her breast against his hand. It had just seemed so natural, as if they'd always been meant to do it.

He put the key in the lock, but the door pushed open at his touch.

He walked in and found Janet in his bed.

Chapter Ten

Rick met Rachel for lunch at the union the next day. He started to lean over her chair and kiss her, as he'd been planning to do all morning. Then he stopped and sat down, not looking at her.

She gave him a puzzled look. "What's that all about?" she asked.

He didn't want to, but he told her what happened.

"So you found her in your bed," she said, and paused. "Did you make love?"

He hesitated. He thought of what she said. No lies. No secrets. "Yes, we did."

To his surprise he saw tears well in her eyes. He also saw that strange look of fear, almost terror, return to her eyes. "And that's why you wouldn't kiss me now," she nodded. He stared at his hands.

She clutched a napkin and pressed it to her eyes. "Is that what you wanted?"

The question took Rick by surprise. He paused, thinking about the question. "No," he said at last. "I didn't want to. I gave in and I shouldn't have. Now I've just abused her again."

"And so you've fallen back into the romance of the century." Rachel's voice caught.

"I'm sorry," he said. "I guess this means I've ruined things between you and me?"

"Did you want to ruin things with me?"

"No," he said without hesitation. "I told you because you said no lies, no games."

"Yes, I did," she nodded. She eyed him for several moments. Then she seemed to make up her mind and drew a breath. "Would you do it again?"

"Would I do what again?"

"The sex with Janet," she said. "If you had the chance to do it over again, would you?"

The question stumped him. "What difference does that make? I did it. I can't undo it."

"Please answer me."

He paused and considered. "I don't think so."

Rachel stood. She extended her hand. He took it, mystified. They walked to a small alcove where no one could see them. She kissed him and a little of the passion from the previous night returned. She stopped and leaned back, still embracing him.

"I don't think you'll remember anything," she said. "Come on." She kissed him. As she did, she took his hand and placed it against her breast. He felt disoriented for a second, and opened his eyes.

He found that they were standing in a cloud. He felt Rachel pressed against him, his hand on her breast. She smiled and pulled his head back down into the kiss—

The cloud cleared and he found himself kissing Rachel outside her dorm. It was dark outside as they stood off to the side of the door to her dorm. He took a quick glance at his watch. 12:18 a. m. "I'd better go in," she said. She reached up and covered his hand with hers, a soft look of joy in her eyes.

He shook his head, feeling strange, a little dizzy. "I know," he said. "Thanks for a great evening, and all your help, Rachel." He lowered his hand from her breast, but she didn't release his hand for a few moments. Then she wrote her phone number on a scrap of paper and put it in his hand. She smiled into his eyes and gave his hand a little squeeze.

"Rick," she murmured. "Please, please remember to do what you really want to do."

He started to ask what she meant with that remark, but she turned and hurried through the door of the dorm.

Rick felt wonderful as he walked home. Rachel again had been bright, witty, fun. He couldn't stop thinking about her and the remarkable ardor of their kisses. He smiled to himself as he thought how comfortable her breast had felt in his hand.

He climbed onto the porch of the house where he lived. A single light bulb illuminated the doorway. He looked at his watch. Not quite 1:00 A. M.

He let himself into his bedroom. He walked in and found Janet in his bed.

Chapter Eleven

The next morning he walked into the union cafeteria. He found Rachel sitting at a table, a huge book open in front of her. She looked up. "Hi, Rick."

He kissed her and sat down opposite her. "Did you eat yet?" he asked.

"You kissed me," she said.

"I think that answer is what's called a *non sequitor*," he noted.

"No, it isn't," she said.

"Did the kiss bother you?" he asked, a bit amused.

"No," she said. "And I didn't eat because I've been waiting for you. Shall we go and get a bite now?"

He sat down. "Wait a second," he said. "I have something to tell you."

She put down her pencil and removed her glasses. They were oversized, with huge lenses. She looked as cute as the dickens in them. He told her so.

"Thank you," Rachel said. "I'd offer to put them back on, but I only need them for reading. If I wore them, I'd see you as kind of a blur. A long haired blur, to be sure."

She giggled. He smiled a little.

"I have something to tell you," he said. "You said no lies."

She crossed her arms under her breasts and smiled. Still her eyes had that strange look of apprehension that he'd seen before.

"Last night after I left you, I went home," he began.

"I guess that makes sense," she nodded. "Better than walking the streets for hours in the cold."

He snickered. "This is important," he said, and she stuck her tongue out at him. He giggled at her, but then got serious. "I found Janet naked in my bed."

Rachel's face fell, but she nodded, not looking surprised. She took her napkin from her lap and folded it. Then she looked up, drew a deep breath and let it out. "Did you—" she paused, swallowed hard, looked at him, then away "—make love to her?"

The question took Rick aback. He stared at the back of his hands for a second, embarrassed. He started to say yes—

But then he realized that he didn't have to. It hadn't happened.

"No," he said. "I have to admit I wanted to, but I made her go home."

Rachel gave a little smile, but pressed a paper napkin to her eyes. She exhaled, like she'd been holding her breath, and he saw that she was crying. What on earth?

"When she walked out of Kam's Saturday night," he said, choosing his words, "I felt that she and I had broken away from one another."

"You did?" she said, in a very small voice.

"We didn't say the words," he said, "but I felt free to ask you to come with me to the gig and then breakfast."

"So you invited me out of desperation, like I was a last resort," she sniffed.

"I didn't mean that—" he started to say, and then realized she was teasing. "I guess I feel free without her. Sex would have put me right back into something I didn't want."

"Can you explain that?" she asked with a tentative smile.

"Janet and I—well, we've meant a lot to each other the last couple of years," he said. "She's been a great girlfriend in every way."

"So. . ."

"So, last night I realized that I don't love her."

"When did you realize that?"

Rick paused. Then, with a big grin: "When you said you had a crush on me."

"Oh," said Rachel. She reached out and took his hand. She picked it up and placed it against her cheek. He felt moisture on his palm and saw tears again. "You've got the verb tense wrong, my friend," she murmured. "I *have* a crush on you. A big one."

"I see," he said.

"Yeah," she nodded, wiping at her eyes with a napkin, trying to be careful not to smear her minimal makeup. "You remembered," she said.

"I what?" he asked, puzzled.

"Remembered," she smiled. "But we can't do anything about it now. I've got a class at 1:00. It's 12:15. Let's get some food."

"Er," he said. "If I were to take you into that little alcove over there, out of the sight of prying eyes—"

"Yes?" she grinned.

"Would you like to make out for a few moments before we get the food?"

"I think I can spare time for that, yes," she said.

Chapter Twelve

Two weeks went by and Rick saw Rachel almost every day. *Strange*, he thought one night after he'd walked her home, *she's become the best friend I've ever had.*

On Friday afternoon, Rachel met him at Kam's for the last twenty minutes of the last set. "Bunch of drunks," she grinned.

"Yeah, it's like that every Friday afternoon," he shrugged. "At least no one threw up on me today."

"Has that happened?" she asked, looking disgusted.

"No," he assured her. "They almost always make it to the bathroom."

He took her to a sandwich place for dinner, then back to his apartment. She waited while he showered and changed for the nine o'clock gig.

She held a paper bag in addition to her school books as they walked in. "What's in the bag?" he asked.

"Never you mind," she sniffed, waggling an index finger and giving him a mysterious grin.

Rachel broke out a book and settled into a chair while Rick took a shower. He came into the bedroom smiling.

"What's up?" she asked.

"How'd you do on your paper?" he asked.

She shrugged. "I got an A," she said.

"Good," he said, and brushed his hair. He wore it longish, below his shirt collar.

"Jerk," she said. "Do you plan to tell me at some point?"

He laughed. "Look in the history book," he said, pointing to the corner of the desk.

She extracted the paper. "An A," she said, with a huge grin.

"Yep. Thanks to you," he said.

"You wrote it," she pointed out.

"Yeah, sort of," Rick said. "But thanks, Rachel."

She decided to stay at his apartment and study while he went to play the Friday night job. He didn't blame her. "Even I get sick of our repertoire," he admitted.

"I'm supposed to be reading Mr. Steinbeck," she said.

"Which one?" he asked.

"*The Grapes of Wrath*," she smiled. "I like it, so I don't mind."

"Yeah, great book," he agreed.

"I'll come over for the last set," she promised. He nodded and left.

At 11:00 that evening, Rick hoisted his guitar strap over his neck and set the instrument on its stand. He walked upstairs to the bar and sat down to wait for Rachel. The biggest crowd of the week always showed up for the last set from 11:15 to Midnight. Students stopped in for beer after parties, or movies, or other things.

"Where's Janet been?" asked Steve, the organist/vocalist of the band. Since they'd been playing in the band together, he'd become a close friend. "Seems like she hasn't come to a gig in a couple of weeks."

Rick hesitated, looking for the right way to say it. "We broke it off," said Rick.

"Huh. Well, I never thought you loved her anyway, Slick."

"You know, someone else told me that," said Rick.

"Who?"

"That girl I've been seeing, named Rachel," said Rick.

"Oh, yeah, the girl you brought to that late party," nodded Steve. "What happened with Janet?"

"I think—" said Rick. He stopped and considered his words. "—I began to resent her."

"How's that?" asked Steve. Karl, who played bass guitar for the group, walked over.

"Oh I don't know," said Rick. "It's just that she'd been on the pill for 18 months, and made me use other contraception as well. But every month she called me to tell me she was pregnant. Then she'd go a day or two and it'd turn out she was *not* pregnant. In the meantime, she'd get hysterical, couldn't sleep, on and on."

Steve laughed. "Yeah. Like you'd abandon her, right?"

"I may be a bum. . ." he began.

"No maybe about it," said Rachel's voice. Rick turned and found her grinning at him. He kissed her and then introduced Steve and Karl.

They laughed and agreed with Rachel's evaluation. The group chatted until the time came to start the last set. "What're you going to play?" Rachel asked.

"We've been working on some new stuff," Rick said. "We've got three songs we want to debut from a British group called Cream."

"Eric Clapton, Jack Bruce, Ginger Baker," Rachel nodded.

"You've heard of them?" said Rick, a little surprised.

"Saw them," she said. "I spent last spring and summer in England. They played at one of the big halls there and my friends took me."

Rick, impressed, turned to lead the way downstairs.

"Now," she said, holding up a finger for emphasis, "if you want a *real* song to perform, I heard it tonight. It's a true classic."

"Oh, indeed?" he said.

"Yes," she said. "And I'll thank you not to be sarcastic, you insensitive lout. I'm tempted not to tell you about it."

"Oh, yeah?" he sneered.

"Yeah," she sneered back, just managing not to smile. "It is very, very lovely, but very, very sad." She gave a deep sigh.

He sighed. "This ought to be good."

"I heard it on WLS just before I come over," she said. "Art Roberts just played it as a matter of nostalgia. A girl falls in love with a motorcycle gangster, but her parents make them break up. Then he gets killed in a wreck. Her life is over." She wiped an imaginary tear from her eyes, struggling not to giggle.

"Right," he said. "I know the song. *The Leader of the Pack* by the Shangi-las. Recorded in 1964, if I remember. Very moving, indeed."

"Well?" she said. "May your fans anticipate the debut performance of this contemporary masterpiece?" Now she couldn't restrain a giggle.

"Well, we'd have some problems," he said. "We couldn't do the motorcycle sound effects, nor could I simulate the sound of a motorcycle wreck."

"Anyone could do the motorcycle sound," she said. "Vroom!"

He considered. "Not bad, I admit."

"But none of you can sing the falsetto, right?"

Now he laughed with her and pulled his guitar strap over his head.

The band played songs by Wilson Pickett and Otis Redding to start the set. Then he went to the microphone.

"Hey," he said. The audience quieted a bit. He said, "We've got some new songs we want to try on you. Bear with us. This group calls itself Cream and they call this song *I Feel Free.*"

After the set, the band packed up and Rachel sat down next to him as he put away his guitar. "Too bad they didn't like the songs by Cream," she said.

"Who says they didn't?"

"They didn't applaud, did they?"

"Oh, that doesn't mean anything," said Rick. "U of I students never applaud."

"What do you mean?" she asked. They stood. He picked up his guitar case and she took his arm as they headed upstairs.

"Yeah," he said. "We led off for the Cryan Shames at the Armory last fall. I talked to them afterward. It frustrated them that the audience—a packed house—didn't applaud. I told them what I'm telling you."

"That must be difficult," she said. They left the bar and headed to his car.

"My ego doesn't depend on the audience's reaction," he assured her.

"I see," she smiled. "What does it depend on?"

He thought for a second. "I don't know. A lot of people come to see us. I know they're having a good time and enjoying the music even if they don't applaud. Also, I have fun just playing music with the other guys. I can use the money, too."

"Again the talk about money," she said.

"Sorry," he said. "When you grow up without money, you get used to talking and thinking about the damn stuff, I guess."

Rick opened the door for her. He popped the trunk and put his guitar inside. Then, he slid into the driver's seat. He started the car, and she said, "Vroom," imitating a motorcycle. He chuckled.

"Tell me about your parents," she said as he pulled away the jalopy away from the parking space.

Rick thought for a moment. "Oh, they're good folks, and I love them, for sure. They just grew up scared of money. Both of them lived through the Great Depression and lived in terror of the money running out. So my dad always worked ridiculous hours—out the door before sunrise, home after we'd gone to bed, no vacations, and so on. I have awful memories of my birthdays, for example."

"Why?" she asked.

"I guess because Mom and Dad seemed to resent them," said Rick. "Like they resented Christmas, and things like that. Remember, they never had much in the way of finances. One year on my birthday, I guess my eleventh or twelfth, I came downstairs in the morning and found my mom crying. I looked around for a gift."

"And. . ." she said. Rick felt his eyes tear a little.

"She didn't have one. Or a card. She looked furious, like she wanted to bawl me out. Instead, she gave me a ten dollar bill. 'Here,' she said. That was it. Not even 'Happy Birthday.'"

"No gift? How about a birthday cake?"

He shook his head. "No. Just the money."

Rachel stared at him for a few moments, then shook her head.

"That must have hurt your feelings," she said.

He nodded, noticing that even ten years later, the wound of that birthday still ached. "She did apologize later," he said. "But it still hurt at the time."

"Can we agree that we won't do things like that with our kids?" she asked.

Rick started to answer. Then he realized what she said. He looked at her. "Our kids?"

"Yep," she said. "Answer the question, Dopey."

"What question?"

"About birthdays," Rachel said. "They should be special things for kids to look forward to, you know."

"Oh," he said. As he thought about it, the question seemed reasonable. "Yeah, we can agree to that."

"Good," she said. "I've been thinking about something else."

"Yes?" he said.

"Rather than going to Mel Root's?"

"Yes?"

"Remember I said I'd tell you when the time is right?"

He said, "What time..." Then he understood. He stared at her, stunned for a few moments. He grinned. "I do remember," he said.

She laughed and took his hand as he steered the old car toward his apartment.

Chapter thirteen

The next morning, he took her for breakfast at Uncle John's Pancake House, not far from the Assembly Hall. He thought through the wonderful evening he'd spent with her.

Rachel had set the room up for them. Candles burned, she'd put satin sheets on the bed and set out a bottle of wine, a couple of glasses, and some cheese and crackers.

"So this is what you had in the bag?" he smiled.

"Uh, huh," she said. "Shall we sample the wine?" she said with that teasing little grin.

"Not on your life," he asserted. "That can wait."

Rick's thoughts turned back to driving. He stopped at a stop sign, not hurrying. He looked at her. "That was so—" Rick murmured.

"So what?" she turned to smile at him.

"—So—I don't know—different," he decided.

"In what sense?" She took his hand.

"You didn't seem to be afraid," he said. "Not at all."

She laughed. "Why would I be afraid? You didn't rape me."

"Well, about pregnancy, and so on," he said.

"Rick," she said. "When people make love, fear doesn't come with it. Never. When people just have sex, they worry. That's what made the difference."

"So we love each other?" he asked.

"I can't answer that," she said.

"Why?" he said.

"Because," she said, sliding over next to him in the front seat and squeezing his arm. "Because I know that I love you. I can only guess how you feel based on what we did last night."

"That makes sense," he said with mock contempt, teasing.

"Jerk," she said.

"Punk," he said. She giggled at the name. For the rest of her life, he would address her by that name.

"Did you ever read the Bible?" she asked. She took his hand and pressed it to her face.

"Yeah, in church."

"You went to church?" asked Rachel.

"All my life," he replied. "My parents took me so that I'd be exposed to it. I guess they figured I'd be free to reject it or accept it when I grew up if I knew about it."

"Hmm," she said. "Anyway, in one spot it says, 'There is no fear in love, but perfect love drives out fear.'"

"Right, I know the verse. First John." Rick thought about the passage. "Does that refer to the love of a man for a woman? Or mankind's love for God?"

"Does it matter?"

He thought. "I guess not."

"So, do you feel afraid now?" she smiled.

"No," he said. "No, not at all."

"Do you understand why what's her name—"

"Janet," he prompted. "You knew that," he added, turning a corner.

"Yeah, right—why sex scared her all the time?"

He shrugged. "Because she thought I only wanted sex, not love."

"That's right," she said, with an approving nod. "She could feel that you didn't love her. But she loved you and wanted to keep you so she did the sex thing, hoping that you'd fall in love with her."

He considered this. "So you're saying I treated her like a complete creep."

"You have to decide that," she smiled.

They grew silent as she leaned against his arm, hugging it. He thought for a second or two about the night. At one point in the lovemaking, he drew back a little from her and said, "Nothing you could ever give me would be better than this."

She stroked his face and smiled back at him. "I love you, too."

As they waited at a stoplight, she asked, "Do you understand why Janet made love to you?"

"Maybe," he noted. "When she came to the apartment that last time. . ."

"She didn't want to make love that night. She wanted you to learn to love her," Rachel said.

"And do you worry about me loving you?"

"No, I'm not worried. And pregnancy would be inconvenient, to say the least, right now. I doubt that you have a venereal disease. But I know that we were meant for each other. I've known it since I saw you for the first time."

"You have, huh."

"Yeah."

"When did you see me for the first time?"

She didn't answer. Instead she turned around and sat back, silent for some time, staring out the side window. "Is something wrong?" he asked.

She leaned over and embraced his arm again. "Would you like to marry me?" she asked, her voice husky.

"Yes," he said. "I would. I want to spend my life doing what we did last night."

"I'd like to marry you, too," she said. "Does that mean you love me?"

He turned and looked into her eyes. No fear, he noted. "Yes, it does," he murmured. "I've loved you since the first moment I saw you at that fraternity. That's why I came to see you in the hospital so often."

She hugged him, and the light changed. They drove in silence for a few moments. "Why won't you answer the question?" he asked.

"What question?"

"I asked, 'Something wrong?'" he said. "Before that, I asked when you first saw me."

"Oh, yeah. Now I remember."

"Well?"

"I don't want to answer."

"Why?"

"Because the answer scares me."

Rick started to respond, couldn't, took a deep breath. "Scares you?"

"Uh, huh."

"You said you didn't feel afraid with me."

"I'm not afraid of you. Never."

"Then what?" he asked, mystified.

"Not now," she said.

They drove in silence. He recalled lying on his back, Rachel's head on his chest. She'd gone to sleep, embracing him, a smile on her face. Rick thought how contented he felt, how comfortable, how—

His eyes jerked open. "I've said that before," he thought. "I said that thing about the gift she was giving me. But how could I?" Rachel shifted her weight a little. He stopped thinking then and relaxed.

As he was pulling into the parking lot, he realized, to his surprise, that he'd slept better than he had in months. He also didn't dream.

Chapter Fourteen

Rick would always remember that the next few months seemed to pass like lightning. He and Rachel saw each other almost every day. They ate meals together when they could and spent the night together often.

A few nights before Rachel graduated in June, they sat together at dinner. "Rick," she said.

"Um, hmm?" he mumbled, cutting a piece of potato.

She averted her eyes and said, "Would you please not be hurt if I ask you not to come to the graduation ceremony?"

He looked up. "Why?" he asked, surprised. "I'm proud of you."

"I know," she said. "And I do appreciate that, and I do want you there. But please, Rick. I don't want you to meet my parents just now."

"Harumph," he grumped. "Does that mean you're ashamed of me?"

"Not even in the slightest. This just wouldn't be a good time," she pleaded. He chuckled and agreed to honor her request.

"I guess we'll have plenty of time, huh?" he smiled.

"Sure," she said. She didn't look very confident. She looked away and he swiped a piece of chocolate cake from her. He'd only taken one bite of the cake before she turned back, realized the extent of his indefensible theft, laughed and demanded immediate reparations.

Rachel decided to stay in Champaign to start work on her master's degree and be near Rick after she graduated. She spent most nights at his apartment and they ate most of their meals together, taking turns cooking.

A few weeks into the summer session, she sat down with him. "Rick, I have to go home tomorrow," she said. "Will you drive me to the train in the morning?"

"Sure," he grinned. "I don't have to like the idea, do I?"

She gave him a wan smile and squeezed his hand. He had the sense that she was trying to draw strength from him.

"How long you going to be gone?" he asked.

"Just a couple of days, I think," she said, with a little wave of her hand. "I don't like to miss class, but this is important."

"What's up?"

She hesitated. "I'd rather discuss it later," she said. "Later this summer, okay?"

"Sure," he said. "I just wish. . ."

"I want to tell you and I will when the time is right, okay?"

Rick chuckled. He agreed and took her to the train early in the morning.

He found himself lonely for her, far more than he anticipated he would be. He picked her up at the train three days later. She climbed into the car and kissed him, but looked tired and upset. He asked if everything was okay.

"Yeah, fine," she agreed. "Let's go home."

He shrugged.

She continued her reluctance to discuss her parents or her family. One night he asked, "When can I meet your parents?"

She didn't respond. She looked away, out the kitchen window.

"Why?" she whispered, after a clear struggle.

"Because I think I ought to ask their permission to marry you?"

Again she didn't speak for a few moments. Then, "Rick," she said, taking his hand. "I'm thinking that I'd prefer that we just get married and not involve families until afterward. Long afterward."

"Why would we do that?"

"Yes," she said. "I've given it quite a bit of thought. I'd like to get married. Take our friends, go see the judge, I do, you do, kiss, and go out to dinner. Tomorrow would be fine, for example."

"I'm sorry," he said. "I can't agree."

"Why not?" she argued. "We're both over twenty-one, we can vote, drink and buy liquor, and on and on. Why not get married and get going with our lives?"

"For one thing, my marriage would mean a great deal to my family. I'd also like them to meet you and welcome you to our family. They're going to be crazy about you."

"I'm looking forward to meeting them," she said. "But. . ."

"Besides, I have no way of supporting you now," he said. "I don't want to get married until we have some way of living on our own."

She brought up the idea of eloping several more times, but Rick had strong feelings that he didn't want to keep their marriage a secret from their families. At last she acquiesced. Her disinclination for him to meet her family continued to puzzle him.

On the Fourth of July weekend, the holiday fell on Thursday and the University cancelled classes for Friday as well. Rachel invited Rick to accompany her to the wedding of her best friend, Donna Marino, to Barry Riske.

The camaraderie that Rachel had with these two seemed somehow to transcend friendship, but he'd come to like them. For their part, they welcomed him, making it clear that they valued him and his friendship. They'd never forgotten how Rick had come to their aid that night they'd taken the strange hallucinogen.

But the friendship between Rachel and Barry puzzled him. Rachel and Barry never made much eye contact with one another. Still they laughed and seemed to enjoy being together with the two people they loved.

Rick and Rachel saw them with some frequency at the University before Barry and Donna graduated and Rick enjoyed his time with them. They were a striking couple. Donna was tall and beautiful as well as a fine student, and Barry was handsome and intelligent. Rick and Rachel enjoyed watching as the love of Donna and Barry developed into lifetime devotion.

Rachel picked him up after Wednesday morning classes and they headed toward north central Indiana.

"How about now?" he asked her as they drove past the airbase in Rantoul, twenty miles north of Champaign.

"What now?"

"Why not tell me why you went home?"

She nodded and composed an answer.

"When I finished student teaching in January, three boys from the school assaulted me."

"What!" he said.

She nodded and began to cry. "The leader was a boy who had failed my class," she said, "while I was student teaching. He recruited a couple of thugs to help him. They ambushed me as I left the school the last day of my work at the school. It was the day before Christmas vacation. They attacked me as I reached my car. It was dark and no one was around."

"Did they rape you?" he asked, all but quivering with anger.

"No," she assured him. "They roughed me up and hit me, and stretched me out face down the back seat of my car, but they didn't get the chance to rape me. A group of basketball players rescued me. They'd just completed basketball practice and they saw the creeps grab me."

Rick pulled the car off the road. He turned to her. "Why didn't you tell me?"

"I don't know," she said. "I suppose I thought you'd think I was cheap or something."

"That's silly, Rachel."

"I guess it is," she said.

"Why did you go home?"

"Oh," she said. "They caught the three boys who did it. I had to go home in case I needed to testify at the trial."

"I see," he said. He took her into his arms.

"What happened?"

"There was no trial after all," she said. "The boys confessed and took plea bargains. They got big fines, probation and community service. They also can't come within a certain distance of me, or the boys who saved me."

They sat on the side of the road as Rachel stumbled through the story of the attempted rape.

"I'm so sorry, Honey," he said.

"I know," she said. "I think I'm okay. Being with you makes me feel safe."

They arrived in Culver, Indiana in the late afternoon. Donna and Barry greeted Rachel with affection. The warm closeness he saw between Rachel and her friends touched Rick.

Not long after they arrived, Barry and Donna joined Rick and Rachel as they sat in the living room visiting with Donna's parents.

"Rick," said Barry. "I could use a favor."

"Sure," said Rick.

"We've been friends for just a few months, I know, but—" Barry hesitated.

"What?" grinned Rick.

Barry looked at Donna, who smiled to encourage him and nodded.

"Look," said Barry. "Donna and I talked this over and I'm not making an idle request, not at all. Would you consider serving as my best man on Saturday?"

Rick stared at his two friends, then turned to Rachel, who beamed at him. "Er," he mumbled. "I—uh—Do you mean it?"

"Yeah, I do," said Barry. "My brother Ted agreed to do it, but. . ." He and Donna grinned at each other.

"What?" asked Rick.

"He just came down with the measles." Donna and Barry just managed to restrain a laugh. "He feels silly, you can imagine. The rest of my siblings and I had the measles when we were little, but he had to pick this weekend. . ."

Donna giggled. "We feel terrible for him," she assured Rick and Rachel. "But it leaves us a man short."

"Well, sure, of course I'll do it," blurted Rick. "And I'm very honored. But I don't have a tux—"

"Use his," Barry said. "He's about the same height and weight as you."

"Jeez," said Rick. "Don't you have. . ."

"I've got five guys, including my two other brothers," said Barry. "But the thing that made up my mind doesn't have anything to do with convenience."

"Yes?" said Rick.

"Rachel glows when she's with you. Donna and I would like to have that glow surrounding us at the altar."

"I'm honored," said Rick. "I don't know what to say—"

"Say 'thank you', Dopey," said Rachel.

Rick turned to Barry and extended his hand. "She's right. Thank you, Dopey." Barry shook his hand and gave Rick a polite chuckle for the terrible joke.

So they settled it. Rick and Rachel stood next to the couple on Saturday afternoon for the wedding. Donna looked radiant in an ivory gown with a beaded bodice and a long train.

But Rick had to struggle not to spend the whole time staring at Rachel, whom he was seeing in a formal gown for the first time. Donna had selected a pastel blue for her bridesmaids' dresses and the pale color flattered Rachel in particular. The afternoon sun filtered through the stained glass windows and enveloped Rachel in a halo of light.

During the saying of the vows, the sunlight streamed through the church windows to illuminate the entire bridal party. As the minister of Donna's church asked the questions, Rachel turned her head and caught Rick's eye. As Donna said, "I do," Rachel mouthed the words to Rick. He nodded with a smile and whispered "I do" as Barry said his vows.

After the ceremony, Rachel took his arm to recess down the aisle. "Someday," she said.

"You bet," said Rick. "Soon."

Chapter fifteen

Rick received straight A's for the summer semester as he had for the spring term and graduated in August. Both Rick and Rachel decided to move back home with their parents though Rachel again suggested that they just get married. Then, she argued, they could find a place of their own. Though tempted, Rick begged her to let things proceed without eloping.

With the Viet Nam war looming, he moved back into his parents' home in a southern suburb of Chicago and Rachel to her parents' home in Winnetka.

The second day they were home, Rachel came to visit early in the morning. Rick stared in envy at her Pontiac convertible with the top down.

"Don't get too excited," she said. "I inherited it from my Grandmother."

"It's a '62 Bonneville," he muttered, running his hands over the white leather upholstery. "Candy apple red."

"You like cars?" she asked, amused.

"I used to work on them all the time," he said. "This is just beautiful, Rachel." She laughed and took his arm to go to meet his parents.

His parents liked her at once, but Rick's attraction to her seemed to puzzle them. They had a pleasant day, a fine barbeque dinner and a game of bridge after dinner. Rick's mom partnered with Rachel and they beat Rick and his dad without difficulty. The two women subjected the men to merciless teasing.

"She seems so different from Janet or any of the other girls you've dated," said his mother, when Rachel had left to drive home late that night. "But you seem so happy around her."

"I am," Rick grinned.

"What sort of family does she come from?" asked his dad.

"Almost a broken one," he said. "Her parents have been threatening to divorce."

"Where do they live?" asked his mom.

"On the North Shore," he said. "Winnetka."

"Oh," his father said, as if things had just become clear. "So she comes from a lot of money, right?"

"What do you mean, Dad?"

"If her parents live in Winnetka, they've got money," said Dad.

Rick thought for a second or two. "We've never talked about that," he admitted. Rachel had never wanted to discuss her parents and he'd never pressed her. "She's never flaunted her money, if she has it."

"Hmm," shrugged his mother.

"Mom, Dad," he said.

They smiled at him.

"I'm going to marry her, you know," said Rick.

"That would be fine with us, son," said Dad. "She's a remarkable young woman."

Mom nodded and hugged her son, a little tear in her eyes.

Chapter Sixteen

Rick took a long walk with his father early the next day. Rachel had asked him to come to meet her parents at about 6:30 that evening. Again, her worried expression troubled and puzzled him. What could be so bad about her parents?

"Dad," he said, "my car needs some major repairs."

"So. . ." said his father.

"I hate to ask, but do you mind if I borrow your car tonight?"

"No, of course I don't mind," said Dad. "But why don't you buy a decent car and get rid of that wreck?"

"I hate to invest any money right now," Rick shrugged. "I hear Viet Nam calling. It seems likely I'm going to get drafted. I don't think anyone would hire me."

Dad shrugged. "I understand," he said. "World War II started when I was in my first year at college. I didn't graduate because of the war."

"I know," said Rick. "I'm glad they let me finish. But my student deferment ended when I graduated. I can't get it again even if I enrolled in grad school."

His dad nodded, looking very sad. Rick took the keys and headed north.

He followed Rachel's directions and arrived at what looked like a mansion in Winnetka, a few blocks from Lake Michigan. He hurried up the long walk to the front door, smoothing his hair. The size of the house daunted him as he rang the bell.

At his mom's suggestion, he picked up a bouquet of flowers for Mrs. Farrell. Mom also told him that on such an occasion, a corsage for Rachel would be appropriate.

He glanced at his watch. 6:30. Right on time, he thought, and pushed the doorbell button.

Rachel opened the door almost at once and stepped outside in the warm August night, dressed in a black slacks outfit.

"Oh my God," he said. "You look terrific."

"Thank you, Rick." Her voice was subdued.

"Here," he said, handing her the corsage. "I hope you like it."

"How sweet, Rick," she said. "It's lovely. Help me put it on." He did so, though she slapped his hand with a giggle a couple of times. "What's with the other flowers?" She nodded at the bouquet.

"They're for your mom," he said. "I thought she might like them."

"What a thoughtful gesture," she said and came to his arms for a hug. "She'll love them."

She felt tense, a coiled spring in his arms. "Is something wrong?" he asked, puzzled.

She shook her head. "Come here," she said. "I'll be okay."

"Swell," he said. "I come to meet the parents and I show up flushed and aroused. Some impression I'll make."

"Shut up," she snickered, and pulled his head down into a kiss.

"Okay, let's go in," she said a few moments later.

"Can I stop in the washroom first?" he asked.

"Of course," she giggled. "I'd recommend it." She pointed to a powder room off the main hallway.

Rick splashed cold water in his face, combed his long hair, and tried to compose himself. He found Rachel waiting for him down a long hallway.

She took his arm and he could feel the tension in her touch.

"Something the matter with you?" he asked, amused.

"You'll see," she said.

"Well, relax, will you?" he said. "You're making *me* nervous."

They walked into a living room that was almost the size of his parents' home. Rick felt uncomfortable at once: dark and musty with uncomfortable furniture, the room stank of old tobacco. The walls, lined with bookshelves, were paneled with a dark oak and Oriental rugs covered gloomy oak floors. Rick detected a faint musty smell from the books, many of which were leather bound. Rachel's mother played idle, minor chords at a piano on one side of the room and her father lounged on a leather sofa on the other side of the room. Each parent glanced at him and then looked away.

"Mom, I'd like you to meet Rick," Rachel said.

Rick returned Mrs. Farrell's cool handshake. He held out the flowers. He noticed that they seemed to be the only colorful items in the room.

"Mrs. Farrell," he said. "I brought these for you."

"Oh," she said, without enthusiasm. "How—uh—thoughtful. . ." She didn't make an effort to take the bouquet from him. After an awkward silence, he turned to Rachel, who gave him a wan smile and took them out of his hand. She laid them on a side table.

"I'll get a vase in just a second," she said.

"Okay," he said, puzzled by Rachel's mother and her rudeness.

Rachel took him to the other side of the room and introduced him to her father. Mr. Farrell glanced up, nodded and looked away. He ignored Rick's outstretched hand. Rick stood bewildered for a moment, and dropped his hand to his side. What the. . .

Rachel took his hand and offered him a wing chair next to the sofa. Rick ran his hand over the smooth, impeccable leather of the chair, noting that it was one of the most uncomfortable chairs he'd ever sat upon. "Dinner will ready in a moment," she said.

"Okay," said Rick, not sure what to make of things. The parents' attitude didn't inspire confidence in him. Tension seemed to hover in the room's air.

Rick tried to make some chitchat and Rachel responded. The parents, however, ignored the younger couple. They sipped at martinis, ice clinking in the glasses. Nor did they offer the younger couple anything to drink.

"Mom," said Rachel. "Could you come over here?"

With a weak attempt to disguise a sigh, Mrs. Farrell rose and crossed to another wing chair at the other end of the large sofa. Rick had the sense that she wanted to maintain a distance from Mr. Farrell. "Dad, Mom," said Rachel, standing next to him and holding his hand. "Rick wants to ask you something." Her hand felt cold in his.

They looked at him with little interest. Mrs. Farrell's glance lingered on his long hair.

Rick cleared his throat. "I'm glad to meet you at last," he began. "Thank you for allowing me to come. You have a beautiful home."

Silence.

"I didn't have any trouble finding your house," he said, "but the drive seemed to last forever. My parents live south of the city, and. . .uh. . .you know, traffic. . ."

He paused, embarrassed at the lack of response. More silence. Neither parent looked up or acknowledged him.

He decided to try a different tack. "I'm sorry we haven't met before," he said. "I hope you'll understand. See, I became intent for months on finishing my degree. Also, my job as a musician made it difficult for me to leave Champaign, because I worked several nights each week, including—ah—weekends. . ." His voice trailed away.

Neither parent said anything. Nor did they look at Rick or Rachel. Mrs. Farrell inspected her unimpeachable manicure. Mr. Farrell shifted his weight and leaned forward, staring into his martini. Neither smiled.

Rick wasn't even sure Rachel's parents heard him. He glanced at Rachel, who nodded and smiled in encouragement.

Rick had played to some tough audiences. He'd faced hecklers, loud mouths, and indifferent responses to his hard work in the bands with which he'd performed. Never, however, had he ever felt less up to a situation.

He couldn't remember feeling more uncomfortable. *Well,* he thought, *let's get it over with.* He decided to abandon the speech he'd rehearsed in the car the whole way.

"I don't want to appear premature and presumptuous, to ask such a big question the first time I'm meeting you," he began. The parents looked up. He thought maybe now he had their attention. *Okay, here goes*, he thought.

"Rachel and I have fallen in love," he said.

Neither parent responded. Rick glanced at Rachel, baffled by the parents' coolness toward him. She gave him another little smile.

"I want to assure you that I'm a good person, a hard worker," he said. The parents still didn't look up. After a little pause he said, "And I came here tonight to ask your permission to marry her."

An uncomfortable silence greeted his words. Several moments passed wherein the parents said nothing and Rick began to get annoyed. He asked, "Mr. and Mrs. Farrell, are you listening to me?"

They glanced at him for a moment. He decided to go back to his rehearsed speech.

"I don't know what Rachel has told you about me," Rick began. "I feel—"

Farrell looked up. "When?" he asked, interrupting Rick.

Rick hesitated. "Er. . .what?"

"I asked you, 'when?' Not a difficult question. Only one word," sneered Mr. Farrell, his voice acid with sarcasm.

Rick looked at Rachel, unsure what to say. "I don't. . .I mean..." he stammered. Then he said, "I'm sorry. I don't understand what you want to know."

His fiancée spoke up. "As soon as we can," said Rachel. "We're pretty crabby when we can't be together. It's miserable—"

"How sweet," snorted Mr. Farrell. "How cute. Wait until you get married." He jerked a thumb toward his wife. "Then you'll learn the true meaning of the word misery."

"Shut up," snapped Mrs. Farrell.

Rick could only stare for a moment, taken aback by the rudeness of the parents. "Er. . ." he fumbled.

Rachel squeezed his hand. She murmured, "Don't let it bother you."

Rick paused to regain a little composure. "Er..." he managed. Then he took a breath and pressed on. "Rachel and I want to spend our lives together. We've seen each other almost every day since early spring."

"Oh, well, that's just swell," said Mr. Farrell, sarcasm dripping.

Rick didn't stop. "I don't have a job right now but I do have a degree, and . . ."

"And now you're waiting to be drafted into the Army?" asked Mr. Farrell.

Now Rick paused, trying to gather his wits again. "Of course we need to discuss that. It seems probable, yes," said Rick. "That's why I haven't started my career search yet. See, I've been thinking—"

"So you get married. What's she supposed to do while you take off to Viet Nam?" Mr. Farrell interrupted.

"Well, I—" Rick began, but Mr. Farrell again cut him off.

"And say you get your keester shot off in Viet Nam," said Mr. Farrell. "Then what?"

Rick struggled, now speechless for a few seconds. He turned to Rachel, and saw a tear in her eye. "I'm sorry," she murmured, her chin trembling with pain.

Rick leaned back in the uncomfortable chair. He'd run out of things to say. Rachel had told him that her parents had been having difficulty with one another, but he hadn't anticipated their harsh reaction to him and his request to marry their daughter.

Then the truth dawned, leaving him feeling empty and sick. He understood that her parents intended to forbid him to marry Rachel. *What did I do to deserve this?* He wondered.

Mrs. Farrell rose to her feet. "Rachel, we need to talk to you alone," she said, her tone making it clear that she had to struggle to be civil. "Would you please excuse us, Paul?"

"Rick," Rachel corrected her mother.

"Oh yes, dear, excuse me," said Mrs. Farrell, not sounding sorry. "Could you show—er—Rick to the den, Rachel?"

Rachel now stammered with surprise for a few moments. Then she nodded. "Of course, Mother," she said.

Rachel took Rick's hand and he stood. She led him to the hallway and to a room with a television and a stereo system. "This won't take long," she said.

"What do they want?" Rick asked her. He felt sick to his stomach.

"I—uh—don't know," said Rachel, not looking in his eyes.

She started to go. "They're going to tell you that they don't want you to marry me, aren't they," he said, his voice dull. "They just didn't want to say it to me."

She came back and embraced him. "Please don't be upset, Rick," she said and kissed him. "It'll be okay, you'll see."

Rick squeezed her hand and managed to give her a smile of reassurance. He saw her distress at the way things had transpired.

Chapter Seventeen

Rachel closed the door behind her and left Rick considering the impolite reception of the parents to him and his request to marry their daughter. The rudeness left him bewildered. His mind felt like a cloudbank.

The room into which Rachel had shown him seemed to be a den, with a television and a stereo system on one side. It didn't, however, look like anyone ever used the room, and again the stale smell of cigarette smoke seemed to have penetrated everywhere.

Rick sat on a couch and looked around him. A window had blinds drawn against the hot August sun, but the temperature of the room couldn't be called comfortable. It felt like it was 85 degrees in the room.

Rick walked over and turned on the television and flipped a channel or two. He found the White Sox game and returned to the sofa. He tried to watch but found he couldn't focus. He loosened his tie.

The downright rudeness of the parents had left him bewildered. That they would treat him like this hadn't even occurred to him. *Did I say something? Do something?*

His mind wandered to the sweet, lovely nights they'd spent together at the University that summer. They'd gone to Allerton House for picnics with friends, taken long walks, played tennis and golf, and studied together.

He recalled the Fourth of July weekend when they'd driven to Culver, Indiana for the marriage of Rachel's best friend, Donna Marino. The Fourth fell on a Thursday, and they arrived late

Wednesday. The rehearsal for Donna's wedding would be held Friday night, the ceremony Saturday morning. Donna asked Rachel to serve as the Maid of Honor and Rick agreed to serve as the Best Man.

They spent Thursday and Friday on Lake Maxinkuckee, swimming and boating and water skiing. Just before suppertime on Thursday, Rick and Rachel joined their hosts on the ski boat. The group had been water skiing all day, and he'd dived off the boat into the lake. He surfaced about twenty yards away and grinned back at Rachel and her best friend Donna who lay on the deck sunning.

Rachel looked up, their eyes locked, and she smirked at the look on his face, knowing what he was thinking. Every time he saw her in her two piece swim suit he felt dizzy.

She dove in and swam over, surfacing right in front of him. She embraced him and said, "Oh Rick, I love you so much." They'd kissed. . .

His thoughts fled away and he returned to the den in the home of Rachel's parents.

Rick's bewilderment now turned to anger. He struggled to fight the irritation down, without much success.

He gave up on the effort. He stood and walked back to the living room, where he heard voices raised in an argument. He stopped outside the room in the hall, listening.

Mr. Farrell was speaking. "And I thought the *last* boyfriend was a loser." He gave a sardonic laugh. "You can't be serious. Where did you dig this clown up?"

"Rick is not a clown," Rachel declared, anger in her voice. "Dad, how could you say such—"

"That hair, for one thing," interrupted Mrs. Farrell. "Disgraceful."

"His clothes, too," scoffed Mr. Farrell. "Cheap garbage, Robert Hall."

"Rick comes from a fine family," said Rachel. Rick could hear the pain in her voice and the effort she had to make not to yell in anger. "He graduated from the University of Illinois and paid almost all the expenses himself. He worked summers in the steel mill on an open hearth furnace. He played with his band five, sometimes six nights per week during the year. He still received good grades and graduated. He doesn't own any better clothes because he couldn't afford them—"

"—And you'd be guaranteeing yourself a life of poverty," said Mrs. Farrell. "You must be able to see that. No doubt he's incurred considerable debt from college."

"That's not true. Rick has almost no debt from college. He worked his way through school—"

"You're missing my point," interjected Mrs. Farrell. "You've become used to a certain level of living with us. You'll never have financial security with this boy."

"Rick may not be rich," Rachel went on. "But he works hard at everything he does. He's had an income since he was eleven. He washed cars in the summer for neighbors, delivered papers and caddied at a country club. He always bought his own school clothes, paid for proms, and now he financed his college expenses. He—"

Mr. Farrell interrupted. "He'll always be a lower middle class oaf."

"Correct," said Mrs. Farrell. "A loser," she added.

"Mom!" said Rachel. "How could you say such. . ."

"Let's get down to business," Mr. Farrell interrupted. "What does he figure he's going to get from us?"

"Get from you? What on earth—" said Rachel. Rick, now seething, could hear the bewilderment in her voice. "He doesn't want anything from you—"

"He knows you come from a lot of money," scoffed Mr. Farrell. "I know this type. He figures he'll be cut in for a fortune. Won't have to work a day in his life."

Now the anger exploded. Rick had heard enough. He walked back into the room.

Rachel stood with her back to the door and didn't see him. "I never once told him that you had money," Rachel was saying. "I never told him that we lived in Winnetka either until we were in love. He never reacted. He has . . ."

Mr. Farrell spotted Rick. He interrupted Rachel without a pretense at politeness. "Young man," he sneered. "We made it clear that we wanted a private talk with our daughter."

"You can talk all you want," Rick said, struggling to keep his voice level. "I'm leaving this house right now. I just stopped in to say goodnight and thank you for allowing me to come."

Rachel turned to him, tears on her cheeks. "No," she said. "No, you can't go. You stay right here." The command in her voice tempered her struggle to remain calm. She breathed deep and took a calmer tone. "Let me work this out," she said. "Sit down."

"No, I won't, Rachel," Rick asserted. "I didn't come here to be insulted."

"I'm sorry to hurt your feelings, young man—" began Mr. Farrell.

"I didn't mean to give the impression that you hurt my feelings," said Rick. They had, he saw, classified him as perhaps a stable boy, a hired hand, seeking the master's permission for the impossible union with the master's daughter. "I may not be the man that you envisioned for your daughter. But that damn sure doesn't give you the right to insult and abuse me. Good night."

The parents looked shocked by his impertinence. Rick turned and started for the door.

"You did it to her, didn't you?" said Mr. Farrell.

Rick turned back, perplexed by this question. Mr. Farrell's expression had turned stony, angry. "I don't know what you mean," said Rick.

"You got her hooked on drugs, didn't you," nodded Mr. Farrell. "You turned her into a junkie."

"A junkie!" Rick gasped, stunned at the accusation.

"Father!" said Rachel, appalled.

"I thought so," nodded Mr. Farrell, taking Rachel's comment as confirmation. "I ought to have you arrested."

"If you believe that, then I demand that you call the police," said Rick. "Go ahead. I have nothing to hide or be ashamed of. I knew Rachel had struggled with drugs but until this moment I never knew that she'd been addicted. It breaks my heart to learn it."

Mr. Farrell gave a loud sarcastic guffaw and took a swig of his drink.

"The notion that I would or could harm your daughter couldn't be more absurd," Rick continued. "On the contrary, I have never taken a drug, much less sold one. I drink very little alcohol and don't smoke."

"You expect us to believe that?" chortled Mr. Farrell.

"Look, at this point I don't give a damn if you believe me or not," yelled Rick, his temper ready to explode. He checked himself and forced himself to speak in a calm voice. "But you seem intent on disliking me. If you think I'm lying, I insist that you check it out."

"Your hair. . ." began Mr. Farrell, disapproving.

"I wear my hair long because I work as a musician. It's part of the job. I had no intention of offending you."

"What do your parents do?" asked Mrs. Farrell.

"What does that have to do with anything?" demanded Rachel.

"I'm not sure why you think my family would be any of your business," said Rick, speaking to Rachel's parents. "But I will tell you about them. My father fought in the South Pacific in World War II. He went to college, though he had to drop out when I was born. He taught me the value of working hard at whatever I do. No matter what, he always supported our family. He works as an investigator for a law firm downtown. My mother graduated from a local college and teaches high school English near our home, though she stayed home until my siblings were in school."

"Okay, okay," interrupted Rachel's father, waving his hand, an expression of vast boredom on his face. He took a sip of what appeared to be a large martini. "All right," he said, nodding his head. "I don't want to waste the whole evening on this. Let's get down to business. What's it going to take?"

Rick paused for a moment, but found he couldn't answer. "I don't understand what you want to know."

Mr. Farrell drained the martini. He rose and crossed to the bar. He poured gin and vermouth into a shaker, added some ice, and shook the mixture. Pouring some into his glass, he crossed to his wife and poured more into hers.

Then Mr. Farrell crossed to a desk and unlocked a drawer. He pulled out what appeared to be a large notebook. When he opened it, Rick realized it was a checkbook.

"One hundred dollars," said Mr. Farrell.

Rick remained baffled. "What do you mean?"

"Cut it out," said Mr. Farrell, his voice dripping with contempt. "I know damn well why you came here and what you want from Rachel. Okay, two hundred."

"I don't . . ." began Rick. Then the light dawned. "I see," he said.

"Five hundred," droned Mr. Farrell. "And you never talk to her again."

Rick looked from Mrs. Farrell to Mr. Farrell. He took Rachel's hand and squeezed it. He forced himself to be calm. "I can't imagine what I did to create such a terrible first impresson on you both," he said. "I'm sorry for whatever I did. I assure you I'm not interested in your money. I don't want it nor will I ask for it in the future."

Mr. Farrell gave another derisive bark of laughter. Rachel began to sob. Rick put his arm around her waist.

"I want to say something before I go," said Rick. "I came here tonight excited to meet my new mom and dad. I thought my new parents would treat me with respect and kindness and welcome me to the family when they saw the devotion I have for their daughter—"

"One thousand," sighed Mr. Farrell, weary of the banter.

Rick forced himself not to acknowledge or react to Mr. Farrell. He paused and went on: "Rachel has changed my life in every way for the better," he said. "Thanks to your daughter and her constant encouragement, I finished my last two semesters at college with straight A's, despite working forty or more hours per week. Over the last several months I've realized that I love her. I will always remember Rachel as the best thing about college—."

"Enough," said Mr. Farrell. "Look, I'll give you two thousand dollars. Consider it my last offer. I urge you to take it. We will never give a blessing to this marriage."

Rick felt tempted to tell the man to shove his blessing, but bit down the scathing rejoinder. He turned to Mrs. Farrell. "Does your husband speak for you too?" said Rick.

She snickered with disdain. "Of course," she scoffed.

"I see," said Rick. He turned to Rachel. He saw her weeping into a handkerchief. "Rachel," he said. "Forgive me. I think I should leave."

"Yes, that would be the best thing you could do," said Mr. Farrell. He signed the check and rose to his feet. He crossed the room and handed it to Rick. Rick stared at the amount on the check: two thousand dollars. "We'll say this is for your—ah—trouble. Take the check and leave. I would recommend that you cash it as soon as possible."

Rick could only gawk at the check, amazed. Rachel came to him.

"These people hate me," he mumbled, just able to speak. "Your parents despise me."

"They don't hate you," she said. "They just don't know you. Please—"

"They just made it clear that they have no interest in knowing me," he interrupted.

"Rick," Rachel pleaded. The pain in her eyes brought tears to his.

Now he recovered from the shock and the anger took him. He released Rachel.

Rick turned and walked to Mr. Farrell, who gazed at him with loathing. "Sir, you and your wife have insulted me and my family," he said, struggling to maintain some composure. "No one has ever treated me like this. I'll leave now, without your money." Rick tore the check into several pieces and dropped the pieces onto the carpet. "I would feel stained and dirty if I accepted. I won't see Rachel again, as you wish."

Saying that, though, cost him his poise. He just managed to check a sob as he turned back to the love of his life. "Goodbye, dearest Rachel," he mumbled. "I'm so sorry."

He made it out of the room before he started to cry.

Chapter Eighteen

At the front door, Rick found he couldn't manage the deadbolt lock, which required a key. He turned and found Rachel behind him.

"Please don't go," she said. She took his arms and held them tight.

The two young people stood in the hallway, Rachel staring up into his eyes. "Please," she said again.

"I can't get out," he said. "Someone locked the door."

"I know," she said. "I did. This is why I wanted to elope. I saw this coming."

"I want to leave," he said. "Please unlock the door."

"No."

"What do you mean, no? I don't need. . ." he stopped when he looked into her eyes. The terror he'd seen the first time he met her, absent for months, had returned. The joy had fled.

She put her arms up around his neck and clutched him. "No," she whispered. "No, you can't go. Please."

He pushed her back, trying to be gentle but firm. "Rachel," he said. "Rachel, I didn't know your parents expected you to marry a prince. I could never live up to what they think I should be. Now I have to figure out how to live without you."

"I can't face the fear without you," she said.

"What on earth do you mean?"

"Not on earth," she asserted. She released him and stepped back. "The Others," she said. "They're after me. They come for me if I'm not with you."

"Who?" he demanded, feeling a chill of dread run through him.

"Who comes?"

"Rick," she said. She stared at the floor. "I've told you what happened to me the night you saved me."

"Yeah, the dreams of the demons, and that. . ."

"But not just that," she said.

Rachel took a shuddering breath. "You remember that I told you that I was almost raped on the Friday I finished student teaching. Three men caught me and assaulted me but some basketball players intervened."

"Yeah, of course I remember."

"Yes," she said, "but in my dreams, they catch me again. They terrify me as much, or more, as they did at the time. Then I'm yanked back to that horrible fraternity and the night you saved me."

"God, Rachel, why haven't you told me?"

"Because I always feel safe with you. I'm not afraid. You protect me, and care for me."

"What kind of nonsense—" he fumbled.

"You think I'm crazy now, don't you," she said. A statement. Not a question. "Just like my parents do."

"I consider you the sanest person I've ever met."

She started to answer, but paused and wiped her eyes. "Thank you so much," she said.

"I mean it, Honey," he said.

"Then trust me. I can't face the terror without you."

He tried to press her. She shook her head. "I let them in," she said. "I made a mistake, and the Others came for me."

"Rachel, I don't. . ."

"In my dreams, I'm assaulted again, terrified, hurt, and sometimes they rape me," she asserted.

"If you're not with me, you mean."

She nodded.

"Why haven't you told me this?" he asked.

"I've wanted to," said Rachel. "But the memory scares me too much to relate it. Like it's doing now."

"But—"

"My parents think I'm crazy," she said. "They tried to commit me. I persuaded them to let me go back to college. I saw you and realized you could keep me safe. When I'm with you, the Others can't get me."

Rick felt a dull chill of fear. "You keep saying that," he said. "What do you mean, The Others? Who? What Others?"

"I can't tell you," she said.

"Why not?"

"Give me a chance," she said. "I'm going to try and see if I can fix this. . ." She took his hand and turned. . .

Then, Rick couldn't move. He found himself in a cloud of vapors, swirling and white, with flashes of color.

"I'll be right back to get you," said Rachel. She released his hand, and then embraced him. "Please don't be scared. And whatever you do, stay right there. Don't follow if you want to be safe."

He stood as if rooted to the place she'd left him, scared and bewildered.

Chapter Nineteen
Rachel

The cloud, the pain, the lights and the confusion cleared. Rachel stood in the upstairs hallway of her parents' huge home. The afternoon sun filtered through the western windows and bathed the hall in light. She glanced at her wrist watch and found that it was 3:43 P. M.

She heard her mother in her bedroom and knew that her father would be in the spare room, watching the game or something. Rachel walked to her mother's bedroom.

"Mom," she said. "I need to talk to you and Dad. Stay here, please."

Her mother started to protest but Rachel didn't stay. She walked into her father's room. She walked in without knocking, crossed to the TV and turned it off. She ignored his objection and said, "Come with me."

Her tone left no doubt that she expected him to follow. She walked back to her mother's room with her father in tow.

"Sit down," she told them, and they complied, puzzled by her tone of voice.

"I've Stepped back," she said. Their mouths dropped open.

"Rachel," said her mother. "What does this. . ."

"I don't like to do that, but I had to," said Rachel. "I'm ashamed of you two. I had to come back because of the way you treated Rick when he came. You disgraced yourselves and me. You insulted, embarrassed and hurt the feelings of a fine man."

"You can't talk to us like—" began her father.

Rachel waved a hand and went on. "You also humiliated me. You behaved like petulant, snobbish children and I'm ashamed of you."

"Now look," said her father, but Rachel held up a hand.

"I don't think you understand how important this man is to me," Rachel said. "I haven't told you everything. All summer he asked me to bring him to meet you. I didn't because I knew you'd be just hideous to him. I begged him to elope, but he refused again and again. He insisted that he wanted to meet you and ask your permission."

The parents sat in silence, looking back and forth at one another. Rachel didn't stop.

"Let me tell you what Rick means to me," she said. "I've told you about the night the fraternity drunks assaulted me, only a couple of months after those three punks attacked me at the high school. Rick protected me even though at that point I was a perfect stranger and meant nothing to him. . ."

Rachel went on for several minutes. The parents sat listening, trying to interject from time to time without success.

"Okay," she said at last. "Here's the story. If you can't be nice to Rick and to each other, tell me now. I can still call him and tell him not to come."

"Now, Rachel—" said her mother.

"If I do, let me explain what this will mean," she continued. "I don't want to do this, but I promise you I will. I will pack everything I own and go and stay at Rick's house. His parents love me already and they'd welcome me. Rick and I will get married and we will never see you again and I mean no contacts, no Christmases, no grandchildren, no future."

"Aw, stop being melodramatic. . ." began her father.

"Dad, I promise you I'll do it. I want to marry Rick. He loves me and would give up everything for me. He is gallant, honorable and a true gentleman. If you give him a chance, you will come to love him as a son.

"But you never gave him a chance," she went on. "You treated him like he'd broken into the house to rob you. I've never seen such rudeness and such arrogance."

Mom and Dad said nothing.

"That's all I intend to say. Decide now, because I have to call him in the next few minutes and tell him not to come."

Rachel's mother and father stared at her for several moments. "Okay, you've made your decision," She said. "Goodbye. I'll be gone in half an hour."

"Wait," said her mother.

"Why?" demanded Rachel. "You've given me your answer."

"I don't want you to go," said her father. "I love you, Honey."

"Dad, I don't want to go," she said. "But I can't and I won't allow you to wound Rick—"

Then she saw the anguish on her mother's face. She turned to look at her father.

Both people just stared at the ground, not able to speak. The agony of divorce, she knew, was a reality for these two. They were hurt, disappointed, as they saw the life they'd tried to build about to end: Not only their marriage, but also their only child was about to leave.

"Look, I'll tell you what I'll do," she said, softening just a little. "If you two cooperate, if you can be civil and kind, I'll reciprocate."

They looked up.

"I know that you've wanted me to go into treatment," she said. "Okay, I will. Name the doctor and the program and I'll go into it."

"Oh, Rachel," said her mom, and now she began to cry.

"Not only that," she said. "I'll help you out."

"What?" they said in unison, looking up.

"I've been watching you," she said. "You told me you'd wait until summer to get divorced. Well, you haven't filed, even though it's August. That tells me that you don't really want to get divorced, and I think you're tired of beating each other up."

Rachel's parents didn't speak or look up.

"I'll use the Step back," she said. "You tell me when things started to go wrong between you. I'll Step back to that time and warn you."

Rachel's parents couldn't speak for a few moments. "Oh God," said Dad.

"Honey," began Mom.

"I can't let you," said Dad. "This hurts you, this Stepping back, right?"

"Well, yes," said Rachel. "It's awful. The dreams I'll have tonight and for the next several nights will be hideous. But I can live with it if I'm with Rick. He protects me, somehow."

Her parents were silent for several moments. Then Mom cleared her throat and choked back a sob. "Brent," began Mom, but had to pause for a few moments. At last, she said, "Brent, let's make an agreement. Why don't we at least pretend that we just got married? That we still feel the love that Rachel feels for this young man?"

Dad looked back and forth between his wife and his daughter. "Rachel," he said, his voice husky. "I think your mom and I need some time alone."

"All right," said Rachel. She left the room and pulled the door shut.

Rachel walked back to her room and sat on her bed, propping her head in her hands. Would she really have walked out? She wondered.

Then she thought about Rick and smiled with anticipation. She'd aired out the guest room and put fresh sheets on the bed in the room earlier that day. She knew they'd make love later after dinner. It had been several days.

Her black blouse was damp with sweat at the intensity of the conflict with her parents. She stripped off the clothes and took a quick shower.

Then she pulled out a blue miniskirt outfit Mom had bought her for graduation, which Rick had never seen. She grinned, thinking of how much Rick would like the outfit. He'd stare at her from time to time, she knew. She wriggled with pleasure as she thought of how much he liked her two piece swim suit.

That was one of the best parts of the way Rick loved her: the way he *looked* at her. The sweet, almost goofy smile, the eyes, his appreciation of her. . .

About quarter to six, she saw. She walked downstairs and tried not to squirm with impatience.

Chapter Twenty
Rick

Rick stood in the cloud, puzzled and unsure of what to do. He heard a doorbell ringing somewhere.

The cloud disappeared and he found himself standing on the front Step of the Winnetka house. The door began to open.

Rick felt dizzy and disoriented, as if he didn't know how he'd gotten there. He looked at his watch. 6:30 P. M. His jaw dropped. *What on earth. . .*

Then his mind settled down. He thought, *Everything has to be okay.* He'd just driven here. He'd climbed out of his dad's Buick and walked to the door. He held a bouquet he'd brought for Rachel's mom and an orchid corsage for Rachel.

Right.

Rachel came out and pulled the door shut behind her. "Hi," she said, hugging him. "It's about time you got here."

"What do you mean?" he chuckled. "I'm right on time."

Rachel wore a pale blue top, with a matching skirt and a pair of white tennis shoes. "You look great," he said.

"Why, thank you," she said.

"This is for you," and he handed her the corsage. He pinned it on, with Rachel giggling and slapping his hand once or twice.

The door opened and her parents joined them on the front porch.

"Mom, Dad," said Rachel. "I want you to meet Rick." Rick, still feelng dizzy, took Mr. Farrell's outstretched hand.

"Welcome, son," said Mr. Farrell, smiling a welcome.

His wife leaned up and gave him a hug. "I'm so glad to meet

you," she said. She laughed with delight at the flowers Rick presented her. "How thoughtful," she smiled.

Rick turned to look at her. He felt a chill of something like horror. He had a distinct memory that Rachel had greeted him dressed in a black slacks outfit. Now, she wore a short blue skirt and sweater.

Mr. Farrell saw him staring at Rachel. He chuckled and winked at Rick. "Okay. I get it now," he said. "I know why you're distracted."

"You do?" said Rick.

"I don't know what to tell my daughter about her hemlines," grinned Mr. Farrell. "I don't approve . . ."

"Dad!" said Rachel, but she laughed as she said it.

"You don't approve," sneered Mrs. Farrell. "What baloney. You'd have loved to see me dressed in a skirt like that when I was Rachel's age."

"I don't doubt I'd like it now," said Mr. Farrell. "Why don't you go up and change?"

Rick couldn't get his mouth to work as Rachel's mother and father hugged.

The parents chatted with him on the porch. Mr. Farrell indicated the trees on the property and told Rick how old they were and which ones he'd planted.

Rachel's mother asked him about the drive from his home on the south side. He described his route, chatting about a traffic jam on the Dan Ryan Expressway. Mrs. Farrell chuckled a little, nodding her sympathy.

Then, at Mrs. Farrell's signal, everyone started inside. Mr. Farrell shut and locked the door.

Chapter Twenty-one

Rick drove home, happy and beaming, the car radio playing in the background. He thought through the lovemaking in the guest bedroom, the gentle touch of his fiancée's hands, the silky feeling of her skin against his. When they got into bed together, Rachel told him that she'd aired the room out that day and put fresh sheets on the bed—

And a strange memory rose up. He saw himself chatting with Rachel's dad in the library after dinner. Without warning, Farrell's face contorted and he snarled a curse at Rick: "You're nothing but a gold digging son of a bitch."

Then everything changed. Farrell was no longer scowling in fury. He smiled and chatted with Rick as if nothing had happened.

Mr. Farrell called me a son of a bitch. I couldn't have heard it wrong.

The welcome, the gracious dinner, the table setting, the enthusiasm of the parents for the wedding—all might have come from a dream of how such an evening would go. Rachel almost glowed with a joyful radiance and an excitement.

Her elation touched Rick. He had a hard time believing that such an impressive, even brilliant girl loved him, and wanted to spend her life with him—

Her father called me a gold digging son of a bitch.

He jerked his thoughts back to the good night kiss. They would talk tomorrow, of course. Rick would see her in two days, when they planned to go to the beach for the day.

He smiled, thinking of when they'd first met. He recalled that Rachel once asked him if he was in love with Janet. He responded with something like, 'how do you know?'

Now he knew.

She promised that the wedding would come off as soon as possible, but it would take at least a few months to organize. Then Rachel and Rick could be together all the time. She'd signed a contract with a school district and would start her teaching career in a month. She assured him that he would hook up with a company or something.

A gold digger? I didn't ask for any money.

Kids. They talked about kids tonight, when they would start a family, how many did they want, had he picked out names, wouldn't it be great to wake up together to little kids running into their bedroom, hopping into bed with Mommy and Daddy—

"Why would he say that? And then not remember that he said it?" Rick spoke out loud.

The trip home went much faster than the trip to Rachel's home, since he didn't have to fight traffic late at night. He took a quick shower and trooped off to bed, dead tired.

Despite his joy, however, his mind swirled with nightmares. He saw himself in the Farrell living room, both of Rachel's parents drinking, giving him a bitter rejection of his request to marry Rachel, forcing him to leave in tears of hurt and frustration.

He jerked awake several times. In the strange way that dreams hold a person, he saw himself again and again in the Farrell living room, facing antagonistic, even hostile people who insulted him and his family.

It never happened, he told himself over and over.

At last he got up and went to the kitchen. He drank a glass of ice water. Then he remembered the other nightmares.

This had happened before, these dreadful dreams. Beginning the night he met Rachel, he'd had nightmares that he'd gone on a crummy date with Janet.

That didn't happen, though.

Then, a day or two after he'd met Rachel when she came over to him at Kam's after a Saturday night gig, he began dreaming that he'd gone back to Janet. He'd found Janet stripped naked in his bed and made love to her. No. The image of what he'd done didn't match the phrase. He couldn't even say he'd had sex with her. He couldn't bring himself to say the coarse word that provided the best description of what he'd done to Janet that night—

But that didn't happen, either. No. No, it couldn't have. He hadn't gone to bed with her. He'd done the right thing. He'd stopped abusing Janet, apologized, and set her free to let her find a guy who would love her and cherish her the way he couldn't. Then, he realized that he had fallen for Rachel . . .

Why do I keep having these dreams?

He wanted to marry Rachel. He loved her, from the way she wrinkled her forehead when she didn't approve of something he'd said, to the way they made love, to their intellectual bond, to the joy he felt when he was with her. When he couldn't be with her, he felt miserable.

He shut his eyes. In his mind, he saw Mr. Farrell crossing a dark, contentious living room to him, handing him a check for $2000, more money than Rick had ever held in his hands at one time.

Rick saw himself tearing the check up and leaving the room, wounded, hurt, dazed by the animosity Rachel's parents showed him—

He forced himself to think about how much his mother and father liked her. They saw her as bright, gifted and charming. She'd make a fine mother. He grinned to think of himself as a father.

He returned to his bed and laid his head on the pillow. He fell asleep, fixing his thoughts on Rachel.

"One hundred," said Mr. Farrell.

"Two hundred," said Mr. Farrell.

"Five hundred and you never see her again."

He jerked awake again.

It never happened, he told himself again and again. *It couldn't have happened.*

Two days later, Rick got his draft notice.

Chapter Twenty-two

Rick visited several recruiters and decided to enlist for a four year hitch in the Marines. Since he had a college degree, the Marine recruiter arranged for him to go to Officer's Candidate School.

Rick and Rachel agreed to put the wedding on hold. As they kissed good-bye the night before he had to report they wept, knowing that they might not see each other again.

Despite the pain it cost, he suggested that if she wanted to date other men while he had to be away, he'd understand. Anything could happen, he argued. She laughed and told him not to be silly. She'd never date anyone except him again, she said over and over.

But she would be wrong.

***

Rick went to OCS at Quantico, Virginia. He volunteered to go into the Force Recon and received intense training in self-defense and martial arts.

Despite the invigoration of his military career, he missed his fiancée every moment. They wrote to one another almost every day and talked on the phone whenever they could.

Three years passed. Rick received several promotions, achieving the rank of Captain in the last year of his enlistment. He saw Rachel on leave whenever possible.

The Marines assigned him to command a company in Viet Nam for the last several months of his hitch. Rachel came to join him in Oahu the weekend before he shipped out to Southeast Asia and they had a tearful parting at the airport. The memories of that weekend in the Hawaiian paradise sustained him for months.

Until the night he died.

***

Rick returned from a mission one gloomy, murky night about a week before Christmas. He and his men had helped a helicopter crew retrieve a company of GIs from a jungle ambush. The Viet Cong had killed a few of the GIs and wounded several others. He climbed down from the chopper when it returned to the base and watched as medics off-loaded the broken and wounded bodies.

Near tears, he walked to what the flight crews called the "piss ditch" adjoining the landing strip. Three hours in a helicopter with VC fire all around him had scared him, as it always did. He never thought about basic human needs when he was up there. Now, he stood by the ditch where the chopper pilots relieved themselves after missions—

—And all Hell exploded behind him.

He didn't think. He dove headlong into the outdoor toilet. Something hot and lethal hit his leg.

Rick screamed, realizing he'd been wounded. He found that he couldn't move. He lay in the ditch, sure he was bleeding to death. He began to talk out loud to a woman who he knew wasn't there. He lost enough blood that he passed out.

Chapter Twenty-three
Rachel

The telephone rang early Sunday morning. Rachel heard her mother speak into the receiver.

A few moments later, her mother tapped at her door.

"Honey," said Mrs. Farrell. "Mrs. Howell wants to speak to you on the phone."

Rachel stumbled out of bed, puzzled at the call at seven o'clock in the morning. She picked up the phone in the hallway. "Hi Mom," she said, expecting to hear a customary chuckle of pleasure at the other end.

"Rachel," said Mrs. Howell, her voice subdued. "Could you come down here?"

"Now?" asked Rachel, still stretching a little.

"Yes, please, Honey," said Mrs. Howell. "Please be as quick as you can. I promise you it's important."

Rachel drew on some clothes and accepted a piece of toast from her mother. "Something wrong with you?" she asked, seeing the expression on her mother's face.

"Nothing, Honey," said Mrs. Farrell.

"Do you want me to come with you?" asked Rachel's father.

"Thanks, but you don't have to," said Rachel. "This won't be a big deal. We've been planning Rick's Christmas present. We're going to send him a cake, some racks of ribs from Gino's, a few other things. I'm sure that's what she wants to see me about."

"Yes," said Mrs. Farrell and turned her head away, wiping at her eyes.

Rachel, puzzled, poured some coffee into her favorite cup, one that Rick that had given her in college, and climbed into her little car that she'd purchased about two years ago when the Bonneville she'd inherited from her grandfather gave out. The new car was okay, she guessed, but she still missed the power of the Pontiac's huge engine, the comfortable ride and the memories that went with it. She put the Pontiac into storage, knowing that Rick would be excited to rebuild and restore it when his Marine enlistment was over.

The Sunday morning traffic amounted to nothing. She knew the route well.

As she drove, she thought about the week coming up. Christmas break started Friday after a half day of attendance for the students. Then she could relax for a couple of weeks, do the leftover shopping, sleep a little in the morning. She sighed, enjoying the prospect of some relaxation.

This would be, she reflected, her last Christmas with Rick away. She missed him so much on big holidays, much more than usual.

Eight months and then it would be over. Rick would come home to stay.

At the back of her mind, she saw her mother and father, and the expressions on their faces that morning. She wondered if they'd started fighting again, though they'd been at peace for a couple of years. Huh.

She pulled into the Howell driveway. She didn't notice the inconspicuous car parked on the street across the way.

She knocked on the door and Portia, Rick's kid sister, opened the door. In the dim light Rachel noticed that the girl seemed upset.

"What's wrong?" she asked, but Portia hurried away without answering. Rachel shrugged, puzzled. On a normal day she had a hard time getting a word in with the talkative girl.

"Mom? Dad? I'm here. . ." her voice trailed away when she walked into the living room. Rick's dad and a tall, handsome soldier with a gold cross on his lapel stood. A chaplain, she realized, and smiled at him. Then, she got it.

Everything stopped.

She couldn't move.

Rick's dad and mom came forward. "Rachel, Honey," said Mrs. Howell, coming over and hugging her. Mr. Howell joined them in the next moment and also embraced her. "This is Chaplain Gordon from the Marines. He needs to talk to you."

"Is Rick hurt?" she mumbled. He didn't speak at once. Rachel looked into his eyes and knew.

Her empty coffee cup fell from her numb fingers and shattered on the oak floor of the entranceway. For the first time in her life, Rachel Farrell fainted.

Rick's body arrived two days later. They held the funeral the next day.

Rick's will instructed them to cremate his body. Rachel and her parents joined the Howell family at Lake Michigan and scattered Rick's ashes into the lake.

Chapter Twenty-four

Rick's death tore Rachel to shreds. She couldn't concentrate in the classroom or on her other duties at the high school. The principal offered to get her an aide until she could recover.

Rachel thanked him and discussed the situation with her parents. At their suggestion she applied for and received a leave of absence for the second semester.

Her parents did all they could for her. One morning, her mother came into her bedroom.

"Rachel," she said, sitting on the bed. "Dad and I would like to take you to Florida with us."

"What? Why?"

"I think that a change of scenery, some sun and the ocean might help bring you out of this depression," Mom said.

Rachel considered. "I don't know," she said.

"Honey," said her mom. "Please believe me now. I learned how depression feels when your dad and I were fighting. Now, I don't know what you're going through. But depression is to a great extent anger, maybe some frustration. I think Palm Beach might give you some perspective."

The offer touched Rachel with its demonstration of love and concern. Rachel agreed, smiling.

Mom and Dad took her to Florida in early February, where they stayed at a fine resort. She lay by the pool in the sunshine, reading novels and writing to her friends, Donna and Hollis.

She did go on dates with a couple of men she met at the pool, to the delight of her parents. They hoped that she would find her way out of the depression that had surrounded her.

She dated a man named James Carmichael several times, going to the beach with him during the day and to dinner and dancing in the evening. One night, she went back to his hotel room with James and to her great surprise, got into bed with him.

The next night, they walked together, hand in hand, on the beach on a dark and lovely night. They found a blanket next to a dark dune and had sex again.

During this sexual encounter, in the height of the passion, she had a flash of illumination. James didn't regard what was happening as recreational or casual sex at all. On the contrary, he was really *making love* to her.

He's fallen in love with me, she realized. *Really, and truly in love.*

She found the relationship exciting and pleasurable. He treated her well, with patience and thoughtful consideration. She knew he wanted to continue the relationship and wasn't surprised when James asked her to come home with him to New York and meet his family.

She said that she'd consider it. The request was tender and sincere, delivered with intense devotion and *love.*

But the next morning, the pain set in. The profound love making reminded her of how much she missed Rick. She felt terrible. She couldn't respond that way to James. She liked him and liked the sex, but she didn't return his profound feelings.

She couldn't continue to lead James on. She'd been cruel.

When she told James that night that she couldn't continue to see him, she knew at once that she'd hurt him.

"This is crazy," James said, his eyes tearing. "Crazy. We could have a life together. You weren't married. You aren't a widow. You don't have kids. I don't give a rip what happened or who you dated in the past. You can get your life going again."

"I can sense how you feel for me," she said, trying not to be unkind. "But—"

"But think of last night and the night before," he said. "Think of how we did together."

"I'm so sorry," she told him. "I just can't."

James took a deep breath and stood. He gave her a curt nod and walked away, angry and wounded, without another word.

Still, every day that passed meant another day away from Rick. His face faded in her memory.

When she returned to Winnetka, she took a couple of graduate school classes. To her parents' delight she completed her master's degree, which meant a raise. Mom and Dad had a party for her to celebrate.

But she grieved that Rick didn't share in the festivity.

Rachel dated on occasion but didn't sleep with anyone for several months. She couldn't bear the memory of what it had been like with Rick.

She left on an airplane for Portland, Maine, on the fifteenth of June. She spent the summer in Augusta, Maine with her two friends, Donna and Barry Riske. They ate lots of lobster, went to clambakes, and explored the rocky coast of Maine from Kennebunkport in the south to Mount Desert Island and Bar Harbor in the north.

One cloudy day, the three of them visited the lighthouse at Pemaquid Point. Her friend Donna promised Rachel that she'd be visiting one of the most poetic places on the planet. Rachel sat with her friends watching the surf crash on the huge rocks, sending spray fifty feet or more in the air.

"What a wonderful, horrid place," she said to Donna, who nodded.

"I know what you mean. My friend Jeri brought her parents' ashes here from Texas. They came out here with her and told her that when they died, they wanted their ashes scattered here."

"Perfect," said Rachel. "I wish I'd done that with. . ."

And the hurt returned. "Oh, God," she said, weeping again at the loss of Rick.

Donna and Barry hugged her and let her cry for a few moments.

When she regained some composure, her good friend continued the story. "The ash scattering plan sounded good on paper," said

Donna. "However. . ." she paused and rubbed at the side of her nose, suppressing a chuckle.

"Huh?"

"Jeri and her family came out here on a beautiful day last summer. A lot of sightseers visit the place in the summer, of course. Jeri and her family sat on the benches over there. They had a little prayer session and the kids walked to the cliff to scatter the ashes. . ." she paused, and began to giggle.

"Yes?" said Rachel, when her friend didn't go on.

"The wind shifted to on shore," said Barry.

Rachel got the picture. "Oh, no," she said, putting her hand to her mouth.

"Uh, huh," said Donna. "An awful lot of people met Jeri's mom and dad that day."

Rachel and her friends giggled, then she let go and laughed until she had trouble catching her breath.

The healing had started, she thought.

Chapter Twenty-five

Rachel had never been fond of flying. Taking off didn't bother her, but landings found her clutching at the armrests with white knuckled anxiety. However to her surprise, the airplane ride home from Maine couldn't have been much more pleasant.

Rachel boarded the plane early and found her seat about halfway back in the airplane, watching people walk down the aisle, storing their gear in the overhead bins. A man looked down at her and smiled. "Hi," he said as he pushed a knapsack into the bin above the seat and sat down next to her. "Chris McBain," he said, extending his hand.

"Hello," she said. "I'm Rachel Farrell."

"Going home?" he asked.

"Yes, I am," she said. "I spent the summer in Maine."

"Wow. Pretty nice."

"Yes, I had a lovely time," she agreed. They continued to chat as the plane took off.

Rachel realized about halfway home that she considered this man next to her the most attractive man she'd met since Rick had died. Tall and handsome, he had classic Italian good looks. He wore an impeccable, well- tailored suit that couldn't have cost less than $1500. She found him witty and personable and his interest in her flattered her.

"So your fiancé died in the attack?" he asked.

"Yes," she said. "I'm starting to heal a little. Maine helped take my mind off it. It's so beautiful on the coast, you know, sitting and watching the ocean, eating seafood, and spending time with friends. I felt myself healing up."

"How so?" he smiled.

She considered her answer for a few moments. "I gained some perspective, I guess," she said. "I'd forgotten how beautiful life can be. Over the last few months I've been learning to put grief in its proper place."

"Maine's a great place to do that," he said. "What do you do back home?"

"I'm a high school English teacher," she told him. "I start work day after tomorrow. I haven't been into the school for months, though. I took a semester off after Rick died."

"Understandable," he nodded and she felt touched by the sympathy in his eyes.

"Oh I don't know," she shrugged. "Maybe I would have been better working through it. As things stand now I feel nervous about starting the job again."

"Yeah," he said. "I'm not surprised you feel that way."

"Tell me about yourself."

"Oh, not much to tell," he said. "I sell for a large chemical company." He told the story of his job. While he worked to finish his degree, the chemical company had recruited him and he'd come aboard.

She learned that he owned a townhouse in Lake Forest, a suburb next to her parents' home in Winnetka. She liked the fact that he didn't live too far away.

Rachel found herself a little disappointed when the plane landed at O'Hare Airport. She realized, as it taxied to the gate, that she hadn't even clutched at the armrests. "Could I offer you a ride home?" he asked.

"Do you mean it?"

"Sure, we're neighbors on the north shore. I left my car in the parking lot here. So if you want to retrieve your luggage, I'll pick up the car and we can drive home together."

"Thank you," she said. "That would save my parents a drive. I planned to call them when the plane landed, but I'm sure they'd be relieved."

As he suggested, she retrieved her luggage while he picked up his car. She wheeled the large suitcase out to the lower level of the concourse and found Chris waiting by a beautiful black Porsche 911. She stared at his car as he popped the trunk and loaded her suitcases in. He held the door and she sank into the comfortable gun-metal gray leather upholstery.

She noticed that he only had one little knapsack, no carry-on luggage or other baggage. Somehow, that struck her as strange. She decided to ignore her little alarm bell.

The ride to Winnetka didn't seem to take much time. They chatted together with good humor. They pulled up in front of her home at about six o'clock.

"Would you like to come in?" she asked, as he helped her in the door with the suitcases.

"Thanks, I'd love to," said Chris. "That's very kind."

Rachel's parents greeted her and extended a cordial welcome to Chris. After cocktails, Chris invited her to accompany him to dinner. She asked her parents if they would mind. . .

"No, not at all," said her mother and even looked a little delighted. Rachel excused herself and went upstairs to her room, where she changed from her slacks outfit into a skirt and light sweater. The evening had turned a little chilly, she thought.

Chris took Rachel to dinner at a quiet, elegant restaurant in Lake Forest. The wait staff knew him and treated them with what struck her as special courtesy.

He drove her along Sheridan Road, along Lake Michigan, in the light of a full moon. He stopped at a parking lot near a pier.

"Like a little walk to settle our stomachs?" he said.

"Sure, that would be great," she said.

"Wait a second," he said. He reached into his glove box and removed some little packages that he slipped into his pocket.

She took his arm as they walked along the pier in the moonlight for a pleasant few moments before stopping in front of a small cabin cruiser.

"Why are we stopping here?" she asked.

"I wanted to show you my boat."

"What?" she said, incredulous.

"Yeah," Chris said. "It's a 1969 Chris Craft Constellation Cabin Cruiser. You like it?"

"Cool," she said.

"Come on aboard," he said.

Chris opened the cabin and they went down inside. He reached into a refrigerator and extracted a bottle of Champagne, which he opened with a loud pop, the cork flying off into the harbor. She giggled, and they sipped the fine wine together on the deck. She'd never tasted any champagne like this, with a toasted almond taste. The wine almost exploded in her mouth with a delightful effervescence. When he was looking the other way, she managed a surreptitious look at price tag on the bottle and realized that this bottle of champagne had cost him more than eighty dollars.

They sat on the bench at the stern of the boat, the conversation proceeding as it had all day. She felt no pressure to entertain him but found him a sympathetic ear. He lifted his arm and she moved over next to him. He draped his arm over her shoulder and she snuggled against him.

"This must be pretty fast," she said, looking around at the cabin cruiser.

"Uh, huh, real nice boat," he nodded, and told her about the specifications. "I'd offer to take you out for a spin, but I'm low on gas, and I don't know where I'd get any now."

"That's okay," she said, giggling.

He finished his champagne and put the glass on a small table. She turned and smiled up at him.

He took her face in his hands and kissed her, a gentle press of his lips against hers. Then the kissing became serious. It continued for some time but at last she managed to draw back, breathing hard. "I forgot to ask," she said.

"Yes," he said, smiling in the moonlight and stroking at her hair, her lips and her forehead.

"Please tell me you aren't married."

He laughed. "No, of course not. Not even a current girlfriend."

Again a little bell rang in her mind. "No?"

He gave a rueful chuckle. "It ended a couple of months ago," he said. "I learned that she had a boyfriend in Dallas that she went to see all the time. I'd been figuring we'd get married. Then she married this other guy."

"So she used you while maintaining this love affair in Texas?"

"Yeah, she traveled there all the time for business," he said. "I didn't even suspect. . ."

"How terrible," she said. "I'm sorry I brought it up."

"No," he said. He brushed her hair back from the side of her head and nibbled at her ear lobe. "No, you have no reason to be sorry. I understand your concern. Now. Will you relax?"

She did. She let herself enjoy the kissing and then his intimate caressing, absent from her life for so long.

At last he picked her up and carried her down to the cabin. He drew back the covers on one of the beds. He loosened her skirt, and helped her remove the rest of her clothing. His clothes came off as the kissing continued.

They lay back together on the bed. Then he extracted one of the little packages he'd brought along. She realized it what was and she watched as he tore open the wrapper and rolled on the prophylactic.

She thought that she ought to protest. Somehow her mouth didn't work.

When they lay back together on the bed, the night had become chilly.

That had to explain the discomfort she felt, she thought, as he drew the covers over them and he dozed off.

Rachel lay awake for some time, relishing the faint soreness and excitement. She thought of James, the man she'd met in Florida and how he'd made love to her. Different than this man, she decided. Not better, just different.

And Rick's face rose up in front of her. She shut her eyes and a tear trickled down her cheek.

I have to let him go, she told herself. With a determined effort, she let herself flow off to sleep.

When she woke, the sun was up. Chris smiled down at her. In a few moments, he and Rachel resumed the lovemaking.

Later that day after he'd dropped her off at her parents' house, she waved goodbye—

And the guilt hit. *I've never done anything like that before. Sex the first time I've even met the man—*

But then memories of that dreadful Champaign drug experience jolted her back to reality.

The drugs. The revolting heroin pusher—what was his name? Rudy, of course. She hadn't had sex with him, thank goodness, but she'd done everything else, breaking all the dorm rules, breaking the law with the drugs, and even crashing a new and awful pathway in her mind.

Her behavior couldn't be called exemplary.

Chapter Twenty-six

Rachel drove to the high school two days later for meetings and to prepare her classroom. Chris needed to go out of town on business for a couple of days, so she hadn't seen him since the night on the boat, though he had called her three or four times. She puttered in her classroom, setting out books and putting up posters.

A student showed up at her door. "Ms. Farrell," said the student. "You have a delivery in the main office. Can you come down?"

"Sure," she smiled.

Rachel walked through the hall, exchanging greetings with teachers she hadn't seen for several months. The warmth and kindness of her colleagues brought her near to tears.

One of the secretaries, Michelle, met her in the hallway and opened the office door for her. Rachel, puzzled, walked in. "What's going on?" she asked.

Michelle smiled and pointed. Rachel gasped as she saw a magnificent bouquet of long stemmed roses waiting on the counter. A beautiful crystal vase held the roses and a card in an envelop lay on the counter.

"Someone sent those to me?" she managed.

"Yes indeed," said Michelle.

Rachel opened the card. "See you at four o'clock," read the card. "Hope you're having a great day". The card's signature read 'Chris.'

Chris met her at the main office at four o'clock as promised. They kissed, embracing with passion.

She took his arm as they left school together. He followed her home while she changed into a formal outfit. Then he took her to another special dinner.

They drove along the Outer Drive, south toward the Loop. He took her to the Ambassador West and a wonderful dinner in the Pump Room, one of Chicago's most famous and lovely restaurants.

She brought him to her parents' home and led him into the guest room for another lovely time of sex. Still, she didn't ask him to spend the night. She felt the slightest twinge of coldness and decided not to push things.

She slept in the guest room that night. As she drifted off, she recalled that the last time she'd slept in this room. It had been after Rick came to meet her parents. Tears rose and she brushed them away.

The next night, Chris took her to a movie. Then they fell into seeing one another almost every day.

He took her to his condominium one Friday for pizza, a cobwebby bottle of an extraordinary Cabernet Sauvignon, and then a few hours of enjoyable intimacy. The condominium stunned her. He had decorated it with leather furniture, glass tables, and a king sized bed with a modernistic headboard.

They wound up in the bed for some of the most breathtaking sex of her life. When it concluded, he laid back, grinning. She snuggled up next to him, since the bed felt cold. She felt intense gratitude to him for his tenderness and concern.

She drove home sometime later and went to her own bed that night glowing and happy. Having Chris in her life had raised her spirits a great deal. He'd listened to her stories about teaching with avid interest.

Chris, on the other hand, never talked much about his job, except to say that it involved high pressure and equivalent high pay.

She woke up shaking with terror at 3:00 A. M.

When she calmed a little, she wondered what had scared her. Don't be silly, she told herself.

Nonetheless, she considered the evening and the whole sexual relationship with Chris. She felt somewhat disturbed that she couldn't feel the love that she'd felt for Rick and the sex didn't reflect love and devotion as it had with Rick. With Chris, making love never transcended his skilled technique. But Chris treated her well and seemed to want to please her and—well, maybe she'd come to love him.

By the end of October, she'd convinced herself that they had something special going.

Rachel chaperoned the formal Turnabout dance at the high school the Friday after Halloween. At this dance, the girls invited the boys, so she asked Chris to accompany her. He wore a charcoal gray pinstriped suit, a well-starched pink dress shirt with French cuffs and a soft, understated tie. His cufflinks were black onyx with a small diamond in each one and his watch was an Oyster Perpetual Rolex. Though Rachel wore her best outfit, she felt a little underdressed next to him. Still several of her fellow chaperones commented that they made a striking couple.

A student, one of her favorites, asked if her boyfriend could take a picture of Rachel and her together. Rachel posed with her arm around the student, smiling and laughing as the girl's date snapped the picture.

Then Rachel turned back to Chris and took his arm. "Smile," said the boyfriend and snapped a picture of Rachel and Chris.

"Hey," said Chris. He sounded annoyed.

"What's wrong?" asked Rachel.

"I don't like having my picture taken, that's all," he said, surly.

A little alarm bell went off in Rachel's mind. He looked handsome to the point of being stunning, and could have modeled for a major fashion magazine. She chose to ignore her misgivings, as she always did. He had a good reason for not wanting his picture taken, for sure.

The next week, the girl came in with copies of the two pictures. Rachel had a bulletin board devoted to pictures of students in her classes and she pinned the picture of the girl on the board.

Rachel put the photo of Chris into her purse, intending to share it with him later. Then, remembering that he'd gotten a little upset when the boyfriend snapped the picture, she decided that maybe she shouldn't show it to him.

One Saturday just before Christmas, she made the long and still familiar drive to Rick's parents' home. They embraced her and welcomed her. She sat between them on the couch and they hugged her with profound affection and concern.

They asked how she was doing, and she kept the conversation as light as she could, smiling and laughing as much as she could. At last, she knew she had to tell them.

"Mom and Dad," she began, but then stopped, choked up a little. "No, I mean Mr. and Mrs. Howell."

They laughed a little and Mrs. Howell squeezed her hand to reassure her. "I wanted you to know," she said. "I've met someone."

She thought she saw a flicker of – regret? Anger? – in their eyes, but dismissed the idea. No. They were too gracious and loved her too much.

She showed them the picture. "I met Chris last summer," she said, "on the way back from Maine. I think we have something special."

She told them about Chris, how they'd become serious, that she anticipated a proposal and a ring, perhaps at Christmas.

"How wonderful," said Mrs. Howell.

"Yes," she said. "And I'm so happy. . ."

Then she couldn't go on. She wept, then sobbed, her heart breaking again at seeing the pain in the faces of the two people who had almost become her in-laws. They held her, loving her, letting her cry.

When the storm abated, Rachel dried her eyes and went to the washroom to fix her makeup. She came back to the Howells and removed her picture of Rick from her purse. She handed it to Rick's mother. Rachel also gave her an envelope with all the snapshots she'd taken with Rick over the time they'd been together.

"We're very happy for you, Honey," said Mr. Howell. Rachel had a hard time speaking, seeing the haunted sorrow of these two people for their son.

The worst moment came as Rachel gave Mrs. Howell the engagement ring Rick had given her. Rachel knew that he had saved for it, putting money aside with every check for a couple of years. It was a small, delicate diamond in a white gold setting. She sobbed as she removed it from her ring finger and gave it to Mrs. Howell. It was the first time it had left her possession since Rick had given it to her.

As she left a little later, Rick's mom hugged her, perhaps for the last time. "'Farewell, Ophelia,'" she said. "'I hoped thou hadst been my Hamlet's wife.'"

Chapter Twenty-seven

That evening she managed to shrug off the melancholy and puttered around her bedroom, excited that she would see Chris in a few moments. Her mother called her to the telephone. To her delight she greeted her old friend Donna calling from her home in Atlanta.

"How's your practice developing?" asked Rachel. Donna had received two advanced degrees in Social Work and Psychology, and worked for a school district as a drug and alcohol counselor.

"Things have gone well," said Donna, and filled her in on several things that had been going on with her, with her family and her husband Barry.

They chatted about one thing and another until Rachel said, "I've got something to tell you."

"Yes?" said Donna. "Does this involve romance?"

"It does," said Rachel, and told her best friend about Chris and how the love affair had been proceeding. She told her about the meeting on the plane, the dating, the dinners and the romance.

"What does he look like?" asked her friend.

Rachel described him in some detail, including a little scar that ran through his left eyebrow. She noticed that Donna had grown silent. "Donna?" she smiled. "Are you still there?"

"A scar," repeated her friend at last.

"Yes," said Rachel. "I tend to kiss it when we become…er…involved." Donna giggled with her a little, but not with much humor.

"Do you mean you've been sleeping with this man?" asked Donna.

"Excuse me?" said Rachel, laughing. "Donna, really—"

"Please, Rachel, I'm serious," said Donna. "And this may be important."

Rachel paused for a moment with her surprise. "Well, I don't want to discuss particulars, but yes. We've been intimate for some time," said Rachel. "He's been wonderful, very patient and respectful. However. . ."

"Yes?" asked her friend when Rachel didn't go on.

"He's leaving tomorrow morning and he's going to be traveling all week. I think I might spend the night with him Friday and come home Saturday."

"Hmm," said her friend. "Do you have a picture of him you could send me?"

"What?"

"I assure you, I think it could be important, Rachel," said her friend. The urgent tone in Donna's voice surprised Rachel.

"Well, I only have one snapshot," said Rachel. "Yes, I know that sounds kind of strange. I used to take pictures with Rick all the time. But I guess I could send it off to you if you insist. . ."

"Please humor me and do so. I'll return it at once, I promise," said her friend. "But you're right; it's probably nothing at all."

"Okay," said Rachel, puzzled at the urgency she heard in her friend's voice. Still she made a note to send it off at once.

After chatting about other matters for a few moments, Rachel hung up. Chris picked her up ten minutes later.

She mailed the picture the next day.

On Friday, she dressed in a nice pair of jeans and a new camel hair sport coat she'd just bought to please Chris. Her parents smiled at the outfit and told her how nice she looked. Mom complimented her on her hair, which Rachel had allowed to grow out for several months.

She smiled her thanks and told her parents not to wait up for her. They exchanged glances.

"You seem serious about this man, Honey," said Mom.

"Yes, I think this might be special," Rachel said.

"Rachel, please be careful," said Dad. "You've been lonely since Rick died, I know. . ."

"Chris has been very considerate," she said. "I think he respects my need to take it easy until I feel okay. . ."

"Well, you do see him almost every night that he's in town," said her mom. Her tone held the merest hint of disapproval.

Rachel didn't reply at first. "Mom, Dad," she said. "I'm not making a commitment I can't fulfill, I promise." Her parents looked unconvinced, but nodded to her. Rachel noted that their initial good impression seemed to have soured, for some reason. She sensed that they hadn't become quite comfortable with Chris.

Come to think of it, she didn't feel quite comfortable with him either.

She shrugged away the feelings. Chris had been wonderful to her. Why shouldn't she happy?

But the strange thoughts wouldn't leave her. She planned to marry Chris. She planned to build the rest of her life around him.

But the love affair had never seemed quite right.

For one thing, she kept feeling he somehow looked familiar. That was silly, of course.

Well, he'd gone to the University of Illinois at the same time as she, at least for a couple of years. She didn't think he had a diploma, though. She'd never seen one on his wall—

Come on, she thought. Maybe I saw him on campus, or in a class.

She realized she'd thought through this several times. When she'd mentioned it to Chris, he assured her he didn't remember her, and that if he had met her, he would remember her beyond any doubt. She smiled at the compliment.

Rachel shrugged away the strange feeling, and packed a little suitcase to take with her. She had a strong feeling she wouldn't be coming home that night.

Then she left to drive over to Chris's townhouse, humming to herself. She hadn't shown her parents the provocative negligee she'd bought to please Chris.

Chapter Twenty-eight

The car drive seemed to take forever, Rachel thought. She tried to focus on Chris and his firm, hard body. . .

But she began to think about Rick.

She remembered the last time she'd made love to Rick: the summer before last, over a year before, she stayed with Rick at a hotel in Oahu for a weekend together. He'd have to ship out on Monday for Viet Nam.

She never dreamed it would be the last time she'd ever see him.

She thought through the passionate meeting at the Honolulu Airport, the lovely Friday night with the soft Hawaiian breeze wafting through their hotel room, the golf on Saturday, a fine meal, and then the night together in the room in the hotel. Sunday, they'd had brunch and gone back to the room. They had about two hours until checkout. She recalled how they'd undressed and gotten back into the bed together. . .

"Rachel," said Rick.

Rachel jumped, terrified. "Rick!" she said. She spun and looked in the back seat of her little car—

Of course she didn't find Rick in her backseat. He died what, a year ago?

She pulled off the road into a parking lot, trying to calm her jangled nerves. She'd never been so startled.

She calmed a bit and tried to reason this out. She'd been thinking about sex with Rick, the most precious thing that had ever happened to her. She recalled how they lay together in the bed that Sunday morning, staring into one another's eyes. She teared up, thinking how long it would be until they could do this again. . .

"I wish I could tell you how much I miss you, Rick," said Rick's voice, and Rachel almost screamed. "At night I come home and cry sometimes. I want to tell you all the things I'm doing and it's so hard to have to write them like this. . ."

She recognized the words. She'd written them in a letter about three years ago.

Rick recited the 91st Psalm: "A thousand may fall at your side and ten thousand at your right hand..." Tears ran down Rachel's face, hearing, for the first time since Oahu, the psalm that had been their favorite.

She went cold, thinking about how the Psalm had linked them together. They'd agreed that each night at bedtime, they would think of one another and recite the 91st Psalm. But, she now realized, she hadn't recited the psalm for many months.

Then Rick's voice said, "I know I'm dying, Rachel. And I know that you have no way of hearing these words. But I want you to know a few things. First I love you and I have since the first time I saw you. Nothing ever made me so happy as being together—" He screamed now, the pain and terror in his cry raising the hairs on the back of Rachel's neck as she sat in her car, staring through the windshield. Tears started from her eyes at the sound of pain.

At last the pain in his voice eased. "Okay, I think I can talk. Please don't grieve for me. Find someone. . ."

Then silence again.

Rachel sat, scared, until the chills faded. She wiped the tears of pain and horror away. That had to be him, she thought. No one else would recite that psalm to me. No one would know how we felt about that psalm.

She got out of the car and took several deep breaths. When she felt calm enough, she resumed the drive to Chris's house, shaking and nervous.

But she couldn't stop thinking about what she'd heard. *Why did I hear this now? How could I have heard it?*

She remembered, then. Exactly one year ago, Rick had been killed. She had suppressed the memory in the excitement of the affair with Chris.

Then she found herself in front of Chris' townhouse. Now she didn't feel sure she could go through with her plans for sex that night. She took a few more deep breaths, and talked out loud to herself. She climbed out of her little car and took her overnight case up to the door with her.

"Hi," he said as he opened the door.

She looked at him, a bit jarred. He'd just come from a shower and he toweled his hair. He wore only a white bathrobe which he hadn't bothered to close. "Oh," she said.

"I'm sorry," he grinned. "I just didn't have time to—ah—change—" his voice trailed away.

"I see," she said, and again, her little mental alarm went off. She fought with her instinct to turn and run to the car—

"You look pretty pale," he frowned. "Do you feel all right?"

She took a deep breath and made an effort to give a big smile. "Sure, I'm—er—fine," she lied.

"I thought we'd order a pizza," he said. "But unless you're starved, I think that can wait."

He took her hand with one hand and took her overnight case with the other. "Come on," he said and led her to the bedroom.

They kissed for some time, standing next to his bed. Still shaken by what happened in the car, she tried to concentrate on relaxing. He began to remove her clothes and she remembered the negligee.

"Wait," she said. "I have a present for you."

She took her overnight case into the bathroom. Standing in front of the mirror, she touched up her makeup and laid out the negligee. She had just slipped the negligee over her head—

"Rachel," said her best friend Donna.

"Hah!" Rachel blurted.

"Don't speak, please," said her friend. Rachel looked around but didn't see Donna.

"No," said Donna. "I'm at home in Atlanta. I'm using the thought channel. Listen to me."

"Okay," whispered Rachel, understanding now. Donna hadn't used her unique mental skill in years. She resisted using it because of the fearful nightmares that accompanied it.

Whatever she wanted, Donna had to be serious about it.

Knock at the bathroom door. "Hey," said Chris. "Everything all right?"

As quick as lightning she hit the lock button. "I'm okay," she yelled through the door. "I'll be out in just a second."

"Well, hurry, will you?" he whined.

"Are you okay?" Donna's voice spoke in her mind again.

"Yes," said Rachel in as soft a voice as she could. "I'm locked in his bathroom."

"Rachel," said the voice. "Please. You have to get out of that apartment now. He's dangerous."

"Huh?"

"It's why I asked you to send the picture," Donna's voice resounded in her mind.

"What—" began Rachel.

"He's using a false name," said Donna in Rachel's mind. "I know him as Dominick Cianni."

"Dominick!" said Rachel, aghast. Of course. Things began to fall into place. The party. The drugs. He was there, with Donna.

"I dated him in Champaign and broke it off with him," Donna spoke in her mind. "He knows what I can do and maybe what you can do."

"I don't see. . ."

"You have to get away," said Donna in her mind. "I tried to read him, but I can't get a clear lock. I know he wants something from you. I don't know what. He may try anything."

"I don't know how. . ." began Rachel.

"Could you climb out the window in the bathroom?" asked Donna, the urgency in her voice terrifying.

"I don't think so," whispered Rachel. "It's too small."

"Let me call the police," said Donna. "Maybe you can pretend to be sick? Just until they get there?"

"Hey, come on," yelled Chris/Dominick through the door.

"Okay, just a minute," shouted Rachel to Dominick. She whispered to her friend Donna. "Here's the address." She gave it to her friend.

"Get away if you can," said Donna. "For God's sake stay away from him."

"I can't—"

"I'm just about to get into the car with Barry now," said her friend. "We're dropping the kids at his parents and we'll be there in the morning."

"How—"

The door crashed open. Chris had kicked it open, shattering the lock.

Chapter Twenty nine

Chris stood outside the door, staring at Rachel in the stunning negligee. "Well, well," he said. "What a spectacular present."

"Chris," she said. "How dare you. . ."

"You're right," said another voice, speaking with a pronounced downstate accent. Chris Stepped aside and Rachel saw a small man with bright red hair leering at her. "Very attractive. Too bad I'm married."

Rachel grabbed a towel and clutched it in front of her. "Chris, who's that?" She said, horrified. "What's going on?"

Then she remembered. She'd seen the little weasel at the fraternity party that night she'd taken Keith's poison. He was Keith's associate and friend.

"I saw what you did," said Chris.

"What?"

"That night in Champaign," said Chris. "When you were unconscious, I followed Keith out. I saw you and your buddy kill Keith on the quad."

"We'll deal with him next," interrupted the little man.

Rachel went cold, paralyzed with terror. "Now," said the little man. Chris lunged forward and grabbed her.

Rachel struggled, but she had no chance against the two men. They dragged her to the bed and secured her wrists to the headboard with handcuffs. Then they tied her feet to the baseboard.

"This won't take long," said the little man. He took her face in his clammy hands and looked into her eyes.

Rachel lay as still as possible. She felt the man probing into her mind as Donna could. She threw up mental blackouts in all the areas he tried to probe.

After a few moments the little man stood up. He reached down and stroked her leg, beginning at her knee and roving up her thigh, leering.

"She blocked me somehow," said the little man. "No one's ever done that."

"What?" said Dominick, incredulous. "How. . ."

"I don't know," the little man said. "But we'll go the other way." He turned back to stare into Rachel's eyes.

"We intend for you to die, Rachel," said the little man. "You may choose how it will go. If you wish a swift, speedy death, you will tell us where to find what we want. Otherwise, you face hideous—er—discomfort."

"Go to Hell, you miserable little creep," shouted Rachel. "I'll tell you nothing."

"All right, then," said the little man, nodding to Chris.

"You know, I really enjoy. . ." began Chris, with a glance at Rachel's bare legs.

"You can have any woman you want after we get them," said the little man.

"You bastard," snarled Rachel. "You never felt anything for me?"

"Oh, I had some fun making out with you," Chris shrugged. "But now. . ."

He dropped a wet towel over her face. She couldn't breathe as the two men held it in place over her mouth and nose.

An eternity passed. Chris removed the towel. "Now," he said. "Where. . ."

She choked water out and screamed a profanity. Chris replaced the towel. Just before she passed out, he removed it again. "Come on, *ma petite*," the little man said. "Just tell us. We'll get them and you can buy yourself some more time to live. You'll wait here, alive, until we get back."

Rachel had never been so terrified. She managed to curse him again as he replaced the towel.

He lifted the towel. The little man laughed. "Don't make it so hard on yourself," he said.

She heard a loud banging in the other room. "What on earth?" said the little man.

"I don't have any idea," said Chris. "I'm not expecting anyone. . ."

"I called the police, you bastards," screamed Rachel. "Help!" she shrieked. Chris dropped the towel across her face. She felt a cold draft as a window opened, then heard a splintering crash from the other room as someone kicked the door open.

Rachel, again near panic, whipped her head back and forth. The towel, with no one holding it, fell away from a corner of her mouth and she sucked air. "Help!" she screamed again. Someone lifted the towel from her face and she gasped.

"Okay, Miss," said a kind voice. "Be calm. Police. Where did he go?"

"The window, I think," she wheezed.

The handcuffs came free as a patrolman unlocked them. He untied her feet. Rachel sat up and the cop put a robe around her shoulders. He helped her to the bathroom where she changed back into her clothes. "We'll get them," he promised. He began to question her.

Rachel called her mom and dad who arrived in the midst of the questioning.

"What did they do, Honey?" asked Mom. Rachel tried to explain, but kept crying, the terror of the evening not yet receding.

"The miserable bastards," said her dad. "Do you know what they wanted? Just sex?"

"It could have been, Dad," she said. "Please just take me home."

Her mother drove her home while her dad followed in Rachel's little car. That night, she slept on a cot in her parents' bedroom, managing only a little troubled sleep.

At two o'clock, she woke up from a nightmare about sex. She almost screamed when she heard Rick's voice again, speaking in her mind as he had earlier that evening. "I've really been having problems with some of the boys in a couple of my classes," he said. "They seem to have a terrible time relating to women. . ."

Rachel jerked upright. She knew now that she'd heard Rick reciting letters that she'd written to him. He'd memorized them, like he'd memorized the 91st Psalm. Now his voice continued: he began to recite the 23rd Psalm, his personal favorite. He struggled when he got to the famous prayer: "Even though I walk through the valley of the shadow of death…"

Then silence fell. Tears flowed down Rachel's cheek. She realized that she might have just heard his last words.

But where did his voice come from? She heard it as if he were standing in the room.

Rachel knew she hadn't dreamt the voice. No. The message had been too clear.

She realized, now, what she had to do.

Somehow she had to figure out how to use the Step and save Rick. Her life depended on it. Dominick and the vicious little redhead wouldn't stop coming after her.

Rachel knew what they wanted, also. But they couldn't get them without her, for sure.

Hiding from the little redhead wouldn't be possible, she knew it. But she knew now that she could shield certain knowledge from him.

Chapter Thirty

In the morning, her mother awakened her. "Rachel, Honey," she said, sitting on the bed with her daughter and stroking her hair. "I'm sorry to wake you. Your friends from Atlanta just arrived. They must have driven all night. I've been telling them what happened. . ."

Rachel seized a robe and threw it over her pajamas. She ran downstairs without even pausing to brush her hair.

"Donna," she cried, embracing her good friend. "Barry," she said, hugging him.

Rachel led them to her bedroom where she collapsed on the bed, weeping with fear about the evening mixed with relief at seeing her best friends.

"Dominick did this, didn't he," said Donna, sitting next to her and stroking her hair.

"Yes," said Rachel. "I didn't remember him at all. I only met him for a moment that night, and he dyed his hair a different color and I think I recall that he had a beard—"

"Yes, he did," nodded Donna. "I broke up with him after the three of us had to be hospitalized."

"I remember you told me," said Rachel.

"I'm sorry I didn't contact you sooner," Donna apologized. "I got home late from a conference and found your letter. I'd suspected it when you described him."

"I'm okay," Rachel assured her. "They didn't really hurt me, just scared me."

"I'm so sorry," said Donna. "I should have warned you."

Rachel told them about the attack and how the police had arrived in the midst of the torture. Barry nodded. "Thank God you came away okay," he said. "Why didn't you Step away?"

"I couldn't get my mind to focus at all, they scared me so much," said Rachel.

Barry nodded. "It would have scared anyone," he said. "Did the police catch those two mutts?"

"We haven't heard from the police, and I'm sure they'd call," said Rachel. "Dominick and Rolf are still out there and they'll attack me again if they can. Then they said they'd come after you."

Barry shuddered. "What can we do?"

Rachel stood and paced. At last she said, "I think I need to find a way to Step Back and save Rick," she said at last. "Then go to the morning when I found out he died. Then I'll contact you. I hope we can find a way to take care of Dominick before he finds me and hands me over to this Rolf creep."

Her friends stared at her, not moving or speaking, mouths open. At last Donna stirred. "Rachel, you can't," said Donna. "You'd be putting yourself in way too much danger. You could be killed."

"That's correct," said her husband. "Donna's quite right. You've never Stepped that far, or that long. Besides, you can't bring someone back from the dead, you know that."

"But maybe I could Step Back to the morning before the attack, call him or send a telegram over there and warn him?" Rachel pleaded.

Barry thought. "No, I don't think so," he said. "I can't imagine him paying attention to such a warning. He doesn't understand the Step Back. He wouldn't comply. He couldn't. He has a job to do."

"I agree," nodded Donna.

"Then I have to find a way to go to the helicopter pad," Rachel choked. "Maybe I can Step there the night it happened." Rachel had a hard time saying this. Fear clutched at her insides.

"I don't think it's possible, given what we know about the Step," said Barry.

"But I do have something I haven't told you," said Rachel. She related the intense episodes of hearing Rick's voice last night and then in the early morning. Her friends stared at her open-mouthed.

"You heard Rick?" said Donna.

"Just as well I hear you now, yes," said Rachel. "I thought about the last time he and I made love. The thoughts became intense. Somehow he called to me. I heard him reciting letters that I wrote to him while he was over there."

"What would have brought that on now?" asked Donna

Rachel considered. Why had she heard it? She'd had sex with a couple of men and this hadn't happened.

At last she said, "I don't know if I can answer, Donna. But as you know, sex is the most powerful communication possible between two people. With Rick and me, sex always became emotional for the last four years when we saw each other for leaves and for Christmas. We never knew if it would be the last time."

Donna took Barry's hand. "I thought maybe only Barry and I got that serious," she said.

"No, and it isn't related to that hideous drug we took, either," said Rachel. "Last night I planned to make a commitment to Dominick. I thought I'd discuss marriage with him and try to set us on the path to our wedding. I thought he was waiting for me to make up my mind to move ahead with my life, to put Rick behind me. Boy did I read that wrong." She gave a rueful shake of her head. "He was trying to locate that creep Rolf, wasn't he?"

Barry nodded. "I'm sure of it," he said.

"Oh, brother," said Donna.

"Yes, and it's kind of strange. Sex never got as intense with Dominick as it had with Rick. I think because I really didn't love him."

"I think I understand," nodded Donna.

"Besides, I don't think Rick ever really comprehended what I can do. And I haven't used the Step for—what? Four years? Five?"

Barry nodded. "How can we help?" he asked.

Rachel looked from Donna to Barry. She took a deep breath. "If it turns out that I can Step Back and save Rick, I want to do it," she affirmed. Her friends nodded, looking a little reluctant. "And then I'll

Step Back to the morning when I learned that Rick died. As soon as I can, I'll contact you two."

"Okay," said Donna.

Rachel thought for a second. "I'll be the only one who remembers this conversation, and what happened with—er—Dominick, won't I?"

"Yes," said Barry. "I think so."

"Okay," she said.

"Right," said Donna, "but how. . ."

"Donna, I'll have to tell you and let you see this whole episode so that we can be warned. You can show Barry then, I imagine."

Rachel's friends nodded. "Remind me then of what I'm about to say now. We need to try to protect each other if we can," said Barry. "I think that maybe Donna and I should move up here."

"I hadn't thought of that," said Rachel. "It would be great if you could."

Donna's face brightened. "I think maybe I can help," she said. "Excuse me a second." She left the room and ran downstairs. She came back with a small suitcase. She removed a framed picture from the bag and handed it to Rachel.

Rachel began to cry at once. The photograph showed Rick standing in front of a helicopter, smiling in his combat fatigues. He looked as he always had wearing that same shy, goofy smile that Rachel had always loved. "Where did you get this?" whispered Rachel, as tears flowed down her cheeks.

"I'm sorry I upset you," said Donna, hugging her shoulder. "Barry had a friend who wound up stationed at the same base as Rick in Viet Nam. When we realized the coincidence, we asked this friend to see if he could take a snapshot of Rick."

"Why?"

"We intended it to be a surprise," said her good friend. "We planned to mail it with a Christmas card and give it to you for a present last Christmas. Then we heard that Rick had. . ." her voice trailed away.

"How thoughtful," murmured Rachel, looking deep into the eyes of the young man whose ashes she'd scattered on the shore of Lake Michigan many difficult months ago—

—And she felt it begin. The pain and confusion, the disorientation—

She stood at the site in the picture. Rachel Farrell dropped to the ground, terrified as she heard gunfire and explosions.

She fought for control and forced the panic down. When she achieved some composure, she Stepped away and again stood in the bedroom. "I don't want to be presumptuous," she heard Donna saying.

Good, Rachel thought. No time elapsed.

"I talked it over with Barry," Donna went on. "We didn't know if you wanted pictures like this around anymore. So we waited. We thought that you ought to be the one who made the decision of whether the photo should be destroyed or not. His friend took the picture on the base," said Donna. "Not too far from where Rick took the shrapnel hit."

Rachel sat staring into the eyes of the young man she'd loved so much and thought she'd never see again. "Donna," said Rachel. "I just felt it happen."

"Yes?" Donna's eyes widened.

"I just went there," Rachel said. She told them what she'd witnessed, feeling intense terror. She'd never seen such a dreadful scene, or even imagined what a firefight looked like. *My God, Rick lived with that every day.* "I think it must have to do with the bond we've established with one another."

"Rachel, please forgive me," began Barry. "I'm sorry. I don't think I should come with you. I think two of us would louse up the time line. . ."

Rachel waved him off. "Never mind," said Rachel. "I understand and I agree. Now. What do you know about this place?" She pointed to the photo.

"Just what our friend told me," said Barry.

"Tell me! Quick!" demanded Rachel.

Chapter Thirty-one
Rick

Rick Howell knew he was dying. He began to talk, saying whatever came to his mind. He started reciting letters from Punk, anything to keep his mind going. His leg felt numb, and he found that he couldn't move it.

Then he found himself floating in Lake Maxinkuckee, in North Central Indiana. He couldn't swim, an overwhelming pain in his leg all but paralyzing him. He realized he might drown. He recited the 91st Psalm, the one he and Rachel shared, which they'd promised to say each night before they went to sleep.

It was the day before the wedding and he had promised to be Barry's best man. People were counting on him. And Rachel. She'd be devastated. No, he couldn't drown.

But he felt the call of the peaceful darkness, the oblivion of sleep and rest. He hadn't had much sleep in the last few weeks. It would feel so good to. . .

"Rick!" screamed a voice.

Rick looked up and saw Rachel at the back of the boat, right by the ladder. She wore that two-piece swim suit he loved so much.

"I know I'm dying," he said to her. "I don't want to leave you—"

"No!" she screamed. "No! No, you aren't dying! Your body is lying to you! Come up here! I'll take care of you!"

"Punky," he said. "Just let me—"

"No!" she cried. "No, I won't let you! Rick! Give me your hand!"

A voice next to him in the ditch spoke. "Do as she says, Rick. I'll help."

Rick turned and saw a man next to him in filthy fatigues. He managed to say, "Okay—I'll try." He felt the man put a hand on his shoulder and his back and help him up. Warmth spread through him, healing and kind.

He reached out and felt his best friend grip his hand with both hands. She began to pull him up the ladder into the boat. "My leg," he said. "I can't move it, Honey." The man reached out and touched his wounded leg. Rick felt the pain ease and turned to look at the man.

He saw that the man had the most compelling and unusual eyes he'd ever seen. They were almost metallic, a gold that seemed to radiate peace. Then Rachel spoke.

"I know it hurts," she said. "But you have to do it! Push with the other leg!" He obeyed. First, he stepped on the bottom rung with his right leg, the good one. With insane pain rocketing through his system, he pulled the other up next to it.

Then the next rung. The next. The next.

Then he'd climbed out of Lake Maxincuckee and stood in the boat. He shook his head and beamed at Rachel. "Isn't it beautiful?"

"Rick!" she slapped him hard. "Rick! We're in danger!"

—And Lake Maxincuckee vanished. Rick knew he stood next to the latrine ditch where he'd dived to escape a blast. He saw darkness, fire, explosions.

"My God!" he yelled. "Get behind me, Rachel!" He pulled her arm. He looked around for the soldier with the golden eyes, but he didn't see him.

He didn't have time to worry about it. He drew his sidearm. He saw figures dressed in black running up the little hill.

He took aim and began to fire.

Chapter Thirty-two

Rick Howell jerked awake, trembling with fear, in an evacuation hospital, his leg burning. *Where the Hell am I?*

A Colonel stood over him, grinning. "Welcome back, Boy," said the Colonel.

"Colonel Spencer," he said, and tried to sit up. He stifled a scream as his leg erupted in more pain than he'd ever felt.

The Colonel held his shoulders and he and a medic lowered Rick to the pillow.

"Relax, Boy," drawled Spencer in his south Mississippi accent. "Doan move 'at leg now. They goan take care of you."

"Who?" asked Rick.

"This man and his friends," said Spencer, indicating the medic.

"That's right, Captain," said the Medic. "We're almost ready for you. Thought you were going to leave us for a few moments there."

"What happened, Sir?" Rick asked, a dreadful fright almost overwhelming him. Spencer squeezed his shoulder.

"Calm, Boy," he said. "You be okay now. And I ain't never been more proud of anyone than I am of you right now."

"Thank you, sir," said Rick.

"Okay," said Spencer. "I gotta talk to your guys. The whole company's outside waiting to hear." He stood and gave Rick a salute. "Good job, Boy," he said and left.

The medic leaned over and pulled a blanket around him. Rick choked back a scream of terror. He seemed to have a memory of someone pulling a blanket over his face—

The medic saw his reaction. "Easy, sir," said the medic. "You're going to be okay, really you are. Two MPs just brought you in. You've been unconscious for several minutes, but we got plasma going in. We're about to work on that leg. We'll do our best to save it, I promise."

"But—"

"You're safe, sir. Honest."

"Thanks," said Rick. "Is that me that stinks so bad?"

"Only temp, sir," grinned the medic. "That's what you get for diving into a sewer. But we'll get you cleaned up, first thing."

Rick began to calm. The terror began to recede and he became aware of violent pain in his left leg.

"My leg," said Rick. "It hurts." He began to weep with the pain.

"Not surprised," shrugged the medic. "You've got a hunk of shrapnel in your leg, sir."

Rick now became ashamed of his tears. He'd spent the night retrieving the bodies of young guys who would never see their fiancées or girlfriends again. Who would never hold them. Never have children with them. "I'm sorry," he said, feeling like a big baby.

"Sir?" asked the medic.

"Yes," Rick managed.

The medic stood and snapped to attention. He gave Rick a crisp salute.

Rick, baffled, returned the salute. "What's that all about?" he asked.

"For what you did, sir," smiled the medic. "You ready to sleep?" Rick nodded, and the medic injected him. "I'm giving you a little morphine, sir. It'll cut the pain, I promise."

Morphine was fabulous, Rick realized as he slipped away. No dreams, no pain, no troubles—

Then he found himself lying on the deck of a ski boat floating in Lake Maxinkuckee, near Culver, Indiana. "Rick," said Rachel. He turned his head and saw Rachel wearing her two piece swim suit and beaming at him from the ladder at the back of Donna's ski boat.

He stretched up a hand and she came to him and grasped it. She lay next to him, stroking his hair on a beautiful day, bright, warm, and sunny.

He remembered, now. A few moments ago, Rachel had pulled him into the boat because his leg hurt more than anything he'd experienced in his life.

"Hi, Punky," he managed as he embraced her.

Rachel beamed at him. "I heard you were hurt," she said.

"Yeah," he nodded. "My leg."

"You'll be okay," she said.

"How are you, Punky?"

"Scared. They're here after me, as usual when I'm not with you. I'm fighting them off as best I can. I'm resting and waiting for you to come back."

"Who's after you?" he said.

"I love you, Rick," she said. "I'll be there soon. Go to sleep. You need your strength." She placed her hands on either side of his face and stroked his face with those long pianist's fingers.

"Okay. . ." said Rick. Oblivion descended and he thought no more.

Chapter Thirty-three

"Come on, Captain, wake up," said a voice. Someone pushed some ice chips into his mouth.

Rick jerked awake, trembling with fear. A nurse, tall and blond and smiling, stood over him. "What?" He managed. She took his hand and spoke gentle words to him for a few moments.

His mind began to clear. He'd had a miserable nightmare of the firefight. In the dream he'd felt himself slip away in death—

"Where am I?" he asked.

"Base hospital, sir," she said. "Calm down. It's okay."

Rick breathed deep and composed himself. Another god-awful nightmare. An attack. A dive into a filthy ditch. Pain.

Dying.

No, he told himself. *I can't be dead. I feel pain.* He winced.

"Does your leg hurt?" the blond nurse asked him.

"Do I still have it?" he asked, scared of the answer.

"You sure do," she said. "You're lucky. We had a light night when they brought you in. Sometimes we amputate just because we don't have the time to do what we did on you."

"Thanks," he said, not feeling lucky with the pain in his leg.

"Can you stay awake for a few moments, sir?" she asked.

"Yeah, I think so," Rick smiled. She waved her hand and in a few moments about twenty people—Doctors, nurses, other patients— came to stand by his bed.

"Ten-hut!" yelled someone. At once the whole group came to attention. They all saluted.

"At ease," croaked Rick, returning the salute. The entire hospital ward began to applaud. He heard whistles and shouts. Two orderlies, being as careful as possible, lifted his shoulders so that he could see. Again he saluted, puzzled.

At last the applause died down and the orderlies returned him to the pillow. Rick didn't know what to say.

"What just happened?" he asked.

"You're a hero, sir," grinned the nurse.

"I'm what?"

"Most of us think you'll get the Congressional Medal of Honor, sir," the nurse said.

"What?"

"The way I understand the story, you climbed out of that toilet ditch as the VC attacked the chopper base. You grabbed your pistol and killed six or seven of them. Then you crawled to your rifle and shot at the rest of them until our guys could rally and the VC retreated. Then you collapsed. We had to fight to save your life."

"My God," he said. "I don't remember that."

"That's okay," said the nurse. "Lots of other people will never forget it. Your whole company stood around until we came out and told them you would be okay. Several of them gave blood, also. We were afraid that if we didn't save you they'd turn into a lynch mob." They chuckled, Rick touched and gratified by the news.

"What hit me?" he said.

"Shrapnel," she said. "I thought you'd like to see it." She picked up a hunk of metal from the table at his bedside. He held the shard and stared at what had almost killed him. About six inches long, it felt as sharp as a scalpel. "If that thing had hit your femoral artery, your parents would be making arrangements for your funeral."

"No," he said. "I have to get back to someone."

"You mean Punky?" she grinned.

"How do you know about her?" he asked.

"She's all you've talked about for days," she chuckled.

"Her name is Rachel," he said.

"Is this her picture?" asked the nurse, pointing to the snapshot he kept in his shirt pocket. Someone had propped it against the lamp on the bedside table. He nodded.

"What a lovely girl, sir." She smiled and propped the picture so he could see it. "That's about all that we could salvage of your uniform, I'm afraid." She made a face and waved her hand in front of her face as she mimed the smell of his clothes when he'd been brought in.

Rick grinned and thanked the nurse. "Where am I?" he asked.

"The hospital," she said. "You're going home, though."

"What?" he asked, hoping he hadn't heard it wrong.

"Yeah," she said. "The war just ended for you. You're leaving here to go to Japan for a few days. Then, you'll be rehabbing in Camp Pendleton for some time, sir."

"Are you serious?" he asked. "I'm going to California?"

She grinned. "Wouldn't joke about that," she said.

"Thanks," he said. Rachel. Near.

An hour or so later, a Marine captain entered the room and crossed to Rick. "I'm Mike Robbins," he said, shaking Rick's hand. "I've been assigned to take over your outfit."

Two hours later, Robbins stood and shook hands. "I'll take care of your guys, I promise, Captain."

"Thanks, Mike," said Rick, feeling much better. "Tell them I love them all."

The next day the hospital wheeled him onto an airplane. He entered the Naval Hospital at Japan.

Chapter Thirty-four
Rachel

Rachel heard a quiet knock at her bedroom door. "Honey?" said her mom's voice.

"Yes, Mom, come on in."

Mom came in and sat on the bed for a moment, smiling with some difficulty. "Mrs. Howell wants you on the phone," she whispered. She embraced her daughter for a few moments.

Rachel returned the hug. "I'll come right now."

Rachel climbed out of bed. She had to struggle for a few moments to re-orient herself as she pulled on her robe.

She hadn't scattered Rick's ashes or gone to Maine. No trip to Palm Beach with her parents. No sex with James, the man from New York, in his hotel room or in the moonlight on the beach. No dating and she hadn't hurt his feelings.

She hadn't met the creep named Dominick. She hadn't let him strip her clothes off. Nor had she climbed into bed naked with him time after time.

The memory left her feeling empty and dirty. The technical skill Dominick brought to their bed had never replaced the feeling of love she'd had with Rick.

She shuddered, feeling like she needed a long, hot shower. That would have to wait. She had something to take care of.

Almost a year of her life had never happened. She'd saved Rick. They had a second chance.

She turned. The picture of the two of them, standing next to a tree in Allerton Park on a summer picnic, arms around each other, stood on her bedside table where she could see it before she turned out the light in her bedroom at night.

Rachel looked into her mirror and fluffed her hair a little. Seeing the hair short again surprised her. She'd let it grow out for several months at Dominick's request. He liked long hair.

Rick liked *her*, she thought as she made her way to the phone. He'd love her if she had a crew cut.

Then she remembered and looked at her hand. The precious little diamond engagement ring was there. She hadn't given it to Rick's mom, of course not.

Down the hall to the phone. "Hello, Mom," she said into the phone.

"Honey, can you come here right away?" said Mrs. Howell, the strain in her voice obvious.

"Yes, I'll be there in no time."

Rachel returned to her room, where she threw on jeans and a sweater and then went downstairs. Her mom handed her a large china mug filled with coffee.

Rachel paused, feeling tears start to her eyes. She stared with delight at her old coffee mug, one that Rick had given her in college. She hadn't dropped and broken it.

She sipped the coffee, trying not to cry. She looked up. "I have to go to see Rick's parents," she said, and a tear fell. She choked a little, thinking of Rick delirious, in terrible pain so many miles away. "Rick's hurt, I think."

"Yes, Honey," said Mom, a look of intense concern on her face. She and Dad exchanged glances.

"Do you want me to come with you, Rachel?" said Dad.

Rachel turned to him. "Yes, please, Dad," she nodded. "I'd appreciate it if you'd come."

Mom looked up. "Rachel?" she asked.

"You too, Mom," she said. "Please. I'd like you to be there."

Chapter Thirty-five

The drive to the home of Rick's parents went by with agonizing slowness, almost all of it in silence. Though her father drove at or just above the speed limit the whole way, Rachel's impatience to get there all but stifled her.

Dad drove his huge Oldsmobile and they'd just gotten onto Route 41 when Rachel remembered. She took a piece of paper and wrote some company names on it.

Before she'd Stepped Back, she and Barry had made a list of companies that had done well on the stock market. She memorized the list and promised she'd share the names with him when she saw Donna and Barry.

"Dad," she said. "Here are some companies that a friend told me about. He works in the stock market and recommended them for investment to me."

Dad took the list and glanced at it as he drove. "Well, I've heard of some of these outfits, but not others. Are you sure—"

"Yes, for certain," she said. "I've saved up enough to invest about five thousand dollars. You should buy some of these, too."

Dad shrugged okay and put the list in his pocket.

Rachel sat back. The companies would pay off well this year. Dad would be pleased.

Rick's kid sister Portia opened the door and embraced Rachel, her face covered with tears. Mr. and Mrs. Howell came up from behind and enfolded Rachel, murmuring welcome to her. "Welcome Brent and Joyce," said Mr. Howell. "I'm so glad you came, too."

"Hi, Jack, Ruth," said Dad, shaking hands. Mom hugged Rick's parents. Mrs. Howell had been crying.

The group moved into the living room. A tall, handsome Marine stood and Rick's parents introduced Captain Carter, a Marine chaplain.

"Is Rick dead?" whispered Rachel. Her mother and father tightened their embrace on her on either side.

"No, not dead," said Captain Carter.

Rachel put her head down and smiled just a little. Nobody in the room would ever know why.

She'd saved the life of the man she loved.

"Captain Howell lies in the hospital now with a very serious leg wound," said Captain Carter. "But he's out of danger and we think he's going to be fine. He may walk with a limp—"

"No, he won't," said Rachel. "I won't let him." The tension eased a little. People even chuckled. "But, Captain, isn't it unusual for you to visit when a man is only wounded?"

"Yes, but there's more to the story," said the Chaplain. "Our base commandant wanted me to come and tell you what happened in person."

"What do you mean?" stammered Rachel.

"We're very proud of your fiancé," said Captain Carter. "Captain Howell repelled a Viet Cong attack almost single-handed."

"He what?" blinked Rachel.

"The base commandant has submitted his name for the Congressional Medal of Honor, Miss Farrell."

Rachel Farrell stared for a few moments. "Yes," nodded the Chaplain. "He saved the lives of several men before he passed out from loss of blood."

Rachel stood in shock, silent, every eye in the room on her. She hadn't just saved Rick. Many more young men were alive this morning because she had Stepped Back.

For the first time, she began to think that maybe her ability was a blessing.

Chapter Thirty-six
Rick

Rick lay in the hospital bed in Honshu, Japan, feeling sad and homesick. He'd been trying to telephone Rachel and his parents, but the phone lines had been terrible and the connections wouldn't go through.

Loneliness for home had him at the point of downright bitterness. The mail from Rachel hadn't caught up.

He got a few novels and tried to read, but had trouble concentrating on the plots.

Three days passed. He lay in a bed, the pain throbbing in his leg. He could see the sky through the window.

"Hi, Rick," said a voice. He turned—

—and began to cry.

Chapter Thirty-seven

Rachel leaned over the bed, hugging him and kissing him. She too began to cry.

"Punky," he murmured, embracing her and weeping into her shoulder. "I didn't think I'd ever see you again."

"It's over," she said. "It's over. You're coming home to stay. It's okay."

"Why did you come over here?" he asked. "I didn't expect this, I really didn't."

"The Marines sent a chaplain to your parents' house," she said. "We thought you'd died." She told him about the Sunday morning trek to his parent's home, Captain Carter, all that had happened.

"I started right away to make arrangements to come," she said. "I decided this was important enough to raid our savings. In light of the circumstances, the school district gave me a couple of days off. Christmas break starts today, so I can stay with you for the next two weeks."

Rachel released him and pulled a chair over. She sat down. "Rick. The chaplain didn't have all the details. What did you do?"

Rick began to blush. "Here's what I understand," he said. "I only have a shallow memory of it." He told her the story of his defense of the base. The look of pride on Rachel's face moved him to tears again. When the story ended, she embraced him and murmured her love and delight.

"When we heard that you'd been wounded," she said, "I came to you as soon as I could. I hope I comforted you."

He listened to what she said and thought about the words. "You came? You hope you comforted me?"

"Do you have a problem with that?"

"Didn't you just get here? I mean, you didn't come to me over there, did you?"

She grinned. "Not now," she said with a wink. "Here. Look what I brought you."

She stepped out into the hall and returned with a case. "My guitar!" he said, delighted.

"I hope you like it. I couldn't bring that gigantic amplifier on the plane, of course. . ."

But he didn't hear. He'd begun unpacking and tuning the old Gibson.

A couple of days later, he received a transfer to the hospital at Camp Pendleton, just south of San Clemente. Rachel came with him and remained with him for the next week as he began his convalescence and rehabilitation. His leg had been improving every day, but he walked leaning on a crutch with her support.

The night before she had to return home and resume teaching, he took her to dinner at the officers' club. A jazz combo played some nice dinner music and he listened, enjoying hearing live music and wishing he could join the group.

When they returned to his hospital room, Rachel helped Rick put on his pajamas. "How are your parents?" he asked. "I haven't seen them in so long."

She smiled a little. "I talked to them this morning," she said. "They've been working hard on their reconciliation. They've seen counselors, taken trips together, started going to church—things they'd never done before."

"Huh," he said. "Talk about good news."

"Yes," she said. "They give you credit, you know."

"Me?" he said.

"Yes," she said. "They started to reconcile the first night you came over. Remember Dad teasing me about my skirt? They used to be like that all the time. Then they stopped. Now they do it again."

He grew silent, unsure about how to talk about what was on his mind. "What's wrong?" she asked at last.

"Rachel," he said. "Something happened to me."

She arranged her skirt and edged forward on the chair next to his bed. "What?" she grinned, taking his hand.

"I don't know how to explain it," he said. "I sometimes feel like I'm going crazy."

Her grin faded as she saw the serious expression on his face. "What on earth do you mean?"

"Many times, when I've been with you," he stumbled, "I think several events in my life since I met you have had—er—well, something like alternate outcomes."

"What?" she said, laughing. "Don't be silly. How could that be?"

"For example, right after we met. Do you remember that girl named Janet?"

"Rick, it hasn't been that long. Of course I remember her," she said. "And I don't like you talking about her. It hurts to think of you with someone else. It hurts a lot. How would you like me to bring up past sexual experiences with you?"

"I'm not talking about sex."

"Then what?"

"I don't know. I kept dreaming I took Janet out on a date rather than play that gig at the apartments, even though I knew I hadn't. I took you to the gig and then to that diner—"

"Mel Root's," she smiled.

"Right. Then, a night or two later, I began to dream that I'd made love to Janet. I came to tell you. You cried and said I'd broken your heart or something."

"I don't remember that," said Rachel. "I remember you meeting me somewhere—"

"The union cafeteria, yeah," said Rick. "I remember that I told you she'd come to my apartment. I turned her down and she went home."

"That's when I began to think maybe things would work between us," she smiled.

"Yeah, but that gets at the main problem. For several days I had dreams that I'd had sex with her."

"Well, did you or didn't you?"

"No. I mean, I remember that I didn't. But I thought for days that I had."

Rachel didn't say anything. She stared at her hands.

"I remember a couple of other times, too. Like when I came to your house to ask your parents for permission to marry you. Everything happened the way I dreamed of it happening."

Rachel stood and looked out the window.

"But then," he said. He paused for a second and composed himself. "But then I began having these dreams. I'd see your mother taking offense at my hair and clothes. I kept seeing your father giving me a check to go away and never see you again. I tore it up. I couldn't get out of the house because you'd locked the front door."

She didn't speak. She continued to stare out the window.

"The last time it happened," he said. He stopped, choked up for a few moments. "It started when I stood next to an outdoor toilet beside the chopper port. I'd gone on a mission to save a company that the Viet Cong had surrounded. We had a Hell of a fight, but we got the guys out.

"I got out of the chopper and walked over to the piss ditch. The VC opened fire and the sky turned red. I dove into the ditch and got hit in the leg."

"Yes," Rachel nodded. "I remember."

"Then I climbed out of the ditch, and you know the rest of the story, I guess."

"Yes," she said. "I'm so proud of you."

"Thanks, but I have to tell you something else."

When he didn't go on, Rachel said, "Well?"

"I keep dreaming that you've told me you can control time."

"Oh," she said.

"Not only that. . ." he said and couldn't go on for a few moments. "Rachel, I keep having dreams that I died."

Rachel covered her face and began to weep. "Honey?" he said.

She didn't reply. He got up and limped to the window. He put his hands on her shoulders and turned her to face him.

"Honey?" he said. "Am I supposed to be dead?"

She spoke at last. "Don't talk like that, Rick."

"Then help me," he pleaded. "How has this stuff happened?"

He dropped his hands. He sat on the edge of the bed.

She came to him and took him in her arms. "You're not dead," she said with emphasis. "You're fine. You got wounded saving the lives of other people. My parents fell back in love because of you. You set Janet free to find someone who'd love her like I love you. Can't you just relax in that?"

Her gentle voice soothed him. He reached up and embraced her arms, but the tears wouldn't stop.

"I can try," he said. "But these dreams are horrible. Just dreadful. This idea has haunted me so that I have a hard time thinking of anything else. Let me tell you what I remember. I lay in that filthy ditch and I couldn't move, not at all. I knew that if I didn't get up and pull myself out of that ditch I'd die right in that stinking toilet."

"Rick," she said. "Don't do this to yourself."

"I started to lose consciousness. I fought it by thinking about you. That made it easier. I dreamed of you at night and talked about you to the guys. I tried to remember every word we ever said to each other. I would read every one of your letters about fifty times, until I had them memorized and could recite them. I was so damn scared that I'd never see you again."

"Rick, no," said Rachel, now begging.

"I recited the 23rd Psalm, then I remember starting on the 91st, which I still say every night before I go to bed…"

"Me, too," said Rachel. "Every single night. And during the day, every time I think of it."

"I looked up and saw you standing on the edge of that ditch, which I thought was a ski boat. Of course I figured I had to be delirious, but you called to me. You said that I couldn't give in. I had to pull myself out and save myself.

"I didn't think I could move," he said. "Then the man stood next to me, helped me up and gave me some strength."

Rachel stared at him. "A man?"

"Yeah," he said. "He was dressed in fatigues, but had real long, almost white hair, like mine used to be in college. He also had incredible eyes, an unusual brown. They almost looked like they were golden."

Rachel covered her mouth with her hands and her eyes filled with tears. She murmured something that sounded like "Curiel."

"What?" he asked. "Did you see him too? Was he there? I mean, was I hallucinating?

She waved her hand, then shook her head. "No," she managed. "Please, not now."

"I reached up and began to crawl on my good leg. You took my hand and pulled. I made it out and rolled away. Then you slapped me."

She didn't say anything.

"I know, I know, this sounds crazy, it couldn't have been you, but I would swear I saw you. Somehow I got out and rolled away, stinking and miserable. I saw the VC, yanked out my sidearm and started firing. The adrenaline got going, I guess, and I grabbed my rifle and fired until I'd used a clip."

"My God, Rick," she said.

"Then I slapped in another clip and kept firing. The VC had to hesitate, and that gave our troops up there a chance to rally and come back at them. A couple of MPs saw me just before I passed out. I turned to grab for you, but you weren't there. The MPs dragged me to the medical tent. They risked their own lives to do so. They told me later I kept saying 'Punky, Punky', over and over."

"Rick," she said. "Please calm down."

"I'll try," he said. "But I know I didn't die because of you."

She smiled and reached up to his cheek. She wiped the tears away.

"Everything's going to be okay, Rick," she said. "It's okay."

He stood and took her shoulders. "Why do these things happen, Rachel?"

"Rick, stop talking like this. Come on."

"No," he said. "No. Help me. Am I supposed to be dead?"

Rachel began to cry. "Please, no, Rick. Please don't. . ."

He embraced her and wept with her, the terror of the nightmares recurring again. Janet. The check. Dying . . .

"Did I die?" he asked.

"Don't," she said.

"Tell me!" he all but shouted. "I can't live with this! I'm going nuts! I know something is wrong, damn it all!"

She turned and walked to the window. He stared at her back.

A long time passed. "Okay," she said at last. "Okay, you agreed to marry me and I know you love me. I need to let you know what you'd be marrying."

"What does *that* mean?"

"I don't want to tell you this," she said, and stopped talking.

"Tell me what?"

She breathed deep. "Before I tell you, I want you to know I do love you. It isn't just that I'm safe with you. I really do love you and have ever since I first saw you."

"Thank you. I love you too," he assured her.

"Remember I told you right at the beginning, no lies, no acts, no games?"

"Rachel, I've always been as honest with you as I could—"

"I'm not talking about you. It's me. I've been lying. Lying the whole time I've known you. Every day, every minute."

Rick stared at her, stunned. At last he managed to say, "What are you talking about? You've intentionally lied to me?"

Rachel sat in the institutional easy chair, not meeting his eyes, staring out the window. She looked up and nodded, still without making eye contact with her fiance.

Some time passed.

"It may help to tell you that it's a lie of omission," she said. "I just haven't ever told you everything at a time when you could remember it."

"But why? Why would you. . ."

"It's very complicated," she assured him. "I'll try to tell you everything now. Maybe that'll make up for. . ." Her voice trailed away.

When she spoke again, he could only just hear her. "Do you have any memory of my father accusing you of being the person who got me hooked on drugs?" she asked.

He thought. "Yes," he said. "In the dream, he said he thought I'd turned you into an addict. That's always puzzled me. I've never considered the possibility of you being a junkie. Your life seems so disciplined. . ."

"Not always," she said.

Now he stopped. "What do you mean?" he stammered.

"In January, 1968, I finished student teaching," she said. "First those creeps tried to rape me. The leader wound up in prison, we learned."

"I can imagine what his parents said this time," grunted Rick. "They no doubt think someone framed him."

"Oh I'm sure," Rachel sighed. "Anyhow, then the boy I'd gone with for a couple of years dumped me..."

"The first guy you ever slept with," he said.

"Well, yes. But right before I went back to Champaign for the spring semester and summer, my parents asked me to join them in the library."

She paused. "Go on," he urged.

She nodded. "My mom said, 'Honey, we want you to know before you leave. I've asked your father for a divorce.'"

A tear started down her cheek. "I turned to my dad. He said, 'don't look at me. I'm not taking credit for her idea.' I looked back at Mom. 'Yes,' she said. 'I've met another man, someone I work with. He's divorced. We began seeing each other when your father went out on one of his business trips. We just met for dinner, I swear it.'"

She wiped her eyes. "I knew better," she said. "I could tell that she'd been having an affair with that man. I don't know how long the affair had gone on. I knew my mom and dad had been having problems. No kid can ever think about his parents having sex, you know what I mean. But I remember that they had lots of fights in the bedroom. That night, I began to suspect that my father had been having affairs right along, too."

"I see," he said. She nodded.

"Then my dad told me he planned to move out. My mom told me she intended to talk to a lawyer. I pleaded with them not to do anything until I could get back."

"I'm not following this," he said. "What does this have to do . . ."

"You'll see," she said.

"Okay," he said. He came over and embraced her. He brought her back to the bed and they sat together. He held her while she stared at her hands.

"They devastated me," she said. "When I got to Champaign, I got into marijuana with my friend Hollis and the guy she was dating."

"Uh, huh," he said.

"I liked the way reefer made me feel. I took a lot of others: speed, LSD, whatever. I didn't discriminate. Then Hollis's boyfriend hooked me up with someone who let me try heroin a few times—"

"Heroin!" he gasped.

"Yes," she said. "I had no trouble relaxing when I took a shot of heroin, I can tell you."

"I know," he said. "The medics gave me morphine for my leg. Same thing."

"Yes, but heroin affects you even more. I got scared and stopped shooting that stuff. It took real will power. Even today, if you offered me a shot of heroin, I'd have to fight not to take it."

"I'm so sorry," he said.

"It gets worse," she said.

"Oh, God," he said.

"One night Hollis invited me to a party at a fraternity house. She said there'd be all kinds of dope and liquor. Why didn't I just come and smoke some marijuana?"

"Uh, huh."

"So I went," said Rachel.

She broke off, unable to continue. They were silent. At last Rick said, "Can you try to go on?"

She nodded, but it took some time before she could speak again. "That's the night the guy offered me the psychedelic on the blotting paper."

"You mean the dope that put you in the hospital."

"Yes," she said, "the night you saved me. At that point, I'd take anything. I think I just about had taken everything. I almost left the party, but I guess—I know—I couldn't resist any kind of dope in those days. Anyhow I said 'sure' and he gave me a small piece of blotting paper."

"Did I hear that right? Blotting paper?"

"Yeah, the pusher put a drop of the stuff on the paper. I let the paper dissolve on my tongue, as he said." She stopped again and looked out the window. In a soft voice, she said, "It turned out that it wasn't an hallucinogenic. It was a device, designed to change the chemistry of the brain, probably for the rest of my life. I had a very bad trip."

"Yeah," he said, because he couldn't think of anything else to say.

"But not just scary. Terrifying. Horrible." She paused.

"Go on," he said.

She still hesitated for a few moments, biting her lip. "Have you been reading the Bible I gave you when you went in?" she asked.

"Yes," he said, nodding to a worn leather-bound book on the bedside table. "It kept me company all the time I spent over there, too."

"One passage talks about the supernatural forces of evil, you know. . ."

"I remember. Ephesians, right?"

"I think so. Anyhow I met them."

"Them?"

"Yes," she said. "The supernatural forces. They were horrible. Twisted, mangled, distorted creatures of indescribable evil, smoke, terror, fear—all those things snarled together."

"Gack," he said. He felt his skin crawling.

"Rick, you have to understand," she said. "I know you didn't see this. You saw a bunch of horny twerps dragging a drunk coed into a bedroom to take advantage of her intoxication—"

"Come on, I never said that..." he interrupted.

She waved a hand. "Of course you didn't. You didn't see what I did, I know. But this vision transcended dreaming. This stuff happened. Several of these things—they didn't even have human shapes; they were more like dark fires, if that makes sense—"

"I can't picture them. Must have been horrible."

"Yes. The vision became dreadful beyond belief. Several of them grabbed me and dragged me with them. I couldn't help myself or resist them."

"Where did they drag you?"

She turned to him. Her mouth worked for a few seconds before she could speak. "To Hell. Not a figurative Hell. The literal Hell. It looked and felt and smelled so real that I could touch it. I could feel the icy blast of perdition and hear the screams of the damned."

"Rachel, I. . ."

She put up a hand. "Rick, wait. Please let me finish the story. When they'd almost pulled me through the black gates, someone— you, it turned out—stood there, not afraid, blocking their path. I couldn't see your face at first, but I managed to yell in desperation, 'Oh Jesus!' Just a reflex, I guess. But the creatures screamed in agony and fury. I can still hear it. I yelled 'Jesus!' again and they let go. You came forward, fought the creatures off and picked me up."

"Rachel—"

She waved a hand. "You carried me to your car, then to a meadow with flowers and blue sky, and then you disappeared. I looked up, and felt Someone with me. I saw a bright creature of absolute purity. His name was Curiel."

"Curiel?" he asked. "Is this…"

"Yes," she said. "That's why I reacted when you told me about the person who helped you in the ditch. When he came to me in the field, he said, 'Find this person, the man who carried you away from Hell,' and pointed. I saw the basement of Kam's at the University of Illinois. I saw the guitarist of this rock band."

"You saw me, in other words."

"Just as well as I see you now," she said. "You stood between me and the black gates. You saved me from Hell."

"Me? I saved you?"

"You kept me from being raped, but also from dying that night, Rick."

"I did?"

"Yes," she said. "I know that if I'd gone through those gates, I'd have died. I don't know how I know that, but I do."

"Jeez, I didn't even suspect."

She nodded. "The creatures seem to be afraid of you," she said. "I don't know why."

He considered for a few moments. "So when you talk about 'them'," he said, "you refer to those—uh—creatures, huh?"

"Uh, huh. Anyhow, the Person with me said that the drug affected my brain."

Rick stared. "He said the dope turned on a switch in my brain," said Rachel. "I could—sort of—undo situations. I asked him to turn it off. He said no, he couldn't. My behavior had consequences, and I had to live with them. I begged him. He said I had to see what happened as a judgment. He warned me not to use the gift if I didn't want to suffer flashbacks to that acid trip."

She grew silent. He stroked her hand.

"I woke up in the hospital, you remember," she shrugged. "The hospital contacted my parents, and they came down to Champaign as soon as they could. When they came to the hospital, I was in a coma and remained unconscious for a couple of days. Mom and Dad were frantic about me, of course."

"Rachel. . ." he began.

"No, let me finish," she said. "I came around pretty well. That's when you came to see me—"

"And we kissed for the first time, too," he smiled.

"Of course I remember that," she said. "Only a day or two later, I felt well enough to go home. During that time I told my parents what had happened. They wanted to bring me home, but I insisted on staying and finishing my classes."

"You said your parents wanted to hospitalize you—"

She nodded. "Yes. They thought I needed to be committed to a mental institution. I persuaded them not to do that."

"Yeah," he said.

"Mom and Dad spent quite a bit of time together during that time. They sort of had to, you know, with me unconscious. I know they filled that time with a lot of animosity, blame, cursing at one another."

"They were together, though. . ."

"Yes, you take my point. When they had to spend time together, face-to-face, and confronting a mutual problem—me, in other words" Rick nodded while Rachel wiped at her eyes "—they couldn't ignore one another. So Dad decided not to move out of the house, just take a separate bedroom. They began to talk about getting some counseling."

"How did that go?" asked Rick.

"Things didn't improve much. They were too hurt and angry with one another. You never met them before, even at my graduation, because I didn't want you to see them bickering and nasty. You remember, I wanted to elope—" he nodded—"but then you insisted that you had to ask their permission to marry me. I thought I would be a disaster. And I sure got it right."

"So. . .that happened? That horrible meeting where your dad offered me money to go away? I didn't dream it?"

"No. They did treat you the way you remember it in the dream."

Rick considered. "So what happened that night?"

"I came to you while you were standing by the front door, which I'd locked, you remember. . ."

He nodded.

"And I Stepped Back a couple of hours."

"Stepped Back?"

"I call what I do Stepping Back. I don't know what else to call it. The process hurts a great deal. When I do it, I'm the only person who knows what has happened in the future, or in the past, most of the time."

"So what do you do?"

"I think about a scene until it becomes real to me. Then I take a Step or two forward and things change."

"I see," he said.

"Anyhow I Stepped Back to two hours before you arrived. I went up to their room and made them sit down with me. I told them about the vision of Hell I had with the drug, that you had saved me, that I'd found you at the University, and that I knew you could protect me."

"Protect you?"

"Yes. See, in the hospital, I talked to my parents about the bad trip, the Black Gates, and the creatures. They came to understand that I'm condemned to spend my life being pursued by these demons, or whatever those things could be. No, they've never seen them. Then I told them the rest of the story. I told them the part I'd never told them before. That you'd protected me and kept me from being dragged through the black gates."

"I see," he murmured, and kissed her cheek. She turned and embraced him for a few moments.

"What else?" he asked at last.

"I told them about how you never took drugs, that you didn't drink much, attended church, and worked hard at so many jobs to get through college."

"Uh, huh."

"I told them that I loved you, and that I wanted to spend my life with you. . ." she choked and he hugged her. "I said that I would go into any sort of treatment program they wanted, or see any doctor, or cooperate in any way that they wanted. But please, just for the night, be nice."

"What then?"

"I threatened them. I said that I'd move out. But I softened it a bit when I told them that if they wanted, I could do a Step Back and undo things that had happened for them."

"Did you do that?"

"No. They refused the suggestion. They know what it costs me to Step Back—"

"What does it cost you? What do you mean?"

"Never mind that for now," she said, waving a hand. "Mom and Dad didn't say anything for a few moments. I think they had to think through the depth of the offer I'd just made them. I know they were touched. Then Mom started to cry. She said, 'Brent, let's make an agreement. Let's try to pretend we just got married and that we love each other. That we can still feel the love that Rachel feels for this man.'"

"Yes?"

"Dad seemed to think it over and agreed. He said, 'Rachel, I think we need some time alone, your mom and me.' I left the room and shut the door. I don't know what happened. They stayed together in their bedroom for almost two hours. They might have made love. If they did, it would have been the first time in years, I think."

"That sounds good, Honey."

"Anyhow, it worked," said Rachel. "They came out as I'd just finished dressing. Mom had been crying, I could see. By the way, I took a shower and put on clean clothes. I think that's how you knew something had changed. You seem to be different from most people. Whenever I've done a Step Back, no one except for you ever remembers what happened."

"Huh. What do you think causes that?"

"I don't know. But I think that every time I've done it with you, your memory of the Step Back gets stronger. I mean, it's like you remember it better."

"Why would that be?"

"I don't know for sure," she said. "You have a more distinct grasp of memories than most people. Maybe that's why we fit together."

"Fit together? What do you mean?"

She shrugged with a little smile. "I think we've always been meant for one another, ever since we were born. I did some study of theology the last year of college, and since you've been gone, too. I'm almost finished with a master's degree in theology, you know."

"Yeah, and I'm very proud of you," he nodded. "But I don't get .."

"In the story of Adam and Eve, you remember, God put Adam to sleep and took a rib from him. . ."

"I remember."

"Yeah, but an ancient legend says that God took out more than just a rib. According to this legend, He took out the parts that make up female emotions and reactions. So when Adam saw Eve, he saw more than just a woman. He saw the parts of him that were missing. When he came together with her, the woman supplied the parts of him that he lacked, what he needed to be complete."

"I'd never heard that story before," he shrugged. "It isn't in the Bible."

"Yes, well, I don't insist on it," she said. "But when I overdosed, Mom and Dad agreed to put their divorce on hold until I got home, then, until I graduated. Then, they agreed to wait until I got married."

"You think they still plan to divorce when you and I marry?"

"No, I don't think so. . ." she broke off and looked at him. Her mouth worked, but no words came out. At last: "Do you know what you just said?"

"Sure," he said. "When we get married."

"Rick, do you still want to marry me?" Her eyes welled up.

"Of course. Why wouldn't I?"

She embraced him and cried. "But I lied to you. I. . ."

He spoke words of comfort until she calmed down. "Rick, you

don't have to do that," she said. "I'll set you free. I promise. You can end it here and now, and I'll leave—"

"What are you talking about?" he interrupted. "I don't want that."

"Now you know what I can do—what I did. . ."

"I'm no better than you, Sugarplum."

She spoke in a very tiny voice. "You never abused drugs like me. You never whored like me. You. . ."

"Whored?" he said. "What do you mean?"

Rachel stared at the ground. She didn't say anything, just bit her lip and shook her head. "Anyhow I'm no paragon, Honey," Rick said. "Don't kid yourself."

"Can you really—I mean really—get past the things I did?"

"Of course I can," said Rick. "I'm not a very good person myself."

"You're the best person I've ever known," she said.

"But. . ." he choked on the question he wanted to ask. "I'm sorry, but I have to know."

She looked up. He couldn't say it for a moment or two. At last: "Rachel, you haven't told me everything. Am I supposed to be dead?"

She didn't answer.

"Rachel," he affirmed, and she looked up. "Rachel, you have to tell me."

She sat, framing her answer. At last she said, "I don't know how to answer you."

"Rachel, please. Did I die? Did you interfere? Is that why I keep having these horrible dreams?"

She stood and walked to the window. When she spoke at last, he almost couldn't hear her. "I'll try to explain," she murmured. She turned and looked at him for the first time in a little while. "Your mom called and asked me to come right away. I thought she needed to see me about your Christmas present, never dreaming that you'd been hurt. I drove down to the south side to their house. I hadn't heard from you for a few days. . ."

"Yeah. We'd been in the midst of an offensive. Three hours of sleep at a time felt like a luxury."

"Yes, he told us that."

He paused. "Who told you? What did he say?"

"A Marine Chaplain named Carter. He came to your parents' house."

Rick stared for a few moments. He looked out the window and said, "Tell me."

Rachel wiped at her eyes. "Captain Carter stood up, looking grim. I knew what had happened the moment I saw his face. I guess I fainted."

"Oh, jeez—"

"When I came to, I found that your parents put me between them on the couch. They'd had to help me to the couch. Your mom hugged me on one side and your dad on the other. Captain Carter said that you had died in the service of your country the night before. The MPs found your body in a ditch where you'd been struck in the leg by shrapnel. You'd bled to death." Now she sobbed, the horror of the moment overwhelming her for a few moments.

Rick felt a chill. He remembered the incident, the dive into the ditch, the attack, the screaming, everything in every fiery, horrid detail.

"Go on," he said when he gained a little strength.

"I ran sobbing to the washroom. Your mom came in and embraced me for a long time, comforting me, even though she needed to be comforted as much as I did."

"They love you like a daughter," he said.

"Your mom and dad couldn't have been any kinder. A couple of days later, the Marines shipped your body home. We had your funeral and scattered your ashes as you requested."

"And?" She didn't speak for several moments. "Honey?" he tried again.

"Rick, please, if I tell you about the next twelve months—"

"Twelve months!"

"Yes, Rick," she said.

"I was dead for a year?" he mumbled. She nodded.

"Please, I don't want to tell you what happened," she said.

"How could that be even remotely possible?"

She resisted, but after a few moments she gave in. "Okay," she said. "I guess I'd better tell you."

Rachel stumbled through the story of the man in Florida who wanted to take her home to New York. She cried her way through the story of Dominick.

"So," he said. "You were—er—with those two guys?" He felt like his stomach might explode with the pain.

"Yes," she agreed, tears flowing. "In the case of Dominick, a lot more than just once or twice."

"Were you in love with this guy?" he mumbled.

Rachel shook her head. "I never fell in love with him," she sobbed, unable to talk with clarity. "Ricky, I promise. On the other hand, yes, I did things with him I thought I'd never do with anyone but you."

"Oh Hell," he said.

Rachel held a handkerchief to her eyes. "I'm so sorry, Rick."

Rick made a conscious effort to breathe, trying to calm the ache in his chest and stomach. "Okay," he said, holding her for a few moments. "Let's try to get past it. We weren't married. And it hasn't happened yet, as I understand things. You didn't get pregnant, did you?"

"No," she said. "Not pregnant. No disease, either, thank God. He always used. . .er. . ."

She trailed off. A long pause ensued, wherein Rachel cried and blew her nose.

"Okay," he said. "You thought I had died. I did die. You did what any attractive girl would do. You started looking for someone else. It looked good at first, but then it didn't work out so you came back and got me—"

"No!" she shouted. "No! That's not what happened! I've never been as miserable as I was when you were—" she paused and struggled for control. "Then I met him. We went together until he assaulted me. . ."

"What!"

"It's a long story," said Rachel. "It happened on the one year anniversary of your –er—death." She related some of the story, Rick sitting in horror. "I got away because of Donna, who called the police."

Rick sat down, now afraid that his head would explode. "And you heard me talking from that ditch?"

"Yes," she said. "Somehow when I thought about how intense our lovemaking had been that weekend in Hawaii, last summer you remember—" Rick nodded "—I began to hear you."

"Then what?" he murmured.

"My parents took me home," she said. "I slept on a cot in their room, next to their bed. I've never been so scared, not even. . ." she broke off.

"Never mind," he said. "I know what you mean."

"Well, Donna and Barry drove in the next day from Atlanta. I told them that I'd heard you speaking to me. We decided I had to Step Back and try to save you."

"You mean your friends helped you?"

"Donna gave me a framed snapshot of you at that helicopter pad." Rick stroked her hand, murmuring encouragement.

"I couldn't bring you back from the dead, I know. But I could do a Step Back. So I did. And. . ." Again she choked on the emotion, shuddering as she relived the horror of that day.

"Yes," he said, embracing her. "Keep talking."

"I went to you."

"You did this Step Back thing?" he asked. She nodded.

"I'd never done that before, I mean, go somewhere I'd never been. I've always gone back to locations I've been in."

"Like when we were in college," he nodded.

"I've only done it a handful of times. I did a few of them with you. Once when we first met and I gave you a second chance to play a late-night gig. One time when you went back to Janet and changed how you handled the situation. With my parents that night you came. The night you. . .died. Once I Stepped back with Barry—" she paused and didn't go on.

"What happened that time?"

"Please," she said, looking away. "Please never ask me to tell you about that one."

"Okay—"

"I'm sorry, Rick. I just can't tell you."

He shrugged in assent. "Did we go to the future together once?" he asked.

"What do you mean?"

"I seem to recall that we were married, that we had children, Christmas, a bedroom—"

She nodded. "I thought you might have come with me on that. The night I woke up in the hospital, you and I hugged. I Stepped forward about ten or fifteen years and found us married."

"Yeah," he smiled.

"But promise you won't ask me about the other time," she pleaded.

"Okay, I promise."

"Thank you," she said. "Anyhow I thought about you. I focused on your face in the picture and I saw you standing next to that ditch. The vision clarified as I stared. I Stepped back to a place I'd never been, the longest Step I've ever done. I found myself next to that ditch. It smelled so horrible."

"Yes, it did."

Rachel sighed. "I saw the firefight start. I stood there terrified for several moments. I ran over and saw you lying wounded at the bottom of the ditch."

"I understand," he said. "You gave me your hand and helped me climb out."

"Yes," she said. "Well, you know the rest of that story. Once you were out, I Stepped back to the time I left to drive to your parents' house. I didn't know what you did. Again, I went to your parents' house. This time, I took my mom and dad with me. The Marine

Chaplain stood up."

"How did that go?"

"Well, at least I didn't faint. Your parents hugged me. This time, though, the chaplain said that you'd received a serious wound, but that the doctors treating you expected you to make a full recovery."

He embraced her, considering for a while. "Did you do the right thing with the Step Back?" he asked.

She shrugged. "I don't know the correct ethics of the situation. No one's ever done this thing except me and one other person. But I think that if I can save someone's life, I ought to, despite what it costs me."

Rick thought this over. "What do you mean, what it costs you?"

"The Angel warned me when I saw him," she sighed. "He told me not to use the power. Whenever I do, I open an area of my mind I should never go to."

"An area that protects you?"

"Yes," she said. "I have to let down the barriers that keep evil away. It takes me weeks to gain control again. Whenever I do a Step Back, the demons, or whatever they may be, come for me when I fall asleep that night. I'm tormented every night for weeks, not able to fall in a deep sleep, scared, standing again at the black gates, surrounded by creatures and terrors. . ."

"Every time?"

"Yes," said Rachel. "Each time the torment gets a little worse, too, a little more terrifying. That's why I try so hard *not* to use it. The Step Back seems to play into the creatures' desires because, after all, the Step Back falls outside the natural order of things, of course. I shouldn't have this power, whatever it should be called."

For a long time neither person said a thing. There didn't seem to be much to say.

She murmured, "Okay. Now you know the worst. You know all that I know. You have a decision to make. Could you live with someone who—"

He interrupted. "Someone who would walk into Hell for me?"

She looked up. She didn't speak for a moment. "What?"

"Someone who loved me enough to give up her freedom, her ability to sleep, someone who would suffer unspeakable terror at night, who would see sights beyond what humans, should see, just to save me? What do you think I feel for that person?"

She didn't say anything for a few moments, but leaned her head against his chest. "Rick. I'm sorry I didn't tell you that I'd Stepped Back. I should have told you right away."

"It's okay, Punk."

"I didn't tell you because I thought I wouldn't use the Step Back ever again. I thought I could control it. But when I heard that you'd bled to. . ." she couldn't say the word.

"Okay," he said, as she sobbed. "Okay."

"And I'm sorry about Dominick. I just missed you so much. . ."

"I know," he said. "You saved my life, Rachel. I think I can deal with that guy."

At last she said, "I'll try not to use the Step Back again. I'll be as normal as I can, I swear it."

"Fine," he said. "It's done."

"No," she choked, with tears of pain on her cheeks. She composed herself for a few seconds. "You have to sleep on this, for several days. When I'm not here, and you can think about what I told you with a clear mind. We never got married. You can call it off."

He tried to assure her that he would never love her less than he did, but she insisted that he wait for at least two weeks to make a decision.

Chapter Thirty-eight

Rick kissed her good-bye the next day. Rachel had to go back to her job. She promised to return at spring break if she wanted her to do so.

Rick stood at the window of his hospital room and watched as she climbed into a cab for the airport. He waved, knowing that she couldn't see him, of course, but saying good-bye all the same.

He thought about how they had struggled to make love during the visit. His leg hurt too much to be too active, but the coupling had been sincere, joyful and as loving as ever. Would they do it again? He wondered.

"Rick?"

He turned to the voice and saw an officer standing in the door. He recognized Larry Knodle, also from Illinois and a captain like him. They'd met and become friends during physical therapy.

"Come on in, Larry," said Rick, wiping at his eyes. "I apologize for the emotion. My fiancée just left, so I'm not doing too well."

"Maybe I can help." The captain limped into the room. "Your fiancée left, huh?"

"Yeah," said Rick. "She teaches school back home, and Christmas break ends today. She had to go home."

"I'm sorry, Rick," said Larry. "You must be hurting like crazy."

"Yeah, I'll say," said Rick. "Anyhow, Larry, your visit comes at a good time."

"I didn't come just to visit," said Larry. "I wanted to talk to you about that guitar over there. You any good with it?"

"Earned my way through college with it," said Rick. "I'm a little out of practice, but I can still play, sure."

"I thought so. Can you read music?"

"Sure," said Rick. "I began taking lessons at the age of nine."

"I play piano and organ, Rick," said Larry.

"Neat. Maybe we could play together sometime. . ."

"I think we can do better than that."

"Huh?"

"You know the officer's club on base, right?"

"Yeah, I took Rachel there two nights ago."

"I'm in the combo that plays there several nights a week. Not a lot of money but the guy who plays guitar for us gets discharged in a couple of weeks."

"Yeah?" said Rick.

"Like you, we all played with bands in college and we play a lot of jazz, blues, you know. I thought maybe you might like to try your hand with us."

"Hell yes I would."

"What kind of guitar do you have?"

Rick nodded to the case standing by the wall. "I have an old Gibson. ES 335, thin hollow-body. Good axe for rock or jazz. . ."

"I know the instrument, yeah. Look, could you come with me now? We're going to rehearse in about twenty minutes."

"I get tired pretty easy, Larry. . ."

"I understand but this might help you feel better about everything, not just your girl. You know the invigoration that comes with playing."

"Yeah, I do," grinned Rick. He grabbed his crutch. "I hate to ask, but could you. . ."

Larry nodded, reached for the guitar and hoisted it. They started down the hallway.

The band set up on a stage at the officer's club. Rick met the other musicians, including the guitarist. When he began to play, Rick realized at once that his new friend played a superb jazz guitar. "Why don't you sit in with us for the next several nights?" suggested the guitarist. "You know, get the feel of it?" Larry grinned and seconded the motion.

Rick joined the group that night and followed the songs on the sheet music, playing the chords.

"How'd you do?" asked the guitarist.

"I stank," said Rick. "I'm way out of practice."

The guitarist chuckled. "Why don't you take some of the music back to your room? You'll smooth out."

"You mean you want me to come back?"

"Hell yes," said Larry. "We didn't expect you to be perfect. Tonight, anyhow."

Rick laughed and took some of the sheet music back to his room. Every chance he got, he rehearsed the songs.

At the end of the week, the guitarist spoke to him.

"Big improvement," he said. Rick thanked him.

"Yeah, if I follow the music, I can play the arrangements okay."

"You'd better," said the guitarist. "Tomorrow's my last night."

Rick Stepped in and found that he loved playing with the group, even enjoying the grind of rehearsals. A few weeks along, he started adding some of the songs he'd played with the band at college: James Brown, Cream, and others. The officers received it well.

His leg healed well without infection. Still he had to sit on a stool to perform with the band. It felt a little awkward and unnatural, but the music worked in his soul as it always had.

One night, Larry spoke to him. "How you feeling?"

"You were right," shrugged Rick. "Playing with the band has helped me out a lot."

"What's that thing about music hath charms, huh?" grinned Larry.

"Yeah, like that," said Rick.

Chapter Thirty-nine
Rachel

Rachel returned to her home and resumed her teaching career. She called Donna a few nights after she'd returned home. "We have to see each other as soon as we can," she said.

Donna hesitated. "What's up?" she asked.

"I have a lot to tell you," she said. "I can't do it all on the phone."

Rachel told her about Rick being wounded and how she'd started her Christmas vacation at the military hospital in Japan—

"You went to Japan?" Donna sounded incredulous.

"Yes," said Rachel. "Then back to California. I returned home Sunday."

"Oh my," said Donna.

"When can I see you?"

They managed to meet in February in Nashville, Tennessee, when Rachel had a long weekend off from teaching. They met in Centennial Park, not far from the Vanderbilt University campus. While she waited for her friends, Rachel toured the Nashville art museum, a reconstruction of the ancient Greek Parthenon.

They sat on a park bench with a long view in every direction. They chatted about school and families for some time until Donna took Rachel's hand. "Okay. Now what's this all about?" asked Donna. Barry looked grim.

She told them about Japan, and Rick, how she stayed with him during Christmas break.

"Why didn't you just get married in California?" asked Donna with a smile. "Rick's back in America to stay and he's not in danger now."

"He wanted to," said Rachel. "But I really felt and still feel that he has to decide without me there, when he can see the whole picture."

"Rachel," said Barry. "Rick loves you to distraction. There's no way he's going to dump you."

"Of course not," added Donna. "But I don't think you wanted to see us because of that. We could have handled that on the phone."

"Okay, you're right," said Rachel. "I have to tell you something very strange. I don't know if you have any memory of any of this."

Rachel started with Rick's death, and related the story of the trip to Maine, then meeting Dominick and their love affair. Donna and Barry stared, mouths open as she filled them in on the alternate time line.

"So you fell in love with my old boyfriend?" asked Donna, incredulous.

"I don't know about love," said Rachel. "Infatuation, I guess. The thought of being with him now nauseates me."

"I can imagine," said Donna.

"Something else," Rachel said. "Another man showed up that night and he and Dominick tried to torture me."

"What?"

"Yes," said Rachel. "Small, red-headed, pronounced downstate accent. . ."

Barry looked grim. "I might have known," he said.

"You told me you know this man," Rachel told him.

"Yes," said Barry. "Rolf Something-or-other, I forget his last name. He was good friends with Keith at Champaign. I'm certain he also took the same drug we did."

"Do you know what he's capable of doing?" Donna asked them.

"Not quite," said Rachel. "I seemed to be able to resist him, though."

"I think he's like Donna," said Barry, "only much more so. I'm guessing that Rolf forced Dominick to help him find you and torture you. Like I say, Dominick knew him while we were in Champaign."

"What do we do now?" asked Rachel.

Barry thought for some time. "Did he love you?"

"I don't know, I really don't," said Rachel. "It's possible. He seemed affectionate and considerate. But. . ."

"Yes?" asked Donna.

"I never did feel at ease with him," said Rachel.

"What did Dominick tell you he did a living?" asked Barry.

"He told me he worked for a drug manufacturer as a sales rep. He made a lot of money, had a bunch of expensive stuff. . ."

She broke off when she saw Barry and Donna staring at her. She thought about Dominick and his pricey suits and ties. The silk underwear. The cabin cruiser. The Porsche. The fabulous townhome in Lake Forest. Its exquisite furnishings.

At last, the truth opened up. She saw now how she had refused to look at it. She began to get the picture, then. "He doesn't, does he," she said. "Oh my God. What an idiot I've been. He sold—sells—*illegal* drugs." Her friends gave her a wry smile.

"I'm sure of it," said Donna. "He became very involved with drugs while I was seeing him. I suspected at the time that he'd begun selling them to support the turning on he liked to do while we were in Champaign."

"But he didn't take Keith's acid. . ." began Rachel.

"I know," said Barry. "I think Keith tipped him off."

"Oh, of course," nodded Rachel. "It makes sense now. Oh, I feel like a fool. Why didn't I see it right away?"

"We have to keep Dominick from hooking up with Rolf," said Donna. "Dominick must have been under his control. The Dominick I knew wouldn't have had the courage to attack you alone."

"Why do you care?" said Rachel, puzzled.

"About Dominick, nothing," said Donna. "But I do care about you. Rick isn't here to protect you. He won't be for months."

"True," said Rachel, "but what does. . ."

"He came at you one way when he thought you were a grieving fiancée," said Barry. "He set up the meeting on the plane. He seduced you and built up your trust until he could get Rolf involved. He'll find another way, perhaps even kidnapping you."

Rachel sat down on the bench and stared, considering. "You're right, I think," said Rachel at last.

"What can we do?" Donna asked. She turned to Barry. "I don't want Rachel living in terror that some thugs are going to attack her."

"Neither do I," said Barry. "I think I might have an idea."

Chapter Forty

Rachel and Donna sat in Donna's car in the driveway of the apartment building where Dominick lived. They saw him park his exquisite Porsche and walk toward the entrance.

He looked astonished when two women climbed out of a car and walked toward him. In the dim light of the parking lot lights, they could see him appraising them: one was tall and graceful, the other petite and attractive.

Rachel stared at the man with whom she had been intimate for months, with whom she'd shared her deepest feelings, whom she had expected to marry. The physical attraction that she'd felt had vanished, replaced by revulsion.

"Hi, Dominick," said the taller girl.

Rachel watched Dominick almost choke as he recognized his former girlfriend and bed partner. "Donna," he said. "What the. . ."

"I know it's been a long time," she said. "I'm wondering. Do you remember Rachel?"

He turned to the Rachel and stared for a second. "Yes," he said. "Yes, I do remember you from the fraternity that night you. . .er. . ."

"It's been a long time," said Rachel. "Too bad, I heard you'd been looking for me."

"How did you find me?" asked Dominick, with some difficulty.

"I remembered where you lived," said Rachel. "From the times we came here for sex."

They could see Dominick's bewilderment. Although he'd enjoyed making love with Donna many times before she'd dumped him, he had no memory of sleeping with Rachel. "What can I do for you tonight?" said Dominick.

"I told her you could get us anything we needed," said Rachel, nodding toward Donna.

"Then maybe we could share it in your apartment?" asked Donna.

Dominick cleared his throat. "Well, what'll it be?"

"What have you got?" purred Rachel.

Dominick unlocked and opened his briefcase and showed them a selection of marijuana, amphetamines, and several other drugs. "I can give you any of these things," he said.

"No," said Donna. "We'll pay the going rate. We insist."

Dominick shrugged. He extracted some marijuana. "Maui Wowee, honest," he said. "Some of the best pot in the world. I get $25.00 a bag for this stuff. Yours for—" he paused. "—say ten a bag?"

"Sold," said Donna. She extracted a twenty dollar bill and placed it in his hand. She took two bags of the marijuana. Rachel also took a couple of the bags.

"Let's go," said Dominick, having some difficulty speaking. "I have a couple of bongs upstairs, a water pipe. . ."

"Very interesting," said the plainclothes cop who had come up to stand behind him. "Thank you, ladies," he said to Donna and Rachel as he snapped cuffs onto Dominick's wrists. Another officer confiscated the brief case full of dope and then took the marijuana from Rachel and Donna. "We'll take it from here. We got it all on film and tape. We've had our eye on this creep for some time." Another detective pulled a small card from his shirt pocket and read Dominick his Miranda rights.

Rachel watched Dominick being loaded into a waiting squad car, handcuffs binding his wrists. She thought about being shackled to the exotic stainless steel headboard of his modernistic bed while Dominick and his partner held her down and tortured her. She recalled the weasel face of the little creep named Rolf.

Will I be safe from Rolf now? Or will he come at me another way?

Dominick would be out of the way for some time, they knew. The two women turned and walked back to the car.

"Damned skirt," said Donna, as she climbed into the front seat next to her husband.

"What's wrong with it?" asked Barry as Rachel shut the door behind her and settled into the back seat. He started the car.

Donna made a sincere, though futile, attempt to pull her skirt down to a modest length. "It's way too short," she complained.

Her husband reached over and laid his hand on her thigh. "Oh no it isn't," he said.

Rachel relaxed and giggled. She didn't need to be scared tonight.

She leaned forward and squeezed the shoulders of her two friends. "Would you like me to drive?" she said. "You two can have the back seat if you want."

Chapter Forty one
Rick

One night Rick called Rachel before he went to the club. After they had been chatting on the telephone for some time, she grew quiet.

"Something wrong there?" he asked.

"No, I. . ." she stammered.

"Why'd you get so quiet all of a sudden?"

She said, in a voice choked with tears, "Have you made your decision? About us, I mean?"

He said, "Oh, that."

"What do you mean, 'Oh that'?" she said, a hint of anger in her voice. "You call the most important thing in my whole life 'oh that'?"

"Yeah, I know what you mean," he chuckled at her indignation. "Mine too. I've been doing a lot of thinking."

She hesitated. "Yes?"

"How long until you come back out here?"

"You know that I've been planning on Easter," she said.

"I've gotten to know the chaplain here on the base," he said. "He's a good guy. If he'd marry us then, would you stay? I don't think I could stand to have you leave again."

"I don't know," she began. "I'd have to quit my job. . ." her voice trailed off.

"Well?" he asked when she didn't speak for a few moments.

"Rick, do you mean it?" she sobbed.

"Of course I do. I miss you so much my whole body hurts. I'm getting out in August. We can move back home then."

"Oh," she said. "Okay. . ."

Rachel couldn't talk much after that. She managed to agree that they should get married.

She arrived early on the morning of the day before Good Friday. Her school district had granted her a leave of absence for the remainder of the school year.

Rachel's parents flew into town the next day, Good Friday. Mr. and Mrs. Farrell took them out to dinner that night.

Rick noticed how happy Rachel's parents looked together. They were delighted with the marriage of Rick and Rachel.

Rick's parents and his siblings arrived the morning of the wedding. They told the young couple that they also were thrilled at the marriage and at Rick's recovery. He walked with a cane now and expected to have complete mobility within a few months.

The base chaplain married Rick and Rachel the day before Easter.

When they moved back to the Chicago area in early August, Rachel resumed her teaching career there. She called Donna.

"I think you'll be happy to learn that Dominick received a sentence of ten years for drug trafficking and possession," said Donna. "He took a plea bargain at that."

"So he's out of the way for the time being, huh," said Rachel.

"I sure hope so," said Donna. "By the way, we're moving in two days. Barry took a teaching job at the same high school you're in."

"That's great," said Rachel.

"Well, at least we'll be together," said Donna. "We should be a bit safer. I hope so, anyhow."

"We're not safe from his creepy little friend yet, though," said Rachel.

"No," said Donna. "But he won't have Dominick to help him, anyway."

At that moment Rachel's husband slipped his arms around her from behind. "Er," said Rachel.

"Yes?" said Donna, amusement in her voice.

"Can I call you later?" said Rachel, speaking with some difficulty.

"I think I understand," said Donna, laughing. "Sure you can."

PART III

Mind Sifter
Geneva, Illinois
Many years later

Chapter Forty two
Donna

Donna Riske jerked awake, scared and trembling, at the sound of the phone ringing. The terror struck so hard she just manage to refrain from screaming.

"Yes," she muttered into the receiver.

"4:30 A. M.," intoned the bored, resentful voice of the motel night clerk.

Right," she managed. She hung up the receiver, forcing herself awake. The day had come.

And now, the real terror set in. Her stomach ached.

They were coming for her, as they had been since they'd murdered Barry. She tried to hide, tried to assume a new identity, and moved around the country. Somehow they always found her. Donna went to the window and looked out. Only a few cars stood in the motel lot and she could see no one in them, thank God. No one stood by her door—

Of course not. If they knew she was there, they'd kick the door open and come in.

Donna stepped out of her pajamas and went into the shower, which she made as hot as she could stand. She stood under the near scalding stream for a few moments, and then turned the control to ice cold, trying to get going. She was going to meet the man who could protect her. She had to be alert.

Donna's teeth chattered as she toweled off. She was hungry and wanted a scalding cup of coffee and a huge hot blueberry muffin, slathered with honey and butter—

That would have to wait. She had to get going.

She hadn't slept well. She'd driven in from central Oklahoma yesterday, arriving after suppertime and grabbed a quick sandwich. She found this little motel on the outskirts of Geneva, Illinois, a charming community on the Fox River about forty miles west of The Loop. Her best friend had lived in this town for many years, though Rachel had died some time ago.

She'd insisted on a room hidden from the street so that no one could see her car. Even though she'd rented the car, she had no idea if they'd traced the rental to her. They were uncanny in their ability to find her, no matter where she went.

Donna put on a little makeup. She dried her hair, dressed and rushed out to her rental car.

Seven minutes later, she pulled up in front of an apartment building, still feeling chilled. She looked up on the second floor. No lights.

She debated with herself. She could go and wake him up, of course. But no, that didn't seem like a good idea. No sense both of them being exhausted. Let him sleep.

"I'll go for coffee," she decided. "Both of us could use it."

She put the car in gear and drove back to State Street, the main drag in Geneva. She'd spotted an open coffee shop. She'd be back in a few moments.

As she drove away, Rick Howell came out of the apartment building.

Chapter forty three
Rick

The thugs tried to kill Rick on the second anniversary of Rachel's death.

Rick jerked awake early, before the sun rose, as usual. After a struggle he realized he felt too miserable to drift back off.

Rick felt tears just behind his eyes. Two years ago his marriage, which had meant so much to him for over thirty years, had ended in a debacle.

He drew on his cotton sweat suit, a wool cap and some heavy socks. After tying up his Nikes and pulling on some jersey gloves, Rick drank a little bottled water and went outside, intending to jog five miles. He stepped into the windy predawn of a cold day, typical of March in the Midwest.

He saw a car turn the corner at the end of the block, but didn't pay too much attention. Still it seemed a little strange that a neighbor would be up this early, he thought.

As he jogged along he tried to form some plans for the day. After his run, he'd return home, stretch his muscles and lift some weights. Then he'd drive over to the cemetery with some flowers.

You won't find Rachel there, said the voice of reason in his mind.

I know, he said to the little voice. *It's just that I want to make up now. Even though I'm several years too late.*

She'd died before he could tell her that he'd forgiven her, that he loved her and that he'd always love her. He hadn't told her before her mind crumbled.

Not for the first time, he reflected on how strange her last two years had been. His wife had been coherent one day, chaotic the next. Her mind seemed to have just—what could you say?—given out. He had to commit her to a mental institution, the most painful thing he'd ever done.

He began to jog along the dark, quiet streets of his neighborhood. He noticed the trim gardens, dormant against winter, waiting for spring.

He thought about the house he'd shared with Punk and their kids long ago. He shook his head as he remembered cruising by the house when he'd first moved back from the West Coast. All Rachel's gardens that she'd nurtured, fussed over, fertilized and watered now lay overgrown, full of weeds, dismal, and forgotten by the current owners.

Rachel would have been furious.

He ran at an easy pace down the quiet street, taking it easy and letting his muscles limber. The dark windows in the houses along the street suggested that no one in the neighborhood had stirred from their comfortable beds yet.

I need to get a hobby besides running and working out, he thought. *Exercise helps, but I can't work out all day. Maybe stamp collecting, or coins, or baseball cards. Something to take my mind off Rachel during the day.*

He thought about the long, lonely nights of solitude when he'd wake up and not be able to fall back asleep, feeling the appalling absence of Rachel's warm, lovely body next to him. . .

He jerked his thoughts away. *Jeez, what a miserable, cold morning,* he thought. *Twenty degrees and a wind.*

He chuckled. *Funny thing about running in the Chicago area: No matter which way you run, you face into the wind.*

Rick had kept himself in good shape for a man in his 60s. As Rachel lay dying in the nursing home, he and his old commanding officer Colonel Spencer had worked out together for months. Rick lifted weights, stretched and renewed his long dormant skills in the martial arts. When he'd moved back to the Midwest, he had continued to work out and maintain the skills he'd learned in the Marines.

Huh, he thought. *At least I'm ready to take on someone who wants to fight a guy in his sixties.*

Rick jogged at about a nine and a half minute pace. He could do better if he pushed himself, of course.

But he found he couldn't push himself. Not today. His body and soul ached with the loss of the dearest thing in his life, the remarkable woman he'd married more than three decades before.

At the end of the block, Rick noticed a huge Ford SUV sitting by the curb with its parking lights on and its engine idling. Two men sat in the car and they turned to look at him—

—Almost like they'd been waiting for him?

Nah, he told himself. *Don't be silly.*

His mind registered in an abstract way that the car seemed odd. Why would two guys in a car sit in the neighborhood at least an hour before anyone else woke up and watch a man run down the street? With the car running?

Leaving for a fishing trip? Nah, too cold.

Picking someone up for an early trip to the airport? Maybe.

So they sat there, scrutinizing a lone nutcase who'd gone out to run in the dark and cold way too early—

A nutcase who couldn't sleep because he missed his wife so damned much.

Rick, trying to be polite, smiled and waved at the men in the SUV as he went by. They didn't wave back. He shrugged. *Nice guys,* he thought with irony.

Rick reached the end of the next block before it registered that he had a car following him. He turned right onto one street, then left and right again, each time sneaking a peek at the car.

Yes. The Ford SUV he'd seen sitting next to the curb seemed to be pacing him, perhaps fifteen or twenty yards behind him. The parking lights had been turned off.

Huh.

Now Rick became aware of a strange sensation. He thought he heard someone speaking to him. *Rick,* the voice said. *Rick, pay attention. You're in danger. You have to get away.*

"What the Hell?" he said aloud.

I missed you at your apartment. I'm so sorry.

"Who is this? How are you talking to me?" Rick asked, baffled.

Listen to me, said the voice. *Please listen. Those men in the SUV want to kill you. You have to hide, get away.*

"This doesn't make any sense," he said to the voice in his mind. He thought, *Am I crazy?*

No, not crazy, said the voice. *Not at all. Please believe me.*

"Okay," he said aloud, mystified. He thought for a moment and understood.

They wouldn't go for him in the neighborhood. They'd wait until Rick moved out in the open, away from the neighborhood houses, where no one could hear him yell for help.

He shot a glance over his shoulder and saw the SUV still tracking him. *Yes,* said the voice. *They plan to wait for the right moment. You have to escape.*

Rick decided to take charge of the situation. He ducked between two houses and headed through the yards to a retention basin. He rushed down the bank of the basin, sprinted across to the other side, up the hill and again between two houses. He hid in some bushes next to a house and looked back over the basin.

The SUV appeared between two houses and drove through a yard and down into the basin. A spotlight flashed around the basin and the houses that encircled it.

Rick began to tremble. He remembered having that reaction to combat situations when he'd been a soldier in Vietnam: cool, in control until the danger had passed. Then, the terror would hit and he'd start to shake.

The situation scared the Hell out of him and he didn't mind admitting it. A fight didn't scare him. Rather, he feared what he couldn't comprehend.

Who the Hell would be after me?

No jogger carries anything worth stealing.

My watch cost $12 at Radio Shack.

I bought my shoes on the clearance rack at Kohl's Department Store. They sure aren't Michael Jordans.

My sweatsuit doesn't have any value at all.

And why do I keep hearing voices?

The SUV drove through a yard a few houses down from where Rick hid. The car turned on its headlights as it turned back onto the street, and began traveling at a slow pace. The man in the passenger seat scanned the houses with a powerful flashlight while the driver manipulated the searchlight mounted near the outside rear view mirror.

Rick's cool returned. He wouldn't push a fight now. Instead he burrowed back into the bushes while the SUV passed. They didn't see him.

When they were past, he emerged and took off again, heading down toward the Fox River. He stayed alert for any motor sound or light.

The voice spoke. *Did you get away?*

"For the moment," he said aloud. The voice went silent.

Puzzled, he tried to reason through this situation. Then, he put it together. The guys waiting in the car. Following him.

Hell, those creeps came looking for me, he thought. *Me in particular.*

You're right, said his Guardian Angel. *Don't go home yet.*

"Why?" He said.

You're still in a great deal of danger. Where did you plan to go?

"I'm planning to go to the River Walk, east side," he said.

Okay, said the voice. *I know where that is. Head south and I'll meet you at Island Park.*

"Okay," he said aloud, feeling foolish. Still, the voice sure seemed real.

Rick jogged down a side street in the dark, and headed across the pedestrian bridge to the trail where he ran four or five days a week.

He calmed as he went, the adrenalin subsiding a little. He took a peek over his shoulder from time to time. No SUV. They couldn't get down to the trail to follow him. Yeah, he'd lost them for sure.

He thought again about Rachel and the pain returned. Punky had died, gone, lost forever, after being tormented her whole adult life with fear—no, with unspeakable terror—because of a youthful mistake.

Rick realized for maybe the two millionth time how much he'd loved her. How much he still missed her. How lonely his life had become without her.

Sure, the neighborhood he'd moved into had a bunch of nice people, some of whom had reached out to him. He'd met and gone on dates with a few women, a couple of whom he met at church, once in a while a fix up with some friend of a friend.

He shook his head. One or two of the women claimed to be interested to learn that he played guitar to help pay for college and still filled in with jazz bands on occasion. Once in a while, he played a show for an amateur theatre group in town.

His heartache returned, the encounter with the SUV fading into the background.

Rachel and he had gone through that rough period, to be sure. He felt pretty certain she had an affair that she concealed from him some years ago. He'd tried to confront her, and she refused again and again to confirm or deny his suspicions.

He winced at the thought of how he tried to provoke her.

One night he'd been downright cruel. "You screwed that Dominick character lots of times, right?" he sneered. "When I got out of the way, you went right after him."

Tears started in Rachel's brown eyes, but he didn't let up.

"What's the matter?" he demanded. "You decided after all these years I wasn't good enough after all, huh?"

"Oh, Rick," she sobbed. "Please. . ." She ran from the kitchen up the stairs to the bedroom and shut the door. He followed and could hear her sobbing through the door.

She'd locked the door. "Let me in," he demanded.

"No," she howled, miserable.

He'd never apologized. Never. Now he couldn't apologize, not ever again.

But he could never make sense of Rachel having an affair. He'd never known a more loyal, more principled person than she. He thought of how adultery devastated Rachel when they were seniors in college. She learned that her parents were planning to divorce over infidelity. The contention between her parents and the divorce proceedings had all but wrecked the two of them.

She couldn't have forgotten. Could she?

He jerked his thoughts back to his run, trying to forget what he did and said to his beloved wife, unable even now to bear the thought of hurting her.

He ran on the asphalt path until he reached Island Park. No cars were parked in the lot and he saw no sign of life anywhere. He shrugged and jogged across the bridge to the island and across another bridge to the west side of the river. The path had woods all around.

Rick felt in his pocket for the squirt gun he always carried. A couple of idiots near the path owned big dogs and the owners sometimes let them run free. Once in a while the damn things barked and snarled at him.

Rick and Rachel had owned dogs and he loved them, but he sure didn't relish a fight with a Doberman or a Rottweiler. Or even a toy poodle, for that matter. So now he carried a squirt gun with a weak ammonia solution in it.

Okay, a dog attack seemed remote. He sure wouldn't go after one of the things.

But if he did have a confrontation with a mean dog he could shoot it with the squirt gun.

Right. Rick Howell, big game hunter.

He wouldn't blind the creature with the stuff, but he figured that the smell would scare it off.

Rick's enthusiasm for running had gone away, but the Angel had said she'd meet him at the park. He ran down along the path to the Fabyan Road Bridge, where he turned and headed back. He'd jog home to some weight training.

The Fox River, shallow and narrow, flowed next to the path on the east side of the path, its bottom layered with mud and goose droppings. A skin of grayish ice covered the river near the path.

He started back across the bridge and saw a fair stand of cattails left over from last year. The park district burned the weeds next to the river almost every year. *They'd better do it soon,* he thought in an abstract way, *before the redwing blackbirds begin nesting.* They were aggressive little birds when they were in rut, or whatever birds went into. The little creeps would hide and jump out, scaring the bejeezus out of—

"Stand still, old man," growled a voice.

Chapter Forty-four

Rick looked up, jarred and startled. Two men had stepped from hiding and now stood blocking the jogging path a few feet ahead. Rick had just enough light to see that one of them wore a scrawny beard and held a knife pointed at Rick's gut. The other wore a black watchcap pulled down almost to his eyes.

"What the. . ." Rick began. Then he dropped into combat cool. He hadn't had a chance to try out his martial arts skills at combat speed since his days in the Marines when he'd fought for his life many times with some very tough people.

Since Rachel's affair he'd worked his way back into fine physical condition. A couple of cheap muggers didn't scare him.

Still the thugs looked pretty big in the dim light. The knife was about three inches long, he realized, but looked like a bayonet.

He took off his glasses and folded them, never taking his eyes of the creeps. Placing the glasses in his left pocket, he removed a big bandanna and wiped his nose.

Then he replaced the bandanna into the pocket and put his hands inside his jacket pockets. His hand closed on the squirt gun filled with the ammonia solution. He pulled it to the edge of the pocket so he could yank it free. The toughs didn't notice.

Rick saw that these two clowns appeared nervous and apprehensive. Like they'd never mugged anyone before.

Puzzling.

He said, "Look, guys, I don't have a damn thing to give you—" But one of them interrupted.

"Here's what's going to happen," said Beard, the one with the knife. "You tell us where to find the letters. If you don't, we kill you. We'll take our time—"

"Like Hell," snarled Rick. "I tell you nothing."

The two men looked surprised. They hadn't expected resistance from a man old enough to be their father by a handsome margin.

They also seemed taken aback that he didn't seem to be afraid of them. These punks figured people would be cowed by their size and intimidating actions.

"Come on, Pop," said Watchcap. "Don't make it hard on yourself. Things can get very unpleasant if we have—"

"What letters do you mean, Little Boy?" sneered Rick.

The men cast their eyes skyward as if imploring heaven for assistance and Rick saw his chance. He yanked out his squirt gun and squeezed a jet of the ammonia solution right into Beard's eyes.

The creep yelled and rubbed at his eyes. Rick attacked with a scream. He slammed the blade man with a scissors kick to the jaw that knocked him backwards.

Watchcap, shocked, didn't react at first. Before he could adjust, Rick ducked and spun a whip kick to his temple. Watchcap staggered, stunned by the kick. He threw out his hand to steady himself.

Rick grabbed the arm. He yanked it upwards and his simultaneous kick struck the thug in the armpit. Watchcap screamed as his shoulder separated.

Rick twisted the arm, spun underneath it and launched another kick, this one to Watchcap's kidney. The kick drove the air out of the man's lungs and he went down.

As Watchcap sprawled on the asphalt path, Rick turned to Beard. This one, bent over with pain, howled as he tried to clear his eyes. Rick kicked his temple, knocking this man to the ground, stunned. Beard dropped his knife.

Rick grabbed the knife and stamped his foot hard behind the man's left knee. The man would need surgery before he walked on that leg again.

No more than a few seconds had elapsed.

Rick turned to the man trying to get his breath. He shoved the knife under Watchcap's chin and yanked him to his feet. He pinned the thug against a tree so that he could keep an eye on the first man. Now he cut the second man's throat just enough to draw blood. He held the knife in front of the man's eyes and Watchcap's eyes widened at the sight of his own blood on the blade.

"Hands on your head," he snapped. Watchcap stammered and Rick poked him with the knife point under the chin. The thug's head crashed back against the tree and he began to whimper. Watchcap put his hands on top of his head.

"You need to look for a different line of work, Sonny," Rick mocked. "Now. What do you want?"

"Your wife's letters," he groaned. "Like we said."

"I don't have any letters from my wife," Rick snarled. "She died two years ago."

"Yeah, well, we're going to get. . ." began the creep, trying to regain some bluster.

Rick kneed the thug in the groin. Watchcap gasped, whimpering as the hideous pain incapacitated him. "I'm in charge here, Stupid," Rick told him. "You speak when I tell you to."

The man nodded.

"Now speak," barked Rick. "One more time. What letters do you mean?"

"I. . .uh. . ." mumbled the man.

Rick realized, surprised, this clown didn't know anything. Rick tucked the knife into his belt and shoved the thug down the embankment into the pond. Watchcap crashed through the skin of ice and fell forward into the unspeakable muck.

Beard gasped for breath as he tried to stand up and gave a hoarse scream as the agony of a ruined knee hit him full force. In the next second Rick seized him by the back of the neck and kicked him down the little hill. Arms flailing, Beard fell into the freezing river next to his buddy.

These two wouldn't present a threat for a little while. Rick took off across the bridge.

What the Hell? He thought. *Those two goofballs wouldn't survive the first cut at a mugger's training camp. What a couple of imbeciles.*

He came to the top of the bridge. In the glow of the parking lot lights he saw three cars twenty yards down the parking lot. One appeared to be the SUV which had followed him earlier. He figured it had to belong to the two creeps.

In the gathering light he pulled out his glasses again and put them on. He saw three people standing around the other two cars.

His vision cleared and he spotted two large men menacing a woman. She looked terrified. "Hey," he yelled.

The two men jerked around when they heard his voice. Rick saw the woman yank a canister up. She sprayed one of the men with a mist that Rick assumed had to be mace or pepper spray. This man clutched at his eyes and screamed.

The other man turned back to her and lifted his hand as if to backhand her.

To Rick's surprise, this man fell to his knees, screaming with terror. The thug covered his head, whimpering and pleading.

"Rick," cried the woman. Rick stopped, surprised that she knew his name.

"Yeah," he growled, still in attack mode.

"We have to get out of here," she said. "Get in my car." She pointed to a white Buick. He remembered seeing the car turn the corner at the end of his block at the beginning of his run.

"Those cars belong to the thugs, right?" he asked, indicating a black Chevy and the SUV.

"Yes," she said.

Rick drove the knife into the sidewalls of two tires on each of the cars. Then he turned to the two assailants, one blinded and the other still terrified. He grabbed the two incapacitated men by their hair and bashed their heads together. They went down hard.

The woman had fired up the Buick. She threw open the passenger door. He dove in and she sped off down the parking lot.

Chapter Forty-five

Rick's glasses had fogged up. He took the bandanna from his jacket pocket and cleaned them. He put them back on and got his first good look at the woman as she turned onto Route 25. "Donna!" he said. "Donna Riske! What are you doing here?"

"Hi, Rick," Donna said with a weak smile. She still looked terrified.

"Jeez," Rick wheezed, out of breath. "What just happened?"

She removed a mitten and extended her hand. He took off his glove, wiped his hand on his sweatshirt, and shook her hand. "Welcome to my life," she said with a rueful smile.

"What do you mean?" Rick asked, baffled by this whole morning so far.

"I'm faced with that every time they find me. They haven't caught me when I was that vulnerable for quite a while, though."

Rick regarded her for a few moments.

"Why are they after you?"

Donna paused for a few moments and turned onto State Street, headed west.

She shrugged. "Do you remember that Rachel and Barry and I took that drug in college?"

"Sure, of course," he said. "It altered Rachel forever. I lived with that for thirty some years, after all."

"These clowns want the secret of the drug, the one that Keith guy used on us."

"You mean the guy who formulated it to begin with?"

"Yeah," she nodded. "They think they can get it from me."

"Oh brother," he sighed.

She hesitated for a few moments. Then, her voice shy, "It's nice to see you," she commented. "How long has it been?"

"Several years anyhow," Rick said. "We moved to Palm Springs almost five years ago."

"California?"

"Yeah. When Rachel retired from teaching we decided to get away."

"Well, you went a long way from Chicago, all right," she said. She hesitated a second or two. "How did you get away from those guys?" she asked.

"What guys?"

"The two that went over the bridge after you."

"You knew about that?"

"I just missed you when you left your house this morning," she said. "I saw you duck away from the creeps in the SUV. Then I headed over to the river."

"So you followed me too? Jeez, what is this?"

She nodded. "I watched you go over the bridge. I parked, thinking I'd wait for you to come back. Then, those two cars pulled up and two thugs ran off after you. The other two brutes confronted me and forced me out of my car. They sure scared me, believe me."

"Do you have any idea what they wanted? The two who went for me demanded letters from Rachel."

"I know what's going on, yes. They've been after me for quite a while."

"Donna, I don't get this. These guys have been chasing you?"

"Answer my question first. How did you get away from them?"

"Maybe you remember I served in the Marines, the Force Recon during Viet Nam."

"Force Recon?" she asked.

"Short for Force Reconnaisance, a Special forces unit, like the SEALs or the Army Rangers," he said. "So when Rachel became—er—sick, I met up with my old commanding officer and we worked out together for a couple of years. Then Rachel died and I moved back here. I've tried to keep my skills up to date."

"Okay."

"Those two in the park were refugees from Amateur Night. They threatened me. I broke one guy's knee and shattered another guy's shoulder and tossed them into the river. They'll be out of commission for a while."

"You might have killed those two in the parking lot. . ."

"I don't think so," he said. "Concussions, I hope. But they'll sure have headaches for a couple of days, too."

"Impressive. Very impressive."

"Get out," he said, waving his hand. "We weren't up against pros. They're a bunch of oversized dorks who think they can make a living intimidating and roughing people up."

"They've made my life Hell for the last few years."

They grew silent for a few moments. Then Rick asked, "Why did you follow me?"

"Let me get my breath for a while," she urged. "I can answer that later."

"Something else," he said. "I think I heard you talking to me when I was running in the neighborhood. How did you. . ."

"Same deal," she said. "Later."

Rick shrugged okay.

"Rachel died," she said.

"Yes, two years ago."

"Uh, huh."

"She died in Palm Springs," he said. "She insisted in her will that I have her body cremated. I brought her ashes back to bury her here, near our old home."

"I knew she was gone," nodded Donna. "What became the cause of death?"

"Dementia," said Rick. "The last two years of her life."

"I remember now," she said.

He nodded. "It came on a couple of years after we moved. I had to place her in a home for the last two years. Her mind exploded, I guess you could say. She—" he paused and choked on the memory for just a second. "She didn't know me at all during that time."

She nodded. She reached across and squeezed his elbow to comfort him. He remembered, now. Donna communicated a great deal by touching. Never overbearing or obnoxious.

"Can you recall her last words?" Donna asked. Rick turned and stared at her, surprised at the question. "I'm sorry, but it might be important."

"Yeah," he said. "Yeah, I do remember. She said a strange word: 'Curiel'."

Donna nodded. "Tell me," she said.

Rick felt a lump develop in his throat. He cleared his throat and said in a husky voice, "The doctor told me it wouldn't be long. I sat next to her hospital bed and held her hand, but I don't think she even knew I was there. I saw that she was ready to go and I started to recite our psalm."

"Which one?" she asked.

"One of her favorites, the 91st," he said. "When I was away during Viet Nam, we said that psalm every night as we went to bed. It was a way of having a connection, even though we were apart."

"What a lovely arrangement," whispered Donna.

"As I watched, her eyes focused on the far wall. She lifted her free hand and smiled, the first time I'd seen her do that in months. It was like she saw someone standing at the foot of the bed. She said, 'Curiel.' She extended her hand and turned to me. She looked in my eyes and smiled—" Now he couldn't continue.

"I'm sorry, Rick," she said. "And then she was gone, I suppose." Rick nodded.

The car was silent for a few moments. "Why did you ask?"

"Barry said the same word to me," she said. "Right at the end. 'Curiel.'"

"Do you know what it meant?"

Donna shook her head. Again they lapsed into silence.

"You called her Punky, right?" she said, a few moments later.

He laughed a little, thinking of how precious that name had been to him. "Yeah. She called me—well, she called me a lot of things, including Fat Ass—'"

"Fat Ass?" she said, grinning.

"Yeah," he said. "I've lost about fifty pounds in the last four years."

"I was about to say, you look pretty trim to me."

"Thanks. I began losing it when we moved west. Then I decided to get back in shape when her mind exploded. I had a friend from the Marines help me. . ." His voice trailed away since it looked like her mind had become occupied elsewhere.

The conversation stalled for a few moments. At last he had to know. "Donna?"

"Don't ask," she said.

"Don't ask what?"

"Don't ask how Barry died. Not right now."

He blinked. How did she knew what he intended to ask? *Well, maybe that would be the logical next question—*

"Did you have breakfast yet?" she said.

"No. I woke up early and lay there for a while. When I accepted the idea that I couldn't fall back asleep I came out for a run."

"Want to get a bite at a restaurant?"

"I'd love to, but I didn't bring my wallet."

"I've got money. It's on me."

They didn't speak for few moments. In the meantime, he reviewed what he knew about Donna.

After their wedding, Donna and Barry lived in Atlanta for some years and moved to the Chicago area about the time Rick received his discharge from the Marines. He'd see Donna with her husband Barry at some parties, he remembered, Christmas maybe, a summer picnic, Saurday night bridge and dinner together. Their spouses had taught together at a high school. Rachel and Donna had kept up a nice friendship since college.

"What did your husband teach?" he asked.

"History. He worked part-time as a dean, too."

"Yech," he said, making a face.

"I know. He spent a lot of his day dealing with real misfits, I remember."

"He'd retired, then?"

"Yes," she said. "As you know Illinois has a pretty good retirement program for teachers. Barry left teaching at the age of fifty-five."

"Not bad," he nodded.

"Your wife retired from the profession, right?"

"Yeah, for the most part. When we moved to California, she liked to take on substitute days from time to time. Until the dementia. . ." he stopped talking, the lump forming in his throat again.

She nodded with a sympathetic smile. "Did you pull her pension money out when you moved, then?"

He paused. "No," he said. "No, I forgot all about it."

"You're entitled to some sort of a pension from it, I think," Donna said.

"You may be right. I'll look into it."

"Well, so something good has come from this, right?"

He laughed. "More than just getting a few bucks," he said. "It's nice to see you again, too."

"Thank you," she said. "Pardon me while I blush prettily."

"What do you do?"

She hesitated. Then, "I fuss over my grandkids when I can. Dabble in this or that."

"I seem to remember that you have college degrees."

"Oh yes. I have a master's degree in sociology. I worked as a drug and alcohol counselor until I also retired." She steered the car into a parking lot. They made their way to the entrance of a breakfast café. "Oh good grief," she said, stopping at the door. "Do I look awful? I forgot."

"You look better than me," he assured her. "I look like a bum. I haven't shaved or anything."

After they ordered, the small talk continued for some time. After a brief pause, she seemed to make up her mind. She asked, "Why did you move to Palm Springs?"

He hesitated. "Well, I guess no harm can come now. She wouldn't care." Her face took on a puzzled look.

He started to speak, but it didn't come out for a few moments. At last: "Rachel had an affair." He paused, but to his surprise, Donna didn't react. Not even a lifted eyebrow. Rick went on: "It lasted a year that I know about. When I found out, I asked her for a divorce."

"And?"

"She persuaded me to stay on. She apologized but said she couldn't talk about it, no details, anything like that. . ."

"I see," she said.

"Yeah." Rick shrugged.

"So, did you go into counseling?"

"Yeah, we tried it," he nodded. "Seemed to help a little. I agreed to it as a condition of not filing for divorce."

She started to ask a question, but stopped as the waitress brought their breakfasts. He noticed that she asked a little grace before she started eating. For a few moments, they tucked into the food.

"You started to ask something," he said.

She patted her lips with a napkin and took a sip of coffee. Then, "When did this affair occur?"

"I think the year before we moved to Palm Springs in autumn, five years ago."

"So the affair went on during the previous school year?"

"Uh-huh, I suppose so. I never pushed for details."

"Of course not."

"Pretty painful, you know."

She stared into her coffee cup and didn't speak for some time. Then, "Did she ever come back to the Chicago area?"

The question surprised Rick. "No," he said. "She went to Milwaukee a lot, though. Her cousin lives there and they always remained close friends."

She said, "So she'd fly into Mitchell Field in Milwaukee?"

"Yeah," said Rick. "Sometimes four or five times a year."

"Did you go with her?"

"Well, no, I. . ."

"Rick," she said. Then she paused and stared into her coffee cup. At last she looked up. "I don't think she flew in to see a cousin."

"What do you mean?"

"I think she came to see someone else," said Donna.

"Donna—" he began. Then it kicked in. He stared into her face. "You mean—er—your husband and my wife?"

"Yes, that's what I think. That nails it."

"But that couldn't be—ridiculous. . ."

"Yes?"

Rick grew silent and thought it over. "Okay," he said at last. "Maybe, I sort of suspected that she continued to be involved with someone. Or maybe she didn't break it off as she said. But I can't do anything about it now."

"Rick, you have to understand something," she said, clasping her hands together. "I have to tell you. Their relationship had a lot more to it than—than, well, just sex."

"Look, Donna," he began. "For the last several years of our marriage, things weren't great, I agree. We had, if anything, a mistrusting malfunction of a relationship. I never could believe her once I found out about—well, about the affair—"

"See, I'm not sure they had an affair. Or that sex ever became involved."

"So why wouldn't she tell me if it was something else? Why would she let me go along thinking about her screwing some other guy? Do you have any idea how much pain that cost me?"

"Of course I do. I lived it, the same as you did. I got the same confession, the same promises and the same assurances as you did."

"Then why bring it up now? Why come to me with this? Why do you think I need to know. . ."

"Could you maybe lower your voice?"

Rick realized that he'd been near to shouting at this woman. He breathed deep and stared at his fingernails, which, he now realized, he'd stopped chewing.

"A childhood habit," he said, holding up his fingers for her to see. "I stopped chewing my nails when I met Rachel. I hadn't even thought about it until now."

She nodded with a little smile. "Like you were set free from something, right?"

"Yeah, just like." He bit off a small piece of toast and took a swallow of coffee. "Would you please answer some questions, Donna?"

"Sure, if I can."

"How did you find out that they were involved?"

"Some detective work, some deduction, some legwork," she said. "Then you confirmed it just now."

Rick looked up in some surprise. "You mean I said something?"

She hesitated, her discomfort obvious. Then she asked, "You called her 'Punky' even at the end?"

"Yeah," he said, baffled. "My pet name from before we married."

Donna nodded. "I'm sorry, Rick," she said. "I have something to show you." She reached into her purse. "I found these when I cleaned out his desk." She handed him a small packet. "I found them in a false compartment in the bottom of the file drawer of an old desk."

Rick accepted the packet. It contained several letters, most of them in legal sized envelopes, though a few of them appeared to be greeting cards. He pulled one out.

He stared at the address on the first. A post office box in Milwaukee.

"I recognize Rachel's handwriting," he said.

"Yes," she said. "I left a lot more still hidden in the drawer. These represent the rest pretty well, though. I've read them all."

Rick nodded. He extracted the letter from the first envelope. He glanced for a moment at the first paragraph. Dear Stain, it began.

"Stain?"

"His middle name was Justin. I can't think of anything else," she said.

The first paragraph didn't sound intimate at all. It read like a business letter. He commented on it.

"Yes," she said. "I found no hint whatever of romance in any of the letters: nothing mushy or sexy at all, nothing about secret trysts, nothing about love or devotion, nothing that you'd expect from a letter during an affair."

"Huh," he said. He couldn't say much else. His stomach hurt with the old pain of betrayal and anger and hurt. He thought he'd gotten past it.

"Look at the end," she said. He flipped the page.

His stomach fell. He found he couldn't talk.

Rachel hadn't signed her name. Instead she'd written "Punk." His affectionate little name for her.

Chapter Forty-six

An hour later, Rick sat alone in his apartment.

He'd made an idiot of himself with Donna, a lovely woman who didn't deserve such rudeness. Rachel would have been livid that he'd treated Donna that way.

He felt awful about his childish behavior at the restaurant. Once he saw how Rachel had signed the letters, he stormed away from the table, not speaking, red-faced and furious. He stood fuming outside the restaurant while she paid the bill.

She drove him home and insisted that he take her card. "Please," she said. "I know you're upset and I understand. Please call me when you feel better. I'll be waiting."

"You'll wait a Hell of a long time," he snapped. He crumpled the card and threw it into the bushes next to the front door. He slammed the front door behind him.

Now, after cooling off a while, Rick knew he needed to apologize. He walked down to the first floor and went outside. Donna had driven away, of course. He looked under the bush and saw the card lying there, wadded and muddy.

He smoothed it out and pulled his cell phone from his pocket. He poked in the number Donna had written down.

She answered on the first ring. "Rick?"

"Yes," he said. "I called to say I'm sorry, Donna—"

"I understand," said Donna. "I felt the same way. I've had some time to work through the anger, though."

"Well, I just wanted to. . ." he began.

She interrupted. "Could we get together again later? Believe me, it's vital."

Surprised, Rick said, "I figured you wouldn't want to see me again..."

"Listen to me," she interrupted. "I'm not angry. I expected your reaction."

That struck him as strange. Why did everything this woman said puzzle him? "Okay," he said. He took a deep breath, feeling like a school kid asking a pretty girl for a date. "Could I take you to dinner?"

"Sure, that would be perfect."

He could visualize her warm smile. He said, "Great. I'll pick you up. . ."

"No, let me come there. Wear something nice."

"Okay," he said. "Maybe we can make a night of it."

Rick went back to his apartment and lay down on his bed, feeling better. Then, the anger returned. Not at Donna. At Rachel.

"Why didn't Rachel break it off with that guy?" he said. "What did I do wrong?" Startled, he realized that he'd said it aloud.

He remembered in vivid detail when he'd found out about Rachel's involvement with some other guy. Once he learned he couldn't sleep for days. He kept visualizing Punk in bed with some guy, a young man with a smooth, hard body, faceless, nameless. She'd be writhing, smiling, gasping with joy as they surged together, relishing the sex, knowing she was betraying him and not giving a damn.

He'd tell her about that dream, that hideous vision. She'd tell him he had to get over it. He had to let it go. *Stop torturing yourself,* she'd say. *I can't,* he'd say. *I keep seeing you making love to someone else.*

He sat up and reached into his jacket pocket, the one he'd worn that morning. He had jammed the packet of letters into the pocket.

Maybe if I read some of them, he thought, maybe I can dissolve the pain. Maybe I'll find out why.

He found the earliest of the letters in the packet and arranged them in chronological order. He began to read.

Chapter Forty seven

An hour later, Rick finished reading the stack of letters for the third time. He stared at the letters, bewildered.

Nothing in the letters so much as suggested romance. The tone sounded cold, impersonal, lacking anything even resembling emotion.

Rick stood and walked to the window. He couldn't understand. Why would his wife correspond so often with another man? The letters didn't seem even to have been written by one friend to another. They could have been written from an attorney to a client.

Why? Why maintain a relationship with a man with whom you haven't even been romantic?

He paced back and forth. He'd come across a few enigmatic statements about meetings. She'd written about meeting at such and such a street corner, in the back of some restaurant, or a Starbucks, and so forth. Don't approach if I have the newspaper open on the table, she'd written in one of the letters.

Why? That seemed to indicate that they knew they were being watched, that they were in some sort of danger, yeah, okay.

And why had Barry hidden the letters in a desk?

Okay, he could figure that one out. Barry didn't want Donna to see them. . .

So why not throw them away? Burn them? Why keep them?

Rick looked at the clock. 3:00 P. M.

Rick sat on the edge of the bed, aware that he felt exhausted. *And I have a date*, he thought.

He had to smile at that. Other than Rachel, he'd never dated a woman he *admired* as much as Donna. The idea of dating some other women had occurred to him once in a while, during the time Punk languished in the nursing home. Then, however, when he'd go to visit Rachel, she wouldn't recognize him or anything, and lie in her bed muttering nonsense.

His heart would break every time. He couldn't face the idea of dating other women.

He laid down, shut his eyes, relaxed and began to doze off. . . .

He jerked awake. Oh no. I slept through. . . He looked at the clock. 4:45. Okay. He hadn't overslept.

He'd rinsed off under a quick shower when he came home from the meeting with Donna. He decided to shave and shower again, though. He needed to wash away some bad feelings.

The hot water cascaded around him. He'd treated himself to the purchase of a super soaking shower head when he'd moved into the apartment. One of his few self-indulgences, he realized.

I've become a monk, he thought.

He lathered his face and considered again the letters as he shaved.

What would motivate Punk to write to Barry? Why would Barry keep the letters?

He toweled the extra lather off. As he stared into the mirror, it occurred to him.

She got letters from Barry, right?

Were those the letters the hoods in the park were talking about?

Did she *keep* the letters from the man she called Stain?

Why hadn't he seen the letters delivered?

If *he* didn't know about them, why did the hoods?

He dressed in his best suit. He hadn't worn it for some time, but it was still in good repair. He'd had it altered after he'd lost the weight. The trousers seemed a bit too big for him, even now. *I guess I've lost some more weight*, he thought.

Where did she hide the letters?

He looked through his ties. He had one that seemed okay: maybe a little wide, but a nice muted red. He'd seen the guys on the Fox

News Channel wearing something like this, so maybe he wouldn't be too far out of style.

Yeah right, he thought. *As if I ever look like I stepped from the pages of Gentlemen's Quarterly—*

She must've gotten letters from him. Must have. Why didn't I see them?

His good black shoes. He found a little polish and gave the shoes a few licks with a shoe brush. The old shoes brightened.

Am I being resurrected?

He grinned to himself and thought about Donna: smart, attractive, tall, and slim with a lovely figure. He enjoyed thinking that they'd make a nice couple. . .

Could I have overlooked something?

He took a couple of hair brushes and smoothed down his hair. He realized that he was spending more time on his personal appearance than he had since Rachel. . .

What could Rachel have done with those letters?

He looked around the bathroom for after shave lotion and found an old bottle of English Leather stuck in the back of the medicine cabinet, maybe left over from high school. He splashed on some of it, relishing the mild tingle, the sting and the fragrance transporting him to high school and the prom for just a moment.

He heard a soft knock at his door and walked over.

Rick caught himself just in time. He'd been almost ready to gasp.

Donna looked sensational. She had done her hair up and she wore an attractive black dress, the hem about an inch and a half above her knees. "Yeow," he managed.

"Clean up pretty well, don't you?" she teased.

"Me?" he said. "You're the one who looks terrific."

"I bet you say that to all the girls."

"Clichés? Must we?" he said with a breathy British accent.

"That comes from a movie," she said. "But you haven't got the quote quite right."

"Correct," he said. "I took it from Hitchcock's *North by Northwest.* James Mason says to Cary Grant, 'Games?'"

"'Must we?'" they said together.

"Yes," she said. "I remember the scene, just before the bad guys make Grant drink himself into a coma and he escapes in Laura's Mercedes."

"Do you like movies?"

"I love them," she agreed. "You?"

"Ditto."

A silence descended for a moment or two as they gazed into one another's eyes. She smiled a bit wider and broke the spell. "Ready to go?" she asked.

"Sure," he said. "I can't offer you a drink, I'm afraid. I haven't bought any liquor since I've moved back here."

"Don't worry. We can get one at the restaurant."

He pulled on a topcoat and escorted her to the door. "Oh," she said. "Did you keep the letters? Please say yes." She clasped her hands in front of her as if praying.

"Yes, I did," he said. "Do you want them back?"

"Please," she said. "If you've had a chance to read them. Otherwise I can wait. . ."

"No, I'll get them," he said, crossing to the bedroom. He brought the letters over and handed them to Donna. "I read them, but I can't figure them out why anyone would care about them."

Donna nodded. "Same for me. I don't know what to think. Maybe. . . " She bit her lip.

"Maybe what?" said Rick.

She shook her head. "Come on," she said. "We have to go. We should be okay."

"Donna," he said. "Why does everything you say sound so enigmatic?"

"I'll explain," she said, "but not here, and not in the car. Talk about something neutral."

"What on earth. . ."

"Just trust me. Please."

By now, Rick's couldn't have been much more confused. They

kept the conversation at the humdrum level. Anyone who overheard them would think they were two strangers, thrown together, just out for an evening of companionship.

"Uh, oh," said Donna.

"What?" he asked.

"I'm being tailgated."

"Ah, it doesn't mean anything," he said. "Just slow down and let the idiot pass."

Donna slowed down, letting the car coast. The tailgater didn't pass, just maintained less than a one car length interval.

"Now what?" she asked.

"Can you see how many guys are in the car?"

"Looks like three, maybe four," she nodded.

He thought for a second. "Okay," he said. "Head down State Street to First. Then turn south and we'll go to the police station. It's right there."

"Okay," she said. Two minutes later she turned right onto First Street. The car turned with them.

She turned left into the police station.

The car went on past. Rick noted the license plate.

"Looks like a kid," he grunted. "I wish I knew why people thought tailgating does any good." He directed her out of the parking lot and toward the restaurant.

A big crowd waited at the restaurant. A jazz combo played quiet dinner music in the bar area. Donna asked to be seated at a table near the band.

After about forty-five minutes of martinis and chit-chat, the hostess came over to them. She led them to their table.

The waitress, a pleasant young woman named Jackie, handed them menus. "Have you been here before?" Jackie asked.

"Not for some time," said Donna.

"Okay," said Jackie. "We have several specials this evening. For pasta, we have a pumpkin ravioli. Our fish is fresh-caught mahi mahi, and we have a nice twenty four ounce porterhouse steak."

"Give us a few minutes, okay?" smiled Rick.

She left and Donna looked around the room. "Let me ask you," he said. She gave a small smile. "Did you hear this? A horse walks into a bar. The bartender says, 'Why the long face?'"

Donna groaned. "Why the joke?" she asked.

"I wondered why the suspicious look around the place?" Rick asked.

Donna shrugged. "Sorry," she said. "Do you think this table seems safe?"

Rick opened his eyes in surprise. He leaned forward. "Safe?" he said. "What do you mean?"

"Do you think we can be overheard?"

"By whom?"

"I don't know who. No idea, in fact. It could be anyone in the place."

Now he began to get frustrated. "Look, Donna. . ."

"I know. I know. You don't get this at all, and I don't blame you. I walk into your life and all of a sudden everything gets thrown up in the air."

"Right. Where do things land?"

She sighed. "So do you think they can't hear us?"

"I don't have any idea. Who would be listening to us?"

She stared at the back of her hand. "You remember I asked you not to inquire about Barry's death."

"Well, yeah. . ."

"The people I'm afraid of murdered Barry."

Again he struggled for words. All that came out was "Murdered?"

She nodded. "Yes. And I think they killed him because of these letters. And the ones your wife received from Barry."

"How. . ." Rick began. "I mean, er. . ."

"They didn't get me because I took a power walk with a friend," she said. "I was out for an hour and a half. I found him. . ." She swallowed hard. The picture hadn't faded, he knew.

After a few moments, he asked "When did this happen?"

"About two years ago."

"Where?"

"Our home in Wisconsin. When Barry left teaching, we moved to Whitefish Bay, north of Milwaukee."

"Not a high crime area, right?"

"No. Very nice area."

"Wait a minute," Rick said. "Milwaukee?"

"Yes," said Donna. "Now you know why Rachel would fly into Milwaukee. Not to see a cousin."

"To see Barry," he nodded, looking grim.

"Yes, but again, I don't think it involved romance. I don't, Rick."

Rick forced himself to remain calm. "So someone trashed your home and killed Barry?"

"Yes," she said. "He must've fought them."

"What makes you say that?"

"He didn't tell them where he'd hidden the letters," she said.

"Yeah," he said.

"They beat him without mercy, too," she said.

"Good grief. And they've been after you ever since?"

"Yes. I think they just learned about you in the last few days. Otherwise they'd have come for you before this morning."

"Do you think they didn't know where to find me or something?"

"That's possible," she said. "They have a great deal of patience though. They waited until they could locate you. Oh brother," she said, putting her hand over her mouth.

"What 'oh brother'?" he asked.

"I just realized. I may have led them to you," she said. "Oh, I'm sorry, Rick."

He shrugged. "They'd have found me sooner or later. Maybe it would be best to deal with it now."

"Thank you," she said. "Tell me something?"

"Yes?"

"Did Rachel ever use the Step?"

He thought. "If she did, I wasn't aware of it," he admitted. "She may have, and it didn't have to do with me. You remember, when she'd use it, she had a terrible time sleeping. But as a rule, she didn't seem to have any difficulty sleeping once we were married. . ."

He didn't say anything for a few moments. He rubbed his hand against his mouth.

"What?" asked Donna, leaning over and squeezing his hand.

"Well, something strange did happen about four years into our marriage."

"Can you tell me?"

He thought. "Okay," he nodded. He took a sip of water and began the story.

***

Rick lay in bed, next to Punk, unable to sleep. She'd suggested sex, but he claimed to be too tired. She fell asleep, but he hadn't been able to drift off.

Rick had lied to her. He couldn't sleep, scared to his heart. Their finances had never been so desperate. They were just about tapped out.

He'd been out of work for several weeks. They'd mortgaged the house, taken a home equity loan, all that. If Rachel hadn't been working, they would have been in the streets.

He jumped at a sound from downstairs. He tried to identify the noise. . .

Of course. He'd heard the scraping of a kitchen chair.

The dog. Where was Lucy? The dog would have barked her head off if someone was in the house. Maybe they'd killed her?

He disengaged himself from Rachel and grabbed a baseball bat.

He crept down the stairs. The light above the stove shone through the kitchen doorway.

He lifted the bat and walked in.

Rachel knelt on the floor by the table, petting Lucy. The dog, ecstatic, lay on her back wagging her tail, exulting in the furious petting.

"Oh God, Honey." Rachel spoke to the dog in that tender voice she used with this dog. Since they'd rescued the pet from a shelter, minutes before the shelter planned to euthanize the dog, Rachel and Lucy had developed a special loving relationship. "I haven't seen you for so long. . ."

Rick turned on the light.

Rachel looked up and saw him. She beamed, looking wide awake and alert. He almost didn't recognize her. Rachel looked like she'd aged at least twenty years. She looked beautiful to him, of course. . .

"Hi, Rick," she said.

"Rachel," he said. "What on earth. . ."

"Will you please turn out that light?" she said, going over to sit back at the kitchen table.

"Oh," he said. "Sure."

He complied. He saw that she had a tablet in front of her. She'd written some notes on it that he couldn't read. She tore the sheet off the tablet and folded it.

"Rick, you need to go back to bed," she smiled. Lucy laid her head in Rachel's lap and Rachel resumed petting.

"How can you be here?" he asked. "I just left you. . ."

"Don't worry," she said. "Just remind me about this sheet of paper in the morning, okay?"

"Sure, okay," he said. She gave Lucy a gentle nudge and the dog backed away. Rachel walked to the counter and put the paper in the silverware drawer.

Now she crossed to Rick, embraced him and kissed him. They hugged as they always did. She drew back, looked into his eyes and stroked his face with those gentle musician's fingers. "I love you so much," she murmured. "I know you're scared. Believe me now. Everything will be okay."

"Good," he whispered, his word echoing in the still of the kitchen.

"Now take Lucy and go back to bed, okay?"

He complied. He let Lucy through the kitchen door. He turned to say 'good-night'– –

Rachel had disappeared. He almost screamed—

But he heard Rachel cry out from the bedroom. He turned and ran up the stairs back to her.

Rachel thrashed in the bed, whimpering with terror. He grabbed her and she struck out, as if trying to defend herself. She hit him in the arm, the shoulder, and he managed to block a punch to his face.

He held her, whispering to her to wake up. "It's okay," he said. "Punky, wake up. You're having a nightmare." He'd left her curled up and sound asleep. She now looked at him with unfocused, terrified eyes.

"Rick, they want me. They don't want to wait. They're coming. . ."

"No, Punk. Wake up. It's okay."

Then she woke up and stared at him for a moment or two until reality returned.

"Oh Rick," she said, and clutched at him. "Did I hit you? Oh, no," she started to cry. "I'm so sorry. I'd never—"

"Yeah, you hit me, but I'm okay," he said. "Forget it. You didn't hurt me. You just had a bad dream. It's okay."

He hugged her as she cried, apologizing again and again. "Forget it," he assured her again. "You were dreaming."

As she regained some control, Rick thought about the encounter in the kitchen. He figured he'd been dreaming the strange episode in the kitchen. Had to be.

His heart pounded for a few moments as he stared at his wife. She turned her face to him and he wiped away her tears, then kissed her cheeks. At last she calmed down. "What're you doing up?" she asked, stroking his face with those long comforting fingers.

"Thought I heard a noise," he muttered.

"Oh."

"Go back to sleep," he smiled.

"Not just yet," she asserted. "I figure I owe you something for whacking you. Come here, you." She tugged off her nightgown and reached for him.

He snuggled to his wife when she had dozed off again. The dream of the other Rachel in the kitchen hadn't faded, but the warm comfort of her body next to his drove away his anxiety. He drifted away.

When he woke in the morning he found Rachel had left the bed already, but he found her in the kitchen, bustling around.

She looked like she always had, bright and cheerful.

"Hi," she said.

"Hi," he yawned. "I'm supposed to remind you to look in the silverware drawer this morning."

Rachel looked baffled. "What on earth?"

"You told me to remind you, okay?"

Rachel stared for a moment, but then turned to the counter. She opened the drawer and found the paper.

She stared at it, looking puzzled for a few moments. Then her face brightened. "Oh, yes," she said.

"Huh?"

She crossed to the kitchen table and wrote on a tablet of paper. "You have to apply to this company," she said, tearing off a sheet and handing it to him. "This morning."

He looked at the company name. "How on earth do you know about them?" he asked, baffled.

"Not important. You just have to apply. I know it."

"Come on," he smiled. "These guys won't even talk to me—"

"Yes, I think they will. Promise me?"

Rachel left the room and he picked up the note she'd retrieved from the drawer. He found the name of the company she recommended that he contact at the top, circled with the words "Rick. Apply today," written next to them. Three or four other companies were listed below, with the word "Invest" next to them.

It didn't make sense. How did she know about these companies?

Rick called the company she'd recommended about 9:00 that morning. He received an invitation to come in for an interview. He started work for the company at the end of the week.

Chapter Forty eight

"Do you understand what happened?" Donna said.

"I think so," he said. "She Stepped back from the future."

"Yes," said Donna. "She brought back some knowledge that she shared with her younger self."

"You know, the dementia came on all of a sudden, now that I think about it," he said. "I hadn't thought about the Step Back as a possible cause."

"What do you mean?"

"She told me that the four times she did it with me caused such hideous nightmares that she'd think she was going crazy. She survived because I saw her within a short time. The longest interval came when she pulled me out of that ditch—"

He stopped and peered at her.

"What?" she asked, giving him a puzzled smile.

"I just told you a story that wouldn't pass the laugh test on an old episode of *The Twilight Zone*," he said, "and you didn't bat an eye."

"I know," she said. "Maybe you can guess why."

"I don't think so. . ." he began. Then, he got it. "You can do it too?"

"No, I can't do the Step," she said. "Barry could do it. I'm only aware of him Stepping Back a few times as well."

"What happened?"

"He studied in Champaign at the same time as Rachel and me. He also got into a bunch of dope and other 60s type behavior, like us."

"So when he and Rachel wound up teaching at the same high school. . ."

"Right. Their jobs reunited them and not by coincidence either. We—I mean, Rachel, Barry and I—planned it that way. After she saved you, we decided we had to band together."

Rick leaned back. He considered for a few moments.

"What does all this mean?" he asked. "Why did you want to be together?

"I'm getting to that. It's one of the reasons I came to seek you out," she said. "I don't know why they felt they couldn't confide to the people in the world who they loved the most."

Rick shook his head. "This whole thing always has been mysterious."

"I know," said Donna.

"On the one hand, Rachel could be as normal as coffee at breakfast. . ."

"Barry too. . ."

"But sometimes she'd go into depressions that would be terrible to behold. They wouldn't last very long, maybe a day or two, and maybe once every three or four years."

"Yes. That happened with Barry, too."

"So. . ." he said.

"So?"

"So why did you come to me? Compare notes?"

"I guess maybe so," she admitted. "But I think I felt some curiosity as well, though."

"How so?"

"You read those letters. They couldn't be more innocuous. It just seems to me that if Rachel and Barry had been lovers, the letters would include hot messages, discussions of burning kisses and passionate embraces, and plans for secret rendezvous, at least."

"Hmm," nodded Rick.

"It seemed a pure accident that I found the letters, too, as I told you."

"Right."

"I'm thinking that he must have written to Rachel," Donna

suggested.

"I've been considering that," Rick agreed. "I've been trying to think where she could have hidden the letters. Of course she could have destroyed them—"

"I don't think so."

"Why not?"

"Because they had no intention, either one of them, of destroying their marriages," Donna asserted. "On the contrary, Barry treated me with more affection before he went nuts than he ever did before," said Donna.

Rick considered this information. "Wait a second," he said. "Did you say he went nuts too?"

"Yes, I did."

"Dementia, too?"

"Or what passed for it. His mind had all but vanished by the end. He still knew me but his mind had grown feeble."

Rick felt a tear run down his cheek. He felt sympathy for this delightful woman. He knew how the pain gnawed at him for two years before Rachel died. He remembered watching Rachel struggle so hard to remember his name, the man she loved more than anything in the world.

"She always said I'd be the one who would keep her from going through the gates of Hell," he said. Now another tear rolled down his cheek. He brushed at it, angry at himself. "I'm sorry, Donna," he murmured.

"No," she said as she wiped at a tear on her own cheek. "Don't apologize. I know how you feel."

Their dinners arrived at that moment and he poured them a little more wine.

"So you loved him as much as I loved Rachel," he said, when the waitress walked away.

"Yes, I did," she affirmed.

They ate their dinners in silence but Rick couldn't stop his mind from racing, however. He liked Donna a great deal, but the pain of this meeting had made him cry. He missed Rachel so much sometimes that. . .

"I know," she said. "I feel the same way about Barry."

"Yes," he said, and wiped at his eyes with the corner of a napkin.

Then it struck him.

He hadn't spoken aloud.

He thought about it again.

"What the Hell?" he said.

She looked up. "Huh?"

"How did you know what I was thinking?"

She hesitated a fraction of a second. "Give me a break," she said. "You made it pretty obvious, Rick."

He stared at her. "I did, huh," he said.

"Well, yes," she said.

He put down his fork. "No," he said. "That won't get it. This has happened a couple of times. How do you know what I'm thinking?"

Donna took a sip of red wine. She touched her lips with her napkin, thinking. At last she whispered, "Do you remember where Barry and I met?"

"Yeah," he said. "At that fraternity party, right?"

Donna nodded. "Let me tell how I saw what happened and how the stuff affected me."

Chapter forty nine

Ten minutes later, Donna concluded her story about meeting Rachel and the drug overdose that changed her life.

"I see," said Rick.

"Yes," said Donna. "Dominick enraged me at the party. I guess I thought—oh I don't know what I thought. Maybe if one of us got hurt, we could stop this drug insanity. So I did the defiant bit, acted like a martyr. I should have left with Rachel."

Rick thought about this for a moment, again the pain of losing Rachel almost overwhelming him.

"She had a terrible experience, I remember," said Donna.

"Yeah. She spent almost a week in the hospital," said Rick.

"Barry and me too," said Donna. "I came to in the hospital like Rachel and Barry. Once I came down from the drug's effect, I seemed to be all right, at least in a physical sense. Never again in a mental sense."

"What do you mean?" Rick asked. He buttered a roll with idle preoccupation.

She hesitated a few moments. Then she told him, "I hear other people's thoughts," she shrugged. "If I'm careful I can will myself not to do it."

"Do what?"

She shrugged. "When I saw your eyes tear a few moments ago, I let down the guard I try to keep up. I heard you thinking. I felt so miserable for you and your loss—knowing myself what it feels like—that I used the thought channel."

"So you can send thoughts too?" She nodded. "Oh brother," he said. "So that's how you communicated to me this morning when I went out running? You thought those warnings to me?"

"Right. I realized I had the ability when I was in the hospital. I lay in bed, my mind spinning, and Dominick came in. He apologized for what happened."

"I'm guessing you didn't buy his apology?"

"That would be an understatement. I turned away angry and heard him say, 'Thank God I didn't take that acid. I'm glad I waited to see how they handled that stuff.'"

"Ah," said Rick. "No wonder he didn't wind up in the hospital."

"Right. I turned back. I said, 'What did you say?' He looked baffled. 'I didn't say anything. What do you mean?' I said, 'Of course you did. You said you were glad you waited to see how we handled that stuff.'"

Rick blinked. "Did he speak?"

"You take my point. No, he didn't say anything. He thought those words and I heard them."

"My God," said Rick.

"Uh, huh. He stared at me and I tuned in to his mind. He thought, 'Jeez, I wish I could get out of here. I've got places to go.' So I told him to go. I didn't care if I ever saw him again."

"I don't blame you," Rick nodded.

"Well, that freaked him out, as we used to say. He knew that even though he hadn't spoken, I'd heard his thoughts. He beat a hasty retreat—"

"To coin a cliché," grinned Rick.

She shrugged again and gave him that appealing smile. He thought, *Good grief, what a stunning woman. Charming, kind, beautiful, wonderful company—*

"Thank you," she said. "You've been very sweet. I know how hard this day has been for you. . ." She stopped. "Oh damn. You thought that, didn't you?"

"Yes, I did," he said.

"I'm sorry," she said. "I promise I'll try not to do it again. I know it invades your privacy."

He nodded as she apologized for intruding into his mind. "Never mind," he said.

She peered at him for a few moments. "You look a little worse for wear. Want to go home?"

"No," said Rick. "No, I don't. I'm sorry I reacted as I did. Tell me though. What happened to that Keith guy? I never heard."

"He died that night," said Donna. "The campus police found him not far from Noyes Lab on the quad. He'd overdosed on his own dope."

"The stuff he gave you?"

"Yeah," she said. "And it's always seemed strange to me. He saw what *one* of those doses did to the three of us. You wouldn't think he'd even try the stuff."

"Huh," said Rick. "Let me ask. Did you see demons too?"

"Not as such," she said. "I realized a few minutes into the trip that I could hear and see what other people were thinking. So the drug turned on a switch in my brain, too, though a different one than Rachel and my husband Barry."

"You just met Barry that night?"

"Yes," said Donna. "When we came out of the hospital, he asked if he could start seeing me. We fell in love and married that summer, you remember."

"How about the demons?"

"I saw them in Rachel's mind and yanked away. I also saw them in Barry's mind when the hospital transferred him to an outpatient center." She shuddered. "I never dated Dominick again, of course. Barry recovered well, but he'd also acquired the ability, like Rachel, to Step Back and change things."

"Did you ever see him do it?"

She nodded. "I'll always remember one episode," she said. "I went into labor early in the morning with our second child. He left the bedroom and went down the hall to call the doctor, looking very worried. He came back in a few moments. He said, 'Donna, I'm sorry.

I've Stepped Back.'

"That stunned me. He never used the Step Back. I said, 'What do you mean?'"

"'Things went wrong with the birth. The baby can't be born yet,' he said. 'You've gone into premature labor. You have to insist that the doctor stop the labor.'

"'Stop the labor?' I yelled. The pain of the contractions hadn't put me in a very good humor at that point—"

"I understand," he nodded.

"—'How can they do that?' We argued about it, but I saw his intense distress. When we got to the hospital, I did insist that the doctor stop the labor. He protested, but I told him I had started labor at least three weeks early. So they gave me the injections, and labor stopped."

"And the baby?"

"Terry—that's his name, you remember—" Rick nodded, remembering that he'd seen the young man several times at get-togethers—"he turned out fine, thank God," smiled Donna. "He came along a few weeks later, healthy, full-sized, no lung problems."

"Did you. . ." he hesitated to ask. "Did you have the nightmares, like Rachel?"

"Sometimes, though not as often. Talk about brutal. Well, I'm sure you can imagine from Rachel's description. I think Rachel and Barry had far worse dreams than mine, though."

"Visions of demons, eternal perdition, and so on?"

"I can still hear him waking up screaming."

"Did he ever do it again?"

She hesitated, considering. Then she shook her head. "Not to my knowledge. If he did, he never told me."

"Do you have any idea how many times he used the Step?"

"I don't know," she said. "I wasn't aware when he Stepped back."

"I wasn't either," he said. "When Rachel did it, I mean. Unless she involved me."

"Same with me," she nodded. "I don't think he Stepped more than a very few times. He wouldn't talk about it. And he told me that he could never talk about one of the times. He never would," she asserted. "Even at the end. . ." she choked up a little.

"Rachel told me the same thing. She told me that I could never ask her about one of the times she did it."

"Right," mumbled Donna. "Barry said the same thing to me."

They stared at each other for a few moments. "Look, I'm sorry, Donna," he said at last.

"You know what it feels like."

"Yes, I do."

They ate their dinners in silence for some time. At last she spoke. "The letters," said Donna.

Rick nodded. "How did you react to them?"

"Well, if they *were* love letters," she shrugged, "they have to be the least passionate examples of the entire genre."

"I thought so too," Rick agreed. "I can't figure out why they stayed in touch that way."

Donna shook her head. "I never remember thinking that Barry went out and had an affair. I have heard it alleged that women can always tell. I must be the exception to the rule."

"The letters read more like business letters than anything else."

"Yes," she nodded. "Have you given any thought to what Rachel might have done with the letters?"

"I have," he said. "If she didn't destroy them, she must have hidden them. But I moved a lot of stuff back from California, and I never saw anything like a secret compartment, or a treasure map, not even a safe deposit box key or . . ."

He broke off as she looked up. "What?" he asked.

"What does a safe deposit box key look like?"

"I don't know. I don't have one. . ." he got the picture. "You think you found one?"

"I found a very flat key in one of her last letters to him," she said, and reached into her purse for her key chain. She selected a small key and showed it to him. "It didn't have any directions for using it.

Other than these numbers, it doesn't have any identifying marks, either."

He considered. "Do you think. . ."

"I don't know. Barry handled banking and that sort of stuff, like safety deposit boxes for us. I don't even know where the bank would be located."

"Where did you do your banking?"

"First Marine, Oak Brook, before we moved to Whitefish Bay."

"Not far from here."

"No."

"Well, maybe tomorrow. . ." said Rick, but broke off as he realized the band had stopped playing to take a break. He looked up and saw two of the band members standing next to the table.

"Yes?" he said.

"Rick?" said one of them.

Now it clicked. He recognized the voice at once. "Steve? Steve Shay?" he asked. Steve had been the organ player and primary vocalist with his last college band. Rick hadn't seen him in years.

"Yeah," grinned the man. Rick rose and shook his hand. He introduced Steve to Donna, noting Steve's quizzical look. Rick guessed what Steve was thinking: *Where's Rachel?*

Rick invited the two men to sit with them. Steve introduced the other man, the band's guitar player, Roger Manning.

The conversation turned to old times and storytelling. Donna looked amused at the tales of the band and some disastrous gigs.

At last Roger told the group that the band had to get back to work. Steve invited Rick to sit in for a few numbers. "Yeah," said Roger. "I've got a second guitar you can use, a Fender."

"I haven't played much in the last several years," Rick said. "I don't know that I could keep up. . ."

"Aw, come on," Steve teased him. A moment or two later Rick nodded. He turned to Donna. "Would you mind if. . ."

"Not at all," she smiled. "I'd love to hear you play."

"Got sheet music for me?" he asked Steve.

"Of course."

Rick finished his dinner and ordered Donna some coffee and dessert. Then he walked to the bandstand. The guitarist unpacked a guitar for him, a nice Fender Stratocaster. Rick and Steve did a quick tune up. He tried to blend in to the background.

Rick played perhaps ten songs with the group, standards like *Satin Doll, Have You Met Miss Jones*, and so on, following the sheet music. The guitar felt wonderful in his hands. "Want to try a solo?" asked Steve.

"Not on your life," said Rick. "My fingers feel so stiff I'm having trouble moving them now."

Steve chuckled. "No way am I going to let you get away with that. Let's play *Hideaway*." He turned to his microphone. "Ladies and gentlemen, here's a great blues riff from John Mayall and the Bluesbreakers. We're going to feature our guest guitarist Rick Howell on this one. It's called *Hideaway* by Freddie King. Ready, Rick?"

With no visible way out of it, Rick gave a stage grin, turned on the fuzz tone on his amplifier, took a deep breath. He turned to Steve and mouthed, "I'll get you for this." Then he counted down and fired away.

The audience gave him a nice round of applause when he concluded. He bowed and said "Thank you," to them.

The band played a rousing version of *The Lady is a Tramp* to finish the set to the applause of the restaurant's patrons. Steve announced a break for the band, and the people applauded.

"Let me give you my card," said Steve. "Call when you can. I'd love to chat with you."

"Thanks so much," said Rick, handing the Strat back to Roger, who grinned at him.

"Nice job," said Roger as he shook Rick's hand. Rick turned to leave.

"Rick," said Steve in a low whisper. "This may be none of my business. . ."

"You want to know what happened to Rachel, right?" said Rick.

Steve nodded and Rick told the basics of the story. Steve's face fell.

"I'm sorry, Old Buddy," he said. "I've never seen two people more in love than you and Rachel."

Rick promised to call and bring his old band mate up to date. Then, after shaking hands with Steve, he walked back to the table.

Donna had left the table.

He could only stare, unable to speak when he saw who sat in her place.

Chapter Fifty

Rick pulled out his chair and managed to sit down. The whole restaurant seemed to have vanished from his range of sight and hearing.

"Hi," said Rachel. She looked exhausted and her face made it clear that she had difficulty speaking.

Tears rose. "Can it really be you, Punky?"

"Yes, but it's only an image of me. I'm at home in Palm Springs with you. I don't do this much. Step ahead, I mean."

"You've been doing the Step?"

"Lots, yes," said Rachel. "I'm so sorry. It's been necessary."

"What do you mean?"

"I can't tell you now, Rick," she said. "I'm so sorry. Please don't be angry."

He couldn't be angry, he knew. A tear started down his cheek. "Punky, I don't know what—" he said.

"I can see you're heartbroken. I take it, since you're here with Donna, that something has happened."

"Yes," he choked.

"Please tell me you didn't divorce me," she pleaded.

"No," he said. "We never divorced, or separated, at least not exactly."

She hesitated and cast her eyes down. "So that means. . ."

"You died two years ago," he managed to choke the words out. She nodded and leaned back, biting her lip, considering this information.

She looked up and murmured, "You moved back to Geneva?"

"Yes," he managed. "I took an apartment not far from where we used to live."

"What about the kids?" she asked.

He nodded. "Everyone's doing very well."

"How many grandkids do we have now?"

"Seven," he said. "Well, six, with one due in August."

"You're their father. Don't you think the time has come to explain what causes all these children?" Rachel and Rick chuckled at the old joke. "And everyone's healthy, happy. . .?"

"Yes," he said. "Our children have turned out to be wonderful parents."

"Donna just Stepped outside for a few minutes," said Rachel. "I asked her to give us about two minutes."

"That's all I've got to see you?" he choked.

"I'm sorry," she said. "Stepping forward is very hard. I'm struggling now to maintain this. But I had to Step here to see you. I have to tell you two things."

"What?"

"Since you're with Donna, I guess you know about the letters I wrote to Barry."

"Yes."

"He wrote some to me, too. I'm going to put them in a safe deposit vault in Palm Springs, that bank we use."

"Used," he said.

"Right," she said. "You can't imagine the value that they have. Also how dangerous they could be. I put something in them that people would kill for. In that horrid time line, Dominick and his boss tortured me to obtain them. You have to protect them. You can't let these people have them."

"What things are you talking about?" he asked, baffled.

"You say I'm dead," she said. He nodded. "Listen to me. You have to leave me that way. Don't let Barry try to Step Back to save me. . ."

"Barry died too, Punky," said Rick. "Someone murdered him."

She looked surprised. "Oh, damn."

"What happened?" he asked.

"Someone came after us, both Barry and me. We've been trying to stay away from him."

"Who?"

"This man has learned—maybe always known—that Barry and I could do time changing. He believes he can figure out what that Keith guy gave us that altered us."

"Yeah," he said. "Donna told me."

"I see," she nodded. Her face contorted with pain. "Okay, Rick. I just have time to tell you," she gasped, in apparent agony. "I love you—"

"Punky—" he began, but his wife vanished. He slumped back into his chair as his life collapsed around him.

Chapter Fifty one

Rick leaned back, stunned with grief. "Oh God," he said as Donna appeared next to the table.

Donna sat down opposite him. "Want a drink?" she said.

He shook his head. "No, that's the last thing I want."

"I'm sorry," she said. "I'm so sorry. You must be in terrible pain. "

"How did she find me?"

"I asked her. She picked this date because it's the anniversary of the day you met."

He thought for a moment, and realized she'd been right. He hadn't thought about it. "It's also the anniversary of the day she died."

"Oh, Rick—"

"No, no, I'm okay," he said, waving a hand to reassure her. "So how did she get here?"

"She told me that she thought about you playing the guitar. She heard you play *Hideaway*, I think, and remembered how much you loved to play that song. Anyhow, she focused on the music and came."

"Did she tell you anything?"

"No, not much," Donna said, shaking her head. "What about you?"

"Yes. She told me where to find Barry's letters. She also told me the letters contained something else."

"What?"

He shook his head. "She didn't say. Just that it has incredible value."

"Oh," she said, putting a hand to her mouth in surprise.

"What?" he said, surprised at her reaction.

"We ought to go get it," she said. "Someone killed our spouses because of these letters."

Now a little alarm bell began to ring somewhere in his mind. "What do you mean?"

"I haven't been honest with you," she said. "At least, not as honest as I could have been."

"Swell. Start a friendship with lies. Why would you do that?"

"Let me try to make amends now," she said. "Please don't get mad."

He looked hard at her. She met his gaze without wavering. At last, he nodded.

"Do you know anything about the danger?" she asked.

"Very little," he said. "Rachel didn't have time to get too specific."

"I imagine she wanted to protect you."

"From what?" he snapped. "Why would she care? She died, dammit."

"She loved you when she did that Step that you just saw. She loved your whole life together, you know."

"We can't be sure she didn't sleep with your husband," he sneered.

She leaned back, stared at her hands, and took a deep breath. Then, she asked, "Do we have to go back to fighting again?"

"Maybe. Why don't you tell me what's going on?"

She picked up her clutch purse. "I paid the bill," she said. "I took care of it while you met with her."

That surprised him. "You didn't have to do that," he said.

"Yes, I think I did," she said. "Let's get out of here. We have to go. Don't talk in the car."

"Where do we have to go?"

"First to your apartment, then I don't know where yet," she said. "We're getting out of town."

"What. . ." he stammered.

"You have to grab some clothes and a razor," she said. "Then we'll hide out for a while. We need some space to think and regroup."

"Now just a minute. I don't—" But she'd already risen to her feet and headed for the door.

Chapter Fifty two

His apartment looked like it had been turned inside out. Someone had pulled out all the drawers, his closet had been torn apart and the refrigerator's contents lay dumped on the floor. "Oh, brother," he said.

"Yeah, I worried this might happen," Donna said. "Pack and I'll do a quick clean up and put the stuff back in the refrigerator. Come on, hurry," she snapped.

Rick, dazed and angry at the invasion of his home, packed some clothes and a shaving kit. Donna came in the room as he finished.

"Have you got a passport?" she said.

"Yeah, sure, somewhere," he said, and opened a desk drawer. The thieves had emptied it. Rick and Donna scouted around on the floor and found his passport under a pile of tax returns and assorted receipts.

"Do you have a way to lock this place up?" she asked.

"I didn't set the deadbolt when we went out," he said. "They forced the other lock, though. Doesn't look like the burglars had a hard time getting in."

"No, very likely they didn't. That lock doesn't look too sturdy."

"But the deadbolt will hold, unless they drive a car through the door."

"Okay," she said.

He locked the door behind him. *I wonder when I'll come back*, he thought.

*Or **if** I'll come back.*

Donna headed the car out onto the main street in Geneva and told him that they were headed to O'Hare Airport. He noticed that she checked the rear view mirrors with some frequency.

"Wait a second. Don't you need to pack some stuff?" he asked.

"No, I'm all set," she smiled.

"You're what?"

"Rachel knew what would happen to you when she came back. She called and told me what to expect. No, not about the break-in at your place, but that you met me, where I was going, and so on. She told me the date and a little about what happened."

"You mean you knew all this would happen?"

"Some of it. Not where she hid the letters," asserted Donna.

"Why wouldn't she tell you that?"

"She may not have seen it as an issue. Not then, anyhow."

"Where should we go?"

"At this point, we're taking the first plane anywhere."

"Now listen to me, Donna. Damn it, I. . ."

"No!" she snapped. "You listen. In case you hadn't noticed, we've landed in a substantial amount of danger."

"From whom?"

"I don't know. Think about what we know, though. We married two people who could control time. They learned how to go forward in time in addition to going back."

"What does that have to do with us?"

"The people coming after us think that they can use me to find the secret of the drug that we took in 1968."

"How?"

"I'm only guessing, okay?" she said. "But it's what I've come up with."

"Okay," he said.

"That psychedelic stuff doesn't leave the bloodstream. You take that stuff and it remains with you for the rest of your life."

"But I didn't take the stuff. I married someone who did, but. . ."

"Yes, but I *did* take it. That means they can analyze my blood for the chemicals."

"Good grief, that would be astounding chemical work. How could they. . ."

"You have to think bigger. If they capture me, they can drain my blood, analyze my brain tissues and tear my body apart looking for the secret. And it doesn't matter how long it takes or how difficult it would be. If they get the secret they can become wealthy beyond the dreams of Midas."

"I don't see how. The damn stuff has been nothing but a nightmare for you."

"Sure. But suppose they manufacture the stuff. They give it to ten people, say children. What are the odds that they'll wind up with another Rachel or Barry? Someone who can leap back and forth in time? Think their way to other locations like Rachel did with you? Then, come back and report what they saw?"

"Don't be silly. The Steps cost Rachel her sanity. Barry, too, from what you said. Who'd submit to that kind of Hell just to make a few bucks?"

"Not them," she said. "They'd use somebody they kidnap or force, or someone they can blackmail."

"Yeah, but. . ."

"Think of yourself as unscrupulous with the ability to Step Back even a day. You learn the results of horse races or find out what stocks or mutual funds have done well, all manner of things. Then you bring the information back to the people who could bet money on races, or move money to stocks, and even more."

"Yeah. It occurred to me with Rachel that we could do that. The psychological effects of the Step would be prohibitive, though. I could never ask her to do that. . ."

"Did you ever have financial problems?"

He thought for a moment. "No, not really. I can't say we did," he acknowledged. "Things would be a bit tight, I admit, but. . ."

Then he considered. The times that Rachel would go into her depressions coincided with financial problems. He'd think they were in some financial difficulties, but then something would always happen, and they'd be able to pay the bills.

"Remember she wrote some company names on that sheet in the kitchen of your old house?"

"But. . ." he said.

"But what if that was a message to herself about what companies to invest a lot of money in?"

"No, it couldn't—" he stopped and thought.

"What?"

"Well, not long after we were married, her father made a killing in the stock market," Rick related. "It was like he had the Midas touch. He invested a bunch of money for Rachel, too, and we made out pretty well."

"We never had a ton of money either, but we were always comfortable," she said. She hesitated. "We'd always get a check just in time to bail us out of whatever financial difficulties we might have. Then Barry would experience those hideous nightmares. I know what you mean. It would be like a demonic possession."

"But they wouldn't abuse this ability, would they? I can't imagine that Rachel would, that's for sure."

"Neither would Barry," she said. "Unless, of course. . ."

"Unless someone forced them," he said, his voice grim.

They pulled up in front of one of the terminals at O'Hare. "Go in," she said. "Head toward the international terminal. I'll meet you there after I turn in this car to the rental agency."

Rick grabbed his gym bag, climbed out of the car and she sped off. He headed to the international terminal. Donna came in a few minutes later. She looked around until she spotted him and put a finger to her mouth.

"Come on," she said. She pulled him along until they found a ticket line for British Airways. Within five minutes they stood at the counter.

"May I help you?" asked the counter attendant.

"Could you put us on your next flight to London?" Donna asked.

"We have one to Heathrow in. . ." she tapped a computer

keyboard. "Seventeen minutes. Can you hurry?"

They assured the agent that they could. Donna handed the woman a Visa card and the counter attendant put two tickets in their hands in a moment. Donna checked their bags and they hurried through security.

"Did anyone see you?" she asked in an undertone.

"Hell, I don't know," he said. "Look, Donna, I'm no spy. I don't. . ."

"Shh," she said. "We won't stay in London. We'll go into town and register at the Mayfair. Then we'll come back to the U. S."

"Right away?" said Rick.

"Yes," she asserted. "Then we have to go and retrieve Barry's letters to Rachel."

"I can't. . ." he began.

"Shut up and walk," she said, taking his arm. "Don't look around. Just smile and talk like we're going on a Honeymoon."

The flight attendants stood by the door, waiting. Rick and Donna hurried into the ramp and boarded the huge jet. The attendants shut the doors behind them.

"Did we make it?" asked Rick.

"I think so," Donna said. "We were the last ones to board. The thugs don't know for sure where we're heading now, or when we're coming back."

The plane took off in a matter of moments. "Thank goodness we didn't have to wait on the tarmac or at the gate," said Donna. "Now, get some sleep."

"How?" said Rick. "I'm scared to death. I don't know who we're running from or anything."

"I know," she asserted. "Please. I can't tell you who's after us or how they found out about us."

"Us?"

"Okay," she shrugged. "I admit it's obvious they want me a lot more than you."

"Oh, brother," he said. "My life was going along pretty well until I met you. I. . ."

At that moment she grabbed him by the front of the shirt with her left hand. She turned his head toward her with her right hand and kissed him.

Sometime later, she leaned back. "Now," she said, as he inhaled, trying to catch his breath.

"Oh my gosh," he said.

"Does that mean you enjoyed it?" she asked.

"Of course I did," he said.

"Oh, good," she said. "I'd hate to think I wasted a kiss."

He leaned against the window and peered at her. "Did you do that to shut me up? Or to convince me to go along with you?"

"How about, 'I've been wanting to do that all day'?" she grinned.

"Okay, you're right, I'd prefer that," he admitted.

"Maybe we could spend one night in the Mayfair, huh?" she said, grinning.

He sat back in the seat. "Make that a promise," he smiled.

"We'll see," she said, as if speaking to a five-year-old. "Go to sleep, will you?"

"But I don't sleep on command," he said. "Not only that, I haven't been able to sleep much since Rachel died."

She sighed. Again she turned his eyes toward hers and stared into them. His eyes felt heavy almost at once. "What did you do?" he said, drowsy.

"A little something that comes with being able to read minds," she said. "Sleep for a while. You'll need it."

"Okay. . ." he said, and knew no more.

Chapter Fifty-three

Rick felt Rachel shaking him awake. "Not now," he said. "I just got to sleep . . ."

"No, you have to wake up," said another, unfamiliar voice.

Now it registered. He opened his eyes. "Good morning," he smiled at Donna. She looked fresh and alert.

"Hi," said Donna. "Good morning."

"What time is it?" he groaned.

"We're about to land," she told him.

"I slept that long?" he asked, amazed.

"Uh, huh," she said. "You did very well."

"Did you sleep?" he asked.

"Yes," she said. "I snuggled against you. It felt good. I'm disappointed you didn't notice, to be frank."

He grinned. "Okay," he said. "I presume you have a plan?"

"We take three cabs to the Mayfair, register, walk out the back and get back into the cab, and come right back here. I mean to say, back to the airport."

"Good grief," he said. "Don't you think you're being a little dramatic?"

"No," she said. "I've learned to be overcautious."

He shrugged okay. "Then what?"

"Then we go back to Miami," she said.

"Miami?" he asked. "Why Miami?"

"Do you have a better idea?"

"Well, no, but. . ."

"I've got an idea I'm refining," she said. "Be patient."

They didn't talk much while they deplaned and went through customs. They found a taxi and Donna directed the driver where to take them. Two cab rides later, they pulled up in front of the Mayfair.

Donna had Rick use his credit card to register for one night. Taking the key, they went up to the room and entered.

"You know something?" he asked.

"What?" she grinned.

"Er," he said, looking at the bed.

"I know," she said. "I've been thinking about that, too."

"I've had a hard time thinking of anything else," he noted.

"We could wait," she said. "I know a place in Miami—"

"I'm not sure that's a great idea," he said.

She turned and faced him. She put her arms around his neck. "What do you think?" she asked. "Would we be okay?"

"When does our plane take off?"

"Four hours," she said.

"We want to get there at the last minute anyhow, right?" She shrugged. "How much fun would we have just sitting around the airport?"

"Nowhere near as much as we'd have here, I agree," she said. She embraced him and gave him another of those incredible kisses.

"I'd say waiting is now off the table," he murmured.

She took away one hand and unbuttoned her jacket. "I have to warn you," she said. "I'm not very good at this." The kissing resumed as the rest of her clothes fell away.

"Hah," he snorted when they pulled back for a second. "Let me be the judge of that."

"Okay," she said, giving him that smile he'd always enjoyed. The kissing resumed as they worked on his clothes.

"I'm pretty far out of practice," he admitted.

"I'll be the judge of that," she said, shaking loose her hair.

"Perfect," he said, and turned the lock on the door.

Chapter Fifty-four

Three and one-half hours later Donna held Rick's hand as the third cab pulled up to the terminal. They went through security and hurried to the airplane. When they were back in the air, she relaxed a little.

"Want to talk?" she asked.

"I'm still recovering," he said.

She smiled and squeezed his hand. "You were a lot better than you led me to expect," she said.

"You too," he said, and put an arm around her.

"You know something?" she said.

"What?"

"I don't think that was just sex between us," she said.

"I agree, it was pretty special."

"Then I have a question," she said, making herself comfortable against him.

"Please present your question," he grinned.

"Do people fall in love at our age?" she asked, leaning against him.

"Why not?" he asked.

"Because I don't know when we'll be safe," she said. "We could be on the run for a while."

"Oh, brother," he said.

"We might have to hide for a long time," she said. "These people have been pretty determined."

"I see," he said.

"Rick, please don't be mad. I'm sorry I brought you into this."

"So you mean that's the reason that you and I. . ." he waved his hand.

"You mean did I try to bribe you?" she grinned.

He laughed. "I hope that's not all that was involved," he said.

"It wasn't," she said, and gave his arm a hug.

"Prove it," he said.

"Not in the airplane, Goofus," she said. "We'd be arrested."

He laughed. "Put me to sleep again?" he asked.

"I'm not crazy about that choice of words," she said. They both giggled.

Chapter Fifty-five

They woke when the airplane landed at Miami. Donna went into a store and emerged a few moments later with a newspaper and a package, which she took to a post office outlet in the airport.

"What did you buy?" Rick asked.

"Just a few things I needed," she said. "I sent some things to my son Terry."

"Where now?" he asked.

"What about a cruise ship?" she asked.

She led him to a cab, which headed up I-95 toward Fort Lauderdale. She led Rick aboard a large cruise ship called *The Summit* where they found a gracious cabin waiting for them. "I called from the air before you woke up," she said. "We sail this evening."

Rick continued to be amazed at the efficiency of this operation. "You're damned good at organizing things, aren't you?"

"I try," she said, a modest blush coming to her cheeks. "I've had some practice, too." He nodded.

The ship sailed late in the evening, headed for the Panama Canal and then to the West Coast.

They stood on deck, watching the great ship head out to sea. "Did Rachel hide the letters in California?" she asked.

"Yes," he said.

"In Palm Springs?" she asked.

"Uh, huh."

"Okay," she said. "We're headed to California. I don't think anyone followed us onto the ship."

"How could they trace us?" he asked. "Haven't we lost them for sure?"

"Maybe," she shrugged. "I've become pretty adept at throwing them off for the last two years."

"You mean they've been after you this whole time?" he asked. "You've been on the run all along?"

"Oh yes," she nodded. "Since Barry died."

"Why not before?"

"I think because I don't have the ability to Step Back, like Barry and Rachel."

"So—" he said, leading her on.

"I imagine they want the chemical combination that changed Rachel and Barry, not me," she said. "They may not know that we took the same batch of Keith's hallucinogenic."

"But your—ah—gift? Can I call it that?"

"I guess," she said, "though I don't regard it that way a lot."

"Anyway, your gift would be just as valuable in the wrong hands, wouldn't it?"

"Maybe," she said.

"How did they learn about Rachel and Barry?" Rick asked.

She shrugged. "I think someone set us up," she said. "That guy that I told you about, the one who came up with the formula—"

"Keith?"

"Yeah, him—well, anyway, I think he knew what might happen at the party. I think he gave us the same stuff, but I think our individual body chemistries altered the way the drug worked."

"You think this Keith tried it, too?"

She shook her head. "I doubt it," she said. "No drug dealer wants to take a chance on himself. No, I'm guessing he slipped it to people he didn't know and observed what happened to them before he went to put it on the market. I'm not sure he planned to have it work the way it did."

And now Rick understood. "He did this—altered you and Rachel and Barry—on purpose," Rick said.

"Of course it wasn't ethical or moral. But whoever accused a drug dealer of being moral?"

"Right," said Rick. "But why isn't anyone else like you?"

"The stuff might not have worked in its trial stages, you know," she shrugged.

"Yeah," he nodded.

"Anyhow I never heard of anyone else being altered after we took the stuff," said Donna. "To be sure, when Rachel and Barry and I came home from the hospital I didn't look very hard. At that point I still found myself trying to get used to the idea that some guy's science project had altered my whole mental chemistry."

Rick shook his head in disbelief. He reviewed the agony that Rachel had gone through, the horrors to which she had been exposed, the nightmares she dreamed each time she'd used the Step Back. "One more question," he asked.

"Yes?" she said.

"How do we pay for this trip?"

"Oh, don't worry," said Donna. "Barry left me quite well off, I have to say."

"How's that?"

"I have a huge bank account," she said. "Or rather, accounts."

He thought about that for a few moments.

"Do you think he—er—cheated with money? I mean, did he use the Step Back for profit?"

"I don't know," she said. "Like you, our financial problems would disappear from time to time. It didn't happen often, maybe once every five years or so, I guess, at the most. And like Rachel, he'd be a mess for a while with nightmares, horrors and depressions."

"Same as Rachel, right," muttered Rick. "What dreadful times those depressions would be."

Donna nodded in agreement. "So when he died, I found that I had a substantial nest egg," she said.

"You're rich?"

"Oh, yes."

"Is the money safe?" he asked.

"Yes, for sure," she said. "I hid the money in several different accounts. I'm the only one who can access them."

"Did you use off shore accounts and that?"

"Uh, huh," she said, "the Bahamas, the Caymans, and so forth."

"So I don't have to feel guilty about the amount of money we're spending here," he said.

"No, I wouldn't say so," she smiled. "Now. We'll need to rent you a tuxedo for a couple of the nights we'll be aboard. We need some other clothing, too."

"Where do we dock, then?"

"San Francisco," she said. "In fourteen days."

"Er," he murmured.

She put an arm through his and squeezed. "What's wrong?"

"I'm feeling uncomfortable," he admitted. "I'm going to be freeloading on you for two weeks?"

"Unless—" she began.

"Yes?"

She started to reply, stopped, then started again. "I've been thinking," she said. "How would you feel about marrying me?"

He did a double take. "Do you mean it?"

"Yes," she said. "We have a lot of things in common, don't you agree?"

"Like trying to keep you alive?"

She shrugged. "Well, that too," she said. "But I liked what we did in the hotel room in London, I have to say—"

"Me, too," he granted.

"—and I think I'd enjoy that on a regular basis."

"I also concur in that," he said. Then, he hesitated for a few seconds before asking, "Do you think we're moving too fast?"

"I don't know," she nodded. "Do we have some sort of a time limit?"

He chuckled. "Well, we have known each other for many years," he said.

"Yes, we have," she said.

"And we've always gotten along pretty well," he said.

"Yes, we do," she agreed. "Once we got past fighting," she added.

He smiled. "And we were good in the hotel room together, weren't we?"

"So?" she said, cocking her head to one side and smiling at him.

"Should we think about it for a day or two?" he asked.

"I've been thinking about it since we got away from those creeps in the park," she said. "I don't know about you, but I don't like sleeping alone."

"Me neither," he said.

"What a bore, you know?"

"You've talked me into it," he agreed. "How about the first formal night? I'll already be wearing a tux—"

"Sounds good," she grinned. "I like economy of effort, too."

Chapter Fifty six

The Captain married Rick and Donna two nights later.

They spent most of the next morning in their cabin, getting to know one another, exploring each other's minds, reviewing likes and dislikes. They came out for meals and in the afternoon, went up to the pool deck to relax by the hot tub and pool before changing for dinner.

Donna napped on a deck chair while Rick watched the passengers stroll by on the deck. He found himself thinking that a catnap sounded pretty good and he dozed also, covering himself with a deck towel.

He woke after perhaps fifteen minutes, refreshed and feeling alive for the first time in—what? Several years, maybe?

He had a hard time for a few moments understanding the emotion he felt. It had been a very long time.

He understood, then, that he felt happy. The danger to both of them seemed to have been put on hold for a couple of weeks. He stretched out his hand to take his new wife's hand. . .

He turned and looked. Donna no longer lay next to him. Her hat and beach bag lay on the deck chair.

Rick shrugged and figured she'd gone to the washroom. He stretched, stood up and climbed into the hot tub for a few moments. He chatted with two or three people who joined him there.

Ten minutes later, he looked over at the deck chair. No Donna.

He still didn't feel any concern, but more curiosity. He decided to swim in the pool for a few moments. The water felt cool against his skin after the hot tub.

Still no Donna.

Rick began to think about what Donna and he had talked about in the intimacy of their cabin. She'd mentioned something about a massage, hadn't she? Maybe so.

He climbed out of the pool and retrieved his room key. He picked up their beach bags and walked back to their cabin. He let himself in.

No Donna.

Now he became alarmed.

He tried to talk himself out of the fear. First, no one *could* have followed them aboard the ship. They must have lost the creeps on the way to London. If not London, then Miami. Rick himself didn't even know that they were coming aboard a cruise ship.

Think logically, Rick, he told himself. Okay, say the worst happened. Say some guys had followed them on the boat. They couldn't—wouldn't—have tossed her overboard. They wouldn't kill her. They wanted her blood, or her brain, or something.

And Donna wouldn't have gone without a struggle. For sure she'd have awakened him if someone had accosted her.

Also she had the telepathic ability, enough power to frighten them to death if necessary.

So where the Hell could she be?

Rick took a quick shower and put on some shorts and a tee-shirt. Donna had still not returned.

He walked to the front of the ship and looked around the majestic view of the bar. No Donna.

He didn't find her in the Thellasotherapy Pool either. Nor was she in the exercise area.

He went to the back of the ship and strolled through the food court, then walked through the pool area.

He didn't find Donna in any of those places. Damn.

He walked through the dining area at the aft of the ship and to the cocktail area. No Donna.

Now fear rose up.

He found a telephone and called the office of Ship's Security. The man who answered the phone agreed to meet him at the concierge desk on the fifth deck. Three minutes later, Rick arrived and shook hands with the director of security, a ship's officer named Amster.

The man listened to the story of how Donna had been napping on the pool deck and now seemed to have vanished.

"Do you have a picture?" asked Amster.

"No, I. . ." Then he thought. "Yes. Back in the room. We took a picture two nights ago after dinner. I also have her passport in our safe."

Amster nodded. They returned to Rick's suite where Rick gave Amster Donna's passport. Amster went to his office and made a copy, then returned the passport to Rick. He pledged to do his best to find Donna.

Three hours passed.

Amster called every hour or so. Donna seemed to have vanished.

Rick made his way to the buffet and managed to eat a sandwich. He returned to the room. At midnight, he fell into an iffy sleep.

At dawn, he jerked awake. No Donna.

She *has* to be on the ship, he told himself.

But if so, why wouldn't she contact me?

Why not use the thought channel?

He went up to the pool deck and into the men's locker room where he took a long hot shower. He put on clean underwear, cutoff jeans and a tee-shirt.

He didn't feel too hungry but he went to the buffet line for some fruit. He found a table on the aft deck and made an effort to eat. In his worry, the beautiful fruit tasted like paste.

Security officer Amster found him as he struggled to swallow some coffee.

"You okay?" said Amster.

"Yeah, for the moment," said Rick. "Any news?"

"No. Nothing," said the security man. "We're going to dock in St. Thomas in an hour or so. We'll bring the police aboard and attempt another search, okay?"

"Sure, of course," said Rick. Amster started to rise, but at that moment Donna's cell phone began to chime. Amster sat back down.

"Hello," said Rick.

"Let me speak to Donna, please," said a voice.

"I can't," said Rick. "I don't know where she is."

"Who am I speaking to, please?" asked the voice with more than a hint of suspicion.

"Her husband Rick," he replied. "Who the Hell is this?"

A momentary silence ensued. "Yes, I'm speaking to Rick," the voice said.

"What do you mean?" asked Rick.

"Excuse me, Rick," said the voice. "I'm your new Stepson, Terry. You heard me speaking to my wife Becky."

Rick relaxed a little. "Oh. I'm sorry, Terry," said Rick. "I seem to have lost your mother. We went out to the pool deck yesterday, and..."

"I know," said Terry. "She called me."

"What!"

"Yeah. She said I had to call her cell and talk to you," said Terry.

"I'm sorry, Terry," said Rick. "I'm not following this."

"Okay," said Terry. "Where are you?"

"On the ship," Rick said. "We're about to dock at St. Thomas."

"Oh, okay, right," said Terry. "I can see the ship coming in."

"You're on St. Thomas?"

"Yeah, Becky and I arrived here yesterday."

"What. . ."

"Mom called us yesterday afternoon," said Terry. "She told me to get down to St. Thomas. She went into hiding from some significant danger."

"So you came. . ."

"Right," said Terry. "We flew down here last night."

"Okay," said Rick. "Do you know where I can find your mom?"

"I can't be exact," Terry admitted. "She's hiding somewhere on the ship."

Rick felt indescribable relief. "So she hasn't been taken prisoner, then?"

"No, not a prisoner," said Terry. "You know she's up against some pretty rotten guys. Once you and Becky and I meet, you'll find her."

"How did she call you?" asked Rick. "I've got her cell phone."

"Not quite. You've got *one* of her cell phones," said Terry. "On any given day she has three or four of them."

"All right," said Rick. "So now what?"

"Come ashore as soon as you can," said Terry. "Meet me at the chair lift in Charlotte, when the ship docks, Amalie. I'll call Mom, and we'll have security go and get her."

"Why can't I get her now?" said Rick. "Or talk to her?"

"No, please don't insist," said Terry. "We sort of have a drill worked out on this. Please. Believe me and go along with this. You and Mom are in deep trouble on the ship. Please be careful."

Now Rick began to be a bit suspicious. "So how do I know that I'm talking to Terry? That you're Donna's son?"

"I understand your misgivings," said Terry. "We thought about that. We've got family pictures with us. You'll see."

"Just a minute," said Rick. "Tell me what happened with your birth."

"All right," said Terry. He related the story of his premature delivery, his father's Step Back to warn Donna, and his subsequent birth.

"Okay," said Rick.

"Good," said Terry.

"I want to talk to her," said Rick.

"No, not now," said Terry. "Please, Rick. Trust me. You have to."

Terry gave him directions to go ashore and where to meet them. "Bring a security guy with you if you want. I'd recommend it."

Rick agreed. "Terry, I haven't seen you in a number of years. Will I be able to recognize you?"

"I'll know you," said Terry. "See you in a couple of hours." He hung up.

"What's going on?" asked Amster. Rick did his best to explain.

"So when we get ashore, the kid calls his mom, she tells him where she's hiding, and security goes to get her and bring her ashore?"

"I think so," said Rick, nodding.

"Jeez," said Amster. "Are you guys some kind of international spies?"

"Something like that," said Rick.

Chapter Fifty-seven

Three hours later, the boat docked and permitted passengers to disembark. Rick, accompanied by Amster, went ashore.

They spotted a chair lift across from the dock like those found on ski slopes. Rick and Amster climbed into a chair and rode to the top of the mountain.

A man came up to Rick and spoke to him in Creole, a peculiar blend of English and French and several other languages. Rick didn't understand, but Amster grinned. "You can trust him, Mr. Howell," said Amster.

The man handed Rick a note signed by Terry. "Take the cab with this man," the note read. "Robert's a good man. He'll bring you to me."

Rick nodded. The three men walked to a parking lot at the top of the mountain. They climbed into an ancient Ford Crown Victoria taxi, and the driver set off.

Rick, despite his worry about Donna, found himself enjoying the drive. The driver spoke enough English to provide a coherent description of the island as they drove.

At last they came to a structure called Blackbeard's Tower, not far from the dock. "Why did you go all around the island?" he asked the driver.

"I had to see if anyone followed you, Mr. Howell," smiled the driver, speaking in well-modulated, articulate English. Rick's head jerked up in surprise, and the cabbie's grin widened.

Rick gave the man $50 as he exited the cab. The man nodded and pointed to a couple sitting at a picnic table not far from the tower.

Rick and Amster made their way over. When the couple saw them, they stood.

"Hello, Rick," said the young man, extending his hand. "Do you remember me now?"

Once Rick saw Terry, he didn't doubt the man was Donna's son. Rick took his hand and shook it. "Yeah, Terry," he said. "I guess I haven't seen you for a long time, since you were a child."

Terry grinned. "I know," he said. "I remembered you, though." Terry looked a great deal like his mother. He had a crew cut and was handsome and well-built. His wife, tiny by comparison to the young man, impressed him as attractive and pleasant. Rick liked them at once. "Nice to meet you," said Terry.

"Yes. Where's your mom?" said Rick.

"Turn around," said Donna.

Chapter fifty eight

Rick and Amster spun around. Rick grabbed her and hugged her. "Oh, jeez," he said. "You scared the Hell out of me, you goofy woman."

"I'm sorry, Rick," said Donna. "I know you must have been terrified. But I couldn't think of any other way."

"Your son called me on your cell," said Rick. "Why couldn't you?"

"They're monitoring the cell phone you have," said Donna. "I purchased a new one at the airport in Miami. They couldn't trace it. I sent another one to Terry and Becky by Overnight. I had to take precautions against what happened on board."

"What happened?" he asked, bewildered.

"First things first. Thank you, Mr. Amster," she said, shaking his hand.

"You're welcome, Mrs. Howell," he said. "I quite understand the difficulty of your situation."

"What on earth?" asked Rick. But Amster and Robert the driver shook hands, then returned to the cab and drove off, heading back to the ship.

"Let me re-introduce you," said Donna. "Rick, you already know Terry, and I want you to meet his wife Becky. They'll take our place on the cruise ship, at least until it reaches Aruba."

"We left the kids with Becky's mom and dad," said Terry. "They're safe, Mom."

Donna smiled. "Yes, I'm sure," she said. She turned to Rick. "Are you okay?"

"I guess," mumbled Rick, too bewildered to know what to say. Donna turned and picked up her luggage. She hugged Terry and Becky and said Goodbye. Rick also said goodbye, delighted with his new family.

Terry and Becky took a cab back to the ship. "Come on," said Donna. "We have a little walk. We can catch a cab in a few moments."

She stopped by the pier at the east end of the harbor and threw a cell phone into the water. "Give me the other one," she said. Rick complied. She threw this one into the harbor as well.

"Nice arm," said Rick.

She chuckled. "Now we catch a cab to the airport."

An hour later, their plane took off for San Juan, Puerto Rico. From there they would transfer to an American Airlines flight to O'Hare Airport in Chicago.

"Then what?" said Rick.

"Los Angeles," said Donna.

"Okay," said Rick. "Now tell me. What happened on the ship?"

She smiled and nodded. She embraced him and kissed him on the cheek. "I'm so sorry, Rick," she said. "I'm sure you were scared."

"Scared?" he scoffed. "Me? No, I wouldn't say scared. I just couldn't eat, sleep—"

"I know, I know," she said. "I knew how cruel it would be to you. But I had to do that, Rick."

"But—" he asked.

She waved a hand. "I talked to Mr. Amster not too long after we came aboard while you took a shower. I called and he came to the cabin."

"I didn't see him," he frowned.

"I know. I spoke to him in the hallway. I didn't want to take the chance that they might overhear."

"What do you mean, they?" he asked. "Who?"

"The first night we came aboard, I saw one of the guys you brained in the park. He didn't know I saw him, I'm sure."

"How could they have traced us?" he asked. "That's incredible."

"I'll explain," she said. "First, I had to concentrate on not letting my thoughts go astray."

"So you called Amster."

She drew a deep breath. "The second night on the ship, Amster had one of his men pass me a note at dinner," she said. "He told me to meet him at the entrance to the ship's bridge after you went to sleep."

"I see," he nodded.

"I told him about the gravity of our situation," she said. "He and I came up with this plan. He hid me and then brought you to the Tower."

"Blackbeard's Tower," grunted Rick.

"Appropriate, I think," she said.

"Why couldn't you tell me?"

"For the same reason I can't see my son and daughter very often," she said.

"This is intolerable," he said, erupting. "This is ridiculous. Let's have them arrested. We'll go into some program, like witness protection or something, until the police can catch them."

"No," she said. "No, we can't. They'd find us. You don't understand how relentless and desperate they are."

"But how—" he floundered for words. "How could they know where to find us?"

"I just learned how. Their leader. . ." she said and paused.

"Yes?" Rick said.

"Well, their leader has the same ability as I do."

Rick was stunned. "What?"

"Yes. I'm certain now he organized all this. His name is Rolf. I'd forgotten all about him."

"You mean the same guy who assaulted Rachel thirty some years ago?"

"Yes, in that alternate time line. This is confusing, I know, but apparently without Dominick's help, it took years for Rolf to find her and Barry. They managed to hide from him."

"But how?"

"I don't know for sure, but Rachel did tell me something important," Donna asserted. "That night they assaulted her in the alternate time line, she learned that she could shield herself from him. If she could, I imagine Barry could also."

"Did this Rolf take the same drug you took?"

"No, I think he took a prototype, much more potent than the one we all got."

"*More* potent?"

"Yes, it all but killed him. When he recovered, his mind reading powers became profound, even more than mine."

"And Keith slipped him the stuff, huh?"

"I'm pretty sure Keith slipped it to him on the sly. Keith didn't know what would happen at the time."

"So Rolf's been reading your mind? That's why we didn't lose them?"

"Maybe," she said. "He took the drug when Keith first came up with the formula."

"Can't they just analyze his blood?"

"I think they have, but no one could find any trace of the acid. So, more than likely, it lodged somewhere in his brain, like it did with Barry, Rachel and me."

"So he's cooperating with them?"

"More than that, he's the leader of the whole operation," she said. "I just figured that out. Besides, he's not what they want because the stuff was so potent and even more dangerous. Not only that, they want to know how to control time the way Rachel and Barry could."

"But with you—"

"Yes, the hallucinogen exists in me in the form they want. Not him," she nodded. "I'm certain Rachel and Barry asked to be cremated so that no one could violate their bodies. Believe me, they would have."

Rick shuddered and paused before speaking. As he did, a flight attendant leaned over their seat to hand them each a ginger ale and a bag of peanuts. When the attendant moved away, he asked Donna,

"Did you know this guy?"

"I knew that he was friends with Keith at the University of Illinois," she said. "I didn't see him again until I saw him on the ship."

She grew silent for a few moments, and then said, "There's something else," she added.

"Yes?"

"Did Rachel tell you about Dominick?"

He thought. "Do you mean the guy she—er—"

"Yes," she said. "In the alternate time line they had an affair for several months until he tried to kill her."

"Not a pleasant memory," he said.

She nodded. "Rachel and I got him out of the way," she said.

"What do you mean?" he asked.

Donna nodded. "Not too long after Rachel used the Step and saved you, she and I set Dominick up." She ran through the story of the night. "He received a sentence of ten years in prison."

"Why don't I feel any sympathy?" he noted with a wry expression of contempt.

"I know what you mean," she said. "We learned many years ago that he died in prison in one of the early years of his sentence. His death came in mysterious circumstances, almost for sure a murder, from what we heard. However no one could figure out who killed him or why."

"Huh," grunted Rick.

"The planet is better off without him," she said.

"That's for sure," Rick agreed. "How did you find all this out?" he asked.

"I saw Rolf on the ship," she said. "I didn't realize his importance until then. He seemed to be looking for me."

"So he can read your mind without having you in sight?"

"Yes. As far as I know, we've never met each other face to face since that night at the fraternity."

"I don't get this," said Rick.

"He's figured out in the last few months how to tune his mind into mine, I think, because of the hallucinogenic we have in common. I get the impression that he feels his way into my thoughts."

Rick shuddered, angered and revolted at the thought of someone invading his mind. She nodded, knowing why he reacted as he did.

"Anyhow I hid and waited until he passed," she said. "Then I tuned into his mind. I got all sorts of information in one sweep. It took a while for me to find what I needed."

"You weren't napping on the deck, then."

"I put myself into a type of trance, trying to sort through the information," Donna said. "When I found it, I knew that I had to go into hiding."

He got the picture. "So then you used your ability to put me to sleep. . ."

"Right," she said. "And Amster hid me."

"Keep going," he said.

"Amster's people waited until Rolf—that's his name, Rolf Montjoy—followed you and Amster off the ship."

"I see," he said.

"Yes," she said. "And I'd guess that he followed you onto the chair lift but you lost him when you started around the island. I'm sorry you had to go so far out of your way."

"Well, I sure didn't have much fun without you," he grumped.

"You're sweet, Rick," she smiled, touched to her heart. "We're going to have a long and wonderful marriage."

"I hope so," he said. "Do you have any idea how we can bring this to a conclusion?"

"Not at the moment," said Donna. "I hope that the letters Barry wrote to Rachel will give us an idea of how to resolve it."

"Do you know how many people this fiasco involves?"

"You mean with the gang?"

"Yes," he nodded.

"No, I don't know," she said. "I'd never seen those punks that attacked you. They don't seem to know what they're looking for, either."

"Yeah," said Rick. "I remember that the one thug didn't know much other than he wanted Rachel's letters."

"Figures."

"Could you have handled them that morning without me?"

She considered, and then shook her head. "I don't think so," she said. "I can only attack one of them at a time. I do know that they have trouble keeping people on my trail sometimes. If I see them first, I can give them terrifying visions."

"Like what?"

"Did Rachel tell you about her vision of Hell?"

"Yes, she did," he said, then got it. "Oh my God. You can scare them with that?"

"Yes," she said. "It stops them dead in their tracks, as you saw."

"Yeow," he said. "I understand why. What she saw terrified her so much that she never recovered all the way from it."

"Uh-huh," she said. "I can encapsulate it and deliver it."

He mulled this over for some time. "Let's change the subject. Where should we stay tonight?" he asked.

"I'd suggest we stay in a hotel near O'Hare and go on to Palm Springs tomorrow," she said. "They've got your apartment under surveillance for sure."

"That sounds like a good idea," he said. "Would we be safe?"

"I think so," she said. "Terry and Becky will stay in the cabin on the ship tonight, not coming out. The gang will most likely wait to move again until the ship gets to Aruba."

"But then they see Terry and not you—"

"I hope so, anyway."

Chapter Fifty nine

They spent that night at a small hotel near O'Hare Airport. Donna snuggled up to Rick. He realized that he'd forgotten how good it felt to sleep next to a beautiful woman. Leaving behind utter celibacy and loneliness filled him with more joy than he had felt in several years.

Then he jangled back to reality. Their lives were in danger. Donna faced a hideous death by vivisection at the hands of some unknown crooks intent on using the time warp to enrich themselves.

"Oh boy," he said as they lay together in the comfortable bed. "What have I gotten myself into?"

"You didn't do it," said Donna, stretching. "I take all the blame."

"You know, I've been thinking. . ." He paused.

"What?"

"I'm thinking I'd like someone to cover our backs, Donna."

"Like who? Who could we trust in this? Who wouldn't be motivated by the greed and the gold fever we've seen infect these people?"

"I've got the perfect guy, I think," smiled Rick.

Chapter Sixty

The next morning, Rick made a couple of phone calls. "Okay," Rick told Donna when he concluded. "We're ready."

After a quick breakfast at the hotel, they took a cab to O'Hare and found a 10:00 A. M. flight to Ontario Airport, east of Los Angeles and convenient to Palm Springs.

As they boarded the aircraft, Rick took one of the lunch sacks the airline set out for the passengers. Donna eschewed them.

"Why?" he asked, amused.

"Have you ever eaten one of those things?"

"Well, no—"

"Okay," she said, looking smug.

Rick managed to eat the yogurt and one of the cookies. He found a granola bar.

"You'll be sorry," intoned Donna.

He took a bite. "Ah," he said.

"Uh, huh."

"I see what you mean."

"Sort of like, oh, sweetened wood chips, huh?

"I would agree, yes, to a certain generic similitude," he conceded. "However, they're not quite as tasty as wood chips."

"Well, I hope you're happy," she said, indignation ringing in every syllable.

"What?"

"Now, the airline has to put another one of those things in the next bag. They can't reuse this one."

"I never thought of that," he admitted.

"Well, duh," she sneered. "Did you think they intend for people to eat them?"

"Seems farfetched, now that you say it," he said, with a sheepish expression.

"We all have to do our part to keep airline ticket prices down," she sniffed.

"I can only apologize."

The in-flight movie turned out to be something they'd both seen. Rick contented himself with the crossword puzzle in the airline magazine and Donna wrote some postcards to her children and grandkids.

Landing at the Ontario Airport, they waited to be the last people off the plane. Donna handed the packet of postcards to one of the flight attendants and whispered to her.

"What was that?" he asked.

"I gave her some money," said Donna. "Just a little something for her trouble, though of course she'd have done it for nothing. I asked her to mail the cards from their next stop."

They found a cab to take them into Palm Springs. Rick's cell phone rang a few minutes into the ride.

"Rick," he said. He listened. "Okay, we'll be careful," he said and hung up.

Donna looked up at him with her eyebrows raised in question. "They found us," he said, his voice lowered. "Someone picked us up at the cab stand. They're a couple of cars behind us. No, don't look. It's best if they think that we aren't hip to them."

He told the driver to take them to a restaurant. "Try to eat," he said, as the waiter brought their meals. "The creeps won't try anything in this restaurant. We'll force a confrontation later."

Donna looked frightened. "No," said Rick. "It's under control. Don't be scared."

She still looked a little apprehensive, but nodded and ate a fair lunch. "Better than compressed wood chips," she said.

"Much," he agreed.

They left the restaurant and walked into the street. "Okay," said Rick. "Head down this alley."

"What?" said Donna. "Why?"

"It'll be okay, I promise," he said.

They walked down the deserted alleyway about twenty feet. They heard footsteps behind them.

"Here we go," said Rick.

"All right, hold it," said a voice from behind them.

Rick stopped and pulled Donna to the side. Three men had followed them down the alley.

"What do you want?" asked Rick.

"She knows," said one of the men. "Hand them over, Mrs. Riske."

"I have them," said Rick.

The men looked surprised. "Okay," said the spokesman. "Then give them here. You can die nice and easy, Mr. Howell."

"Uh, huh," said Rick. "Okay, here's our deal, guys. If you want the letters, you're going to have to take them."

The men exchanged glances. "Give it up, Mr. Howell," frowned the leader. "You're good, we know that. But you can't be good enough to take all of us."

Rick put Donna behind him. "You have to prove that," he said.

The leader nodded to one of the goons who grinned and started forward. As he did, the sound of a whoosh startled the attackers. The man stopped and clawed at his back. Then he screamed as the full voltage of a taser struck. He fell to the ground, twitching and gasping. The attack left the others startled and confused for a second.

Rick moved on the leader as the taser hit, who didn't quite realize yet that the situation had changed. Rick's gym shoe clipped him just in front of his left ear and sent him spinning. The other man turned and ran into an outstretched arm that smashed his nose. He fell hard to his back.

In seconds, all three men lay on their faces as Rick and another man yanked plastic ties onto their wrists.

"Hello, Boy," said the man, his South Mississippi accent bringing a smile to Rick's lips as it always did.

"Boy?" said Rick, feigning indignation.

"You'll always be 'Boy' to me, Laddie," said the man.

"Donna," said Rick. "I want you to meet Colonel Noah Spencer. He taught me everything I know about martial arts in the Marines."

Donna stepped forward and hugged Spencer. She had tears in her eyes.

"Hello, Donna," said the colonel. "It's okay now. Breathe deep." He stood about five-nine, weighed perhaps 200 pounds, as solid as an oak tree. He hugged Donna with grace and warmth, comforting her, easing her mind from the violence of the fight.

"Where did you come from, Colonel Spencer?" asked Donna.

"I picked you up at the airport," said Spencer. "Rick here called me early this morning. Out of the blue, I should add, thrilled me to hear from him. Good man, this. Saved my life couple of times. . ."

"You saved me too, Colonel," said Rick.

The three men on the ground began moaning. Rick yanked out his cell phone and phoned the Palm Springs police.

"Scandalous," said Rick. "Muggers in Palm Springs. Imagine."

"Disgraceful," agreed Spencer. "If these three dolts were the best they had to send, you've got nothing to worry about."

"I agree," said Rick. "Talk about incompetents."

"See you soon," the colonel nodded. He walked to the other end of the alley, turned left and vanished.

"Where'd he go?" asked Donna.

"He'll stay close, don't worry," said Rick. "These creeps have no idea what they've unleashed."

"But he must be seventy years old," she said.

"I think so," said Rick. "He commanded our outfit during my last tour in Viet Nam."

"When you were wounded?" she asked.

"Yeah," nodded Rick. "After Rachel went into the hospital I called him and he helped me get back in shape. I spent a lot of time working out with him and getting my life going again."

Donna smiled. "Does he have a family?"

"Widower, nice pension from the service, retired from a security company of his own," said Rick. "But the company runs pretty well without him now. His two sons manage it for him. They make him look like a wimp."

Donna chuckled with him. The police arrived in the next few seconds.

"Jeez," said the first officer on the scene. "What did you do to these guys?"

"Cheap muggers," said Rick. "We plan to press charges, of course."

Getting the muggers booked took a little time. They'd be out of the way for a few days.

The watch commander spoke to Rick. "You may find this strange, Mr. Howell."

"What?"

"Not one of these guys has any police record," said the commander. "They haven't been arrested, none of them, for anything more serious than a parking ticket. Anywhere."

"Huh," said Rick. The news didn't surprise him, however.

Chapter Sixty-one

Rick and Donna made their way to the Charter Savings and Loan Bank where he presented the key Donna carried on her ring of keys. The security officer nodded and checked Rick's identification, and then led them to a vault. He pushed one key into a lock, and Rick did the same on his side of the box. They turned, and the large box slid out.

The officer led them to a small room, and told them to let him know when they were ready to leave. He shut the door to afford Rick and Donna privacy.

Rick hesitated.

"What's wrong?" asked his wife.

He turned to her and put his arms around her. "I need to know how you feel about this, Honey."

She hesitated. "I understand. Do you want privacy?"

"No," he said. He thought for a second about how much he'd come to love this woman. He still loved Rachel. Always would. But he loved this woman, too.

"Yes," she said. "Your capacity to love doesn't diminish when you love someone new."

"What do you mean?"

"The more you love, the more love you have to give away."

"You read my mind again, didn't you?"

"Not this time, no. I know what you're thinking."

Rick embraced Donna, stroking her hair. Within a week of meeting her, she had become the most important thing in his life.

"Thank you," she said.

"For?"

"For the hug," she said. "It means a lot."

Rick opened the box. They found a large packet of letters, all addressed to Rachel. Donna glanced through them. "They all seem to be from Barry," she nodded.

He set the letters aside. He found three small bankbooks and opened them. As he did, his jaw dropped.

"What?" Donna asked.

"I seem to be rich," Rick said. She looked at the bank books. The amount of money staggered her as well. He also found stock certificates and letters from a number of mutual funds, all of which listed him as the owner. Each statement reflected a significant number of shares.

"Where did she get the money for this?" asked Rick, mystified.

At the very bottom of the box lay a yellow-brown envelope, about nine inches wide by twelve inches high. He saw that Rachel had addressed the envelope to him. He lifted it and realized that it contained several pages and what seemed to be a video tape. Rachel had sealed the envelope with heavy cellophane tape.

He sat holding the envelope, not wanting to open it.

"Rick," said Donna. He looked up.

"Oh my God," he said.

"What do you want to do?" she asked. "The bank closes soon."

"Okay," he said. "We leave everything except this envelope," he said, holding it up. "We can come back tomorrow for the rest of the letters and the bank books."

"Sure," she nodded. "I agree."

Rick locked up the safe deposit box and returned it to the guard. Donna and he walked to the bank exit.

"I am dying to watch this thing," said Rick.

"I understand," she said, her voice muted.

Rick heard the concern in her voice. He stopped at the door and pulled her aside. He took her face in his hands and kissed her.

"Listen to me," he said. "I took vows with Rachel. They meant the world to me. I'm sure you felt the same way about Barry."

"Yes," she whispered. "Yes, I did."

"But those vows ended when she died. And yours ended when Barry died." She nodded. "I will always—always—love Rachel," he said. "I called her the love of my life."

"I know that too."

"But I'm going to think of her in the past tense. She died. Now I intend to think of you as the love of my life. I took vows with you that will only end when one of us dies. Nothing whatever can change that. Nothing. Nothing in this letter, nothing you say or do, nothing that happens to us. Ever."

She said nothing.

"Rachel put something important in this envelope. I know it."

"Yes," she agreed.

"It may be vital to us and to our children and grandchildren, you know that too."

She could only nod.

"If I have to die to protect you, I'm not afraid to do it," he said.

She looked up, a bit surprised. "I've died before," he said.

She nodded. "But Rachel can't come to bring you back this time."

"Rachel saved me, yes. She came to me when I needed her. She gave me the courage to stay alive and do what I had to do. That's a big difference."

"I know. But she loved you enough to give you all that courage."

"I can't argue. Now, you give me the same courage. If I have to, I'll face death again."

"Okay," she said in a very small voice.

Chapter Sixty two

They opened the envelope in a hotel room. Rick felt surprised at how nervous the event made him. He sat staring at the envelope he now held in his hand. "I'm afraid about what I'm going to find out," he said. "I'm sorry."

She squeezed his arm. "We need to get it over with," she said. "Then we can figure out how to get on with our lives. Our lives together."

"Right."

He opened the package and pulled out the videotape. He loaded it into the room's video player and turned it on.

After a few moments, Rachel's image appeared. She smiled and began to speak.

"Hello, dear Rick. I plan to hide this letter and video tape in the safe deposit box so that you won't find it until I'm gone for sure. I took the Step last night to meet you in the future. I try not to go to the future if I can avoid it. I'm sure you could see the strain it puts on me."

She choked just a little, but then pushed on.

"I am sorry that I won't be with you to see our grandchildren grow up. I'm sorry I'm going to miss old age with you. I'm sorry that I won't see you playing Christmas carols on your guitar for our children and grandchildren when we open presents together.

"But I'm glad for the time we had together," she said with a gentle smile. "I'm glad that you loved me, and that you didn't leave that night when my parents insulted you.

"I'm so glad that you married me.

"Thank you.

"I hope this letter finds you happy and safe. I left you enough money to pay for any care you might need in your old age, to buy Christmas presents, to take a cruise or go again to Hawaii if you want to."

She hesitated, struggling to speak without crying. "I hope you marry my dear friend Donna. I hope she loves you as much as I do and always will."

Now, she looked into the camera. She took a deep breath. "See, Rick, I never told you, but you saved me. You don't know it, but you did.

"The night that I came over to reintroduce myself to you at Kam's, you kept me from—well, from ending things. I mean, killing myself. That night I'd made up my mind to go one more time to see you. Then, I decided, I'd end my life. You can't imagine the state of my mind when we met: Horror, guilt, terror, hideous nightmares—all those things, all the time.

"I had saved up about twenty sleeping pills here and there. They would have done the trick, I know. I decided that I just couldn't live with the terror I experienced when I dreamed every night.

She wiped at her eyes. "I saw you and the band many times, not just at Kam's, but at other gigs. I stood off to one side and watched you.

"Maybe you weren't as brilliant as Eric Clapton, nor as inventive as Jimi Hendrix, nor as innovative as Wes Montgomery when you played jazz. I didn't mind," said Rachel, smiling at the four decade old memory. "I just loved to watch you perform. I've never forgotten the intensity and love with which you played your guitar. People listening to you felt your love for music and that passion entertained them. It saved me.

"I told you that I loved your intensity, and the way you used the instrument. It became an extension of you and your personality.

"You said that playing the music invigorated you so that you couldn't sleep. I remember the first time you said that at the diner in

Urbana. I almost told you then that your music kept me alive. It did. You kept me from killing myself as I'd planned.

"When you brought me back to my dorm from Mel Root's Diner after the pre-dawn breakfast, I kissed you good night—you remember? —and went up to my room. I sat for an hour, just staring at the pills. I tried hard to pray, even though I didn't know much about prayer then. I think I received an answer to that prayer.

"A few days later, when you broke it off with your fiancée, I carried the sleeping pills to the bathroom and flushed them. I tried to pray again. I think my prayers worked. I dreamed of that meadow again—remember I told you about the meadow?—and I felt safe. Safe, for the first time since I went to Champaign that semester."

Rachel hesitated. She again wiped at her eyes. "But now I have to confess what I've never wanted to tell you. You won't like this.

"I didn't tell you everything. In fact I didn't tell you the worst." Another hesitation. At last, she cleared her throat and went on.

"Do you remember in your hospital room at Camp Pendleton, I told you I had used the Step five times? I involved you in four of the Steps. You remember, I'm sure, that I asked you not to ask about one of them. You never did. Thank you so much.

"I didn't deserve that grace, dear Rick." Rachel paused. She opened the cap on a bottle of water and drank.

When she spoke, she didn't look at the camera. "I'm a murderer, you see."

Chapter sixty three

Rick pushed the Pause button on the VCR's remote. He and Donna stared at the screen.

"My God," said Donna.

"I know," said Rick. "But I was afraid the news would be something like that."

"Yes," said Donna. They stared at each other for a moment. Then Rick started the tape again.

***

Rachel nodded, and took a sip of water. "Barry and I killed a man together.

"Barry and I used the Step Back to stop forever the hideous experiments of the man called Keith. Like all dealers in the venom of drugs, he was evil, wicked and amoral beyond expression.

"By now you know that he never showed up again in Champaign after Barry, Donna and I took his latest batch of poison. Barry and I, as well as Donna to some extent, have been tormented for years because of the night Keith poisoned us."

Rachel again took a sip of water. She cleared her throat. "Just after I regained consciousness after the Acid trip, I lay on my hospital bed, just staring at the ceiling. I comprehended that things had changed in my mind, but I didn't know the extent of the change or what I could do.

"Barry came into my room about midnight, dressed to go out in the clothes he wore to the fraternity that night. Looking back, I think—I'm sure—he'd already made up his mind about what we had to do.

"He began apologizing as soon as he came in the room. He wept with remorse, in fact.

"'I don't consider what happened your fault in any way,' I said. 'I took the stuff. Donna and I had just about left to go home. We should have.'"

"'Me too,' he said.

"We talked for some time about how much regret we felt. We came to realize that Keith *knew* that we would become able to do things that humans were never intended to do."

"Then, he grew silent. 'Something else bothering you?' I asked.

"He nodded. 'Yes,' he said. 'I keep seeing other places, other times.'

"He shocked me, Rick. I felt the same way. 'I do too,' I said. "'Do you know if Donna feels the same way?'"

"'She doesn't,' he said. 'But something else happened to her.'"

Rachel paused and nodded. She sipped a little water before she spoke again. "I'm sure you know what Donna can do, Rick. She spent months learning how to control her ability and in some cases, her desire to know what others were thinking.

"'Did she take something different from us?' I asked.

"'No, I don't think so,' said Barry. 'I'm pretty sure it came from the same batch. It looks like the stuff reacts to individual body chemistry. It seems to work on each person who takes it in a different way.'

"We sat together for several minutes, chatting about the effect of the drug on each of us. I never told you everything about what it's like for me. Let me try now. I tend to see other times, other places, even if I've never been there.

"For example, when I Stepped back to try to save you, I thought about you, and I focused on your face, and I saw you on the helicopter landing pad. If I thought further, I could see you at all sorts of different times in our relationship. I saw you when I first met you, when you took me to the late-night party, the first time we made love—all of these things like snapshots.

"So it went that night in the hospital room. I saw my parents standing in the hallway two days before when I regained consciousness. I saw a trip to Disneyland in Anaheim when I must have been ten or eleven.

"All of these seemed far more vivid than mere memories. They appeared—I don't know—*real*. I could see myself standing there.

"Over the years I have tried to suppress this memory ability. I have to. If I focus on these memories for any time, I find myself there. I can interact with the people, breathe, smile—..."

"I hope that makes sense. I mean, these sights become more than visions. They become real."

She looked at her hands for a second. "I told that to Barry that night in my hospital room. 'Yes,' said Barry. 'I've felt the same way.'

"'Does that mean we can go to these places, not just see them?' I asked.

"'If you see things the way I do, then yes, I think so.'"

Rick knew his wife well enough to tell that she had to struggle to keep talking. He felt nervous, suspecting what she was about to say.

Rachel spoke again. "We sat together on my hospital bed, silent for a few moments.

"'Barry,' I said at last. 'How well do you know Keith?'

"'Not well,' he admitted. 'I know where he lives. I know his friend Rolf a little better.'

"'Does Rolf use this stuff?' I asked.

"'No, I don't think so. Rolf seems pretty straight. As far as I know, he never tried any narcotics or hallucinogens. Not even pot.'

"'And he lives with Keith?' I asked.

"'Yes, but keep in mind, I don't think Keith has ever tried anything either.'"

"'What?' I asked, amazed.'

"'Yes,' he affirmed. 'Won't touch anything, but he makes drugs in his labs. He synthesizes LSD, Speed, all that stuff. The component chemicals don't cost much.'

"'He must be brilliant,' I said.

"'Yes,' he said, 'In some ways. But morals don't hinder him at all, on the other hand.'

"'Do you know that for a fact?' I asked.

"'Yes,' Barry said. 'Oh, yes. Rolf isn't any better. He'd do almost anything for money, too. Remember what Bernstein says in *Citizen Kane*? "There's no trick to making a lot of money if all you care about is money."''

"We both sat for some time. 'They have to be stopped,' I said.

"'Yes,' said Barry. 'That's why I came to you tonight. Nothing will prevent Keith from giving this stuff—or even worse—to other people. He'll keep going. I don't think he knows what he created with us.'

"'What he created?' I asked.

"Then I understood." She sipped the water.

"Barry spoke the truth, dear Rick. We—Barry, Donna and I—had become monsters, like the Creature from Mary Shelley's *Frankenstein*. Keith had re-created our minds, re-engineered our brains, with immoral unspeakable science, all based in profit and not in a desire to help others.

"You make me feel, Rick, like maybe I'm not a monster. You love me despite what I can do. I love you for that absolute, unconditional love you always showed me—"

***

Rick again paused the video machine. "What?" asked Donna.

"I'm sorry," Rick said, tears on his cheeks. "She said something like that so many times. It always brought tears to my eyes."

"I know," she said, her voice soft. "It's okay." She stroked her husband's hand. He turned and embraced her until the tears faded.

Rick pushed the button on the remote.

***

Rachel spoke again. "'What can we do?'" I asked him.

"Barry stood, and paced the room. He started to speak several times, but couldn't get it out. Then, at last—'we have to stop him,' he asserted. 'We have to Step Back to that night. We have to kill him as he leaves that building. If we don't, he'll go home and make that garbage even more potent, maybe fatal this time. Then, when we get out of here, we have to destroy his laboratory, destroy his notes, his chemicals, everything.'

"I protested, but then he told me that two more people were admitted to the hospital the night before. They were suffering with the same symptoms of drug poisoning that we had. We both knew that Keith had infected at least them and maybe others.

"Barry urged me. He told me we were the only ones who could make things right."

"I hesitated a bit longer but I knew that he was right. Of course he was. We couldn't do anything else.

"'Even if he went to jail,' Barry said, 'it wouldn't be for long. He wouldn't be discouraged. And he would always have the knowledge of how to transform another person's mind.'

"I agreed. We sat staring at each other for several moments.

"'We have to kill him,' Barry said. 'Right now, before we talk ourselves out of it, and he hurts someone else. He has to vanish, also.'

"'But he already left the building, except in our memories,' I said.

"'Rachel,' he said. 'We can go there. Don't you feel it?'

"I paused for a few seconds because the answer scared me, Rick. I hadn't had the complete experience of the Step Back yet. But I knew.

"I sensed that time no longer presented a boundary for me. Neither did space. I knew that I soon would be able to go places and times that I'd never been, even."

Rachel paused, and took a sip of water. Rick noticed that she had stopped looking into the camera lens. "We didn't know how or even if we could go through with it, Rick. But I nodded. He waited in the hall while I changed into street clothes.

"Then, he came back in, took my hand and we Stepped together back to that night. We found ourselves standing in the street outside the fraternity house. I looked in the door and saw the crowd standing around my body, Barry's body, and Donna's too.

"What a nightmare sensation! I can't describe it. Seeing my own body lying there terrified and nauseated me.

"We didn't go in. We knew that if anyone saw us, they'd be traumatized. Lord knows we didn't want anyone else loused up.

"We didn't have to wait long. Keith hurried out scared and shaking, but grinning. We let him walk past us.

"Then, we followed him. He didn't see or hear us." Rachel sat upright. Now she looked right into the camera.

Rick listened in horror as his wife described the pursuit of Keith to the University of Illinois quadrangle, and how they waited for him to emerge from the Chemistry Building. Rachel told him about the confrontation. "'Hello, Keith,' I said, sounding cheerful and pleasant. He turned and saw me. His face—I can never forget what he looked like; horror, surprise, shock, anger—all of it in one expression. But then Barry grabbed him in a chokehold around his neck."

Rachel grimaced. The horror of the memory made her shudder. She breathed deep for a few moments before she went on. When she spoke again, she related how she and Barry had forced the ineffable pusher to swallow his own poison. "Well, it ended in seconds. Still Barry didn't let up until we were sure he'd ingested the chemicals. Keith died of an overdose of his own poison, his soul wracked with all those emotions."

Rachel sat straight up, and her face took on an expression of defiance. "God help me, I hope his soul burns with torment on the other side of the Black Gates for what he did to us.

"Keith sank to his knees, his eyes wide with terror. I stepped forward and slapped him with all the strength I could muster. Then Barry again grasped my hands and we Stepped back to my hospital room. We heard Keith scream as we Stepped away.

"The dreams!" Rachel shuddered. It took a second for her to gather herself. "I hadn't anticipated them. Oh, Rick—no description I could give you would ever allow you to imagine the horror. The demons dragged me to the Black Gates again and again, night after night. For weeks sleep became a terror and a nauseating experience of grinding misery.

"The day after we Stepped back to kill Keith, the police visited us. We found out that someone had witnessed what we did. This person, that guy named Dominick"—Rachel paused with a little shudder—"followed us and saw what we did. He saw us take something from Keith before we killed him.

"Then he went to the police and reported us. He told them that he'd seen what we'd done. He knew Barry, and he'd met me."

Rachel shrugged. "The police, then, came to the hospital and interviewed us. They asked us if we knew the man known as Keith.

"We told the police that we had met Keith that night for the first time, and that he gave us the drugs that had put us in the hospital. They asked us if we knew that he had disappeared. We said that if he'd died, that would be just fine with us. He'd altered our bodies and our minds forever.

"They questioned us about his death, Rick. We said something like 'We couldn't have been there. At the time you're describing, we were unconscious and being transported to the hospital.' They stopped questioning us almost at once. I'm sure they thought that even to suspect us would be ridiculous.

"When we got out of the hospital, Barry and I went together to Keith's apartment. We burned all of his papers, his books, and all the chemicals we could find. We did a very thorough job. I'm sure that nothing survived that related to his experiments—

"—Except for some pieces of blotting paper. I'll tell you more about them later.

"So we committed the perfect murder. Other than the torment we unleashed on ourselves and which we experienced for nights after that, the murder seemed flawless.

"After all when Keith died, Barry and Donna and I lay unconscious, confined to the hospital. As far as anyone ever knew we never left the hospital until they discharged us.

"I also don't think anyone mourned the loss of Keith except perhaps for one person. His friend Rolf began to lose his mind after

Keith tricked him into taking the drug. I'm not sure how Keith managed the deception. It could be that he spiked Rolf's coffee with the stuff, or injected him when Rolf slept.

"In any case, over the next few years, Rolf went crazy, psychotic. Vicious, and homicidal. He's gotten worse and worse, and of course no one can stop him.

"But he doesn't appear deranged, doesn't give any hint of his insanity. He became obsessed with destroying Barry and me—I don't know if he knew about Donna when he started. When he came after me with that Dominick character—" Rachel gave a little shudder at the memory—"I discovered that I could block him from my thoughts. I don't know why, but Barry could do it too."

"As a result he couldn't find us. He didn't know our names and addresses, where we lived or anything. Without Dominick to help, it took him about thirty years to locate us. That's when our lives fell apart. You couldn't know, dear Rick, what I had to endure. I couldn't confide in you, nor could Barry tell Donna. Rolf would have come for you, and you couldn't have defended yourselves, not even Donna with her ability.

"Because of his unique mental powers, he can get people to help him who would not under any other circumstances. He can cause them blinding headaches and create terror in them that people have never experienced."

Rachel paused, sipped at the water. "Donna, I know, can do some of this. She used to help me sleep when we lived in Champaign, and when we knew each other later. She also has the ability to encapsulate horrors to others.

"But her abilities don't match up to those of Rolf. I have seen him force people to assault me and Barry, people who didn't know us or care about us before he attacked them." She shrugged. "You remember that huge man who accosted us as we were leaving Kam's that first night? Who came to apologize the next day? I'm sure Rolf sent him."

"He's not above capturing those who get in his way, terrifying them, and coercing them to carry out his terror," she went on. "Do not underestimate him, dear Rick."

She held up the envelope, the very one that Rick and Donna had found. She removed a plastic bag. "In this envelope you'll find this plastic bag, which contains several pieces of blotting paper, the ones I mentioned. These pieces are all that remains of Keith's experiments. We salvaged them from his jacket the night we killed him and hid them so that we could retrieve them later."

She shook her head. "One of the things we discussed before we Stepped back involved those little squares. We realized that what we had in our hands could have enormous implications if they were placed in the right hands. We didn't know what to do, though. Neither of us had any background in Chemistry, since I majored in English, Barry in history. We decided to keep them safe until we could figure out how to get them into the hands of someone who could do legitimate, solid research into what the squares could do."

She put the plastic bag inside the envelope. "Those squares of blotting paper are worth far more than you can imagine. You mustn't let them fall into Rolf's hands. When we figured out that Rolf had picked up our trail several years ago, we hid the squares so that if something happened to us, he would never find them.

"But as long as you have them, you remain safe. He knows that we have them and that we've hidden them from him. If you protect them, you might be able to get him to bargain with you.

"That's why we kept them and didn't destroy them. They protected us against him. He knew that if he harmed us—or if he hurt you or Donna—we'd destroy the squares. He wants them, but he fears them, too.

"You can't let him have them," Rachel asserted. "Destroy them before you let him get his hands on them. I can't imagine what would happen if he began to play around with time. What paradoxes would he set up? How would he distort reality?

"I hate to say this. You may have to kill Rolf. Barry and I set out to do that when we found that he'd traced us. He has the capability of destroying someone else's mind. I'm afraid he might manage to do it to me or to Barry.

"I think Donna knows that Dominick died in prison," she shrugged. "I'm not sorry, but I'm pretty sure he contacted Rolf before he died. I also think he told Rolf that he'd seen us kill Keith and take the squares.

"The night he and Rolf tortured me, Dominick told me that he witnessed our murder of Keith, too. I'm guessing that Rolf fixed up Dominick's prison death, though I can't prove it.

"That last night when he and Rolf tortured me in the alternate time line, Dominick revealed that he was the one who witnessed Keith's murder. He couldn't manage to hook up with me in Champaign. So he came looking for me. It took him almost four years to find me. After all, he only met me that one night at the fraternity and only for a few seconds then."

"Barry and I talked about Dominick. We're only guessing, but we pieced together a scenario that we think describes Dominick's efforts to find us. He traced me through Donna, but there again it took a long time. He went to Culver, her home town, and found that she'd married Barry, and then went after us. He found out about you, and bided his time. He made a fortune as a drug dealer, and only worked this search for me and Barry part time. He had to find an opening. When he learned that you had died, he moved in on me.

"He hired some people to watch Donna and Barry, and me too. He found where I lived in Winnetka with Mom and Dad. He made inquiries and managed to learn when I planned to return to the Chicago area. When we met in Maine that summer, he found out and waited until I made my plane reservations to come home. So, he flew to Maine the day before, met the airplane and arranged to sit next to me. He changed his appearance somewhat—shaved the beard, changed his hair color, and so on—and set up the whole snow job."

Rachel shuddered. She sipped at the bottle of water, the rage simmering at the memory of Dominick's seduction.

"Donna will remember that I said that I never felt that he loved me. I'm certain that I never loved him. On the contrary, he had an affair with me only in hopes of finding those squares. I remember him questioning me about that last semester at the University and I told him about my studies, the dope usage, but I gave him no information about my ability to Step Back. He let the affair go on until he got frustrated with not getting the squares and summoned Rolf to help him." She shuddered at the memory.

"Since you are reading this letter, I think all my fears have been realized. Barry and I joined forces and Stepped to several places to try to find Rolf and stop him. We have had only indifferent results."

Rachel pointed a finger at the camera. "Rick," she said in a forceful voice, "I want you to know this now: I never had an affair with Barry, nor did I ever love him. I'm so sorry I didn't tell you and ease your mind. But I couldn't tell you about all this. I just couldn't. I didn't want you to know about this when I joined forces with Barry to fight Rolf."

Now she relaxed and gave a little smile which displayed her great affection for her husband. "I know you. You would have tried to help, tried to rescue me. I love you for your loyalty and your courage.

"But you couldn't have fought Rolf," she said, shaking her head for emphasis. "He would have turned you to his side with ease.

"I lived in appalling danger for that one horrible year until we moved to Palm Springs, where, I gather, I died. Barry and I had to Step Back several times to hide ourselves from him. We couldn't be present when Rolf found us.

"That also explains why you have all the money." She held up a couple of little bank books. "Each time I Stepped back, I took with me some knowledge of stock market successes or investments. Barry and I both set up a war chest. So yes, we began to Step Back to make a profit. I never shared the money with you. If I had, you would have known what was happening, because I would have had to tell you.

"We hoped that we could find Rolf and destroy him before he found us.

"I gather, since I'm dead, that we didn't succeed. But he can't be stopped by ordinary assassins or a rifle. He senses danger and he knows when we come for him. On at least three occasions we've just seen him and Stepped away before he could paralyze us. I cannot overemphasize the terror of one of his assaults.

"I'll give you an analogy. You told me once that when you took our daughter Cara on an Indian Princess camp-out, the camp allowed your group to build a huge campfire, using some old picnic tables they wanted to get rid of. I'm sure you remember. Cara never forgot the experience, anyhow.

"Imagine, though, that you had to jump through that fire to be safe. Perhaps that can give you the feeling for what we did on those three occasions. We had to leap through the hideous flame of his mental shocks to a safer time.

"You caught me that one time in the kitchen of our old house, remember? It was such a thrill to see you as a young man again.

"Now you have the money. I hid it well, beyond Rolf's ability to find it."

She dropped the bank books into the envelope. Then she went on. "Don't try to shoot Rolf or poison him—he'll know what you're trying to do. Nonetheless, somehow, you have to destroy him. His mind—his conscience—whatever was good in Rolf has been warped. I don't know if he can be retrieved.

"Don't see the horror as Rolf's fault. He didn't ask for this hideous result. His nefarious roommate wounded his mind beyond earthly redemption. I don't think anything can help Rolf on this side of eternity. He deserves our pity, of course. But that can't change how you approach him.

"You have one resource. Donna can shield both of you with her ability. She can put a blanket of mental protection around your mind. But even she cannot sustain such a protection for long.

"You have to protect yourself, too. Please be careful."

Now she looked into the camera and again lifted her finger. "Rick: whatever you do, do not be tempted to ingest one of the squares. You cannot anticipate what will happen and how your mind will be altered. Drugs change everyone who takes them. The results have always been far too unpredictable to justify the use of such things. You know that as a teacher I saw many children whose lives were destroyed, either in a direct way or indirect way, by the use of drugs.

"My life would have been ruined if you hadn't saved me. Bless you always.

"As I told you. Do not try to rescue me. Let me rest. I believe that I am safe, beyond the reach of the hideous creatures. I took some Steps to ensure that.

"Remember these words. I know what's coming. I am not afraid. And no matter what happens I shall always love you. Goodbye, Rick."

Rachel held up a remote, aimed it and pressed a button.

Rick watched her picture fade away.

Chapter Sixty four

Rick and Donna sat for some time, staring at the television, aghast and bewildered and saddened all at once.

"Are you okay, Rick?" she asked.

"I will be," he said.

"So," Donna said. "Any ideas?"

"None," he admitted. "I have no idea where to start."

"Barry didn't leave me a letter like this," she said. "I wish he had. I wish I'd known what they were up against. Maybe I could have helped—"

"No," he interrupted. "They did everything they could to protect us from Rolf. Rachel thought I shouldn't even know about things until she died. She even let me think that she had an affair so that I wouldn't ask—"

Tears choked him for several moments. He hadn't communicated with his wife Rachel for years—two years in the asylum, two more since she'd died. Then he'd seen her in a restaurant for just a few tantalizing moments. Now he'd just seen a video made when she still was beautiful, still had her sanity, and was trying her best to protect him.

"So," he said, "It looks like this Rolf destroyed them, doesn't it?"

"Yes," said Donna. "I think he stole their minds, Rachel's worse than Barry."

"Why couldn't he learn where they hid the squares?" Rick asked. "He should have been able to rip their minds open like tissue paper."

"No, I don't think he could," Donna said, shaking her head. "I think they had a great deal of immunity to his probes, though he could launch attacks. They'd figured out how to shield their brains in some areas. I couldn't read either one of them when they didn't want me to do so."

"Hmm," said Rick.

"Your security men could be in serious jeopardy, though. Rolf can smack people very hard."

"Yeah. Somehow we have to warn them not to approach this guy."

"Agreed," said Donna. "You should call Colonel Spencer at once and get this picture of Rolf to him." She pulled a photo from her purse.

Rick glanced at it. Rolf, a small man, had bright red hair and oversized glasses. Nor could he at all be described as handsome, Rick noted.

"How did you get this picture?" he asked Donna.

"I can shield myself pretty well from him, you know," she said. "I snapped that picture with my cell phone aboard the ship last week. He doesn't know I took it."

"Do you have others?"

"Yes, Mr. Amster printed up several copies for me."

"Okay. We give this to the security guys and tell them to stay away from him at all costs," Rick said.

"Without any doubt," she said. "If they know what he looks like, they can run away when they see him."

"Donna," he said. "Could he be tuning into you without you knowing it? Could that be how this crew has known everything we're doing?"

Donna thought. "I don't know. I've tried to hide everything I can from them, but they've found us. He may have learned to tune into me somehow."

"But he didn't see you on the ship. . ."

"I don't think so," she said, shaking her head. "But I can't overlook the possibility that he set me up, that he gave me inaccurate or misleading information."

"Why didn't he come after me?"

"I don't know for sure. Those guys you beat up may have told him that you don't have the letters. That's just a guess."

"Hmm."

They continued to look through the packet. They found a plastic bag. Inside, they saw several pieces of red blotting paper.

Donna's face went white. "Yes," she said. "That's how I remember they looked. The potion turned the center a little darker than the rest of the square."

"Donna," he said.

She turned to him.

"I think I get it," he said. "You've been wrong. They never wanted to submit you to vivisection."

"What?"

"No," he said. "That would have been silly, even with the best of forensic efforts. What they want—what they've always wanted—were these squares."

She stared at him. He saw her struggling to re-orient her thinking. "Could that be. . .?"

"I think so." He took the envelope and turned it over. Something fell out.

Another envelope addressed to Donna lay in the larger envelope. "What on earth?" she asked.

"Open it," Rick said.

Donna opened the slim envelope. A single page was inside.

"It's from Rachel," she said, mystified. She began to read.

Dear Donna,

If you're reading this, you're still alive and Rolf didn't get you. I think I can help you strengthen your shield, if you're willing. I know that you work hard to protect yourself and others from falling into the trap of using the gift. I don't blame you. But let me tell you what Barry and I have learned.

The power—yours and ours and Rolf's—increases with use. You get stronger in the ability until the power gets more and more pronounced, I mean.

I hope you saw my video to Rick. If you have, you know that I am okay with you and him together. I'm sure you can imagine the pain it costs me to write those words, but I mean it. I am gone, and you remain. I will not allow myself to be jealous. I had many years of feeling secure with him.

Please take steps to make yourself stronger. Please. I don't think that you can fight Rolf as your ability stands now.

Rick will protect you. I can't explain why, but I know it to be true. When I'm with him, I feel safe. No—I am safe. I can't explain his strength, his ability to help. You will see it as you go.

Somehow, I believe it has to be related to his music. Please consider this idea and see if you agree. I never had the opportunity to try it out for fear that I would involve him in this horror. I believe that you two now have to fight your way free of this monstrous calamity.

Now. Practice. Work hard. Start to project more. You must.

I can feel Rolf pulling my sanity from me, trying to destroy me. Rolf has become strong enough so that he doesn't need to see me or Barry. In recent days he's become able to attack our minds even when we don't see him. He's assaulting us as I write. He'll get me, soon. But I can shield the knowledge of where I'm going to hide this envelope and the bank books even though it costs me everything. I know you can understand.

Please do not let Rick take the psychedelic. It would be like him to chance everything so that he can learn to Step Back. You must not let him. Instead make him concentrate on protecting you and eliminating Rolf.

Love, your friend, Rachel.

Donna folded the letter. They stared at one another.

Chapter sixty-five

"So?" said Donna.

"She's right," Rick said. "I'm thinking about taking one of these things."

"No," she said. "No, I forbid it."

He looked up, surprised. "You forbid it?"

"You cannot," she said. "It would destroy you for days under the best of circumstances. You'd need to be hospitalized and we can't afford that time now. Your brain would experience permanent alteration, like me, like Rachel, Barry and the others. Nor do we know what the result could be. You might be able to Step, yes, or maybe learn to read minds.

"But those may not be the only possibilities," Donna continued. "What if you acquire some other, even more frightening ability? No, Rick. No, you mustn't."

"Donna, don't you see. . ."

"I see more than you know or can imagine," she said. "You never went in for the horror of drugs. You can't start now. Furthermore, you're a lot older than we were when we took them. Yes, I know, you're in fine condition, but this would affect you even more now."

"But. . ."

"But think of the terror, the vision of Hell that both Barry and Rachel had," she said. "Not just the effect of the drug. You know yourself that Rachel had a terrible time sleeping for years. No, don't put yourself in the hands of the Enemy."

"Okay, maybe," he sulked, a bit sulky.

She softened a little. "You made a lifetime vow a few nights ago," she whispered. "We have a future, we do, I promise. Don't go to the past. Help me and take care of me here."

He embraced his wife. "All right," he said. "I promise." Donna returned the hug and kissed his cheek. He kissed her—

And they made love.

They had done it before and both had enjoyed it, but now something different, even extraordinary happened. The sex became almost violent as two people united with one another in a struggle to build a future of love and respect and mutual admiration. They clutched at one another, desperate to find the rhythm of their own marriage to one another, to let the past be still, to focus on one another for the rest of their lives, to surrender, to please, to supplicate and draw forth joy from the other. The intercourse transcended mere physicality and became spiritual.

As they reached the height of the passion, two abandoned and heartbroken people said goodbye to what had bound them elsewhere and found a new path, a communal power that gave them a mutual joy, an ecstasy, wherein all stress, anger, bitterness and loneliness disintegrated.

They said goodbye to what had been. They became a single unit, joined and bound together.

The lovemaking didn't end when the sexual climax came for both. They continued kissing, embracing and murmuring love to one another for some time.

When they drew back, they lay next to each for several minutes, not willing to let the passion go.

"Hi," Donna said at last.

He caressed her breast and kissed her again. "Hi," he said.

"Thank you," she said.

"I know what you mean," he smiled back. "You're welcome." She nodded with a smile and ran her fingers through his hair, and drew his mouth to hers.

They kissed and embraced while reality returned.

At last he drew a breath. "Let's figure this thing out now. How can we stop this Rolf guy?"

"I don't know," she said. "But Rachel always knew you could protect her. Something about you scared them."

"It can't be martial arts, or weapons," he reasoned. "This Rolf could demolish me before I could get a hand on him."

"Right," she said. She drew a breath and let it out. "You said that she always knew you could protect her. Even from the first time she saw you."

"True," he agreed. "That would have been when she saw me playing with a band at Kam's at the U of I."

"Were you doing something that stood out that night?"

"She never said, but I assume singing and playing my guitar."

"Of course," Donna nodded.

"Can you think of any circumstances under which you can't read someone?" Rick asked.

"I'm trying," she said.

"Let's think about that music thing Rachel mentioned to you," he suggested. "What do you make of that?"

Donna sat up in the bed and thought. "You know," she said. She paused, thinking through what she was going to say. "That night at the restaurant, I sat watching you play when the group invited you to join in. I remember that I focused on you as you were playing for a few moments. I wanted to hear the music through your mind."

"What?" he chuckled. "Do you think music sounds different for me?"

"I didn't know," she admitted. "But I haven't known too many musicians in my life. I don't have a tin ear by any means, but I don't have the hands to make music. Paint, write, yes, but not make music."

"Not tracking," he said. "Better spell it out."

"I couldn't hear what you were thinking," she said.

Rick lifted his eyebrows in surprise. "But why?"

"Because of the music," she said. "I think that's it."

"Was it like—I don't know—interference?"

"In a way," she agreed. "I'd get bits and snatches of thoughts, but nothing complete. That's odd because for the most part I have no trouble hearing your thoughts when I let myself do it."

"That's interesting," he said. "Could that be why our lovemaking just got so intense?"

She smiled. "Maybe," she said. "You remember that Rachel said—she said it to me, in fact—the demons feared you for some reason."

"Yeah," he said, drawing out the word. "I remember it well. I can't think why. . ."

"I think it might have to do with music, or perhaps with sound somehow."

"Huh?"

"Yeah," said Donna. "On the ship I had quite a bit of time to consider you. I sat in that cabin reading, eating the meals Amster brought to me, and so forth. I remember how worried you were. I've been able to focus on you well since the first time we made love. It continues to get stronger."

"Huh?" he said, aware that he sounded like an idiot but not sure what to do about it.

"Look, I don't know what to make of the sound thing. I don't recall that happening before. I've never been around an artist before."

"An artist," he said, a bit surprised. "I'm just a hack guitarist. I don't even play all that well, to tell the truth."

"I don't think the quality affects it," she said. "I think it may have to do with your concentration."

"Interesting," he said. "But did the sound of the band interfere?"

Now she lifted an eyebrow. "That might be something. I do have a harder time reading someone with sound present."

"I wonder. . ." he said.

"What?"

"Could we block the ability to read minds with sound?"

"Hmm."

Rick leaned over and turned on the radio. He found an oldies station, playing something from Tommy James and the Shondells. "Try," he said. He thought of a trip to Kauai, visiting the Grand

Canyon of Waimea, the drive. . .

Donna's face screwed up. "Huh," she said.

"What did you get?"

"A blur," she said. "I had the impression of the ocean maybe. . ."

"I thought about Kauai. I took Rachel there for our twenty-fifth anniversary."

"I think we might be on to something, then," she said. "I can read you pretty well for the most part, but not then."

"Look," he said. "What if we would go someplace where sound could present a problem?"

"Like where?"

He turned the radio up. "Okay, I think I have an idea."

Chapter Sixty six

The plane landed at Cancun the next afternoon. Rick and Donna hurried through Mexican immigration and took a bus to a pleasant hotel called the RIU Playacar in the Mayan Sun Coast region south of Cancun. That evening they enjoyed a meal while chatting and relaxing with other guests. The bartender recommended a drink called a Tequila Boom-boom.

Donna watched in amusement as the bartender poured a shot of tequila into a tall shot glass, then added grenadine and soda. The bartender covered the top with his hand and smacked the glass hard onto the table.

"Quick," he said, handing Donna the glass. She threw the strange mixture down while Rick applauded. Then he took his turn.

One hour and several Tequila Boom-booms later, they staggered into their room.

"Now what?" Donna asked. Rick reached over and turned on a transistor radio.

"You think he knows we're here?" Rick asked. "You did think about coming here enough to tip him off, right?"

"I'm sure," she said. "The security at this place appears excellent, so we should be ready."

"Do you think he suspects a trap?" asked Rick.

"No way to tell," she said. "I can't read him."

"Yeah," he said.

She nodded. He saw her apprehension about what they intended to do in the morning and enfolded her.

They found a bus tour to the ancient Mayan city of Chichen-Itza the next morning. The tour director said that many people would accompany them on the bus. "Though the ride takes about four hours," he told them. "You will find your visit to the ruins far more than worth it."

"I know," said Rick. "I've been there and I've told her about it."

The tour director told them that they didn't need to walk around with the group, of course not.

The bus ride was unusual but striking. Rick napped on the way, though Donna, who hadn't slept much the previous night, remained too agitated to relax.

When the bus arrived at Chichen-Itza, Rick and Donna made their way to the temple which dominated the park. "Go up to the top," he said.

"Look at these steps, Rick," she said. "Our feet won't fit on them."

"Walk serpentine to the top," he suggested.

The steps worked fine when they negotiated them in that fashion. They climbed to the top of the pyramid, the Temple of the Sun. "Now what?" said Donna.

"Now, we wait," he said.

Chapter Sixty seven

An hour passed. Then two.

The tour groups had departed and the sun had almost set when Rick and Donna emerged from the Sun Temple, headphones in place. "What are you listening to?" asked Donna.

"The Byrds," said Rick. "You?"

"Motown," Donna smiled, and adjusted the volume on her I-Pod. She pointed to the ground at the bottom of the Temple of the Sun.

Now four men came forward and stood at the bottom of the steps. One of them shouted up at them.

"Come on down," he yelled.

"No," said Rick, speaking in an ordinary voice. The man looked taken aback that he could hear without difficulty.

"The acoustics here will surprise you, I know," said Rick. "Just talk in a normal tone of voice."

"You're trapped, Mr. Howell," the man said. "If you come down and assume the position, we'll make it quick."

"No," said Rick. "You don't get it. We've trapped you."

"Don't make us come up there, Pardner," said the man.

"If you want us, you'll have to," said Rick.

"Then you die a miserable death," said the man. "I'll take my time killing you. I'll enjoy it."

"Uh, huh," said Rick. "Let me make you a counter offer. You could make it easier on yourself if you ask your boss to come here. We'll meet with him."

The men glanced from one to another in surprise.

"He won't come," said the man.

"Then you have to come up and get us," said Rick. "And you can't imagine what my wife will do to you while you make the climb up here. Again: We'll meet with him."

The men stood at the bottom of the pyramid and talked things over.

"Guys, we're not offering you a choice," said Rick. "Show him, Honey."

Rick almost felt the nightmare singe the air as it shot from Donna's mind to the leader. In the next instant, the man fell to his knees, bellowing with pain and terror. The others backed up, afraid to touch him.

A few long moments later, Donna released the man. He slumped to the ground and vomited, the horror of the vision overcoming him for a few more moments.

"Anyone else?" asked Rick.

"Okay, Mr. Howell," said one of the others. "We'll try."

Two of the men departed, the leader being supported by the other, still not coherent. Two others stayed behind to guard the ancient Mayan Temple of the Sun.

"What did you hit him with?" he asked.

"A little vision of the Gates of Hell," she said. "The visualization of mankind's worst nightmare terrifies most people."

He chuckled but couldn't shake feeling nervous. "You think you'll be okay?" he asked.

"Yes," she said. "I've decided to face it head on with this attitude: If he gets me, I'll be free. If I get him, I'll be free. Either way, I'm free."

The two men returned, following a tiny man. "Yes," said Donna. "It's Rolf."

"Hello, Donna," said Rolf, when he stood at the base of the great pyramid. "You've made a terrible mistake. I'm going to enjoy this."

"You pathetic, sad little man," she said. "Killing people for profit. Trying to benefit from the nightmares of others."

"Come down, now," Rolf said.

"No," said Rick.

"No," Donna added. "No, we won't descend to your level, you crazy little doofus."

Rick put two fingers to his lips and gave a shrill whistle.

Three gunshots.

Three of the men clutched at their backs and fell. The one who remained dove for cover but again a rifle cracked. The man staggered and fell.

"You killed them," said Rolf, looking around for the shooters.

"No," said Rick. "No, not killed. They've been hit with an animal tranquilizer. You can't and won't be able to hit the men who shot at them."

"Oh?" said Rolf with a smirk. He shut his eyes. He smiled a little.

"Show him," Rick said.

A gunshot—the real thing this time—resounded through the huge square. The ground at Rolf's feet exploded. He whirled, searching the ruins.

"You can't fight the sound here, Rolf," said Donna. "The acoustics won't let you and neither will the colonel and his men. You won't see them and you can't touch them with your mind."

Rolf started to close his eyes. Again a gunshot pinged off the lower Step.

"Tell the stupid sumbitch he better not try that again," yelled Colonel Spencer. "We'll drop him next time."

Rolf, now, began to look scared. Until this moment he'd never failed at anything with his mental abilities.

"Give up, Rolf," said Donna. "Now we know how to stop you. We only have to play the music. You can't bend the skill around the music."

"No," he screamed. "No. Never. You still have those squares. . ."

"Give up, Rolf," Rick repeated.

"You have the advantage only for the moment," Rolf said. "I'll just disappear and find you again. I'm in the only place where my mind can't work."

"That's not true," said Rick. "You're not leaving here alive unless you do what we tell you."

"It's over, Rolf," said Donna. "Lie down on the ground. We'll. . ."

"You think I'm going to surrender?" asked Rolf, his eyes wild. "Why would I do so?"

"Because if you don't, you die," said Rick. "Colonel Spencer and his men will kill you right now."

Rolf attempted a laugh. "Idiots," he sneered. "I'm stronger than you can imagine. . ."

"But not here," said Donna. "Here I am stronger than you. Watch this. . ."

Again the air seemed to sizzle and Rolf screamed. He fell to the ground, eyes wide.

Then with an intense struggle he looked up at them. His eyes focused on Rick—

Rachel stood in front of him.

"Rachel," he said. "How did you get here?"

"I had to come," she said. "You have to stop Donna. She's dangerous. She's betrayed you to this man."

Rick stared. Then his thoughts cleared.

"No," he said. "You aren't here. You're dead. This is a lie."

Now Donna took Rachel's place. "Relax and take the music away. I'll protect you—"

"No!" he screamed.

Donna vanished. He turned and saw his new wife next to him, her eyes glazed and vacant.

With an intense effort he grabbed her and embraced her. She screamed in terror.

"Donna!" he yelled. "Fight your way out of it!"

At once everything stopped.

Rick found himself on the altar of the ancient Temple of the Sun. He heard the drums, the chanting. At his side, he saw—

Who was it?

The figure lifted the sacrificial knife. "No!" yelled Rick. He focused on the knife. He pushed back at the knife with his mind.

The knife withdrew and the figure put it by his side. Rick realized that this was the Mayan high Priest, ready to sacrifice him.

"No!" he shrieked. "Donna! It isn't true! You aren't the priest!"

With all the strength he could muster, he reached to his I-pod and turned it up.

The sound almost deafened him but his mind cleared. He wasn't on the Mayan Altar of Sacrifice.

Rick stood on his feet. His mind was clear, the scene was clear, Donna stood next to him.

"Colonel!" he yelled.

Nothing happened.

Rolf had stymied the Colonel and his sons with the mind trick. Rick turned and saw Donna collapsed, her hands clutched to her head.

He embraced his wife and kissed her. He reached for her I-pod and turned the volume up.

At first, she didn't respond. She seemed to be unconscious.

Then, with an abrupt jerk, she came awake.

Her eyes focused. "Rick," she whispered.

"Yes," he pleaded. "Get it back!"

Donna stood. Rolf had come halfway up the Steps, smirking at them.

"No!" said Donna.

The air seemed to screech as Donna's attack thought blasted into Rolf's mind. His eyes grew wide. He screamed.

Then the ancient temple reverberated with gunshots. Rolf's shirt exploded and he looked up at Donna wide-eyed.

"Donna!" he shrieked, his eyes wide with terror. "No, don't let them take me through those gates! Donna! No! I'll—"

He never finished the sentence. Colonel Spencer's bullet ripped into his skull and his head exploded.

Chapter Sixty eight

Rick and Donna started to descend as Rolf's body rolled down the side of the ancient Mayan temple. Colonel Spencer and his men materialized as if from nowhere and twisted plastic ties onto the wrists of the stunned men.

Spencer's sons drove a van up to the great pyramid. "What about these guys, Rick?" Colonel Spencer asked, pointing at the men lying on the ground.

"Never mind them," he said. "Leave them here. Without Rolf, they're harmless." Darkness had now descended at the ancient Mayan site.

Spencer's sons bundled Rolf's body into the back of the truck. All climbed aboard.

The truck drove away. Several minutes later, they stopped at the edge of the Ancient Sacred Cenote, where the victims of the Mayan sacrifices had been thrown.

Colonel Spencer and his sons tied concrete blocks to Rolf's body. They threw the body in and Rolf's body vanished, the last sacrificial offering to the Sacred Cenote.

The Lear Jet Donna had chartered stood waiting, fueled and ready.

The jet took off. Hours later, it landed in southern California and taxied to a private hanger.

Rick and Donna said Goodbye to Colonel Spencer and his sons. A few hours later, Rick and Donna sat in a quiet restaurant in Palm Springs. "That was awful," she shuddered. "Rolf couldn't quite get past the sound. But omigosh, he was powerful, Rick. He was holding five people prisoner at the same time. But when you turned my music up he couldn't adjust for a few moments—long enough for me to blast him, anyway. He must not have known about the music block, or in his arrogance thought he could get past it.

"What on earth did you do?" asked Rick.

"I showed him what Rachel saw at the gates of Hell," she said. "I let the creatures carry him to the black gates. He'd never seen it. When I let him go, they were about to drag him through the gates. It scared him so much that he released Colonel Spencer and his sons from the grip. Thank God they recovered as fast as they did."

"So would he have died even if Colonel Spencer hadn't shot him?"

Donna shrugged. "I don't know," she said. "I know that Rachel and Barry always felt that if they'd gone through the Black Gates, they'd have died."

"Yeah, I remember her saying that," agreed Rick.

"It happens all the time," Donna shrugged. "What happened to Rolf is a side effect of drug abuse. Morality starts to slip away. Soon any type of behavior takes over."

***

The next morning they drove to the bank in Palm Springs, where Rick and Donna intended to put Rachel's financial affairs in order. "Was Rolf doomed from the moment he met Keith?" Rick asked his wife.

"I don't know," said Donna, thinking for a few moments. "He had a chance. He could have re-learned how to make good decisions. That's what we all have to do with situations that are presented to us. He didn't do it, but Rolf *could* have used the ability as if it was a precious gift, not an opportunity for personal enrichment. "

"Like the decision I made when I agreed to marry you," he said.

"And me," she smiled. "The best decision led me to you."

"Donna," he said. He thought for a second, trying to frame a question.

"Yes?" she smiled.

"Look," said Rick. "Do you think that. . ."

He paused. "Do I think what?" she asked, taking his hand.

"Can we learn to let the past go?" He asked. "Carve a new place for ourselves?"

"Of course we can. We're alive, unlike Rolf. Barry and Rachel live in us, in our hearts. We'll live through our children."

Rick nodded. "It's a matter of deciding to do what I need to, isn't it."

"Yes," said his wife. She paused and stared up into his eyes. Then she embraced him and kissed him, the sweet, loving kiss of a mature woman for the dearest person in her life. "Do you feel okay now?"

"I feel fine," he said. "I'm going to let Rachel rest, I think. You and I need to start living, Donna."

She grinned. "What did you have in mind?"

"How about sky-diving? Hang-gliding? Maybe surfing?"

"Well," she said. "It's winter, so the surf ought to be up in Waimea Bay on the north shore now—"

"Jan and Dean," he said. "*Ride the Wild Surf.*"

"Not just surfing, or great seafood, either," she said. "I promise."

"Sounds perfect to me," he grinned.

Chapter Sixty nine

Two nights later Rick woke up from a doze in the hotel room on Oahu. The warm breeze of Waikiki came in like a breath of peace, gentle, soothing.

Rick and Donna had spent the day at Waikiki Beach, learning to surf. She was, like Rachel, a fine athlete, well-coordinated and energetic. Then they enjoyed a dinner of Ahi Tuna, accompanied by an icy Gewürztraminer.

Rick smiled to himself. He'd bought Donna an evening dress in the Hawaiian style of flowers and bright colors. It showed off her figure and legs to great advantage and he saw the looks that she got as they walked across the dining room to their table.

They'd gone dancing after dinner for a while and he again had become convinced that he was in the company of the most beautiful woman in the room.

When they returned to their room Donna lit some candles to accentuate the lovely furnishings. The love making had been relaxed and quiet as the two people again bound together. She'd murmured several times that she loved him. He'd told her that he loved her.

That's what sex is supposed to do, he decided: to establish, then deepen the love of two people. Now that the terror was behind them, their lives lay wide open before them. They'd face that life together.

He drew his knees up and thought about the things they would enjoy together—Christmas, Thanksgiving, birthdays, all the things that would happen as their families got together. Donna's son Terry, his wife and kids. Rick's daughter Cara and Dan his son, their families, maybe he'd take everyone to Disney, or on a cruise, or who knew what?

Donna slept next to him, and he moved a hand to caress her breast. She smiled a little and covered his hand with hers without waking up.

Rick slipped out of bed and walked to the bathroom and then to his suitcase. He found a pair of boxers and a tee-shirt and started to slip them on.

In the dim light, he saw a manila envelope at the bottom of the suitcase.

He pulled it out and opened it. He reached inside and his hand touched a plastic bag.

Inside the bag he saw several squares of blotting paper. He'd almost forgotten about them.

Rick sat on the edge of the bed and looked though the clear plastic at the squares.

Four decades ago, the evil experiments of a crazy chemistry student had altered several people for the rest of their lives. How many lives had been lost, how many reputations had been ruined, how many hopes and dreams stolen away because of Keith's experiments, his greed, his desire to play God?

Then his roommate and first victim, Rolf, had set free who knew how much violence. His life, like Keith's, had ended in violence.

Pandora's Box, thought Rick. Keith and Rolf weren't the only evil ones. We opened the box of Hell in the sixties with our own folly.

Rachel suffered her entire life. Barry, cursed with the same ability to alter time. Donna, the striking woman who was now his wife, had also been changed beyond revocation. The pathetic little man named Rolf had transformed into a homicidal monster. Rick shook his head, peering through the plastic at the squares.

Then it hit him.

They had time now. He could take one of these things. Not now, not tonight or even in the next week, but soon, he could ingest one of Keith's accursed squares.

Yeah. He could have a doctor standing by, an expert in drug

usage, someone who knew what to do. Nurses, hospitals—

Could he learn how to Step Back?

If he could, could he Step Back and save Rachel? Save Barry?

He thought. Things were going well and now, he and Donna knew the secret. First, they'd diminish Rolf's mind trick with the music. Then Rachel and Barry could block him long enough for Rick to take him out. They all would be safe. No ignominious end to the life of either remarkable, wonderful person.

How many deaths could he prevent? How many minds could be freed from insidious distraction and slavery?

He had the tool in his hand. He could just ingest this drug—okay, this hideous pathway to Hell—recover for a few days and then Step Back. Where could he go? He thought.

Then he knew. Of course. He could Step Back to the year that Rolf first came after Barry and Rachel.

The three of them could fight the little creep. Neither Barry nor Rachel had combat training, of course, but Rick knew he could take Rolf out, with a sniper's bullet or even hand to hand with a knife, or a garotte. Hell, Rachel knew how to shield herself, and she could show him what to do.

They could enlist Donna's help, of course. She could paralyze the little man with the vision of Hell. Then they could inject him or shoot him. Or Rick would kill him with his bare hands.

Rolf would never hurt anyone again.

He knew how Rachel would respond. He could almost hear her speaking in his mind. "No," Rachel would say. "No. Let me rest. Let Barry rest. Go on with your life. Love Donna. Care for our grandchildren and children. Enjoy the money I left you."

Behind him, Donna shifted in the king size bed. He turned to look at her.

In the candlelight Donna's body looked even more exquisite. She was an outstanding woman in every sense: not only gracious and kind, but beautiful, intelligent and accomplished—

But she can never be Rachel, he said to the voice in his mind.

Nobody's Rachel, said the voice.

Yeah, but Christmas. The Grandchildren.

No, Rachel had said. No, don't try it.

Rick opened the plastic bag. He extracted one of the squares.

A science project, Rachel had called it. An evil, unspeakable science project—

"Rick," said Donna, sitting up behind him.

"I'm thinking about it," he said, turning to her. "That's all."

"I know," she said. "I know you are. The violence of the thought woke me up."

"Oh," he said, getting it now.

"Rick, you can't," she said.

"She saved me. . ."

"And you saved her. You kept her safe for thirty-some years."

"But Barry. . ."

"I know," she said. "I've thought about him too."

She sat up and embraced him.

"Rick," she said. "They're gone. But they live in us. In our children and grandchildren. They always will."

"Yes, but. . ."

"Honor them," she said.

"Yes," he said.

"Rick," said Rachel's voice.

He turned in surprise. He realized that Rachel hadn't spoken. Donna, his new wife, had spoken to his mind, calling back Rachel's voice. He'd been startled.

Donna had her hand outstretched. "Give the bag to me," she said. "I'm going to take the damned things onto the lanai and burn them in the ashtray. It's more than forty years overdue. Then we're going to make love again." She took hold of the bag, but Rick didn't let go.

Rick hesitated. He felt the tears rise.

"Let them go," said his wife.

He nodded and handed her the bag.

THE END

Title: The Coven of the Spring

- Author: Jeff Lovell
- Publisher: TotalRecall Publications, Inc.
- HARD COVER ISBN: 978-1-59095-113-2 $27.95
- PAPERBACK, ISBN: 978-1-59095-114-9 $19.95
- EBOOK, Nook, Kindle, ISBN: 978-1-59095-115-6
- Number of pages: 336
- Publication Date: 2013

An ancient secret, with frightening new powers, emerges to terrify and destroy.

Grace DeRosa, a gifted research chemist, lives with her husband Jim and their seventeen year old daughter Crissy. Grace finds a hidden spring in the woods near Salem, Massachusetts. She discovers that the consumed water imparts unique and fearful powers that lead to the ability to read minds, create terrifying mental pictures and force the user's will on others.